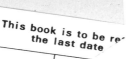

Stephen Gray was born in Cape Town in 1941. For Penguin he has edited *The Penguin Book of Southern African Stories* (1985), to which this collection is a follow-up, and in 1989 *The Penguin Book of Southern African Verse*. In 1991 his novel, *War Child*, appeared. Recently he has published short stories and other pieces in *Passport, Commonwealth, Index on Censorship, Staffrider* and *The London Magazine* — these are collected together in *Human Interest and Other Pieces* (1993). 'Letters to Pratt' first appeared in *Soho Square* in 1992. He lives in Johannesburg.

The Penguin Book of Contemporary South African Short Stories

Edited by
Stephen Gray

PENGUIN BOOKS

Published by the Penguin Group
27 Wrights Lane, London W8 5TZ, England
Viking Penguin, a division of Penguin Books USA Inc, 375 Hudson
Street, New York, New York 10014, USA
Penguin Books Australia Ltd, Ringwood, Victoria, Australia
Penguin Books Canada Ltd, 10 Alcorn Avenue, Toronto, Ontario,
Canada M4V 3B2
Penguin Books (NZ) Ltd, 182-190 Wairau Road, Auckland 10, New
Zealand
Penguin Books, Amethyst Street, Theta Ext 1, Johannesburg, South
Africa

Penguin Books Ltd, Registered Offices: Harmondsworth, Middlesex,
England

First published by Penguin Books 1993

The Acknowledgements on pages 304–305 constitute an extension of this
copyright page.

ISBN 0 140 23726 7

Typeset by Creda Press
Printed and bound by Creda Press

Contents

Introduction

This collection of twenty-seven pieces is designed as an introduction to South African writing in short fictional forms of recent times.

The purpose is to make known to a wider readership as many as possible of the rising figures in what may fairly be called a really new school in the world of South African letters. The emphasis here is firmly on rethinking, renewal. The process is combative and requires invention, transgression. All in all, the work of a highly skilled, daring and very fresh configuration may be seen to be upon us. In one another's company we may realize how, in the last decade or so, this group of steady practitioners has not only arrived, but become the very persuasive current generation.

That is, this anthology postdates *The Penguin Book of Southern African Stories* which appeared in 1985, but which — the way these things lumber along — cut off at about 1980. This one opens there, including all of that decade, and is strongly focused on the 1990s.

But at the time of editing the preceding *Penguin Book* there was no vigorous short story production underway within South Africa: a long-ranging survey seemed appropriate and in order, drawing from a wide geography (South*ern* Africa), a deep history and many languages, with due tribute paid to translators; in short, a way to consolidate a heritage and an exercise in multicultural transactions at a time when apartheid at its darkest had all but closed such traditions down. There the (rather sombre) theme was also enduring achievement, with places of honour held by Nadine Gordimer, Es'kia Mphahlele and other seniors.

Only four writers have carried over from there to here: Rose Moss, Ahmed Essop, Sheila Roberts and Peter Wilhelm. They are exemplary users of the new style and all in mid-career. There were to be others: for example, Richard Rive, who in July, 1987, published in *Contrast* a severely dashing sabotage of the established conventional story with all its usual freight in 'Mrs Janet September and the Siege of Sinton'. This was illustrated (!) with a photo of the character in question he had torn from a magazine. Talk about the crossing of boundaries as he ventriloquized against the authorities in the form of this railing woman. But Rive was dead two years later, tragically . . . on the brink of a powerful creative breakthrough.

There were other precursors. Breyten Breytenbach in *Granta*, No. 14 (in Winter, 1984) in an extraordinary piece called 'Punishable Innocence' seemed to be scrambling the categories with magnificent ease — autobiography, reportage and fictional devices with fantasy mixed in. This exemplified the confusion and collapse of all the old norms in favour of this new mixed-convention, push-and-pull text. Thrilling tactics and compulsive reading. But this was a translation as well, and since there is now such an abundance of material to choose from in English-original the line had to be drawn in a bit closer this time. Anyway, Rive, Breytenbach were also too well established for the purposes of this launching exercise.

But still, a mandate had to be found, a text by which it seemed this new school was charged. Bessie Head wrote one (indeed, several) and although it dates back to 1972 it was not commonly available until it appeared posthumously in 'Dreamer and Storyteller', in *Tales of Tenderness and Power* in 1989 (and also as the Epilogue in *A Woman Alone* in 1990). There she wrote:

> Each human society is a narrow world trapped to death in paltry evils and jealousies, and for people to know that there are thoughts and generosities wider and freer than their own can only be an enrichment to their lives . . . The cheap, glaring, paltry trash of a people who are living it up for themselves alone dominates everything. If one is a part of it, through being born there, how does one communicate with the horrible? That is why South Africa has no great writer: no one can create harmony out of cheap discord.

She chastened us, and she made the challenge all right to those *born* here.

More recently (in a review in *The Guardian Weekly* on 4 June, 1993) Elleke Boehmer in effect spoke for the new South African-born generation which her own work represents:

> There are methods of narration other than the historical which are also valid and illuminating. Indeed, especially at this time of cataclysmic change, there is a specific need in South Africa for new kinds of stories, for plots and characters other than the realistic or typical — perhaps non-heroic or eccentric, plain or strange. More than anything, South African writing requires new forms for thinking about reality. Not history enclosing fictions, but fictions nudging — absentmindedly, even irresponsibly — at history's outer edge.

This requirement has been the main criterion for selection here.

Every anthologizer is indebted to previous editors for the process of filtration and exposure of new items they abet and maintain. Details of the sources of each item are given in the Notes on Contributors and in the Acknowledgements, with special gratitude to book-publishers where appropriate. Some texts have come directly from the authors, been negotiated and in due course finalized, but most are drawn from those journals devoted to the promotion of upcoming work, most especially *Contrast* and then *New Contrast* and *Staffrider*, with *The English Academy Review*, *New Classic* and *The Classic*, *Frontline*, and further afield *Kunapipi*, even *The London Magazine* and *TriQuarterly*. These are the archives of the vanguard, a pleasure to search through for a pattern that appears there only at random and fragmentarily.

Also I must thank the National English Literary Museum in Grahamstown for their record-keeping. Out of their meticulous bibliographies leap . . . well, many possibili for fruitful combination. Their willingness to supply obscure material is always a facilitation.

For the convenience of non-South Africans a Glossary of some recurring terms in the vernaculars is placed unobtrusively.

Stephen Gray, 1993

The Wreck of the Santa Maria

DAVID BASCKIN

With the first wave that crushed the forecastle of the Santa Maria, the Friar Barto turned his thoughts to Job. The second wave smashed the bridge and the mind of his Brother Hieronymous reflected briefly on the circumstances that preserved the life of Noah. But when the third giant wave stove in the galleon's side, came the various realizations to all on board that Hell was cold, Hell was wet, Hell was Greek and Hell was for ever.

Purgatory dawned the next morning with the survivors huddled on a windy shore, some leagues distant from the Bay of Natal. Six months out of Lisbon the Christians found themselves facing a silent group of pagans dressed in skins and feathers. Of the pagans there were many, of the Christians very few. Apart from the two Franciscans, there was Goncales the carpenter, Juao the sailmaker and Jesus, a boy drummer. The pagans kept their distance, standing like a frieze on top of the giant dune that dominated the beach. Jesus, his teeth chattering, kept up a ticking ratatat-tat on his side drum, miraculously saved, undamaged, from the wreck. Friar Barto, his scapular crucifix held aloft, breathed a silent anathema on the distant group. It seemed to work, since the pagans kept their distance.

Providence, with its usual selectivity, had washed up a collection of flotsam on to the beach. Apart from the common maritime stuff of spars and sailcloth, of ropes and seachests, of dead sheep and dead men (both hastily buried in sandy graves), the sea disgorged a small organ of forty pipes, a portable altar and a carved box containing the lectionary of Saint Catherine. These three items had been the sacred furniture of the two friars who had intended presenting themselves to the court of the Maharajah of Goa as an embassy of the Portuguese throne and its present occupant, King John. The altar and organ were to have been the basis of their first church in India, while the lectionary was a personal gift from King John to the Maharajah.

Widely regarded as a miraculous text, the lectionary was more than just a record of Saint Catherine's austere and pious life. When first displayed for sale in the Paris bookshop of the Widow Flambe, passers-by who read it underwent a variety of religious experiences. These ranged from mere grace for the many to profound healings for three cripples, two lunatics, six lepers, an idiot and nine blind beggars whose capacity to read the book in the first place was a miracle in itself. Such was the fame of the lectionary that King John bought up the entire printing and ordered the movable type broken and scattered. All copies of the lectionary were destroyed by the King except one: the gift to the Maharajah. This, it was hoped, would lead the royal Hindoo to reconsider his pagan ways, and embrace the One, True and Catholic Faith.

Unbeknown to the survivors of the Santa Maria, and despite the expertise of Sadiq the Moorish physician and alchemist, King John had succumbed to the plague forty days after the departure of the ship from Lisbon. The Prince, his son, had ascended the throne as King John II. His interests were very different from those of his father, being concerned more with a Hanseatic customs treaty than missionary adventures in the distant East. Consequently, as far as Lisbon was concerned, the unlucky venture of the Santa Maria had already faded from official consciousness.

But on the sands below a massive bluff near the Bay of Natal the five survivors kept their mission firmly in mind as a point around which to rally their hopes, firm their purpose and enrich their sense of human meaning. Friar Barto assumed leadership of the group. Waving his hands above his head, he beckoned at the distant group of feathered pagans. Slowly a small group detached themselves from the mass and approached the Christians on the beach. Speaking slowly and deliberately, the Friar addressed them in Portuguese, telling them of his mission to India and their role in assisting him achieve that goal. Despite the loudness of his voice, the oration had no effect, forcing him to try again, first in Latin, then Hebrew, and finally Aramaic. Exasperated, he let his hands fall against his cassock, so causing the gilded rosary at his waist to clink and glitter in the harsh African sun.

At this, one of the pagans fell on her knees before the Friar and touched the golden chain with one tremulous hand. Jesus the boy drummer played a long, slow roll while the other Christians grew silent. Then Hieronymous spoke. 'It is a miracle,' he said, 'but not a surprise. For did not the Apostles first baptize an Aethiopian, so long ago? So too shall we, on this dark and barbarous shore.' He raised the woman to her feet, detached the golden rosary from Barto's resistant girdle and hung it round her neck. There it lay between her naked breasts, a focus for the sacred thoughts and profane desires of Goncales the carpenter.

The next day, with the forty pipe organ loaded on the back of the pagan woman, the little group of Christians continued their march up the beach, heading for the cool and fragrant harbour recorded on the charts of Vasco da Gama. The organ swayed as the pagan bent under the load, her breasts and rosary forming a triple pendulum pointing at their azimuth, straight down into the centre of the earth. With Juao the sailmaker pumping the bellows, Friar Hieronymous stroked the double manuals, thundering mighty chords on the organ in company with his soaring Kyrie Eleison, his head thrown back in ecstasy, eyes shut, the mouth wide open to the blistering sky.

The rays of the evening fire glittered that night on the shard of glass that Goncales the carpenter used to shave Friar Barto's tonsure. Apart from the crackling of the mangrove twigs in the blaze, the night sounds zoomed and twittered with the shrieks and howls of owls, jars, bats and bloodsucking insects. In a bowl of her own manufacture, the pagan woman nurtured a stew made from the amiable corms and rhizomes she had gathered in the declining evening light. Sustained by it, the Christians slept on the soft beach by the bay, leaving Jesus the boy drummer on watch against the darkness.

With the morning came the plan for work. While Hieronymous praised God with massive arpeggios on the organ, the rest of the Christians under Barto's direction erected the altar and arranged upon it the lectionary of Saint Catherine. At noon the pagan woman fed them once more. Following the celebration of the mass, Juao the sailmaker and Jesus the boy drummer dug an oubliette, the soft sides of which were shored up with green timber cut by Goncales the carpenter. That night all drank a mild ferment brewed by the woman and felt a great calm fall upon them. While the Christians lay on the sands gazing at the unfamiliar stars, with a soft dew settling on their unblinking eyes, the pagan woman sat at the organ and with one hand picked out the melody of the Credo. This she repeated, engaging now the Vox Arcana and using her left hand to invert and augment the treble line. At this, Jesus the boy drummer joined her with a rimshot accented percussive statement on his side drum. The Credo stood on its head as the pagan woman brought in a thundering bourdon bass of such intensity that even the sea was silenced.

Goncales the carpenter, impelled by the rhythm, jumped to his feet and began to dance. The friars, alarmed, tried to stop him but Goncales jerked and capered, shouting out terrible truths about his past life. Between yells of dark incoherence he counterpointed the roar of the organ with a threnody of sin. In his past life he had been a whoremaster, renting the bodies of his women to the sailors of Lisbon. While this had made him rich, it had not made him well. Ripping open the front of his leather breeches, he dragged out his generative member, holding it between finger and thumb. It was a poxy, purple thing with a tricoloured carbuncle the size of a mynah's egg ornamenting the tip. Shocked by Goncales' revelations both moral and corporeal, Friar Barto, his crucifix erect, grabbed the dancing carpenter by one flailing arm and threw him into the oubliette. Goncales lay on the sandy floor of the inverted

8

tower, gazing up at a ring of darkness, randomly pierced by the alien stars of the Natal night.

The next morning the supine Goncales was awakened by the brightness of the dawn sky. His circle of vision framed the sun transected by a canopy of leaves and thick branches. A scarlet narina trogon flew in a flash of red from one vine to another. Into this tiny panorama the silhouette of Friar Hieronymous cut a sudden and sanctimonious outline. 'Goncales!' he said. 'Use your time profitably. Muse on your sins. Repent!' So saying, he lowered on a thin rope the carved box containing the lectionary of Saint Catherine.

Goncales the carpenter stood on tiptoe to receive the printed life of the saint. As his outstretched fingers touched the carved box in which the lectionary was enclosed, he felt a jagged impulse so intense that he fell insensible, the open book collapsing face down across his unconscious visage. To a rolling ratatattat from Jesus the boy drummer the sweating friars and Juao the sailmaker hoisted the absent carpenter from the oubliette and laid him out on the shore of the bay. The pagan woman moistened his pale lips with a leafy infusion and soon his eyes fluttered open to reveal dilated pupils of different size. Then to the amazement of all he began to declaim in French, a language familiar to none of those present. Friar Barto was the first to realize what he was saying. Holding the lectionary of Saint Catherine open, he pointed at the print as Goncales the carpenter recited the entire text — vita prima, vita secunda, de veritate instructa — verbatim.

When this was over Goncales the carpenter rose to his feet, standing alone in the presence of the kneeling Christians. 'My brothers,' he said, 'the day of miracles is not over.' Stripping off his clothing, all could see that his generative organ was healed, the carbuncle vanished, the pox gone, the empurplement replaced by a veritable tower of ivory. All gave praise, the friars marvelling that the power of Saint Catherine was sufficient to transcend continents, not to mention a lengthy submersion in the sea.

As the weeks progressed, with Goncales busy in his saw pit shaping, chamfering and seasoning his store of green planks, it became clear to him that his healing was a mixed blessing. Sometimes he would waken of a morning to find his generative organ so huge that it needed to be carried on the shoulders of the two friars preceding him. On days like this the pagan woman, overcome by the immanence of the scene, attempted to worship it, garlanding it with flowers, only to have Friar Barto beat her off, shrieking his accusations of profanity.

And sometimes it became so small that it gave the appearance of a mons veneris, filling him with an uncontrollable fear that he was turning into a woman. At times like these he would pray with a fervour that amazed all who saw him, and was thus saved by a benign Providence from a fate worse than leprosy.

Then one day it was time to leave, in a boat made of mangrove planks by Goncales the carpenter and rigged with vines by Juao the sailmaker. With the pagan woman at the double manuals of the forty pipe organ, Friars Barto and Hieronymous alternating at the bellows, with Jesus the boy drummer beating out a brave ratatattat on his side drum, Juao up the mast and Goncales trailing his generative member in the water as a tiller, the boat sailed away from the Bay of Natal.

Some say the fourth wave got them. But Malagasy women still sing of a group of Christians who landed on an Indian Ocean island where they lived out their remaining days, capturing and eating the large flightless birds which once populated that distant and idyllic place.

Bibliography

Alain Boureau, 'Franciscan Piety and Voracity: Uses and Stratagems in the Hagiographic Pamphlet' in Roger Cartier (ed.), *The Culture of Print*, Polity Press, Cambridge (1989).

The Prime Minister is Dead

IVAN VLADISLAVIĆ

The Day They Killed the Prime Minister

They killed the Prime Minister during the winter.

I was ten years old. That year my parents and I moved to a house in a new suburb. Granny moved with us. Grandfather said he was too old to move, so he stayed behind in the old house. He gave us a post box and two plastic numbers for the gate, and wished us everything of the best in our new home.

It was an ordinary place. Three bedrooms, a lounge, a dining room. No gnomes. No crazy paving. A reasonable path of solid cement from the front gate to the veranda steps. Laying the path was the first major task my father and I undertook.

When we moved in the house still smelt of raw wood, fresh paint, putty. There was much to be done: the floors would have to be sealed, the fingerprints cleaned off the window panes, splatters of paint scraped off the tiles in the bathroom and the kitchen.

The garden was veld. The builders had simply fenced off a rectangle and cleared a patch big enough to put the house down on. The way to get the grass out is to attack the roots. You can't skoffel with a spade — it grows back. You have to work a fork in around each tuft, loosen the earth, stick a hosepipe in among the roots, turn it on full blast, blow the soil away. Then you pull on the grass until it comes out, roots and all, like a plug. Knock out the remaining soil against the ground, pile all the grass in the wheelbarrow, push it around to the compost heap at the back.

That's what my father and I were doing on the day they killed the Prime Minister. I was loosening the soil and my father was pulling the grass out. He was wearing his old army uniform, as he always did when we waged war against the garden. Granny was in her rocker on the front veranda, crocheting one of an endless pile of woollen squares which would eventually be herded together into a lopsided blanket. She was listening to the radio, silently, through a small earphone.

I was pushing a wheelbarrow full of grass around to the back. As I passed Granny, the rocker lost momentum, stopped. A brightly coloured square dropped to the floor. She hefted her large body out of the chair and stood swaying solemnly, still joined to the radio by the coil of flex. Then she bellowed: 'The Prime Minister is dead! Some madman chopped him up with a panga!'

I carried that thought with me, like a peach pip in my cheek, as I pushed the wheelbarrow round to the back and tipped the grass into the hole my father and I had dug the weekend before.

I see now that the death of a Prime Minister has many consequences.

When my grandfather died he left us a suitcase. There was something in it for each of us. My father got a suit that was too big for him, and a pair of pruning shears. My mother got some newspaper clippings and some photographs, old and cracked like leather. I got a pair of lucky nail-clippers given to my grandfather by an Italian prisoner of war.

When the Prime Minister died he left us a compost heap on which practically anything would grow. Mealies grew there once, all by themselves. Granny speculated that Lazarus, who sometimes worked in the garden, must have thrown away the sweetcorn that she'd given him for lunch.

Once the Prime Minister was dead they started renaming streets after him, and stations, and schools, even pleasure resorts. Then they renamed our suburb after him. They wanted us to live in a monument. It was a new suburb, and no one minded.

When I came back around to the front with the empty wheelbarrow my father was standing to attention and my mother was holding a glass of sugar water to Granny's lips.

She had unplugged Granny from the radio and turned it up so that we could all hear.

Granny finished a blanket that evening, during the seven o'clock news.

The Day We Buried the Prime Minister

We buried the Prime Minister in the spring.

My father and I were planting the orchard on that day. There were thirty trees in all. Three rows, ten trees in each. A platoon of trees, my father called them. The holes we dug were deep and perfectly round. We marked them out with a compass made of two nails joined by a piece of sisal string eighteen inches long.

My father loosened the earth with a pick and I shovelled it out of the hole. The ground was very hard and we had to soak it with water from the hosepipe. Soon my hands and feet were covered with mud. As the hole got deeper the colour of the earth would change.

My father said he had desert sand in the turn-ups of his khaki pants, left over from the war. 'Come,' he would say to me, 'hold your dixie here.' Then I would cup my hands next to his hairy calves, and he'd peel back the turn-ups so that a trickle of sand flowed into my hands. 'Dyed with the blood of patriots,' he said, if the sand was red, and 'Bleached white as bone by the desert sun,' if it was white.

Granny was sitting in her rocker, under a beach umbrella, with the radio on her knees. At three o'clock they were going to cross live to the funeral. We would have a running commentary of the whole procession from the church, through the streets of the city, to Heroes' Acre at the cemetery.

'Numero Uno!' Granny shouted. 'Rotting in the soil. A piece of meat. Shame. He leaves a wife and six children.'

'He leaves more than that,' my father said. And then to me: 'Get in the hole, Private.'

The holes for the fruit trees had to be four feet deep. I was the measuring stick: when I stood in the hole the ground had to be level with the top of my head. We put rocks in the bottom of the hole for drainage, then compost, then a layer of sand sieved through an old mesh gate. Then smaller stones. More compost and more sand. Each layer of sand had to be thoroughly watered. When the hole was almost full we chose one of the saplings that stood ready in the shade next to the house. We left the name tag on each tree so that we would know which was which until it bore fruit.

All the trees grew except for the fig tree, third from the right, in the back row. It didn't die either. It just stayed exactly the way it was when we put it into the ground.

My grandfather came once a year after that to prune the trees. Each time he would stop before the stunted fig tree and shake his head. But he said that it was good that one tree failed: the earth should never be too kind. It spoiled people.

After he died we let the trees grow wild. We were sick of peaches and plums, and chutney, and jam. We let the weight of the fruit snap the branches and we let the fallen fruit rot into the ground.

'I'm pleased the old man isn't here to see this,' my mother would say.

At a quarter to three my mother brought out tea and a plate of biscuits.

'You know,' she said when we were drinking the tea, 'this funeral is a big occasion. We're not likely to see another like it in our lifetimes.'

'Unless they kill the new Prime Minister,' my father replied.

'Don't speak like that in front of the child,' Granny said sternly.

'It won't harm him if it's true,' my father said. 'They're pulling out all the stops on this funeral. Massed bands, tanks, a fly-past of jets. Every citizen issued with a flag, every building draped in crêpe. A twenty-one-gun salute. Now if they kill the new Prime Minister, and I think this is not unlikely, they'll have to do the same, won't they? It wouldn't do if they gave the next Prime Minister a half-hearted send-off.'

'That may well be so,' my mother said, 'but the point is

that we shouldn't think that way. You can't go through life taking the great events of history for granted. When one comes along you've got to grab it with both hands.'

My father put down his teacup, took the beret out of his epaulette and shuffled it back on to his head, catching up the hair that spilled forward on to his forehead. 'What are you getting at?'

'I think it's our duty to let the boy be part of today's ceremony. Look.' She took a page of the newspaper from her apron pocket and spread it out on the ground. There was a map with a dotted path running through it and she traced this route with her finger. 'The procession's passing by just here in about thirty minutes. It's a short walk away. Why don't the two of you clean yourselves up and then you take the boy down to have a look.'

Just then Granny let out a terrifying scream.

My father stood. 'All right, men,' he said to me, 'you've got thirty seconds to wash your hands and feet. Then I want you formed up and ready to move out.'

'You should wash up decently and put on some proper clothes,' my mother protested.

'Nonsense,' my father said. 'In times of war we dispense with formalities. We'll go as we are, stained with combat and proud of it.'

I washed my hands and feet under the tap, then fell in. My father inspected me briefly. Then he ordered me to climb into the wheelbarrow, passed me the newspaper, took up position between the handles, and we set out. Just before we disappeared around the side of the house I looked back. My mother was packing the teacups on to the tray. Granny waved.

The metal wheel of the wheelbarrow clattered on the tar. The sound seemed very loud, because the streets were so quiet and empty. Sometimes as we passed a house I could hear the muted voice of the radio. But there was none of the usual Saturday bustle. No children playing, no one washing a car or working in the garden.

We did not speak for several blocks. When we came to Theo's café, the limit of my world, my father stopped. He took the map from me and studied it. Then he asked me to hold one corner and with his stubby fingers, the nails still caked with mud, he showed me the way. 'We have to go south now for three blocks. Then we have to turn west for another four, and we're there.' We went on.

Now there were fewer houses, more shops and office blocks. The streets began to fill with people, all walking in the same direction we were. They were dressed in suits and church dresses, and they walked along in silence. Some of the men wore black armbands. As we approached the older part of the city the buildings became greyer, gloomier. Here huge columns supported stone pediments. Old statues, the flesh blistered and corroded, stared down at us.

When the tar gave way to cobbles the clanking of the wheel grew even louder and now several people stopped to stare at us. I leaned back in the wheelbarrow so that I could look up at my father. His jaw was as set and craggy as a statue's. His eyes looked stonily ahead. The hair that curved back from under the beret could have been cast in bronze. Then I too looked ahead and tried to mould his hard expression to my face.

We stopped soon at a kiosk where we each received a little flag. Then we rattled on, and at the end of the block I could see a jostling wall of black cloth, splashed with colour — the colours of the flag — and many pale profiles all facing to one side. Some of these faces looked back, annoyed, as we approached. We parked behind the wall of people and my father hoisted me on to his shoulders. Then he climbed carefully on to the barrow.

'We're right on time,' he said.

The wall had absorbed all colour and sound, but now that we rose above it we could see the bright, gleaming procession, hardly a block away, and hear the music.

The procession drew slowly closer. In front was a phalanx of traffic officers, the sun flashing from the windshields of their motorcycles and their black leather boots and gloves. Then came the drum major, shrouded in leopard skin, and the band, all its pipes and tappets bristling. Behind that another machine, a company of soldiers, slow-marching.

And then came a truck towing the Prime Minister, in a box covered with a ceremonial flag, on top of a gun carriage, as if he was a secret weapon captured from the enemy. Behind him another squad of soldiers, and behind them tanks, and behind them more soldiers as far as the eye could see.

This solemn movement, this stirring music, hemmed in on either side by the frozen waves of mourners.

When the first company of soldiers had almost passed us, my father raised his arm in a rigid salute. I waved my flag. The men around us swallowed and stared ahead. Some of the women dabbed at their eyes with the little flags. A child started crying.

Then, as the gun carriage drew level with us, the truck suddenly coughed, jerked, and came to a halt. A cloud of black smoke poured from the exhaust pipe. The soldiers behind faltered. The front ranks began to mark time. Those behind marched slowly and solemnly into those in front. A few of the men dived for cover under the gun carriage.

The band and the first soldiers marched on. Between them and the stalled truck a fascinating gap began to open.

The driver of the truck climbed hurriedly down and opened the bonnet, tinkered with the engine. Behind, the soldiers stumbled and coughed in the smoke. The gun carriage was now completely obscured.

My father snapped out of his salute, jumped down from the wheelbarrow and squatted so that I could climb from his shoulders.

'Private, we must do what must be done.'

He took up the wheelbarrow and, as if they understood our mission, the people parted to let us through.

The box was heavy. The soldiers were already half a block ahead of us. We set off in pursuit, my father pushing the wheelbarrow while I held the box steady. The crowd waved us on. Once the flag got caught under the wheel, and the box was almost jerked from the barrow. My father was breathing heavily by the time we caught up with the soldiers, and adjusted our pace to the slow rhythm of the music.

I looked back and saw that the crowds that had lined the streets had surged together behind us and were following. On the dark surface of that wave the flotsam of the flags and their faces bobbed.

Outside the cemetery a man in white gloves waved the band and the soldiers off to one side into a parking lot. He directed us straight ahead, through the wrought-iron gates, along the stone walkway that led to the grave. On either side the stone faces of the men in the history books looked down from their columns, unblinking, unmoved.

The grave. The black figures clustered together, the man with the book clutched under his arm, the brass railings. They stood as people do on the edge of a cliff.

My father's stride lengthened. I had to run to keep up with him. The box bucked violently. My father began to run. I stopped, panting, and stared after him. He ran towards the hole. The mouths of the people at the graveside opened. The man with the book held out his pale palm like a traffic officer.

My father ran on. At the last moment, on the very lip of the grave, he dug the metal prow of the barrow into the earth and heaved.

Letters to Pratt

STEPHEN GRAY

Not that he stood much chance of getting away with shooting the prime minister.

The facts of the matter are as follows: on Saturday 9th April, 1960, during a cup-giving ceremony at the Rand Easter Show, which in those days was held at Milner Park in Johannesburg, David Beresford Pratt, who was in the members' enclosure because he was exhibiting his cattle, did 'wrongfully, unlawfully and maliciously attempt to kill and murder Hendrik Frensch Verwoerd'. That is how the charge sheet describes the crime. This crime Pratt committed by pulling out his revolver, approaching the seated official party and shooting Verwoerd, the prime minister, in the face.

The photo of Verwoerd going down is horrible indeed. Incredibly enough, he survived the bullet which entered by his nostril and completed its passage by going round the inside of his skull. Pratt was the one who shot him, there was no doubt about that. But the unfortunate Verwoerd had several more years in power to go before he was finally assassinated successfully.

After his attempt on the prime minister's life, Pratt did not have many months to go. He was immediately held in detention under the new emergency regulations. So severe were these that until he was finally charged he was not able even to consult with his lawyer. He was visited a few times by the daughter of his first marriage and by his only other close relative, his sister in Cape Town, to both of whom he was allowed to write a weekly letter about his life in prison — one would pass it on to the other.

Pratt had a bleak style. One such letter reads as follows:

6.00 a.m.   Dress and clean up cell.

7.00 a.m.	Wash.
7.30 a.m.	Daily chores.
8.00 a.m.	Thomas à Kempis and meditation.
9.00 a.m.	Exercise.
9.30 a.m.	Read Knox.
10.30 a.m.	Letters.
11.30 a.m.	Chess.
12.00 noon	Lunch and exercise.
1.30 p.m.	Read light literature.
2.30 p.m.	Chess.
3.30 p.m.	Read Therese.
5.00 p.m.	Thomas à Kempis and thought.
6.00 p.m.	Missel.
7.00 p.m.	Read Knox.
8.00 p.m.	Chess.

Love,
David.

Another is in sonnet form, ending:

Vain desire and self love have no place
Upon these pastures reached alone by grace.

He kept all the letters he received, although these were
rationed out to him at the rate of a small bundle a week.
One of these was usually from his mistress who lengthily
described how she would now have to get a job unless he
could help her out. Since his assets were frozen, he was
unable to satisfy her requests, but he nevertheless kept all
her pleas in a waiting file as if he would fix her up when he
could.

With incoming letters so limited, David Pratt could have
had no real idea of the impact of his case in the outside
world, which of course he would never see again. Also,
everything he received was censored with a purple stamp
obliterating any political reference he might have been able
to use in his own defence. In an extreme case, part of a
paragraph would be clipped out with scissors. Where this is

really bad you would think the censor was some child trying to turn Pratt's letters into lines of cut-out dolls. If Pratt had lasted to Christmas he could have used his correspondence as decorative streamers.

At any rate, the point is that he never knew that the boldness of his deed, which made headlines around the world, among many other things had unleashed a wave of fanatics who bombarded the prison with fan letters addressed to David Pratt, Esq. They came from all over, in different shapes and sizes. None of these fans was known to him, yet they all had this characteristic in common: each wrote to him as if they had known him for years. I am talking about hundreds of letters a day arriving at P. O. Box 410, Pretoria, with their brown 1d. stamps of a wildebeest of the old Union of South Africa, soon enough to become Verwoerd's Republic. Most of them were from lonely women who admired the dashing, handsome cattle-breeder of the press photos and sought to cheer him in the solitude of his cell. Some men wrote; an example is an old school friend who had decided (or been instructed) not to mention too specifically the circumstances in which Pratt found himself:

I returned back to Natal to find the sardines had at last arrived and we had one of the best runs we have had for years. We netted 20 tons of sardines, and other netting syndicates did equally well. The sardines have never been as late as this but the delay was good as it kept the crowd hanging about so the pub did well. We had the most terrible seas last week and our nets were badly damaged so we are busy getting them repaired. This is the first trouble we have had for a long while.

I suppose you do find time drags terribly — I hope things are brought to a head soon for your sake.

There are many such letters from family, friends and business associates, none of whom seem fully able to grasp their correspondent's dilemma: Pratt was awaiting trial on a

21

capital charge with every likelihood of being found guilty.

His most faithful correspondent was one who first signed the name R. Malan and only several letters later with the less formal Rita Malan. What makes her correspondence so extraordinary is that it appears Pratt never replied to her. Probably his weekly allocation was taken up with business affairs and pressing personal demands, particularly when his second wife returned from Holland to get things straight for the sake of the two children they had together. Yet Rita Malan persisted, in the hope that one day she would receive a response.

Dear Mr Pratt, You don't know me from a bar of soap and most probably you never will, but I just want you to know that while you are 'inside' there is someone outside who thinks all the best thoughts for you. Your sincere admirer, R. Malan.

Dear Mr Pratt, Last week I wrote to you. You can tell it's me by the light blue Croxley, which must remind you of the colour of the sky, and the terrible handwriting I have, which this nib only makes worse. I know from my son who is a prison warder (but not at your prison — he's in Barberton of all places) that you may receive limited letters. Where he is they don't give out letters to the blacks at all, but when you're expected to be on death row you do get some. I say this just to lift your heart. An admirer, yours sincerely, R. Malan.

Dear Mr Pratt, This is your admirer again, and you must be wondering who I am and why I so admire you! Well, it isn't just your good looks, you know, and anyway I'm far from being one of these teenagers who just go mad over some movie star's picture. But I have collected every cutting there's ever been on you, and so from my scrapbook I have learnt a considerable amount: you inherited a sweet factory on the Rand which is the basis of your fortune; your fine education, marred only by the blight of epilepsy; playing polo and all and your fine war record in North Africa and

Italy. And how you tried to run for the UP in Magaliesburg where you have your ranch and the first trout hatchery in South Africa too. I gleaned it all from the papers and from your manager; they keep the place in model condition. I went out there to do some research on the ground, as they say.

Soon you'll be able to say a year, a month, a day . . . and I'll be able to say in 1959, May 16th at 12.00 David Pratt did this. Well, on that day you were having a secret lunch with Dr Dönges, weren't you? — putting your money behind a secret plot to get rid of Verwoerd before he brought the country to ruin. By 1.00 p.m. old Dönges had walked out, and so had the other very powerful man: Diederichs, wasn't it? They both walked out, but they didn't tell on you to the police, did they? You see, I have done my detective work. I reckon if you couldn't persuade them to stop him by normal means, you thought you'd have to take on the burden yourself! Am I right? You knew you didn't have much time left anyway, so why not take him with? Yours, Rita Malan.

Dear David Pratt, Forgive my familiarity, but I get to know you more and more. I feel as if I know you, even though we've never met and never will. But there is so much to say in your defence and now you say in the paper you will have no legal team, but will defend yourself. (This isn't said directly because you may not be quoted.) You *must* have defending counsel, because they want to argue under the Mental Disorders Act, No. 38 of 1916, that you were partly incapable, therefore while of unsound mind you committed or attempted to commit a crime for which you had diminished responsibility — and that way gets you off, don't you understand? If you defend yourself you'll be guilty and you'll hang. Oh David, please understand this crucial point . . . Or maybe I don't know you well enough after all, and I've not fully registered how you refuse to hide behind anything crooked. Of course I see it now: if you take full responsibility it means you thought that evil man deserved to die; that you *did* mean to kill him (the rest is cut)

Dear David, I want you to know what very good progress I've been making in unravelling your case and in coming to an understanding of you. I don't think in many details I have been wrong, have I? I found out this terrible story of how you walked into the Magaliesburg pub and called them all Ku Kluxmen and racist bigots and all; well, I've never been into a pub like that, for obvious reasons, but I can just imagine — and you're right of course, these bloody Nationalists will stop at nothing now. So they string *you* up from a lamp-post, a white man, and set your truck on fire and shoot at the support for your feet until you're hanging. They said they put your hands inside the noose so you could stop yourself being strangled. No wonder you hate the bastards! They'll make you swing again, because of what you did to their Nazi leader: so please my (cut out)

Dear David, When I sign 'Rita' it means that's my full name — it's not an abbreviation of a longer name. All the women in your life have had such romantic names — but here am I, plain Rita. 'Mrs' of course — I told you about my son. My husband is dead now, so it is just the two of us to make do, and since my son is in Barberton I rarely see him nowadays. You must miss your children a lot. I know you and your daughter from your first marriage were getting very close when this occurred. Her affidavit before the court says this, when she got custody of your financial affairs. She seems a very sensible girl to me — not a spendthrift like some I know. She pleaded very calmly and logically and made a great impression on the judge. Oh yes, I was there . . . how else would I know those details? The courts are about the only place left in this whole country where a person like me may freely go these days. I suppose now he's got a bullet in his brain (thanks to you!) Verwoerd will try and segregate the courts too! Yes, it's true, there is nowhere a person like me may go any more: bioscope shows, out of bounds; no bus to get to them anyway; no books from the public library any more; no place to stay (thank God my old employers keep me on in the back and I go out to char from there). Now there's a curfew and soldiers in tanks, man. To get to

the courthouse I had to show my pass three times and finally say *my boss* had sent me with an important message, otherwise they wouldn't let me in as myself — a respectable Coloured woman of a certain age. What have I done to Verwoerd that he makes my life a misery like this? You were perfectly justified to act as you did. God made a mistake when He let him recover, if you ask me: ████████
████████

. . . this weekend and my son came, so I feel a lot better. He says even in Barberton even the short-term prisoners are on *your* side. So you're quite a local hero with the black people, my dear! — if you don't mind me being so forward. I don't mean anything by it except to cheer your spirits, as you know. But my dear David, sometimes, although I know I shouldn't, I do wish for a sign from you; some indication of message received. If you get this at all it is only through the ingenuity of my son who is in the prison service and knows how to get these through. Otherwise they'd end up in the rubbish bin like all the other unwanted post and a lot else besides. I don't want my feelings for you to be reduced to ash, at least until I *know* you know of my concern for your well-being.

So let's change the subject a bit: I must keep you informed with all the great events surrounding your famous case. I'm sure you don't know half of it. For example, did you know the night you shot Verwoerd, in the Rand Club (not that I'd be allowed near such a precinct) there was rejoicing until 2 a.m. and you were the toast of the town. Also at Wanderers and Inanda Club (out of bounds to the likes of me). They'd all assumed Verwoerd was point-blank dead. They must have been truly shocked when *The Sunday Times* came out with the news that he would pull through. And I'm now embarrassed for my country, like them, that we have to have this man pull us all into the dirt.

I cannot explain, but I have arranged for a message from you to be delivered to me. Please acknowledge receipt of all the endeavours I have made to understand your case and the esteem in which I hold your suffering. Yours sincerely, (Mrs) Rita Malan.

Dear David Pratt, No sign, no message. I have waited over ten days. The post from Pretoria to Primrose, Johannesburg, does not take *that* long. What am I to say, what am I to do? If you do not wish to encourage my communications, you could not have found a crueller way of saying so. I paid £2. 10s., damn it, and unlike for you, for me money doesn't grow on trees. My costs in this case already amount to a small fortune. My pension money's all gone on the room and food by the 20th so what extra I get has to tide me over, but it isn't much. Damn it, you could have given me a sign. Or do you also consider me too beneath you to be bothered about? Yours in true mortification.

All right, I've calmed down now . . . because, well, what else can I do? I have had to decide how to interpret your silence. I have had to face the very real possibility, as well, that you *cannot* in fact communicate with me. My son says, down a long line of hand-to-hand stuff (it is not easy to get from Primrose to death row), that your old malady has reasserted itself and all you do in your cell is sit cross-legged and answer no one. He found out your glasses were broken when they beat the hell out of you, as they caught you when Verwoerd fell — and his security chief got such a fright he *fainted*! — remember that! They dragged you behind the tent and smashed you up so badly they wouldn't let anyone see you for the next two weeks. Your vision is still impaired in your right eye, hey? Maybe you get all my letters but just can't read them properly. DAVID I PUT THIS IN CAPITALS: YOU ARE NOT ALONE. MORE THAN HALF OUR COUNTRY AGREES WITH YOU. IF THEY HANG YOU, THEY WILL BE HANGING ALL OF US. LOVE, RITA.

Many of Mrs Malan's fervent letters to David Pratt included pertinent detail about the events leading up to the assassination attempt: the massacre of resisters at Sharpe-ville on 21 March that year, the two grand marches into Cape Town of the PAC and the subsequent devastation of Langa and Nyanga, the declaration of the state of emer-gency in most urban magisterial districts by which any tactics were admissible to stop the stayaways and drive the workers back to work. None of this could Mrs Malan have witnessed at first hand, but that did not mean she was unaware of the reasons for mass revolt, nor disassociated herself from it.

Most of this is cut from her letters. Only snippets remain. 'I wish I could send you a photo out of the newspaper of brave Chief L. burning his you-know-what' (Luthuli and his pass-book). 'I wish I could show you S. going to jail' (Sobukwe). The scissors cut out all the main events of a terribly disrupted year, during which apartheid strode in as overseas investments strode out. The scope of Mrs Malan's concerns was reduced by those scissors to her more con-ventional sympathy for the prisoner.

But one wonderful letter got through intact.

My dear David, I imagine you are over your epilepsy altogether, cured as you never could be in this world, cross-legged on your institutional bed with your hair shaven as it must be. I want to talk with you quietly about the sadness of South Africa and share with you from my heart what we outside are going through. You probably knew it was coming: this referendum over whether we should have a republic or not, with obviously guess-who as executive president. You and I have one more thing in common now: you as a classified criminal and me as a classified 'non-white' will not be asked to vote on the outcome. Nor will most of the rest of our country. Can this really be true that an issue concerning each and every one of us is not even to be put to the vast majority? White adults will decide if we are to stay a civilised nation that can hold its head up in the company of the rest of the world, or a little white state in which no one counts but the Afrikaner. I know how incensed you must feel: for if they win their white supremacist state they will surely be expelled from every forum of this day and age, and we with no choice will have to be expelled with them. I never mind the Queen on our stamps; she makes me think of all the millions of other people of colour around the world who share her on their stamps as well. And now, no permission given by the likes of you and me, we shall have Verwoerd on a stamp, so ungracious, like a great fat pig. And he rules by the will of only 9% of the people! At least everyone had a little love to spare for the Queen, don't you agree? I just thought you should know this, my dear. People will remember the sacrifice you made, even if everyone tells you to the contrary, and even if to you it sounds so useless. With respect and affection, as ever, Rita.

The last letter Rita Malan wrote to David Pratt he never received. The date of the Primrose postmark records that it was posted a few hours after his death and it would take several more days for the news to be released by the prison service. In her search for a sign, this was surely it. We may reconstruct: shortly after receiving the letter quoted above, Pratt rolled his sheet into a rope and tied it around his neck, tightening it through the bars of the headboard. Once he had twisted the sheet sufficiently to strangle himself, he managed to turn his body around two more times to make the knot even tighter and finish the job.

In other words, having lost out on every aspect of his plan to halt the rising tide of South African racism, he still reserved the right to act on his own behalf before his own life was taken from him. Many of those who remember Pratt still feel that he was murdered, as even a fit and physically tough yogi like him could not have contrived to end himself in such a bizarre way.

Here is Rita Malan's last letter to Pratt, never read by him. What became of her subsequently is not known. As she was elderly then, chances are very slim that she could still be alive thirty years later. Others involved with Pratt are still very much alive, so obviously one has to use discretion in presenting the papers he left behind. I have mentioned letters of family and friends, but none of them seems to register as well as Rita Malan the full impact of how he stepped out to intervene in history . . . failed . . . and paid the price. He knew he had a short time to live, as his epilepsy had become dangerously bad. By the end everyone had deserted him . . . except for faithful Mrs Rita Malan, this extraordinary woman whom he had never met.

My dear David, You have only one option now that no clemency may be expected: the rest of your days in the Criminal Lunatic Asylum. That's where they get rid of embarrassing cases (my son says). You will wear a pointed hat like a dunce and go up and down on your knees in your pyjamas, with a little board hung on your chest saying: 'I killed Verwoerd and he is forgotten now.' They will medicate you, because they are genuinely humane, but these will be the wrong medicines at the wrong times, and none of them will soothe the trouble in your soul. Your fits will become more frequent and take longer to subside, but at least orderlies will be around to hold you to the bed so that you do not damage yourself. Now that there is no mercy left, my dear, there is only one way.

I will always think of you, your bravery,
             With all my love.

What's Love Got to Do with It?

DEENA PADAYACHEE

The debate in the medical school canteen raged hotly among the ragged collection of exhausted, scruffy medical students.

Satyapil proclaimed, 'Look people, I just don't see the point. We're very much a Third World country. You know we need doctors desperately — look how bad things are in the rural areas. These women,' (the tone of his voice was like a red-hot lance through the brain) 'most of them anyway, will simply get hitched. They'll have kids and then maybe they'll work half a day . . . if they work at all.'

He glared at the students as if daring any of them to challenge him. They only looked back at him sullenly.

Triumphantly he continued in his high-pitched nasal voice, 'Very few of them will contribute effectively to health care in our country once they're married. South Africa cannot afford it — and they occupy precious medical school seats here.'

Satyapil didn't state the obvious: that theirs was the only black medical school in the country.

Like the rest of the group at the table, Gopal belonged to Satyapil's tutorial group. He ruminated about how thought-less Satyapil was being in discussing this point while they were having lunch; it was neither the time nor the place for it.

Satyapil was still talking: '. . . these places could have been occupied by bread-winners who would've had medi-cine as their only career. Look at how difficult it is to get a place here.'

The noise in the canteen was deafening. It was full of nurses, doctors and various workers from the adjacent hospital. The place had a Spartan finish to it and was far too small, but it was the only sit-down eating-house in the area for black people.

Shenaz looked at Satyapil and wondered what she should say. He was a tall, lanky, dark-skinned fellow, whose faded blue jeans and old shirt had seen better days. He was from a very poor family on the North Coast — the family had been evicted from their home in Riverside by the government and had moved up the coast. The poor fellow was always trying to earn some money in any way he could, even volunteering for the often uncomfortable experiments the Department of Pharmacy was always running. He felt his poverty keenly and frequently his resentment towards students who had more than he had became visible. And that included Shenaz.

Shenaz asked, 'So what do you advocate? That women should not become doctors, or that female doctors should not marry?' Her tone was soft, with only the serious look on her face betraying her concern.

'Obviously we need female doctors,' Gopal replied. 'I think many aspects of our work would appeal to the feminine personality, anyway. In countries like Russia most of the doctors are female. I think the medical school applies a quota system. It's obvious that only the brightest girls are accepted into our university.' And he smiled at Shenaz.

Shenaz liked Gopal. He was always polite and careful with what he said. A very studious and hard-working fourth year student, he still managed to be virtually free of the arrogance and condescension that so many medical students were guilty of.

Teboho sighed, 'There are so few girls at this faculty as it is. If there were only men here, what a dull place it would be.'

Gopal grinned at Teboho. The Southern Sotho had a bursary and worked on a very tight budget, but the twenty-three-year-old never complained. His incisive mind and sparkling sense of humour frequently brightened up their tutorial sessions.

Gopal added, 'You ladies bring some colour and warmth to our existence — I'm glad that you're here.'

Satyapil chipped in, 'Look, don't get me wrong; I like having women around as much as anybody else. But the health of our people is a serious business; we must be above emotion in this matter.' He focused sympathetic eyes on Shenaz and continued, 'I hope you don't take any of this personally, but we must be realistic about the situation. The concept of female doctors goes against every aspect of the Indian cultural outlook as we know it. Our society believes that the lady ought to devote herself to her family and home. Work, if it is to be considered at all, ought to be a part-time business. How will a female doctor cope with all the demands that her Indian husband will make on her?'

'I suppose you wouldn't be too happy if your wife was under the orders of another man — now would you, Satya, you old conservative!' commented Gopal with a smile.

'Damn right I wouldn't,' answered Satyapil. 'In any case, I can't see myself marrying a doctor . . .'

Teboho interjected with a laugh, 'I can't see you marrying anybody at all. In second year you were practically hitched to that female cadaver of yours, you spent such a lot of time with it! Now you just about live in the wards. You're married to Medicine, man.'

Satyapil gave a half-grin and replied, 'Well, I like medicine. Besides, I'm not half as clever as you lot. I *need* to study.'

Gopal took a sip of his cooldrink and said in a tired way, 'Don't we all?'

Teboho said, 'But man, there's some real beauties in our class — I could marry a doctor. At least she would have something in common with you. But I think the most important thing is whether our spirits touched, whether we had a certain sensitivity to each other's souls — if she felt when you felt, and you felt when she felt. Now that would be wonderful!'

Shenaz exclaimed, 'Why, Teboho, that's lovely. It's almost like poetry . . .'

Satyapil interjected acidly, 'Well, I'll bet you anything you like more than half our female graduates will be either single or divorced by the time they're thirty-five.'

Teboho grimaced and responded, 'That's a cruel thing to say.'

Shenaz looked calmly at Satyapil. Her slender hands moved expressively as she spoke. 'Medicine is a demanding profession, Satya, for all of us — and yes, it goes against the woman's basic maternal instinct when her career jeopardizes her home and family. But then we have this terrible conflict within ourselves. On the one hand we want to do everything we can and use all that God gave us to reduce pain and suffering; to try and teach people so that disease can be prevented; we want to serve our country. On the other hand, we have this perfectly normal desire to love and be loved by someone very special to us.'

Gopal grinned at the slack-suited Shenaz. 'I'm special, only you have to be very intelligent to notice it!'

Teboho knocked Gopal playfully on his chest. 'And you'll need an electron microscope to find his nice parts!'

Gopal gave his curly-haired pal a friendly poke in the ribs. Then he turned to Satyapil who was digging into a sandwich and said, 'Look, some of our most brilliant academics are women — why shouldn't they also develop their talents? I mean, look at old Fats in Pathology; she's not such a bad lecturer.'

Satyapil said between bites, 'She illustrates my point perfectly: she's cold, hypercritical and virtually devoid of feminine qualities; she's not warm or caring. Do you know that the patients refer to her as the clockwork robot?'

Teboho commented, 'Ja man! Have you noticed how she walks, arms stiff at the sides, moving precisely forward with each step like a real little robot. Here, I'll show you.' He stood up and with a mock serious expression on his face walked stiffly forward, each arm close against his body moving forward in time. The group burst into laughter.

'Can you imagine making love to that iceberg?' Satyapil said. 'I'm sure a corpse would have more feeling.'

Gopal laughed, 'I bet her poor hubby defrosts her each time he has to do it!'

'Come on now boys, you're being cruel,' said Shenaz. 'But seriously, medicine ought to make you more warm and caring, not the other way around. I think Fats would have been cold in any career; I'm not surprised that she prefers to work with microscopes and corpses rather than real, live people.'

'There are cold male lecturers as well — look at Dr Dahl and Dr Halle,' Gopal added.

'Ja, and then there's Dr Chappie and Dr Pazziz,' said Satyapil. He gazed thoughtfully at the students and, with one big ebony hand on his cheek, he continued, 'Ja well, while we look after our patients we have to detach ourselves from their pain so that we might survive. That sometimes translates in some of our colleagues into aloofness, and um — an aura of academic iciness. It's bad when that happens to men, but when it happens to the people who give birth, it's like a fundamental law of nature has been violated.'

Shenaz put her hand on Satyapil's arm. 'I think that we should not allow our personalities to be distorted by our careers . . .'

Satyapil gazed soberly at Shenaz. 'The truth is that all our personalities are modified by what happens to us, good and bad. The laws of our country have changed us, as have our experiences.'

Teboho stood up and, raising a mock serious finger, proclaimed, 'And so we need every citizen we can find to help us fight everything that causes pain in our country. Come on, the wards await us!'

Standing up, Gopal added, 'Ja man, every citizen must develop his talents, otherwise we'll be exploited like cattle.' He stretched his small frame and, with one hand on Teboho's shoulder, began walking out of the canteen.

Teboho told Shenaz as they walked, 'Yes, we need educated men, women, children — everybody! I mean this crazy government has had its fun with us for far too long. I can't believe that this is 1977 and they're still behaving like idiots.'

Shenaz thought of what a lovely soul resided in the cheerful body and rumpled clothes that responded to the name Teboho. She smiled at him and said, 'I'm glad you think that way, my friend. We must try and change those aspects of our culture that make it easier for us to be abused and humiliated.'

'Right on, Sister!' answered Teboho as they walked to the hospital nearby.

Shenaz was one of those very gentle, very dignified young ladies whom many of the male students had some kind of crush on. She appeared to personify the warmth and succour that they all hungered for after coping with the rigorous demands of their training. Yet beyond the casual, flirtatious remark, none of them tried very hard to pursue lovely little Shenaz. The trouble was that she was terribly adept at keeping all of them at arm's length. Like most of the Muslim girls at university, she didn't date. She was a delicacy all the more alluring because she was just out of reach. She was very rigid, even for a Muslim, maintaining all the religious customs from food to dress.

Shenaz, they knew, had a tremendous amount of love and understanding to give the man she would marry. They all agreed that it would be a tragedy if Shenaz didn't meet somebody she could love. She was one human being it would be marvellous to care for.

That evening the boys waited in Umbili Road for the bus to the student residence twelve kilometres away in Wenties. The topic turned once again to Shenaz. She lived in town with her parents and had already left for her home.

'Maybe you should convert,' Satyapil teased Gopal the Hindu.

Gopal grinned. 'No way!' he replied. 'In any case, I'm sure she will only consider a nice Surtee boy with whom she's intellectually and emotionally compatible . . . and she'll love the lucky swine as well.'

Satyapil gazed thoughtfully at Gopal and observed, 'I think that Riaz likes Shenaz.'

Gopal suddenly looked worried. 'What makes you say that?'

'I caught him examining Shenaz a few times; you know what I mean — the skin test. He's interested in her, you mark my words,' said Satyapil.

Teboho commented, 'Now that you mention it, I did notice him giving her the once over. And ja man, she's definitely been looking at him longer than a nice Muslim girl should!' The Sotho student was having a lovely time watching these Indian mating rituals.

Gopal said, 'Well, I can't think of a nicer guy for our little Shenaz. He's so jovial and articulate . . .'

Teboho added, 'He has a terrific quicksilver brain . . . he just glows with his zest for living.'

Gopal responded, 'Ja, he makes people feel good to be with him.'

Teboho asked, 'Well, has he, you know, made any moves?'

'I don't think so,' Satyapil replied, 'and I don't think he will.'

Teboho exclaimed, 'Why the hell not? I mean they're ideal for each other.'

With just a hint of bitterness in his voice Gopal asked, 'Ja, why not? After all, they're both Muslims.'

Satyapil answered grimly, 'She's Surtee and he's Memon. We know they hardly ever intermarry.'

Gopal said, 'Heck, I didn't know there were different types of Muslims.'

Teboho exploded, 'And what's love got to do with it?' He turned and punched the tree he was leaning against. Then he marched off a little way, as mad as hell.

However, the boys noticed the attraction between Riaz and Shenaz grow irresistibly day by day. He was always stopping to chat with her; he'd frequently be found sitting next to her. Occasionally they'd even share their lunches.

They all noticed the change in Shenaz. From the 'Marble Queen' of the class she became a laughing, vital person, sharing their risqué jokes. She appeared to become infected with some of Riaz's zest for life.

The group was gathered in the canteen again, animatedly discussing Riaz who had really set the cat among the pigeons that day. He had told the dean of the faculty at a student body meeting that it would not be ethical for

African, Indian and so-called 'Coloured' medical students to work and study at a 'Whites Only' hospital, as was being contemplated by the authorities. In a measured voice he had said, 'How can you expect us to work in a hospital that refuses to treat our relatives, or us for that matter?'

The tall, distinguished looking dean had no answer.

Riaz had also added that any doctor who prevented sick people from receiving help because of their pigmentation ought to be tried in a court of law for breaking the ethical rules of the medical profession, and for acting against the interests of the South African people. Nobody had spoken to the dean in this way before and the group was very proud of Riaz's effort.

Gopal's voice was exultant, 'Ooh, I like this boy! Only they are allowed to make the rules, and they're always finding us guilty of breaking them. Now Riaz wants to put them on trial. Fantastic!'

Shenaz was anxious. 'Well, I hope they don't victimize him because he stated what we all think.'

Satyapil commented, 'We all pay a price for progress. Let's hope the voters become a little more sensible soon.' Only white people were permitted to vote in their country.

Gopal said, 'He's such an inspiration; when he's around I feel as if apartheid becomes a sick joke that mocks its perpetrators.'

'Ja, and he's bad for our cadavers,' added Teboho in mock serious tone. 'They might decide they'd like to sit up and have a chat with him!'

Gopal said, 'Well, here's hoping he makes more of our scared people wake up. Honestly, so many of them behave like they're dead it's just not true.'

Satyapil added, 'Ja man, it's bad; too many of our people do little more than work and sleep. They're frightened to think, frightened to see more of life, terrified of trying to expand the scope of their lives because of the trauma this might bring from our fellow citizens and from the state.'

'Riaz is a good example of how we must think and act,' Teboho said.

'Well, I think he'd make a terrific family practitioner,'

said Shenaz. 'He's so warm and friendly; he puts you completely at ease. You feel you can talk to him, and he won't laugh at you if you say something silly. I've never met anyone with so much reason to be arrogant, but so completely lacking in aloofness.'

'Yes, but I'll bet everybody will take advantage of him because he's not cold and distant,' observed Satyapil.

'People are not so silly. Who would want to offend such a person and lose such an unusual friend?' responded Shenaz.

Gopal commented, 'It's those who really care who get hurt in this world. The selfish become millionaires. You have to wear your heart in a steel jacket if you don't want to be wounded by your own compassion.'

Teboho's voice was raised a few decibels. 'Oh, get lost, you lot. The rest of humanity is not so evil. It's only a person's sense of responsibility and caring that gives his life some meaning. If we do not achieve something tangible with our lives, if we don't have a sense of purpose, if we don't leave this world a better place . . .'

Satyapil cut in, 'Quick, kick him off his soap-box before his head blows up!'

Teboho scowled happily at Satyapil and continued, '. . . a better place than we found it, then what's it all for? We have to believe in the essential goodness of people.'

'Yes, but those people out there, they live their lives by a different set of rules.' The voice came from behind the crowd. They turned to see bespectacled Riaz. As usual he hadn't shaved for a day or two. He was a small fellow with an infectious grin. 'How's it, people!' he said, and they greeted him cheerfully.

Riaz continued, 'You know I've seen them continually testing our compassion and sense of caring by making unethical demands on our profession.' He paused and then said, 'And there's more than a little envy.'

'What do you mean?' asked Shenaz.

'That uncle of mine, you know the one I mean, the doctor. Anyway, he told me about this woman who wanted a medical certificate for her husband. The doctor had never seen the woman before and the man hadn't even bothered to come to the surgery! Can you believe it?'

They all laughed.

Satyapil asked, 'Did the husband eventually come? I presume he was too sick to make the journey.'

Riaz replied, 'Nothing quite so innocent. Seems the husband was having a bit of an unofficial holiday. His wife was trying to prevent the fellow losing his job.'

Satyapil asked, 'What did your uncle do?'

Riaz answered, 'He turned down the request, of course. Some of the patients behave as if doctors are Christmas Fathers.'

Satyapil said, 'I wonder if the fellow lost his job? It's a difficult ethical situation. I know some of the employers are pretty heartless. Sometimes, you know, the man has something urgent to do, like maybe take care of the funeral arrangements for a dear relative, but the employer will not allow the chap to have paid compassionate leave. A medical certificate may then be the only way that fellow can get paid leave. And sometimes, if he doesn't get a certificate, he might just get fired.'

Shenaz reacted, 'How awful; it's a tough world out there.'

Gopal said, 'Our university constitutes a tough world too, only at least here many of the rules make some sense.'

Teboho observed, 'I was thinking, people, that when the rules are made by crazy people who often have no sympathy for your culture, then our people are forced to make their own rules.'

Riaz nodded sympathetically. 'Yes, and that makes criminals of all of us who live our lives according to a different set of values.'

Gopal said, 'I heard something recently that really was not so funny.' The group turned to look at him. 'Ja, man, seems there was this nurse at this uniracial hospital who asked one of our graduates to make a cross next to the appropriate race on a laboratory form. I mean, can you imagine anybody asking one of our people to worry about the race of a patient?'

Teboho responded, 'That's crazy, man!'

Gopal said, 'Anyway, the doctor told the nurse not to worry, that the lab would still do the test. But she insisted that he make that cross; she said that the rules in the hospital were that the form had to be completed in full. It's one of those crazy hospitals where, if the most innocuous things are left out, the laboratory will not do the test and the patient ends up suffering. But this doctor had made friends with the laboratory staff so they did the test even when he didn't put in the race of the patient. So our doctor told his colleague not to worry — that he would take full responsibility for the test, and that she had done her duty by reporting the omission to him.'

Teboho commented, 'Hell, if she was so worried about the patient, she could have put in the little cross by herself. It's not such a big thing.'

Gopal said, 'Exactly. But she didn't see the bigger issues involved and how ridiculous her little bit of power-play really was. At any rate, she became quite emotional, and with her eyes full of tears she told the doctor that she knew why he didn't want to fill in the race on the form — it was because she was a nurse and he was a doctor and a nurse was telling a doctor what to do. Can you believe it?'

The group broke into laughter that was tinged with sadness.

Shenaz said, 'The poor thing must have had quite an inferiority complex, then.'

Satyapil added, 'And there must have been lots of envy.'

Riaz said, 'All right, the poor thing was ignorant, but did the doctor explain the principle involved?'

Gopal answered, 'I don't think he did.'

Teboho said, 'Well, there's a lesson for us. I think sometimes our people attack us for less than ethical reasons. We should teach them; we should try to understand them rather than mock them or get angry.'

Even though Shenaz and Riaz had become very good friends, they still did not get 'serious'. Teboho, especially, was getting quite angry with Riaz. He told Gopal, 'That fellow mustn't think he's booked Shenaz or something. I mean, I've never seen him so much as touch her. I'm sure I've touched her more than he has.'

Gopal said, 'Maybe you should take your chances with her, Teboho.'

'Maybe I should,' he replied. 'But seriously, Gopal, they're inseparable at the Medical School, yet he doesn't even take her to the cinema. Has he ever been to her house?'

'That's an idea!' Gopal explained. 'Next time we go to Shenaz's place, let's take Riaz along.'

'You mean he's never been?'

'No.'

The opportunity came after the stiff mid-year exam. Even though they'd studied all night, they couldn't sleep. The 'Fruity Four', as Shenaz called them, 'accidentally' dropped in to see Shenaz at her parents' flat. Satyapil normally did the bars after an exam, but he was persuaded to join them. Riaz was noticeably nervous, but he came along.

Shenaz opened the door. The boys hid while Teboho raised his hand in mock salute and said, 'Good afternoon, Ma'am. Titch, the Travelling Masseur. I massage away your troubles. No part of your anatomy is too much work. Special rates for the head . . .'

'And if you massage his great big foot, he'll pay you double! Hi, Shenaz,' said Riaz as he stuck his head out from the side.

With a great deal of laughter and shouting the Fruits burst into Shenaz's home. She was delighted to see them. She too had been unable to sleep. Shenaz's mother came in and quickly took in the new face: Riaz.

Mrs Vawda gave them a big smile and said, 'It's nice to see you.' She looked at Riaz.

Shenaz said, 'Ma, this is Riaz. He's also in my class. Riaz, this is my mother.'

Riaz smiled politely. 'Cosy flat you have here, Mrs Vawda; I like your lounge suite.'

Shenaz's mother smiled broadly. 'Thank you. We used to

stay in Grey Street but then the government said Indians couldn't stay there any more.' She was a fleshy, petite woman whose daughter resembled her quite closely.

After a respectable interval, Shenaz's mother left the lounge to make the tea. While the rest of them chatted, Riaz and Shenaz spent most of the time looking at each other and exchanging thoughts in a quiet undertone that was virtually inaudible to the others.

The next week disaster struck the university. The dean was notified of a government decree which stated that Africans were to be phased out from the Medical School as a separate African one was to be built. The response of the Coloured, African and Indian students was immediate and predictable: they went on an 'indefinite' boycott and they wrote to every medical body in the land, to UNESCO and to the World Medical Association, informing them of this latest abuse of what Teboho called 'unethical power'. If the boycott was not brought to an end soon, there would be very serious consequences, including among other things very few interns to work in many state hospitals.

There was also much disinformation about the real issues and so, at a mass meeting, the students decided to march to town to 'tell the people what was going on'. At that time such marches were illegal and the reaction of those in power was totally uncompromising. It was a very emotional period: the students were furious about the way in which the government was interfering with their university and trying to separate citizens simply because of their race. Few people thought of the inevitable consequences and no student voiced his fears. The decision was unanimous. All six hundred students including Shenaz and the Fruits marched.

The marchers were baton-charged by riot police, the police dogs enjoyed some human sport and ninety-one students, including Riaz, were arrested. The rest of the Fruits spent a restless night together at Shenaz's home.

At the crack of dawn the next day, they joined the huge crowd outside police headquarters. Shenaz's mother came with them. Riaz's parents, Mr and Mrs Essack, were already there. The Essacks were worried, but very proud.

Mr Essack observed, 'The government should be in prison, not our students. The government is supposed to promote education, instead they distort it, and they use our money to do so! If only we could vote them out of office.'

Mrs Essack added, 'Our children love all South Africans. The government should learn from them, instead of putting them in prison. Instead they treat foreign whites better than people born here.'

Mrs Vawda said, 'Don't these young people make you feel proud? My husband too went to jail for opposing racial segregation.'

Mrs Essack laughed and said, 'Mr Essack also went to jail for caring for his people; he demonstrated against segregated schools.'

The old folk continued chatting about the young man they respected so much. Lawyers arrived to negotiate with the state's representatives for the release of the students.

Shenaz, so calm and composed normally, was beside herself with anxiety. There was little her friends could say or do to console her. By 1 p.m. there was still no news. People began ferrying in food to the waiting throng. Police with dogs watched the multitude but did not attack them. Then at about 2.30 p.m. a cheer arose from an underground exit that had very few people in front of it. Some of the prisoners were being released from one of the four exits of the fortress. Parents, students and friends dashed there, but no more students were released.

Then a few minutes later a cheer was heard from an exit on the other side of the fortress which had very few students in front of it. The worried citizens realized what the police were doing and divided themselves equally in front of the exits so that their heroes could have an appropriate reception.

Finally Riaz appeared. He seemed as vivacious as ever. He hugged each of his friends in turn, irrepressibly cracking jokes and sympathizing with his mates for not being fortunate enough to share his experience! Then he came to

Shenaz. She hadn't slept all night and she was the picture of gloom. Her eyes were moist as she looked at him. He gazed at her; then he stepped over quickly and did something nobody had ever seen him do before: he took lovely, exquisite Shenaz in his arms and, in front of more than a thousand cheering, jubilant people, he hugged her very tightly. Shenaz burst into tears.

Teboho patted Shenaz on the back. He glowered at the horrible structure that had incarcerated his friends and said, 'That cold, concrete thing can try to jail us, but all it does is draw us closer together.'

And he hugged his friends.

The boycott continued and the dean of the Medical School suspended academic activity. Still the state would not budge.

It became difficult for the boys to judge how much further the relationship between Shenaz and Riaz had developed. As far as they could see, the pair were not even holding hands, even though it was obvious to everybody how they felt about each other. The debate raged over whether: one, Riaz would finally make his move; two, Shenaz would permit physical contact; three, Shenaz would tell her parents; four, Riaz would tell his parents; five, the two would elope; and six, Shenaz's parents would not transfer their masterpiece to another medical school.

There were still the sceptics who maintained that nothing would come of it, that Shenaz's father had a nice (Teboho insisted on calling him 'little') Surtee boy lined up (a tailor, it was rumoured). Of course there were lots of girls that Riaz could choose from.

Shenaz and Riaz maintained a discreet silence, however. Inquisitive phonecalls from their friends were deftly fielded. But Gopal stumbled on what had happened when he went to the Medical School library to get a book. He was sauntering through the deserted corridors of the university when he spotted two heads in the otherwise empty common room. He went in. Two happy faces looked up from their books at him. They were Shenaz and Riaz. Their elbows were very definitely, very deliberately touching as they sat next to each other. And on Shenaz's finger was a beautiful diamond ring.

Naturally the boys were overjoyed. But how had the two got round their parents' objections? They managed to corner Riaz alone and ask him.

Riaz explained, 'Well, my family had met Shenaz and they liked her; they could see how I felt about her. They didn't even speak about the fact that she's Surtee. So we tackled the next obstacle: Shenaz's parents. I dropped in on a few occasions to see Shenaz, and her mother was not hostile.

'So we decided to take the bull by the horns and visit Mr Vawda in his shop. He was actually quite friendly. He took us to his office at the back and gave us tea. He spoke about what his generation went through in the nineteen fifties and sixties, when they were kicked out of their homes by the laws of the country and black people struggled to get an education. He said he was very proud of our generation and felt sure we would live to see freedom.

'Finally Shenaz said, "Pa, Riaz and I are very good friends."

' "I know," said her father and his eyes were shining. "You choose your friends well."

'I took a deep breath and told Mr Vawda that I wanted to marry his daughter. His face did not become hard, but before he could say anything, Shenaz told him in her quiet way that she loved me and that there was no one else for her. She spoke softly but it was one of the few times that I noticed a certain steel in her voice.

'I'll never forget the way Mr Vawda looked at his daughter then. The old man had a look of admiration and respect in his eyes. He didn't say anything. He just stood up, reached out and shook my hand. Then in his gruff way, he congratulated me! In an emotional voice the old man said, "Welcome to my family, Riaz, we're proud to have you. I'm sure my daughter will be very happy with you." '

Teboho let out a hoot of delight.

Riaz continued, 'He never even said anything about Surtees and Memons. Instead he looked at us and said, "I'm filled with hope that our country can still produce citizens with your values, despite all the repression by the criminals." Then he stuck out his big, hairy hand at his daughter and congratulated her. He took her in his arms and hugged her like a big bear.

'Shenaz began crying and said, "Oh, Pa, I'm so happy!"

' "There there, darling," he said joyfully, "I'm very happy for you. You've chosen well." Then he grinned at me and added, "My baby certainly seems to like the company of ex-convicts! First her father, now her fiancé. Well, young man, you'll find that after prison marriage can be quite fun!"

'We burst out laughing and Shenaz said, "Pa, you're the limit!"

'After that,' Riaz continued, 'my parents were a snap. We'll be married after the final examinations. That's if we ever write them.'

After more than five weeks of boycott and an international outcry, the state finally relented. There had also been much protest throughout the country at the 'needless separation of South Africans who want to be together'.

All the Fruits passed the examinations. And Africans still attend their university. Teboho, especially, enjoyed the wedding, the first Indian one he'd ever been to. But he was rather annoyed at how little resistance had been put up by Shenaz's parents. He was heard to mutter, 'If a goddamn Memon could have married her, I shouldn't have been put off by these Coolie clowns!'

Cardboard Mansions

FARIDA KARODIA

'Chotoo! Eh Chotoo!'

'Ja, Dadi-Ma?' the boy cried from the far side of the yard.

'Don't ja Dadi-Ma me! Come here!' the old woman called from the stoep. Leaning over the low abutment wall, she craned to peer around the corner but her view was obstructed by a pile of rubbish. She stepped back knocking over the chipped enamel pail which was normally kept beside her bed at night. The empty pail rolled out of reach, clattering against the wall.

She waited for the boy, pulling the end of the faded green cotton sari over her head. Her wide, flat heels hung over the back of the blue rubber thongs almost two sizes smaller than her feet.

Dadi-Ma looked much older than her seventy-three years. She was a tall, heavily built woman with slow, tired movements. Her dark brown eyes were set deep in a face scored and marked with age and hardship. The gap in the front of her mouth was relieved only by three stumps of rotted teeth, bloodily stained by betel-nut.

In her youth she had been much admired for her beauty, with her dark lustrous eyes like those of a young doe. But there was no one left to remember her as she'd been then. Sonny, the youngest of her sons, and her grandson, Chotoo, were the only surviving members of her family. Three of her sons and her husband, like so many of the men who had toiled in the sugarcane fields, had all died of tuberculosis.

And now the only ones left to her were her grandchild, Chotoo, and her friend Ratnadevi. Dadi-Ma in her old age was left to gaze upon the world with the patient endurance of the old water buffalo they had once owned in India.

The boy, Chotoo, took a long time coming. His grand-mother waited, her broad, varicose-veined feet and legs planted astride. A rip in her sari revealed a discoloured slip, unadorned and frayed. Her dark eyes stared out from under thick brows, slowly gathering in impatience.

'Chotoo!' she called again and sat down on the step to wait.

The row of shanties was all connected. At one time they had served as a shed, but an enterprising landlord had used sheets of corrugated iron to divide the shed into stalls which he rented to the poor. All the dividing walls stopped at least twelve inches short of the ceiling.

On Saturday night when Frank Chetty beat his wife, Nirmala, her cries swirled over the heads of the other tenants. Some ignored them. Others were just grateful that they were not in Nirmala's shoes. Dadi-Ma's daughter-in-law, Neela, had once remarked to their neighbour, Urmila, that no matter what Sonny was guilty of, this was one thing that he had not yet stooped to.

'Just you wait and see,' Urmila said. 'It'll happen when Sonny loses his job.'

But even when Sonny lost his job he never raised a hand to his wife. Chotoo, however, was not so lucky and in his short life had been slapped many times, often for no apparent reason. Despite this, Dadi-Ma's pride in her son remained undiminished. She could hold up her head and say that he had never lifted a hand to his wife or his mother.

It had come as a terrible blow to Dadi-Ma when Neela had died in childbirth three years ago, leaving Sonny with the boy, Chotoo. But Sonny was hardly ever around and everything had fallen on her shoulders. Somehow they managed. Even when Sonny lost his job they still managed. Dadi-Ma used many of the ideas she had picked up from Ratnadevi who had a real knack for making do.

But eventually Sonny had fallen in with a bad crowd and everything seemed to come apart. Now there was a new element in their struggle, one that caused Dadi-Ma a great deal of anxiety. As Sonny was jobless, there was not a penny coming in any more, yet all weekend long Sonny smoked dagga. Sometimes he drew the reefers through a broken bottleneck making himself so crazy that he'd end up running amok with a knife. At times like these Dadi-Ma and Chotoo had to hide from him until the effects of the dagga wore off.

Without means to pay the rent there was constant friction between himself and the landlord. Sonny, desperate and irritable, pleaded with the landlord until they reached a state of open hostility. The tenants were all drawn into this conflict, all except Dadi-Ma. She alone remained aloof and detached. Sitting on the concrete step in front of their room, she listened in silence to the two men arguing when the landlord came to collect the rent. Sonny's response was always wild and abusive. Although she was afraid that he would harm the landlord, she remained impassive.

The landlord, Mr Naidoo, grew to resent the old woman. He thought that her silence was a way of showing contempt for him. Who was she to judge him, a man of means and property? He often wondered as he drove off in his Mercedes why it was that she never said anything. What thoughts crossed her mind as she sat there, implacable as a stone Buddha? In the end he grew to hate the old woman.

Then one day the inevitable happened: Sonny got into a drunken brawl and stabbed someone. He was arrested, sentenced and thrown into jail. Mr Naidoo saw his opportunity to evict the old woman, but he hesitated, fearing censure from the other tenants, some of whom had contributed to help Dadi-Ma with her rent. He knew, though, that this situation could not continue indefinitely. Those who had supported her were themselves experiencing difficulty. So he bided his time.

It happened that a few months later the old woman fell so far behind with her rent that the others could no longer assist her. Now at last Mr Naidoo could exercise his rights; he gave Dadi-Ma her notice.

She was devastated. She had tried so hard to keep the roof over their heads. There was nothing for her to do now but pack their few possessions. They would have to move, but where to? she fretted. Dadi-Ma's concern was more for her grandson than for herself. She did not have many more years left, but what would happen to this boy who was only starting out in life?

'What took you so long, hey?' Dadi-Ma demanded, feigning severity when the boy finally joined her.

He shrugged, his hands thrust deep in his pockets, emulating the cockiness of the older boys who hung out in the alley. She tousled his hair and he sat down on the step beside her, pressing close to her side where he felt safe and secure.

For a time they sat like this in silence, the boy content with this closeness while his grandmother brooded about the past and the problems which were driving them into the unknown. Her mind moved slowly and ponderously, like an ox picking its way over the stones, lingering on the good times.

Lately her thoughts had started returning to those happy years — to Ratnadevi and Stanger. The two women had shared a friendship that went back a long way. They had arrived on the same boat from India to marry two indentured labourers on the sugarcane fields in Natal. They had lived in the same compound, as close as sisters, sharing in each other's joys and tragedies.

'Why you like the skollies?' the old woman asked the boy, adjusting the sari over her head. 'They no good.'

'Why you say that, Dadi-Ma?' he asked. His enormous brown eyes turned up to her questioningly.

He was so young, she thought, how could he understand that she wanted him to make something of his life? How could he understand that if he didn't try, this was all he had to look forward to?

'Because they bad. They smoke dagga. You best go to school so you can be something, hey?' she said in her broken English.

'We don't do nothing wrong, Dadi-Ma, we just sit out there bullshitting.'

The old woman shook her head wearily.

'They say old man Naidoo going to throw us out. Where we going to go, Dadi-Ma?'

Dadi-Ma felt a deep attachment to her grandson. She had been drawn to him from the moment he was born. It had been Dadi-Ma who took care of him right from that first day, not his mother who was too tired and sickly to care. From Chotoo came the only warmth and caring that life still apportioned to her. All that the boy had known of love and tenderness came from her; not from his mother, whom he could not remember. It was a bond that neither had words for. The only expression Dadi-Ma ever gave her grandson of her feelings was a rare and awkward pat on his cheek, or the tousling of his hair with her arthritic fingers.

The boy, undernourished and small for his age, with eyes as large and expressive as hers had once been, was conscious of his grandmother's love. The others, like his parents, had deserted him. But not her. She was the fulcrum in his fragile existence.

'I was thinking, Chotoo, maybe you and me, we go to Stanger. It will be a good place for us. This place is no good,' she muttered.

'Where is Stanger, Dadi-Ma?' he asked, his voice catching in breathless excitement.

'It's not so far away.'

'How will we go . . . by car, by train?' he asked, in his shrill little voice.

She nodded, smiling down at him. 'We go by train.'

Dadi-Ma had saved some money for just such an emergency. The money, fifty rands, was what she had amassed in her long lifetime. Money that she had artfully secreted. Many times the money had gone for some other emergency but somehow she had always managed to replace it. Sometimes it had been slow to accumulate; money from the sale of a few pieces of gold jewellery brought with her from India, a few cents here and there from what she could scrimp out of the money Sonny had given her to buy food and clothes in the good old days when he still had a job.

These savings were all that stood between them and destitution now. The previous night she had removed the money from its hiding place beneath the linoleum under her bed, and in the dim light of the lamp she had counted it carefully, stacking the small coins in even piles, smoothing out the crumpled notes. Then she had returned it to the hiding place for safekeeping.

After a while Chotoo started fidgeting and wriggled out from under her arm.

'You don't tell nobody,' Dadi-Ma warned him. 'If old man Naidoo find out he make big trouble for us.'

Chotoo nodded. Despite his age, he understood. 'Can I go and play now, Dadi-Ma?'

'Ja, you go and play, but you remember what I tell you.'

'I won't tell nobody, Dadi-Ma.'

She nodded and he sauntered off to the side of the house where the dagga smokers hung out. She watched him go, legs thin and scaly, the knobbly knees protruding just below his short trousers, his feet rough and thickened from going barefoot.

The tenement somehow always reminded Dadi-Ma of the quarters they had once occupied on the sugarcane plantation. There she and her husband had lived in a barracks with dozens of other workers, separated from the rest by paper-thin walls, or frayed curtains. In summer the windowless barracks were like ovens and then when the rains came it was like the monsoons in India, lasting for weeks and turning the compound into a quagmire.

Further north along the east coast was the town of Stanger where Ratnadevi had eventually moved after her husband died. His death had released Ratnadevi and her family from the contract which had bound them to the plantation. When Dadi-Ma's own husband had died and Sonny had run off to the city, Dadi-Ma had also moved to Stanger to live with Ratnadevi.

She remembered every detail so clearly. The wooden shack set back from the road amidst a clump of mango, banana and litchi trees. There had been an abundance of everything on that small piece of property, even the birds flocked to feed off the ripening fruit. It was indeed a wonderful sight and one that Dadi-Ma had cherished since that time.

She had never been happier than during those days with Ratnadevi in that old shack in Stanger. The two of them had managed by taking in laundry from the white people, most of whom were English-speaking. They also used to weave baskets which they sold in the local community, or peddled in the market place where Ratnadevi had a hawker's barrow.

The house was at the end of a gravel road. It was the last house on the street with a larger corner lot where parts of an old picket fence still stood. On windy nights they could hear the pickets clattering and rattling against each other. Each sound had its own particular significance and was like music to Dadi-Ma's ears. Some nights when it was very quiet she imagined she could hear the strains of a flute, the same poignant sounds made by Manu, the confectioner in her village in India, when he sat on the front step of his hut playing to the night.

From one of the big trees in the front yard hung a swing carved from an old tyre. There had been enough room for a large garden and the eggs produced by the hens were taken to the market each day. Dadi-Ma learnt a great deal about survival from the years she had spent there.

Then to interrupt this happiness, something unexpected had happened which irreversibly altered the tempo of her life. Sonny, who had married and moved to Port Elizabeth, sent for her. He was her son; her only son, how could she have refused him? Without the slightest hesitation, Dadi-Ma packed her few belongings and went to live with her son and Neela, her daughter-in-law. Neela, she found, was a frail and sickly girl who was unable to withstand the rigours of married life. Dadi-Ma took care of them all.

Several years went by and to Dadi-Ma's dismay her daughter-in-law, Neela, had still not produced a child. For reasons that Dadi-Ma did not understand the young girl could not carry a single pregnancy to its full term, miscarrying each after only four months.

It was a difficult life but Dadi-Ma never complained,

even though she hated city life and constantly longed for Stanger and for Ratnadevi. The years passed and memories of those happy days began to dim. Eventually she stopped thinking about them. For fifteen years she lived with Sonny and his wife, taking care of them, and suffering constant abuse at the hands of Neela who grew resentful of her role in the house. Then one day, five years ago, Neela gave birth to Chotoo and it was as though Dadi-Ma had finally found fulfilment.

Now, ever since the landlord had given them notice, her thoughts returned again to that little house at the end of the road with the swing in the front yard. She could see the trees and hear the plank veranda and fence creaking in the wind.

Dadi-Ma remained on the step, dreaming. There was a stench of urine and human excrement in the air which came from a blocked sewer. They were accustomed to the stench which mingled with the rancid smell of old ghee and curry.

In a way Dadi-Ma was relieved that they were leaving. It was too difficult to raise a boy in this environment. He needed to run free, to breathe air unpolluted by smoke and odours of decay. Dadi-Ma's thoughts drifted back to the long low line of hills in the north, to mango and litchi trees laden with fruit. She remembered how she and Ratnadevi had sat out on the veranda, identifying the gaily coloured birds as they swooped down into the trees.

She and Ratnadevi had spent so much of their time in the backyard, doing the washing, kneading and scrubbing the heavy linen against the fluted surface of the washboard. In their spare time they sat beneath the tree, weaving baskets. Sometimes they chatted about their life in India, or life on the plantation; other times they worked in easy companionable silence.

Chotoo returned to his grandmother's side, wanting to know more about this place called Stanger. She was smiling to herself now as she thought of how she and Ratnadevi would once again sit out in the yard. She remembered the long washing line and the sputtering sizzle as Ratnadevi deftly spat against the iron. She remembered the smell of lye and freshly ironed laundry.

They could weave baskets again. As if following her thoughts her fingers, now stiff with age and arthritis, fell awkwardly into the familiar movements of weaving. The boy, seeing this, pressed closer to her side. She looked down upon him sombrely and drew his head against her chest. She began to talk to him of the life she had once known. The boy listened and with her words felt a new sense of adventure.

That night Dadi-Ma bundled together their few possessions. Her plan was to leave under cover of darkness since she did not have the money to pay the landlord the rent that was owing.

They caught the train for Durban early the next morning. For Chotoo the adventure had begun. Through most of the journey he was awake, his nose flattened against the window. In the second-class coach they shared their compartment with two other women, who chatted amiably with his grandmother while he remained at her side.

When they arrived in Durban, he grabbed a handful of his grandmother's sari, and hung on while she carried the bundle of belongings on her head. In the street outside the station they got into the bus for Stanger.

It was a long drive and they passed fields of sugarcane. Dadi-Ma pointed out many things to him, drawing his attention to this or to that. He stood against the seat, his nose once again pressed to the window, lurching against her as the bus bumped and swayed. They stopped often to offload passengers on the road and it was afternoon before they arrived at their destination.

Dadi-Ma became excited as they approached the town. She asked the woman across the aisle about the bus stop. The woman told her that the bus went all the way to the market. Dadi-Ma was pleased. She knew her way from there.

They entered the town and Dadi-Ma looked around for familiar landmarks, but things had changed. The market was no longer where she had remembered it to be. It had been moved to a new location. Dadi-Ma was puzzled. She spoke to the woman again, asking where the old market was, but the woman shrugged, saying she didn't know. She did not live here, only visited occasionally.

'Ask the woman over there,' she said.

Dadi-Ma got up from her seat and Chotoo followed her, clutching the end of her sari. In her anxiety she was impatient with him. 'Stay there,' she snapped.

Chotoo's eyes grew large and mournful and she was sorry that she had spoken sharply. She touched his cheek and explained that she would be back in a moment, that she was merely going to speak to the woman over there, near the front of the bus. She told him to remain in the seat so that no one could take it.

Chotoo understood and hung back.

Dadi-Ma spoke to this other woman for several minutes. Chotoo watched her and sensed her unease.

'What is it, Dadi-Ma?' he asked when she returned.

'We will have to walk a long distance,' she told him.

'Why?' he asked.

'So many questions!' she exclaimed. Then she said, 'The market-place where the bus stops is no longer where I thought it would be, they have moved it.'

The boy did not say anything; he sensed in her a new anxiety that bewildered him.

When they got off the bus at the market-place, the woman Dadi-Ma had talked to in the front of the bus asked why they wanted to get to that particular street.

'It is where my friend Ratnadevi lives,' she said.

'Your friend lives there?' the woman asked, surprised.

'Yes, she has a small house with big trees.'

The woman fell silent. Then she shrugged her shoulders. Perhaps this friend was a servant in one of the big houses out there, she concluded.

Dadi-Ma smiled and thanked the woman.

The woman repeated her instructions, telling them to go to the end of the wide road and then to turn to the left and continue on for five more streets to where there was a big store. At that point they were to turn right and walk for several blocks until they reached the area of big houses and mansions. There they were to turn right again to the street Dadi-Ma was enquiring about. 'But there is no small house there like the one you have described,' the woman said.

'From there I will know my way,' Dadi-Ma assured her. She thanked the woman, hoisted the bundle on to her head, and waited for Chotoo to get a good grip on her sari. Then she left. Her feet in the old champals flip-flopped as she walked away. The other woman watched them going.

Dadi-Ma and Chotoo walked a long way that day, stopping often to rest. Chotoo was tired and dragged on her sari and she had to urge him on with quiet words of encouragement. She talked about the trees and the birds, nurturing the anticipation which lightened his step. At the end of the road, they stopped. She took down the bundle from her head and carefully unwrapped it. Packed amongst their belongings was a bottle of water. She handed it to Chotoo who took a long drink, then after taking a sip herself, she screwed the cap back on and returned the bundle to her head.

They turned left and continued on. She recognized some of the landmarks, her heart lurching excitedly as she pointed these out to the boy. Then they turned right and suddenly nothing seemed familiar any more.

Nevertheless they pressed on, following the woman's directions. They walked all the way to the end of the street in silence. On both sides of the street were large houses surrounded by walls and fences. The open field she remembered was no longer there. Her legs automatically propelled her forward. The pain that had racked her limbs through the past few days now gave way to fear which turned her legs to jelly.

They had made the last right turn and supposedly this was the street where she had once lived. Her dark eyes looked out upon an area that was unrecognizable. Slowly and wearily they made their way to the end of the street, but Ratnadevi's house was no longer there, neither were the trees and the groves of bamboo. She took the bundle from her head. The boy raised his eyes to look at her. In her face he saw the bewilderment.

Dadi-Ma was tired now, her legs could no longer hold her weight and she sat down on the kerb, drawing the boy down beside her.

'What's wrong, Dadi-Ma? Where is Ratnadevi's house?'

Dadi-Ma's fingers moved, weaving an invisible basket.

'Dadi-Ma?' he said in a small voice.

'Hush, Chotoo. Don't worry. We'll rest a bit and then we'll find Ratnadevi's house.'

Chotoo drew close to his grandmother, resting his head on her lap for he was tired and sleepy.

The woman must have made a mistake, she thought. Ratnadevi's house was probably at the end of some other street and she would find it. A small house with a plank veranda and many trees with birds. Chotoo would be able to climb trees and pick fruit to his heart's content and sometimes he'd help them to pick bamboo for baskets.

A servant who had seen them sitting there came out of one of the houses. 'Why are you sitting here?' she asked.

Dadi-Ma described the house she was searching for.

'Yes, I remember that one,' the woman said. 'The house was torn down a long time ago.'

'What happened to the people who once lived here?' Dadi-Ma asked.

The woman shrugged and shook her head.

Dadi-Ma sat back, the pain that had nagged her all day, numbing her arms, suddenly swelled in her chest. The woman noticed the way Dadi-Ma's colour had changed.

'Are you all right, Auntie?' she asked.

Dadi-Ma compressed her lips and nodded. She did not want to alarm Chotoo. Did not want him to be afraid. She struggled to get up, the woman helping her to her feet.

But Chotoo saw the expression on his grandmother's face and for the first time in his life he felt insecure and uncertain about the future; felt a dreadful apprehension of being wrenched from the only human being he had ever loved.

'Dadi-Ma, Dadi-Ma,' he sobbed.

'It's all right, Chotoo, it's all right.'

But he knew that it wasn't all right, that it would never be all right again.

Another Story

ZOË WICOMB

Approaching D. F. Malan airport. The view from the window on the right, that is, as you enter the aircraft: it falls out of the blue, suddenly, even with your eyes fixed on the ground rising towards you — a perfect miniature plane, a razor-edged shadow in the last of the sunlight, earthborne, yet flying alongside where before there had been nothing. And then it grows. Because the sun is low and because nothing, no nothing will remain a little toy-thing. (A darling little toy-thing, but that sort of word has no place here and must be excised.) Yes, flying across the earth, it gradually grows larger. Still wonderful while its outline remains sharp, until an ungainly leap in size when overblown, with edges grown soft and arrowed wings blunted, the once-lovely little thing spreads and is swallowed. A simple multiplication and division sum, a working out of velocity, height, angle of the sun, etc., could have foreseen that moment. But she didn't. Or perhaps couldn't. So that was that. And the plane landed with the usual bump and the ping of the pilot's intercom.

To tell the truth, Miss Kleinhans was scared. And Dollie's voice as she leaned over the wild with morning-glory fence rang in her ears.

'If you asking my advice, Deborah Kleinhans, I say stay right here where you belong. You not young, man, and there's no need to go gallivanting after family you don't know from Adam. I mean, family is now family, but the whole point is that family is family because you know them. It's not a stranger who gets to know you through ink and how-do-you-do on paper. And remember Cape Town is full of troubles with people throwing stones and getting shot. And what with you being a stranger in Town. Have you listened to the wireless today?'

Deborah's head spun in an attempt to work out how knowing or not knowing blood relations affected the claims that such people could legitimately make on her, for she had come to see the visit as a duty. Also, the morning-glory trumpets had started yawning and she watched the first fold up neatly, spiralling into a tight spear that betrayed nothing of its fulsome blue.

'Dollie, this thing will take some thinking about. But it's too cold out here for me.' She had not asked for Dollie's advice; she had merely spoken of her indecision. But if only she had listened to Doll who was after all a sensible person, a neighbour she could rely on, even if that husband of hers was a good-for-nothing dronklap. I should have been a spinster like you, hey, Dollie sometimes said in exasperation, but Deborah could tell how the word spinster cut into her heart, for Doll would swirl the remains of her coffee and gulp down the lot as she rose with just that hint of hoarseness in her voice, I'll have to go and get ready the old man's bredie. Or his socks, or boots, or ironing, and even she, the spinster, knew that that was not the worst a woman had to do. She who had worked for years in white households knew more about things than people thought.

There had been two letters. The first simply a matter of introduction. A certain Miss Sarah Lindse from a wayward branch had traced her, a great-aunt, wishing to check the family connection and with Old Testament precision had untangled the lines of begetting into a neat tree which Deborah found hard to follow. Coloured people didn't have much schooling in her day but she knew her Bible and there was no better education in the world than knowing the Bible from cover to cover. Still, enough names on those heavy branches looked familiar, although so many children, dear Lord, why ever did her people have so many children. Family tree! It was a thicket, a blooming forest in which the grandest of persons would get lost. And she pursed her mouth fastidiously; she had a lot to be thankful for.

There were times when you had to face the truth; times like this when you'd made a wrong decision and the good Lord allowed you the opportunity to say, I have been guided by vanity. And in the same breath she found her vindication: for a person who had worked as a respectable housekeeper all her life, but in service all the same, the connection with this grand young woman was only what she deserved. A history teacher at the university in Cape Town. The drop of white blood, no doubt, and she sighed as she thought of that blood, pink and thin and pure trouble. Ag, that was a long time ago and now she had a niece, a lovely girl who was educated and rich and who wrote in the second letter: I'll send you a plane ticket. Come and have a holiday in Cape Town. To her, an old woman whom the child had never even met. And Deborah, who had been timid all her life, who had kept her feet firmly on the ground and her eyes modestly fixed on those feet, for once looked up to see the serpent of adventure wink through the foliage of the family tree. And she was undone. And at her age too, but she replied, keeping to the lines of her Croxley pad with a steady hand, although these modern pens behaved as if light upward strokes and bold downward strokes were the last thing they hoped to achieve: I have always wanted to fly and would like to look around Cape Town. But I don't need a holiday so you can save up the darning and mending and of course I could do the cooking while you get on with bookwork. Thank you for the offer.

It was also that nonsense of Dollie's. She had managed to think it through and it simply did not make sense. Family is family and the whole point of such an unnecessary statement was that you didn't have to know the person. Vanity again: she had proven her ability to reason things out for herself and in showing off to Dollie had brought upon herself this business — this anxiety.

If only she had someone to talk to on the flight. Silence was something still when you were on your own but here with a flesh and blood person sitting right by your side the silence fidgets between you, monitors your breathing, stiffens the body and makes you fearful of moving. So many new things cannot become part of you unless you could say to the person sitting right there, My what a business this is, without of course letting on that you've never flown before.

But the red-faced woman next to her had swung round to the aisle as if she, Deborah Kleinhans, freshly bathed and in her best Crimplene two-piece, as if she had b. o. Ag, it's the way of the world, she consoled herself, these whites don't know how to work things out, can't even run their own blooming homes. If she were in charge she'd have Apartheid to serve the decent and God-fearing — that was a more sensible basis for separating the sheep from the goats, but she sighed, for how would one know, how could one tell the virtuous from the hypocrites, the Pharisees. These days people grew more and more like jackals and the education business only helped to cover up sorcery and fornication.

And here Miss Kleinhans felt once more a twinge of regret, a tugging at her intestines which happily could be diverted from the new niece to the wonderful South African Airways lunch. All nicely separated in little compartments that Dollie could well be alerted to, her with the eternal bredies, day after day everything mixed together, meat, potatoes, tinned peas and veg and then, on the plate, that man of hers would stir in the rice, pounding, as if it were mortar to be shovelled into the cracks of his soul. But it would've been nice just to say to the red-faced woman, Isn't it oulik these little brown dishes like housie-housie things. Last time I flew they were orange you know. Just in case. And she lifted her head high; no one could accuse her of being ignorant, green and verskrik as a young farm-girl. The Goodlord she felt sure would forgive her. Especially after the temptation, the terrible desire to put one in her bag, only the little SAA pudding dish of cream and brown plastic and with the white woman's back virtually turned to her, nothing could be easier. But she didn't. And she praised Dearjesus who resisted forty days in the Wilderness and felt sure that He would not expect her to fast just because He had, not on this her first flight with food so prettily packed.

That was before she thought of the order of eating. She knew that one did not just start any old where you liked. Her De Villiers household always had fish or soup to begin with but how was she to determine the order of things that in fact were the same. A test that would have made the woman, if her back had not mercifully been turned, giggle at her ignorance, for there in the little compartments was tomato and lettuce alone and again tomato and lettuce with meat, and how was she to decide which came first. More than likely the two halves of the same tomato turned into different names on different plates, which only went to show how silly all this blinking business was, but she was grateful all the same for the disdain of the woman who had swung round into the aisle. At what point was she to eat the round bread? Only poor people, her father had always said, ate bread with their dinner, so she would look upon it as a test, like in the fairy tale of a round red apple or something to tempt and catch the heroine out. Why else would the two large black berries have been hidden under the lettuce? She would have arranged it on top to set off the green and red; she had always paid attention to presenting food attractively and Mrs de Villiers never had anything but praise for her dishes.

The pip of the foul-tasting berry proved yet another trap. How was she to get the damned thing out of her mouth and back on to the plate? Would she have to pretend that she was not hungry, that she could only just pick at her food? What nonsense, she admonished herself. This was no boiled sweet destined to dissolve; she could not very well keep a pip hidden in her cheek until God knows when, so she spat it into a paper napkin under cover of wiping her mouth, and niftily tucked it into her sleeve. There was no one watching her; she would tuck in and not waste the poor girl's money; this food — never mind if it didn't live up to the cute containers — was expensive and, what's more, paid for. How could she, a grown person, be so silly and she chuckled audibly so that the red-faced woman took the opportunity to adjust her discomfort, to straighten her spine and allow herself ten degrees that would bring Miss Kleinhans's fork just within her line of vision.

The girl must have been relying on a family resemblance; why else had she not suggested ways of identifying herself. Perhaps she should wave a white handkerchief or something. That was what people did in *Rooi Rose*, which only went to show that *Rooi Rose* then was not for people like her. She could never do such a thing, make a spectacle of herself. It must have been the flight through high air that made her think such unusual thoughts. As if she had taken a feather duster to her head so that those stories, she now clearly saw, were for white people. Which did not mean that she couldn't read them: she was used to wearing white people's clothes and eating their leftovers, so what difference did it make reading their stories. As long as she knew and did not expect to behave like a *Rooi Rose* woman. It was difficult enough just sitting there, waiting, with so many idle eyes roving about. She lifted her head to concentrate on the lights flashing their instructions about smoking and seat-belts until they finally clicked off, the messages exhausted, and felt herself adrift midst empty seats and the purposeful shuffling of people anxious to go.

Deborah looked about and caught sight of the red-faced woman who flashed her a warm smile. What on earth could the person mean? She was not to be lured by a smile of falsehood, here where there was no danger of striking up a conversation. As far as she was concerned it just was too bladdy late. What a cheek, but then, not keeping track of things, a smile leaked from her lips all the same and she had no choice but to incline her head to nod a greeting.

The usual Cape Town wind awaited her, just as Dollie had said, and Deborah smoothed her skirt and patted her head to check that the doekie was still in place. Crossing that space was not simply a question of putting one foot before another. The tarmac felt sticky underfoot; the wind snapped like a mongrel; and her ankles wobbled unreliably above the Sunday shoes. Ahead, through the glass, a tinted crowd waited, waved, and what would she do if the girl was not there? That she could not allow herself to think about. The Goodlord would provide. Although the Goodlord so often got His messages mixed up, like telephone party-lines, so that good fortune would rain into the unsuspecting lap of that heathenish husband of Dollie's, when it was she, Deborah Kleinhans, who had spent the holy hours on arthritic knees, praying. If red-face walking purposefully just ahead of her was expecting no one, you could be sure that some thoughtful niece on the spur of the moment had decided to meet her after all, while she, a stranger in this town . . . But this time, and Deborah was careful to smile inwardly, this time, He got it just right.

Sarah was confident that she would recognize her great-aunt by the family resemblance and indeed the woman walking unsteadily across the tarmac could be no other than Deborah Kleinhans. Who, incidentally, was the only elderly Coloured woman on the flight. Sarah corrected herself: so-called Coloured, for she did not think that the qualifier should be reserved for speech. It grieved her that she so often had to haul up the 'so-called' from some distant recess where it slunk around with foul terms like half-caste and half-breed and she stamped her foot (which had gone to sleep in the long wait) as if to shake down the unsummoned words. Lexical vigilance was a matter of mental hygiene: a regular rethinking of words in common use, like cleaning out rotten food from the back of a refrigerator where no one expects food to rot and poison the rest.

The old woman was stronger, sturdier than she imagined, with the posture of someone much younger. But she was tugging at the navy-blue suit which had got nipped, or so it seemed, by her roll-on, so that her hem-line dipped severely to the right. Also, threatening to slip off, was the doekie which had to be hauled back over the grey head as she struggled with a carrier-bag in the wind. But they met without difficulty.

'So we found each other. Something to be grateful for these days when you lose and search for things that disappear under your very nose . . .'

'And people going missing by the dozens,' Sarah interjected. Deborah looked alarmed. Whatever was the child talking about; not her, she had to get back home; Dollie would be expecting her in precisely one week.

'Ag, they say big cities swallow you up but we're old enough to look after ourselves. Dollie's people,' she added, 'even in Kimberley, you know, after the riots. Clean disappeared. But one never knows with these children. Dollie is now Mrs Lategan who's been my neighbour for twenty years.' Then she chuckled. 'But what if we are not the people we think we are, or no, that's not what I mean. Let's sit down child, I get so deurmekaar and I need to take a good look at you.' They sat down and looked at each other surrounded by squeals and hugs and arm-waving reunions. In the two pairs of eyes, the flecked hazel eyes derived from the same sockets of a long dead European missionary, there was nothing to report. The improbable eyes, set generations ago into brown faces, betrayed nothing, as eyes rarely do, but both claimed to read in the other signs and traces so that they held each other as firmly as the rough and wrinkled hand gripped the young and smooth. Deborah wondered for the first time why the girl had brought her all that way. Sarah thought of her father who in his last years had kept a miscellany of rare physical complaints. A man who knew his viscera like the back of his hand and could identify a feeling of discomfort with self-claimed accuracy — his liver, or pancreas, or lower section of the colon — an unnecessary refinement since the remedy of Buchu Essence served them all. She hoped that her great-aunt would not get ill; those were surely the eyes of a hypochondriac.

The girl was rather disappointing: untidily dressed in denim without a dash of lipstick to brighten her up. There was something impenetrable about her face, a density of the flesh that thwarted Deborah who prided herself on looking right into the souls of strangers. Also, her car was not at all what Deborah had expected but then she did not think any car smart except for a black one. The house that they pulled up at was very nice, but modest, she thought, for a learned person. With so much rain here in Cape Town it seemed a pity not to have a proper garden. Just a little patch of untrimmed grass and a line of flowers sagging against the wall. Yellow and orange marigolds, their heads like torches, so that she turned to look back at the dark mountain and saw the last light gathered in the flaming peak of a cloud.

The medicinal scent of marigolds followed them into the house. Through the passage lined with old photographs. So many people with nothing better to do than stand around and wait for the click of a camera. And right into the kitchen until the marigolds submitted to the smell of coffee. From a blue enamel pot like her very own the girl poured large cupfuls and her heart leapt, for city people, she thought, only drank instant coffee, didn't have time, Dollie said, for Koffiehuis. Washed in a caffeine-induced well-being she felt her feet throb all the more painfully so that she eased off her shoes to find two risen loaves straining under the nylon stockings. Why feeling good should have reminded her of feeling bad she did not know, but oh, she felt like a queen being led to her room with a bowl of hot water in which to soak those feet. But queens get their heads chopped off, so it was not too surprising that in that dream-wake state as she rested before dinner Deborah orbited wildly in a marigold-round, her eyes chasing the pinpoints of light where orange turned to fire and her head threatening to fly off. She rose clutching her throat.

At table Sarah talked too much. Deborah, used to turning her own thoughts slowly round, this way and that, and then putting them away safely for another inspection day, found the girl's insistent ways too exhausting. Like Mr de Villiers's office with rows and rows of narrow drawers packed with papers — the girl's head was like that. And she spoke fast, whirring like a treadle-machine that made her own head, still delicate from dreaming, spin once again. And all these things from the past, the bad old days that Sarah wanted to talk about. Stories folded and packed in mothballs right at the bottom of Deborah's head. To disturb those was just plain foolish, just asking for things to come toppling down.

'Perhaps later this year I'll come to Kimberley. To look around all those places. The old farm, Brakvlei, all those places where the Kleinhanse lived,' Sarah said.

But the old woman would not be roused. 'Nothing there

to see. Not a Coloured person left in those parts. You won't find a riempie or a rusty nail. No, it's years since I left and soon after that the others trekked. The drought, you know. Girlie, this is a lovely bobotie. I haven't had any for so long: being on your own you can't really make such elaborate food.'

The girl was not a bad cook. And the bobotie was good although Deborah liked it just a little bit sweeter. Just a spoonful of apricot jam to set off the sharpness of the dried apricots. That's what she liked about bobotie — the layers, different things packed on top of each other. She always did it in a pyrex dish so that you could see the separate layers of curried mince, apricots and then the thick custard just trying to trickle down to the dried fruit. Almost a pity to eat it.

'No really,' she said through slipping dentures, 'there's nothing like a good bobotie. Bananas are also good you know, but to contrast with the custard, apricot is best.'

In the tall, frosted glass of Fanta the orange bubbles broke merrily at the brim, almost too pretty to drink. On the same principle Deborah's good clothes remained unworn at the back of the cupboard, but today, in her Sunday wear, eating and drinking the beauty of it all, her old heart was content and this Sarah was a girl to be proud of. She would bring Dollie along next time; my, what a time they would have.

Then Sarah said in a preacher's voice, '. . . nothing but an untidiness on God's earth — a mixture of degenerate brown peoples, rotten with sickness, an affront against Nature . . . So that was the farm.'

They had slipped into comfortable Afrikaans, a relief to Deborah whose English pinched like the Lycra roll-on that Dollie insisted had to be worn for the visit. And now the girl had switched to English once again so that she groped and grunted, for syllables from the two languages flew to each other to make wild words; because she did not understand about the sickness and death and because she felt a great weariness, a cloud settling around her head. The girl was surely mad. Everybody gets sick and dies, but Brakvlei was never rotten. Oh no, theirs was the cleanest of farmyards, the stony veld swept for hundreds of yards and even the fowls knew not to shit near the house. In that swept yard a young man rested his brown arms on the latched lower door, leant well into the dark but spotless kitchen with the sun behind him lighting the outline of his tightly curled hair. And Deborah, sick with shyness, packed more wood into the full stove and felt her hem a hot hoop below her knees, for she had outgrown that dress, and she had never been looked at in that way. Even when he offered to cleave a log that refused to go into the stove, his eyes burned and then her Pa came, to see his favourite daughter, his miracle late-lamb, younger than the grandchild, tug at her skirt and he ordered Andries away. That day she tore the dress into rags and braved a beating for she knew that a strip of plain cotton could simply have been sewn on to lengthen the skirt. But a beating has never done anyone any harm and she could thank her Pa now for sitting here where the girl's strong hands came to rest on her shoulders.

'Auntie feeling all right? Perhaps a drop of Buchu Essence?' she enquired, once again in Afrikaans.

'No, I'm all right. Just put a little bit of bobotie on my plate.' Then Deborah remembered the libel. 'Cleanliness is next to godliness. That's what my mother always said. And it was my job every morning to sweep all around the house. Really, it was just rearranging the veld, making our own patterns of earth and stone with the grass broom, but Ma said, The veld will swallow us up if we don't sweep. No, you can ask anyone; Brakvlei was the tidiest little place you've ever seen. If your people thought otherwise, well, then they just don't know what tidy means. All my life I have kept that motto: Tidiness is next to godliness.' And then her anger subsided: her mother would not have quoted the adage in English as she just had, not at home. What had she in fact said? How unreliable words were, lodging themselves comfortably in the memory where they pretended to have a rightful place. Deborah did not hold her memory responsible.

'No, no,' Sarah soothed, 'I'm sure you're right. I have no

doubt that Brakvlei was well kept. But I wasn't really talking of Brakvlei; it was just something I remembered. From a story.' But the young woman's eyes burned so brightly, so busy-bodily, oh Deborah just knew that passion for probing deep into other people's affairs. Who did this child think she was, wanting to pry into her life and she who had never said a word to anyone about Andries, the tall young man whom she saw just once more before her father waving the old shotgun told him not to set foot in that swept yard again.

'People come and go and in the end it's no bad thing. No point in brooding over things that happened a long time ago. I haven't got time for those old stories,' she said firmly.

'A pity really; it's an interesting story that needs to be told by . . .'

'And what would you know about it?' Deborah interrupted. 'It's never been interesting. Dreary as dung it was, sitting day after day waiting for something to happen; listening for hooves or the roll of cartwheels.' But she checked herself. Hearing only the wind howl through the bushes and the ewes bleat, she had made up stories. Of driving through streets lined with whitewashed houses; of friends, girls in frilled print frocks who whispered secrets under the breath of the wind; and of Andries on horseback galloping across the swept yard right up to the kitchen door. But she said, 'You know I have my books — *Rooi Rose* every fortnight, I haven't missed a book since I started working for the De Villiers and when I retired I kept it up. Every fortnight. Good stories that seem to be about real life, but well, when you think about it, you won't recognize anyone you know. They'll give you no useful tips. They're no better than the nonsense I used to make up in my own head to kill the time. My advice, child, is to stick to your business and forget about stories of old times.'

'It depends surely on who tells the story. Auntie Deborah, that's what I must ask you about. Do you know if someone has written the story of our family, from the beginning, right from the European missionary? Do you by any chance remember a woman, a white woman speaking to

71

your mother or brothers or yourself about those days? A woman who then wrote a book? Have you ever heard of the book, of . . .'

'No, I don't believe it. What nonsense, of course there was no such woman. A book for all to read with our dirty washing spread out on snow white pages! Ag, man, don't worry; it wouldn't be our story; it's everyone's story. All Coloured people have the same old story.' And then Deborah slumped in her chair.

Sarah knew it, just her luck, the old woman travelling all this way to put down her head and die at her table. She held a bottle of brandy to the lifeless lips. The eyelids fluttered and Deborah sat up with remarkable agility as if the laying of her head on the table had been a deliberate gesture of exasperation.

'Just tired, child. Don't worry, I'm not going to die here; I'll die respectably in my own house and that not for some time yet.'

Sarah helped her to bed. 'Tomorrow evening,' she said, as she tucked her in, 'I have to go to a meeting. But in the morning we'll go out. Somewhere exciting, but let's talk about that tomorrow.'

'To the Gardens, girlie; that's where one should go first. I've heard so much about the Gardens in Cape Town. Where the fine ladies parade.' And she giggled for she knew it could not be as her mother had described so many years ago. And even then it was a second-hand account, told by her grown-up sister Elmira whom she had never known.

Deborah was not surprised by the knock. Her heart had swollen, filling her chest with a thunderous beat and rocking her entire body as she heard the footsteps steal past her window, round to the back of the house. Skollies with armfuls of stones, just as Dollie had warned her. Then a low, barking voice — Quick. Here. Slowly, she twisted her head to look at the clock. Then Deborah leapt out of bed. She would not await death lying prone in her bed. Oh no, if skollies planned to kill her, well, they would meet her standing up straight, ready to meet her Maker. Her hands groped for the dressing gown but the old arms shook too violently to guide them through the sleeves. She crept out to the hall; she could at least telephone the police. But they were already at the door. What kind of cheeky skollies were these who thought she would open the door to her own death? Why did the girl not wake up? She pulled on the dressing gown. The knock grew louder and someone shouted, 'Open up; it's the police.' They had come for Sarah.

Deborah waited for Dollie in the Lategans' kitchen. Mr Lategan put the kettle on for coffee, making an elaborate display of not knowing where to find things, so that she suggested that he put on his shoes while she made the coffee. That the man should be told to make himself decent, as if she would divulge a word to someone sitting in his socks. And she thought of the folly of having expectations, of how she had imagined sitting at that table with Dollie, telling her story.

But there they sat drinking the coffee she made and Mr Lategan knew exactly where to find Dollie's buttermilk rusks which they dunked. And so she told him, for she could not expect the man to ask again. About the police who came for Sarah at five-thirty in the morning, pointing their guns as if they were in a play on the TV. And how they turned the house upside down and even looked in her suitcase. But they were very polite, especially the big one in command who apologized nicely and said to her, 'You should have kept an eye on the girl,' so that she turned to him triumphantly and said, 'So you don't know everything like you said you did. I've known this girl for less than a day.' Mr Lategan interrupted to say that if they didn't know that, they could so easily have got the whole thing wrong, the wrong house, the wrong woman, everything. Which was exactly what Deborah was about to say, also the wrong Deborah Kleinhans, for she felt as if the story had been playing on the TV. She allowed him to be the author of the observation.

There was also Cape Town to tell about even though she knew that he had been twice. But the city was so big that he could not possibly have been to the same places and he certainly listened with great interest. Sarah had written a letter to her neighbours, the Arendses, and even then Deborah marvelled at the girl's skill, how she wrote like lightning, her hand flying across the paper in such straight lines, even though the big policeman leant over her, checking every word. Busybodies, that's what they were, going through people's things and reading their letters. Mrs Arendse took her to the Gardens but her heart was not in it. Someone else, a young woman whose name she could not recall, took her to a museum to see what the girl called her ancestors. Hottentots in a big glass box, squatting around an unlit fire of all things, so that she left in disgust. But she said nothing to him of the large protruding buttocks and the shameful loincloths of animal skin. No, her heart was not in it and Mrs Arendse arranged an early return flight for there was no point in waiting to see Sarah again. They telephoned many times but there was no point, everyone said.

When Dollie came she told it all again and she did not mind Mr Lategan sitting there until he tried to correct her. If things were slightly different the second time round, well she was telling it to someone different and he should have had the decency to keep quiet. So she went, taking her bag, for she had not yet been home and Dollie shouted after her, 'I'll come with,' just as she unlocked her door.

Dollie lay across her bed while she unpacked. The frock for parading in the Gardens, a bold print of yellow daisies on white, she folded away into a bottom drawer for the nights were drawing in and really it was perhaps too bright for someone of her age. And then she told Dollie. Of how she had offered to make a nice pot of coffee because it was so early and that's just what you needed in order to think clearly. If the policemen burst rudely into the house, well, she was brought up decently. Sarah shouted at her but she knew how a civilized person should behave. And she paused in an attempt to trace the moment when things became muddled but all she recalled was an unmistakable smell of marigold, a weariness and the precise timbre of the sergeant's voice as she finished pouring the coffee: 'Milk and sugar for the other two but just black and bitter for me.' Then without thinking, without anticipating the violence of the act, Deborah Kleinhans took each cup in turn and before his very eyes poured the coffee into the sink. Together they watched the liquid splash, a curiously transparent brown against the stainless steel.

Shakespeare's Image

AHMED ESSOP

When I first went to work for Taurus Decorators (during
the university vacation period) Mr Winterton, the director,
took me around the premises and introduced me to the
staff. This was when I met Don Carlyle, my immediate
senior. He was dressed in a fawn suit, brown shirt, bronze
tie and several pens appeared like a hierarchy of totems in
his coat's outer pocket. His complexion was smooth and
unblemished, his shampooed soft brown hair salon-
groomed above his domed forehead, his moustache and
small beard neatly trimmed. I was struck by his remarkable
similarity to the portrait of Shakespeare that embellishes so
many texts of his plays. And the impression mellowed when
he said, 'How do you do? I am pleased you are joining us
for a while.' His voice had the modulated, cultivated tone of
a professional actor.

I soon came to know Don Carlyle better. As principal
supervisor he was a perfectionist; he demanded an extremely high standard from the workmen who decorated
the homes of the affluent and the offices of millionaire
businessmen in the city. He was university educated and
held a Bachelor of Arts degree. He was a keen student of
modern literature. I listened eagerly to what he had to say
about the authors whose writing he enjoyed.

'One of my favourites is V. S. Naipaul,' he said to me
during a lunch-break in a restaurant. 'Have you read his
work?'

'Most of it.'

'And do you like it?'

'His early work, yes. But I think his recent work set in
Africa suffers from being rootless.'

'Not at all. I think he is a very good observer of

post-colonial Africa, its descent into anarchy, corruption, decadence, tyranny . . .'

I allowed him to go on and later asked him why he had not thought of an academic career.

'And remain a pauper?' he asked, elegantly wiping his mouth with a table napkin.

That was true. Academics, not possessing the thrust of trade union power, had become an effete group in a strident age.

As the days passed our conversation ranged over many topics. Don Carlyle seemed to me a paragon of Western civilization and culture. On art, history, music, films, plays he displayed the subtlety of his intellect. However, his knowledge of the civilizations of Africa and the East was superficial; but then a study of these had no place in the Eurocentric education institutions in the country.

On politics he was well informed and liberal in his views. 'Equal education and equality of opportunity should be the aims of a rational society. But I don't think that we should have a democratic society immediately.'

'When should we have it?'

'When everyone has become literate and can exercise the vote responsibly.'

'That will take a long time. I am sure the ruling aristocracy want to enjoy the country's riches without sharing them equally.'

'That is a pity.'

There were two other supervisors at the firm, but it was soon clear to me that Don Carlyle hoped to become deputy director some day. He deserved the position as he was the architect of the firm's reputation in the city. Not only did he bring his knowledge of every aspect of interior decorating to fruition, but never left at closing time, remaining to finish 'some odds and ends'. He arrived at work in the morning half an hour before everyone else, and when meetings of supervisors and office staff were held he invariably made his contribution on 'working to schedule', 'efficiency' and 'tasteful and harmonious design'.

After a month the director went on a business trip to New

York and left Don Carlyle to manage the firm. As he had very much to do now, our conversations came to an end. Of course he communicated with me when it came to office work and I consulted him when necessary. It was on one such occasion when I went to his office that I saw something that overturned my estimation of the man.

He was not at his desk. But I noticed an airletter that was still in the typewriter and thinking that he would return in a moment to complete it, I went in. I looked at a framed picture of a sailing ship, the ill-fated Mary Rose of Henry VIII, for a while. My eyes then fell again on the airletter which was addressed to Mr Winterton in New York. I am not sure what made me read part of the content of the letter. Perhaps it was an inadvertent glance; perhaps I had acquired the office worker's tendency to examine all letters; perhaps my eyes were attracted by this revelation: 'I suspect our tea-girl Jane is pilfering sugar from stock as more of it has been consumed than formerly. Perhaps she has been surreptitiously taking sugar (and who knows what else) over the years.'

I retreated to my office, filled with a profound sense of disappointment. Deeply perplexed, several questions presented themselves to me. How could a cultivated man perpetrate such an ignoble act? Did he wish to give the director an impression of his vigilance and devotion to the firm? Did his ambition to become deputy director spur him to use Jane as a pawn towards that end? I thought of Rosencrantz who says to Hamlet: 'Take you me for a sponge my lord?' and Hamlet's answer: 'Ay, sir, that soaks up the king's countenance, his rewards, his authorities.' Would Don Carlyle have written that about a white 'tea-girl'? Marcellus's words to Horatio on the battlements of the castle of Elsinore came to mind: 'Something is rotten in the state of Denmark.'

Later in the afternoon Jane came with my tea and asked me if I had any letters to post (going to the post office was part of her daily work). I said no, and then as a thought suddenly sprouted said quickly, 'Jane, I have to go and see someone in a short while. If there are any letters I will post them on my way.'

She went out and returned with several letters. I saw the airmail letter among them. For a moment I experienced the illusion of seeing Don Carlyle, on the stage of the Globe Theatre, chuckling as he handed that damning letter to Jane. I thought of Hamlet and how he had sent Rosencrantz and Guildenstern to their doom:

> Up from my cabin,
> My sea-gown scarf'd about me, in the dark
> Grop'd I to find out them; had my desire,
> Finger'd their packet . . .

I felt tempted to open the letter and add a derisive postscript that would alienate Don Carlyle from Mr Winterton; but, as I was not personally involved, decided not to.

I posted all the letters excepting Don Carlyle's. When I passed a garbage can attached to a lamp-post in the street, I stopped, tore up the letter and threw it in.

Necessary Appendages

TONY PEAKE

'But what about Toby?' asked Graham, staring down at the swaddled shape of their seven-month-old son. 'It's a five-hour crossing and at least another five on the other side. Will he cope?'

'Will I cope, you mean,' smiled Laura, bending over the cot and tucking a final quilt over the sleeping Toby.

'Well, will you?'

Laura straightened up. 'Of course he'll cope. Babies are more resilient than you think.'

'And you?'

Laura closed her eyes, though whether in resignation or so as to conceal some other, more complex emotion, Graham couldn't be sure. 'I thought we'd decided. We both want it. And we need a break. Why go over and over the same old ground?'

Graham shrugged. 'You say we both want it. But do we, really? And Richard? What about Richard? He may hate the idea.'

'Richard,' said Laura, stepping back from the cot, 'will jump at the idea. Believe me.' She slipped an arm around Graham's waist. 'All you have to do is pick up the phone.'

Later, after their usual Thursday supper of pasta and salad, and after he'd shared the last of the wine between their two glasses, lining them up side by side so as to be sure of giving them each the same amount, she said, 'Right. Ring him now.'

He looked across the table at her. In the dim light of the dining room alcove the details of her face were indistinct beneath her helmet of hair, only the precise, red line of her mouth standing out with any clarity.

'You're sure this is what you want?'

She lifted her glass to her lips and took a small, deft sip.

'Surer, it would seem, than you.'

'You're not just doing it to please me?'

She returned her glass to the table. 'Ah!' she said. 'So that's what you think! Just being obedient, am I? The perfect wife.' She challenged him with her eyes. 'It had not occurred to you that of the two of us, I might be the one who fancies Richard most. That it's not entirely yours, this fantasy we're plotting.'

He got up and went to the phone.

'I only hope,' he said, starting to dial, 'that we know what we're doing.'

'What we know,' she countered, 'is what we want. What we don't know is whether we'll get it.'

The phone at Richard's end began to ring.

'Wouldn't you say?'

But before he could answer, Richard's mellifluous voice was purring in his ear. 'Maloney speaking.'

'Richard! It's Graham.'

'Graham! How are you?'

'Fine, fine. And you?'

'Can't complain.'

'Listen! Laura and I were wondering . . . We've been offered the use of this house . . . Winbourn it's called . . . In the west of Ireland . . . We're thinking of going over for Easter and we wondered if . . . Well, if you'd like to come too.'

There, it was out. He waited, numbed, for Richard's response.

'Winbourn? Isn't that Gary Stewart's house?'

'Yes.'

'How the hell do you come to be offered the use of Gary Stewart's house?'

'Well, his daughter Sally's been working at the theatre, and one day last week I happened to mention that since coming to London I've always wanted to visit Ireland, and she said her father's house stood empty most of the year — he's always in Hollywood — and if we wanted to — well, we could have it. There's an old couple, apparently, who live in

the grounds and keep an eye on things but otherwise —
well, it just sits there.'

'Gary Stewart! Shit!'

'So?' queried Graham. 'Can you come?'

'Can I come?' echoed Richard. 'Of course I can come!
Gary Stewart! Jesus! When do we leave?'

Out of the corner of his eye Graham became aware of
movement in the alcove. Laura had been clearing the table
and now she was preparing to take their dirty plates through
to the kitchen. He waited until she drew level with him,
then gave her a thumbs up.

There was, in her answering smile, a flicker of triumph so
personal, so private, that he was left feeling oddly super-
fluous. 'What we know,' she'd said, 'is what we want.' Did
he know, though, had he ever known, what it was that
Laura wanted?

They'd met and married in Cape Town, he in the second
year of his drama degree, she halfway through an MA in
history. Their courtship had been swift and surprising, a
mere three months separating the day he'd collided with her
diminutive form on the library steps, sending her notebooks
flying, and the day they'd presented themselves, he in his
only suit, she in a borrowed dress, at the Register Office,
entering the building as two, giggling individuals, and
emerging from it, a quarter of an hour later, still giggling,
but as one.

'Wasn't he horrible?' she'd said, wrinkling her nose. 'The
registrar? His breath smelt. Did you notice?'

Something about the way she said this, the mere fact that
she'd said it, caused him a moment's unease, made him
wonder if her displeasure was really aimed at the registrar.
What did he know, after all, really know about this small,
neat and disconcertingly intense woman who'd turned his
world inside out by welcoming him with such alacrity into
hers, who made him blush, sometimes, the way she stared
at him, and who called him her knight in shining armour, as
if she needed him to rescue her from something?

'You don't think we've done the wrong thing?' he asked worriedly.

She giggled. 'Well, so they all tell us. But they can't hurt us now. Not now we've got each other.'

'They' were their parents, both sets of whom had reacted with horror to the news of the wedding: hers because, as rigid Afrikaners, they objected to an English son-in-law; his because they viewed twenty-five-year-old Laura as the older woman in embryo, come to trick their impressionable twenty-year-old of his freedom and future.

'Fuck all parents!' she went on. 'Fuck all parents for the way they try to stifle you. But most of all, my love' — and here she lifted her giggling face coquettishly to his — 'fuck me.'

They'd made love a great deal in those early months, exploring and devouring each other with an intensity that left him feeling not sated but emptied, not more himself but, mercifully, less. Laura's obsessive need for him, coupled with the delight she took in his, to him, lank and awkward body, momentarily stilled all his usual neuroses and uncertainties, even that sick and secret part of him that leapt to life at the sight of men in summer shorts, their muscled thighs brown from the sun, or on the beach when, stripped to a triangle of black, these same men hurled themselves into the curling Atlantic breakers.

'You make me so happy,' he'd whisper in her ear as they lay entwined in their chaos of sheets. 'So very happy.' Meaning, of course: so normal, so very normal.

For almost a year he hardly gave the men of Cape Town a thought, and never visited the little shop at the end of Long Street where, in a rack at the back, there was a section on sports: magazines on naturism and body-building.

Then gradually, insidiously, like water finding out the fracture in a vase, his interest in men began to seep back into his life. He would, in the street, be helplessly drawn to the curve of a labourer's neck, or on the bus to the line of an arm lying lazy along the back of a seat, and before long he was visiting the shop again and poring over the magazines. It being South Africa, the men in the magazines were never entirely nude, and not that attractive — slackly middle-aged in the naturist titles, popping with muscle in the others — but he pored over them all the same until, shamed into action by the watchful Greek behind the counter, he would buy one and add it to the growing collection in the back of his briefcase — which was where, hunting for their joint chequebook on the anniversary of their wedding, Laura came across them.

She didn't react immediately. All day she kept whatever it was she was feeling to herself; and that evening, as they sat on their balcony savouring the champagne she'd bought and watching the sun sink behind Robben Island, even if Graham's eyes hadn't been on the sunset, his thoughts on the irony that the lump of rock silhouetted so fetchingly against the sky should be the country's most infamous prison, he wouldn't have noticed anything more than a certain watchfulness in Laura's manner, a certain wariness. It was only when they made their way rather tipsily to bed that he realized anything was amiss — for there, in a neat little pile on his pillow, were the magazines.

'What the hell . . .?' he began.

Laura, who'd slipped into bed before him, cut across his bluster by reaching for the top magazine and opening it at random. 'Show me your favourite,' she said.

He took a step backwards, snagging his ankle on the bedside table. 'Laura, please! You must let me explain.'

'Him, for example? Do you go for him?'

'Laura, please . . .'

But she merely patted the coverlet. 'Angel, please! You can't see properly from there.'

She made him guide her through each magazine, pointing out the men who most appealed to him, which legs he found most sexy, which arms, which stomachs, which chests. When he'd finished, she said simply, 'So much nicer if we share them, don't you think?' — and slipping her hand between his legs, pulled him on to her and whispered in his ear, 'That man in the last magazine. The one in the white costume. Didn't you love his eyes?'

And because, for all his squeamishness about the situation, he had been excited, too, by looking at the magazines with her, he responded eagerly to the pressure of her hand, was more than ready to be taken into her.

'You mustn't mind,' he said afterwards, running a hesitant finger along the set of her jaw. 'I'd hate you to think they were that important. The magazines, I mean. You're what matters. Not them.'

'I don't mind,' she said, 'as long as we share them.'

'You mean that?'

'Of course.'

And it seemed that she did. In the days that followed she made no further reference to the magazines, nor did she seem in the least bit strange or distant. If anything, she was more affectionate than usual, more tender, and she didn't shrug him off, or look at him askance, when he reciprocated her tenderness.

Until, with the advent of summer, on perhaps their third or fourth sortie to the beach, she dug him in the side one morning, and gesturing towards a surfer carrying his board down to the sea, surprised him with a question. 'Now tell me. The guy with the board. Could you go for him?'

It took him a moment to see where she was pointing, by which time the surfer was almost in the water.

He shrugged. 'He's too far away. And anyway, why do you ask?'

'I like to know what turns you on,' she said. 'What makes my baby tick.'

'You,' he said. 'You make me tick.'

She leant over and pinched him, sending a stab of pain up his arm. 'Show me!' she hissed. 'Show me who turns you on.'

He sat up and began scanning the beach. 'All right. That one there. With the brown hair.'

'Why him?'

Now he was embarrassed. 'I can't say.'

'Of course you can.'

'Well, it's — no, I can't.'

'Of course you can.'

'Well, it's partly the shape of his bum.'

'Why his bum?'

'It's firm and it's neat.'

'What else?'

'His pectorals and the hair on his legs.'

'What else?'

'Laura please, I can't.'

'Go on.' It was a command, not a request.

'And he looks . . .'

'Looks what?'

'Well hung.'

Her eyebrows rose. 'That's important?'

'Yes.'

'Very?'

She was staring at him with an odd expression.

He wormed his toes into the sand. 'Well . . .'

'Very?'

He hung his head. 'Pretty much.'

'I see.'

At the end of the day, returning to the car, she caught his arm on the spot where she'd pinched him, making him wince, and whispered, 'There's someone for you. He's — what do you say — well hung.' But though she giggled as the man in question passed them, his light-blue jeans bearing ample testimony to her powers of observation, there was something in her tone that unsettled him, an edge of resentment, anger, even disgust. And in the car on their way back to town it wasn't entirely frivolous, not altogether a joke, the song she made up:

'Keep your thoughts to yourself
And your cock in control
Keep your beady eyes on the crotch ahead.'

'Don't!' he snapped.

She darted him a look of mock surprise. 'You don't like my song?'

'You're making too much of it.'

'I'm making too much of it? You let slip that anatomically

I'm deficient, that I lack a rather necessary appendage, and now you're cross because I sing about it?'

'Laura, please! You're you. I don't want you like them.'

'Ah!' she said. 'But imagine how much more you'd love me if I had a cock!'

They'd drawn up at a set of traffic lights, and she took his arm and gestured towards the man beginning to cross the road. Although the man was carrying a shopping bag which partly obscured his body, there was no mistaking why he was being pointed out — nor any escaping the fact that Graham had spotted him first, had already clocked, with a practised sidelong glance, the promising bulge in his shorts.

'On a scale of one to ten,' said Laura, 'I'd say that was a seven. Yes?'

Graham didn't reply.

'Too much?'

'No, no,' he said woodenly. 'Spot on.'

'This game I like,' she said. 'Especially if we keep score.'

Crotch-watching, she dubbed it; and as the summer engulfed them in its heat and languor, she took to playing it with a vengeance, not only on the beach but on their shopping trips to town, at the movies, strolling along the seafront, anywhere, in fact, where there were men. And although with time he grew more adept at hiding his discomfort, the more obsessively she played the game, the more uneasy it made him, the less he liked her invasion of this particular fantasy — and he was greatly relieved when, towards the end of summer, and hot on the heels of his graduation, he was offered a means of escape: the job of stagemanaging a multiracial theatre in Johannesburg.

'Isn't it fantastic?' he crowed. 'My first application, and I land the job! At one of the most innovative theatres in the country too!'

Though best of all — better, even, than the job, or the fairytale cottage they were able to find within a week of their arrival, or the fact that Laura had no difficulty in acquiring a new supervisor for her thesis — best of all was that at a stroke, the move seemed to work the spell he'd asked of it. Laura gave up crotch-watching, and with her obsession went his. Men ceased to be the focal point of their existence.

'I was right,' he thought to himself. 'It was a stage, a tiny part of me, unimportant.'

And in his relief at being thus released from himself he showered Laura with gifts, was more than usually attentive to her: the perfect husband.

It lasted eight months. Then two things happened. Laura fell pregnant and Graham went to bed with a man.

The man was Graham's assistant stagemanager, a short, dark nineteen-year-old, a silent boy who went quietly about his work, not seeming to take much notice of the outside world. His name was John, he'd recently moved flats, and Graham had promised to help him put up a bookcase.

It was a Saturday and Laura had gone shopping with a friend, leaving Graham the car and instructions to be back by six because, she said, she might have news for him.

John's flat was in Hillbrow, on the sixteenth floor of a once sleek, now decaying block over which there hung a faint but persistent smell of food. John had moved in only the week before and the flat was still barely furnished — two chairs and his stereo in the living room, a mattress and a tea-chest in one bedroom, nothing at all in the other.

The fridge, however, was well stocked with beers and they drank a couple and looked through John's record collection before turning their attention to the bookcase, a do-it-yourself affair in cheap, streaky pine which John had bought as a kit. They worked silently and in expert, practised unison, and it wasn't long before the bookcase was up and Graham was helping John unpack his books.

'*Giovanni's Room*,' he said. 'What's that?'

'It's about two guys, an American and an Italian, in Paris, in this room, they get involved . . .' John tailed off.

'You mean they're queer?'

John shrugged. 'It's about love, certainly.'

Graham felt a sudden constriction in his stomach, an unexpected and unwelcome surge of excitement and lust. He opened the book at random and read: 'He seemed — somehow — younger than I had ever been, and blonder and more beautiful, and he wore his masculinity as unequivocally as he wore his skin. He made me think of home — perhaps home is not a place but simply an irrevocable condition.' He shut the book quickly.

'You can borrow it if you like,' said John.

Graham shook his head and stuffed the book on to the shelf. 'I've already got something on the go.'

They finished unpacking the books.

'There,' said Graham. 'Looks good.'

'Yes,' said John gravely. 'Thank you.'

Then he stepped forward and, taking Graham's face in his hands, stared intently into his eyes — and reading there what he expected to read, pulled Graham towards him and kissed him.

Although he stiffened, Graham didn't pull away, nor did he protest when John took his hand and led him into the bedroom, where he unbuttoned Graham's shirt, unbuckled his trousers, then undressed himself and, pulling Graham on to the mattress, nestled his short, furry body against the larger contours of Graham's pale, hairless one.

They lay in silence for a long time, not moving, then John felt between Graham's legs.

'What is it?' he asked softly. 'Don't you want to?' And when Graham didn't reply: 'Well, that's fine by me. We can just lie here. That's nice too.'

The hour hand on the clock by the bed went from two to three to four; and gradually for Graham the almost nauseating excitement he'd felt when John had begun to unbutton his shirt settled into a sort of peace, a sense of rightness, as if his whole life had been aimed at this point, everything he was and everything he'd done designed to bring him here to John's room to lie in John's arms, and when John eventually felt for him again, he was ready.

When the clock reached five, he said, 'I have to go.'

John lifted himself on to his elbow. 'You're beautiful,' he said quietly.

'I must go.'

'That's all right,' said John. 'I know.' And he jumped up and threw Graham his clothes.

At the door to the flat, he touched Graham's arm. 'Wait a minute!' He vanished into the gloom and returned with *Giovanni's Room*. 'Here,' he said, 'take this.' He pressed the book into Graham's hand. 'You'll find it interesting.'

'Thank you,' said Graham. 'That's very sweet of you. Thanks.'

Though no sooner had he reached the street than he dropped the book furtively into the nearest bin.

Arriving back at the cottage he was relieved to find Laura still out. He wouldn't have been able to cope, he realized, had she been there to greet him. It made him feel quite odd enough, not wholly himself, displaced, just to see her knitting on the arm of her chair, the remains of their morning coffee on the tray by the sofa. He ran himself a bath, and getting into it, began to wash himself meticulously. He was still in the bath when Laura burst through the door crying, 'Guess what? I'm pregnant!'

The euphoria lasted a month. Laura was so patently thrilled, her customary spikiness and occasional bad temper, her uncertainty and her fear of strangers, transformed into such cat-like contentment that he couldn't help but be pleased too — and he discovered within his pleasure a nugget of something else, an atavistic delight in the fact that he was continuing the family line, that he was doing what sons were brought into the world to do.

Then, at the end of the month, and coinciding with the onset for Laura of morning sickness, an unaccountable unease took hold of Graham. With Laura pregnant, he knew he had to get away from the theatre, from all that was known and familiar. Now that he was going to be a father, he had to start anew.

He broached the subject one evening as he and Laura were taking a dip in their neighbour's pool. They'd dived in together and as they swam for the shallow end, he said, 'I think we ought to move to London.'

'London?' In her surprise, Laura took in a mouthful of water.

'Well, I've got a British passport and now you're pregnant we have to think again about South Africa. Things are changing, I know, but not that fast. This isn't a good place to bring up children. Imagine if it's a boy. He'll have to do his military training on the border.'

'There may not be a war on the border by then.'

'But we have to think of these things.'

They reached the shallow end and Laura stood up, shaking the water angrily from her head.

'Why are you saying this really?'

'Don't you think it's a good idea?'

'What about my thesis?'

'You can do that by correspondence.'

'And your job? How will you get a job in London?'

'I've got contacts.'

'But London's horrible. Everyone says so. Cold and wet and crowded.'

'That's only what they say.'

'How can we bring up a baby there?'

'How can we do it here?'

'But this is paradise!'

'On the surface, sure. But visit Soweto and what do you find?'

'We don't live in Soweto.'

'What happens in Soweto affects what happens here.'

She looked at him. 'So we're going to London then?'

'Don't you think it's for the best?'

'And when will we stop running?' she asked. 'Or does it go on for ever? A new city each time you can't face yourself?'

Their parents took the news equally badly, but nothing anyone said could change Graham's mind. He found out about flights, he got the manager of the theatre to write on his behalf to a handful of London theatres, he wrote himself to the people he knew about accommodation, and when he'd done all this, even though nothing definite had come back, no word of a job or a flat, he booked the tickets.

'Contrary to what you think,' he said to Laura, 'I'm doing this for the baby. For you and the baby. Not me at all. So please be with me.'

'Oh, but I am,' she said. 'That's exactly it. I'm your wife, after all. With you all the way.'

They arrived in London in the autumn and stayed with a friend in Chiswick, in a large house off the high road, where they were told they could have the attic for as long as they needed it. Fortune smiled on them, though, and within weeks Graham had found a stagemanaging job and flat in Tufnell Park.

'See!' he said. 'I told you things would work out.'

Even the weather treated them kindly, running, on their arrival, to a fortnight of Indian summer followed by almost a month of crisp, clear days during which the trees in the parks began, with slow magnificence, to go over.

'See!' he repeated. 'I'm not such a lousy husband.'

They were well entrenched by the time the weather changed and a dull, grey sky came down to trap the city in its own cold and misery. Though by then they hardly noticed, for Laura was almost due — and on 17 December she gave birth to seven pounds four ounces of screaming, healthy baby: Toby Jonathan Andries; the Toby for them, the Jonathan for his parents, the Andries for hers.

They had a perfect Christmas and New Year, cocooned in the flat by the weather and Toby, taking it in turns with the feeds and the nappies, and coming sometimes to stand jointly at the bedroom door just to stare in wonder at the cot and the fragile, miraculous proof it contained of their future.

Then, in the second week of January, Richard exploded into their lives. A new show was coming into the theatre and Richard, twenty-four and just out of drama school, had landed the job of understudying the star.

Graham was coming down the stairs from the dressing rooms on the morning of the first read-through, a clipboard under his arm when, barrelling up the stairs, came a matinée idol in a massive and somewhat moth-eaten fur coat.

'Maloney!' he panted. 'Richard Maloney. Not late, am I? For the reading?'

There was something so touchingly defiant and out of place about the tattered opulence of Richard's coat that Graham warmed to him immediately. 'No,' he said, laughing. 'You've plenty of time. Follow me.'

Within days they were friends, nipping out together to the pub for a lunchtime drink, fetching each other sandwiches or cups of tea from the café on the corner, gossiping in the stalls. Graham learnt that Richard came from Ireland but had lived in London since the age of ten, had gone from school to Hamburg, where he'd managed a band before deciding he wanted to act because, bowled over by his looks, a stranger in a bar had come up to him and said he had a face the camera would love. Returning to London, he'd landed a place at LAMDA, from which he'd just graduated. He had a bedsit in Islington, rode everywhere on a bike and, the fur lobby notwithstanding, was inseparable from his coat, harbinger of the lifestyle to which he aspired.

He'd recently broken up with his girlfriend and though he affected not to mind, Graham sensed that he was lonely — and because he and Laura, Toby apart, were lonely too, he said, 'Why don't you come for supper on Sunday? Nothing special. Pot luck. But you can meet the family.'

And so it was, that Sunday, that Richard came to supper — and so successful was the evening, so immediately did Laura and Richard take to each other, that they asked him back, and before long they'd become a fixture, their Sundays together, and expanded into a ritual: a lunchtime drink at the Flask, a walk on Hampstead Heath, then tea at the flat, supper and an hour or two of television.

Laura broached the subject first. 'Tell me something,' she said over breakfast one morning. 'Do you fancy Richard at all?'

'I beg your pardon?'

'Richard. Do you fancy him?'

'Well, he's awfully nice and he's frightfully good-looking, but I really . . .'

'Don't be coy,' she said. 'You know what I mean.'

'Why?' said Graham. 'Do you?'

She didn't reply but that night, in bed, she slipped a hand between Graham's legs and said, 'I wonder how he's hung?'

Graham began to watch Richard in a different way, to study the particular and pleasing configuration of his face, the way his voice seemed to caress the words he uttered, the startling power and grace of his body.

'You know what I think?' Laura said one Sunday after Richard had left and they were washing up. 'I think you're a little in love with him.'

'Nonsense.'

'Your eyes,' she said. 'They're what give you away.'

'I like him, sure. He's a good friend. And yes, I find him attractive. But to suggest I'm in love with him!'

'I wouldn't mind, you know,' she said. 'As long as we shared him.'

'I'm not enough for you?'

She looked at him. 'Did I say that?'

A fortnight later Sally Stewart offered Graham the use of her father's house.

They met, as arranged, at Euston, boarded the train for Holyhead and, after an unscheduled delay of two hours at the other end, were decanted at midnight on to a ferry that carried them, pitching, through a turbulent sea to Dunlaoghaire. They landed at dawn, tired but triumphant, picked up their rented car, and with Graham at the wheel, Richard navigating and Laura jiggling a fretful Toby on her lap, headed west. They reached their destination mid-afternoon.

They stopped in the local village to shop, then, following Sally's directions, took a narrow road that skirted a lake until they came, as promised, to an imposing set of wrought-iron gates and, turning through them into a tunnel of rhododendrons, followed the drive until it opened out before a large, square Georgian house, its brick façade warm and inviting in the afternoon sun. To the right of the house the land fell in a series of lawns to a boatshed and a jetty, whilst to the left it had been transformed, by turns, into a garden, a tennis court, a pool.

'My God!' breathed Richard. 'This is unbelievable.'

The front door opened and a small, pert woman with greying hair appeared.

'Welcome to Winbourn,' she said. 'I'm Mrs Worral. Now don't you be worrying with your bags. Mr Worral will fetch those later. What an adorable baby! How old is he? Or is it a she?'

They were led inside and given a tour of the house. The ground floor consisted of an L-shaped drawing room which overlooked the lake, a book-lined study, a dining room that boasted twelve foot of gleaming, mahogany table, a billiard room, a snuggery and, at the back of the house, a scruffy games room. Upstairs there was a glut of bedrooms, all en suite.

'This one's Mr Stewart's,' said Mrs Worral, 'and Sally uses this one but any of the others are yours. You choose. It's no skin off my nose where you sleep. All the beds are made up.'

They chose rooms opposite each other at the far end of the corridor, and then coming downstairs met Mr Worral in the hall. He'd brought in the bags.

'Now you just tell me,' he said, 'if you'd like to use the boat and I'll show you where everything is. The tennis rackets and croquet things are in the rec room by the tennis court.'

'And if you'll come with me, miss,' Mrs Worral said to Laura, 'I'll show you the kitchen.'

'We're in the house behind the pool,' said Mr Worral. 'You've only to call if you need anything.'

Richard and Graham took their cases upstairs whilst Mrs Worral ushered Laura into the kitchen.

'I still can't believe it,' said Richard, coming into Graham's room. 'It's like a fairy tale.'

'Pretty bloody grand, eh?' smiled Graham.

'This is what acting's all about.'

He crossed to the window. Graham joined him.

The grounds fell in a series of plateaux to the lake, to be echoed on the other side by a purple mass of mountain, lightly iced with snow.

'Stunning, eh?'

Graham nodded.

Richard turned, and taking Graham in his arms, gave him a sudden, sharp hug. 'It's good of you to have asked me.'

'It's great you could come.' Graham's voice was thick in his throat.

'We're going to have a ball.'

'An absolute ball.'

Later, after Graham had bathed Toby and Laura had fed him and put him down in his carrycot in a corner of the kitchen, they opened a bottle of wine and set about preparing an elaborate supper.

'We must do this in style,' said Laura. 'Otherwise we'll offend the house.'

They ate at the massive table in the dining room, giggling at each other across its gleaming length and marvelling at the silverware, the crystal, the gloomy oils on the walls.

Afterwards they settled in the drawing room and tried to feign nonchalance about the snapshots dotted about on the sideboards and mantelpiece: Elizabeth Taylor standing where Graham was standing by the fireplace; Richard Dreyfuss and Dustin Hoffman on the jetty; Mary Dunaway, Gary Stewart's first wife, striking a pose by the pool.

'The very rich,' intoned Richard, 'are different to you and me.'

'I'll say,' said Laura, investigating a cupboard in the corner. 'They have better liqueur for a start. Look at this.' She produced an expensive-looking brandy. 'Shall we?'

'Why not?' said Graham, and giggling again he poured them each a glass.

'A holiday to remember,' toasted Laura.

'A holiday to remember,' echoed Graham.

Graham and Laura slept until Toby woke them at six. Going to the window, Graham drew the curtains on a perfect day: a powder-blue sky and lake, the promise of sun.

Descending to the kitchen to make tea, he found Mrs Worral putting some milk in the fridge.

'From the farm,' she explained. 'And I've put some eggs in the pantry. Will four pints be enough?'

Graham nodded. 'Looks like it's going to be a perfect day.'

'You've struck it lucky, all right,' said Mrs Worral. 'In the seventies they say it'll be, before the week is out.'

And indeed, it was already warm by the time they'd had breakfast; and when, later that morning and with some help from Mr Worral, they took the boat out on the lake, both Richard and Graham were able to take off their shirts.

'Such views on this boat!' said Laura. 'I wish I had my camera.'

That afternoon they walked to the little church they'd sighted on the hill beyond the house and that evening they ate another elaborate meal in the dining room.

After supper Laura said she fancied a stroll.

'I'll listen for Toby,' said Richard.

Laura and Graham went out on to the lawn. Although there was no moon, their eyes soon adjusted to the dark, and they followed the fall of the lawns all the way down to the jetty.

'Well,' she said, 'when are you going to ask him?'

'Ask him what?'

'You know.'

'When the right moment presents itself. I can't just spring it on him.'

'Why not?'

'I just can't.'

'And what if the right moment doesn't present itself?'

'Then we do nothing.'

'You mean we come all this way and do nothing?'

'If the right moment doesn't present itself.'

'What a waste.'

'Why? Aren't you enjoying yourself?'

'Of course I'm enjoying myself.'

'So what's wrong with this? Just as it is.' Graham gestured to where, high above them, brilliant cubes of light spilled on to the lawn from the drawing room windows.

'It's not what we want,' she said. 'It's not what we came for.'

The next afternoon Laura announced she was tired and was going to take a nap.

'In that case,' said Richard, 'I'm going back to the church to take some snaps of the graveyard.'

'I'll come too,' said Graham, 'if I may.'

'Of course,' said Richard. 'That would be nice.'

Graham sat on the wall and watched whilst Richard moved like a cat between the gravestones, clicking away with his camera. Then, out of film, he joined Graham on the wall.

'I really needed this break,' he said. 'I know we're always whinging, and you must be sick of it from work, but it isn't easy being an actor, always waiting on others, at their beck and call. You and Laura are very special to me.'

Graham cleared his throat. 'I'm glad', he said, 'because you're very special to us.' He kept his eyes fixed on his feet. 'In fact,' he went on, 'we would have been heartbroken if you hadn't come.' He didn't dare look up in case he met Richard's eyes. 'In fact, we'd both like it, Laura and I, if we could all go to bed together. You know, sleep together. If you'd like to, that is. We don't want to force you.' Graham found he couldn't go on. He tailed off and there was silence.

'Well,' said Richard eventually, 'I hardly know what to say.'

'You don't have to say anything,' said Graham hastily. 'You don't have to do anything. Not if you don't want to. We just wanted you to know.' He slithered off the wall. 'It's up to you. Entirely up to you.' Now, at last, he was able to meet his friend's eyes. 'I suppose we'd better be going back.'

They didn't say much on the way, and when they got to the house, Richard went to his room. Laura was in the kitchen making tea.

'I've spoken to him,' said Graham.

'And?'

He shrugged.

'What did he say?'

'Not a lot. But he didn't seem too horrified.'

'What next?'

Again Graham shrugged. 'Don't ask me.'

'We must behave,' said Laura, 'as if nothing has happened.'

'Isn't that a touch British?'

'It's the only way.'

That evening at dinner none of them made any reference to the afternoon and though there was a slight tension in the air, a few less giggles than normal, Laura's prescription worked: they got through the meal unscathed.

After dinner they played snooker, then they watched television, then Graham stood up and said, 'Well, time for bed.'

'Indeed,' said Laura, standing up with him.

Together they looked at Richard.

'Me too, I guess,' he said. 'This country air. It tires you out.'

They turned out the downstairs lights and went upstairs. In the corridor outside their bedrooms, Richard said, 'Well, good night, you two!' — and planting a clumsy kiss on Laura's cheek, darted into his room.

Graham looked at Laura and shrugged. He opened their door and turned out the passage light. Laura followed him into their room.

'He's shy,' she said. 'That's all. You'll have to go and invite him.'

'I already did,' he said. 'As good as.'

'You have to make it absolutely clear.'

'Why me?' he said. 'Why not you?'

'It has to be you,' she said. 'You're the man.'

He began to undress. 'No,' he said, 'I don't want to.' But when she got into bed and reached across for him, his body betrayed him.

'So what's this, then?' she crowed. 'Of course you want it.'

'All right,' he said, throwing back the covers. 'I'll go.'

He went into the bathroom and fetched a towel.

'Check on Toby,' she said as he came back into the room. He went to the cot. 'Out like a light.'

He went to the door. 'What am I going to say?' he asked. 'Just invite him over. That's all.'

He went into the corridor. There was a line of light under Richard's door. Graham hesitated a moment before knocking. There was no reply. He knocked again, a little louder this time, and Richard said, 'Yes?'

Graham opened the door. Richard was lying in bed, propped up on one elbow, reading.

'We'd like it,' said Graham, 'if you joined us.'

It came out more as an order than a request and it didn't surprise him when, almost meekly, Richard folded down the corner of the page he was on, closed his book and stood up.

He was naked, and Graham caught his breath at how neatly Richard's body contained its own masculinity, how perfectly, how succinctly it announced itself. Graham's masculinity, or so he'd always felt, leaked rather than emanated from his untidy, gangling frame.

Expressionless, Graham walked to the door and, taking Richard by the hand, led him like a child across the corridor and into their bedroom.

Laura had thrown back the covers and was lying full-out on the sheets. When he and Richard reached the bed, she lifted her arms and said, very softly, 'Come!'

Richard let go of Graham's hand and leant over Laura. Her arms came up and clasped him round the neck. He fell on to her, their two bodies merging into one.

Graham remained standing by the side of the bed, suddenly at a loss over what to do. Then, rather hesitantly, he lay down next to the rise and fall of their bodies.

'Yes, yes!' Laura was whispering in Richard's ear. 'Oh yes, like that, like that!'

Graham extended a tentative hand and encountered Richard's back. He let his hand slip to the globe of Richard's bucking buttocks, and from there to his inner thigh. He met no obstacles to his exploration of Richard's body but neither did he feel it to be welcome. He removed

100

his hand, whereupon Laura clutched at it, her nails digging painfully into his flesh.

'Oh, yes, yes, yes!' she was moaning. 'Like that, like that!'

The pressure from Laura's nails increased, the springs of the bed began a vulgar creaking, and then, just when he thought he couldn't stand the pain any longer, Laura's hand went limp, there was a long sigh, and he heard her say, 'Oh, that was good. I needed that. Thank you.'

Graham reached out for Richard, but as he did so, Richard rolled off Laura and got to his feet. 'I'm sorry,' he said. 'I think I should go back to my room.'

'Not on our account,' said Laura. 'We'd like you to stay. Wouldn't we, Graham?'

'I don't think I should.' His body dematerialized into the shadows.

Graham heard the door click shut. He lay very still for a long time and then, very hesitantly, he put out a hand to feel for Laura. As he touched her, she twitched away from him, and lashing out with her foot kicked him sharply on the shin.

'Laura?' he queried.

But there was no reply.

He lay absolutely motionless after that, not moving at all, until at five o'clock he heard Toby stir in his cot, and getting up, took his son downstairs to warm his bottle.

At breakfast both Laura and Richard were very subdued. When he attempted to give Laura a good morning kiss, Graham found himself kissing not her cheek but the empty air, so quickly did she sidestep his embrace; and Richard was equally loath to be drawn into early morning pleasantries.

After breakfast Richard said, 'I promised I'd ring my agent. Do you think they'll mind if I use the phone?'

And after five minutes in the study, he reappeared in the doorway and said, 'You won't believe this but I've got to go back. I'm up for a part in the new Simon Gray.'

'When?' said Graham. 'When must you leave?'

'This afternoon. Isn't that a bummer?'

'It's because of last night, isn't it?' said Graham.

Richard laughed. 'Of course not. Last night was just fine.' He came properly into the room, and walking over to Graham, gave him a clumsy hug. 'You're a lovely man, you should know that. You too,' he said to Laura. 'I'm honoured that you like me. Good God, flattered! But you know how it is. Work is work. Now what about trains?'

Laura, who was winding Toby, said simply, 'Mrs Worral. Ask Mrs Worral. She'll know about trains.'

They had an early lunch, after which, in virtual silence, they drove Richard to the station. Despite the sinking sensation in the pit of his stomach, Graham managed to be reasonably matter of fact about their leavetaking; every bit as matter of fact, he noticed thankfully, as Laura.

As they pulled out of the station forecourt, he patted her on the knee and said, 'For the best, I suppose. I mean, where would we have gone from here? When you think about it, I mean.'

She didn't reply, just said, in a low, dull voice, 'I'd like to see where you asked him.' So he made a detour to the little church and they went into the graveyard and he showed her where he and Richard had sat on the wall. She ran her hand slowly along the stone, then turning to the baby in her arms said, 'Well, Toby, time for your supper, I suppose.'

Back at the house, she went into the kitchen to prepare Toby's supper whilst he went upstairs to prepare Toby's bath.

'Don't forget,' he said as they went their separate ways in the hallway, 'we still have each other.'

He heard the scream as he was bending to turn on the tap. For a second he thought his ears were deceiving him; then, as the scream — high-pitched and agonized — continued and grew, he knew that they weren't, and dashed downstairs and into the kitchen.

The first sight to greet him was Toby in his feeding-chair, his chubby hands waving, conductor-like, in the air: a miniature maestro coaxing his mother through her aria of grief. Then, beyond the baby, huddled like an animal at bay in the corner of the room, he saw Laura, her eyes fixed blankly on a point in the middle distance, her mouth open in the scream.

He ran up to her and shook her, but that didn't stop her; it was as if she hadn't felt his hand on her shoulder, was oblivious to his presence. He took a step back and slapped her hard across the face. Only then did she stop screaming.

'Laura,' he began, 'my angel, you mustn't . . .' But even as the words formed on his lips and other words queued up to join them, he realized that nothing he could say could ever make good the damage.

'I'm sorry,' he whispered. 'I'm so sorry.'

Still she didn't acknowledge his presence, so crouching down opposite her, he took her hand and pulled her upright, and putting his arm around her shoulder, guided her towards the table where Toby, perhaps to fill the silence that had settled so oppressively on the room, had set up a howling of his own. With his free arm, Graham scooped up the baby, and it was thus that Mrs Worral, who'd come up from her house in the grounds to investigate the scream she thought she'd heard, saw them: a perfect family grouping, mother, father and son, thrown into glowing relief by the late afternoon sun streaming in through the window.

The Exile

ANTHONY AKERMAN

We were giving the model a rest when the telephone rang. After thirty minutes under the lamps peering down into my Mamiya, I also needed to give my eyes and back a rest. I was in the studio kitchen making tea so Trudy, my stylist, answered. I normally don't take calls during a session with a model. I know it's a cliché, but in commercial photography time is money. Trudy came into the kitchen and told me that Sipho was on the line. He'd offered to call back if I was busy, but she said it sounded as if he had a problem. I remember feeling irritated. Immortalizing a fifteen-year-old model for the cover of a glossy magazine was giving me all the problems I could cope with that afternoon. I left Trudy to finish making the tea and took the call in the studio.

'I'm sorry to worry you,' said Sipho. 'It's just something I must tell you.' His voice was flat and toneless.

'What's the problem?' I asked. I looked up and saw the model watching me with her doe-like eyes. She smiled.

'Samson is dead,' said Sipho. 'Samson Kunene.'

'When?' I asked.

'Last night,' said Sipho. 'It happened last night. I had to go there and fix things up.'

'How did it happen?'

'He took his own life,' said Sipho. 'It was a suicide.'

I don't know exactly what I felt. Mostly disbelief I suppose, if that's a feeling. I was trying to make adjustments; adjusting to a new idea, the idea that I'd never again pass him in a street or see him in a café. I didn't know Samson Kunene all that well. I try to avoid South African exiles. I left the country eight years ago. When I say I left it, I mean I left it behind me. Amsterdam is my home now. My life is here; my woman and my job. Next year I'll have a Dutch passport and that's that. I didn't ask to be born in South Africa and I had no intention of dying there as a soldier on the border.

'Is everything all right?' asked Trudy.

'Oh yes,' I said and I smiled. I had to snap out of it. I wanted the model to look seductive and sophisticated, not serious or sad. I threw the mental switch and went back to work. The pictures were good and the magazine commissioned me to do another cover.

Saskia had left for Breda before I got home. She's an actress and in the Dutch theatre they tour everything. She was in a play by some East German writer. I had a steak and a glass of wine and sat down to write a proposal for a potential client. If I landed this job it would pay for our summer holiday in Greece. I made two abortive attempts to get started, but I didn't have an idea in my head. I turned on the television. As usual there was nothing worth watching. I was reading *Ragtime* (I always get around to bestsellers ten years after they've been published) so I poured another glass of wine and sat down for a read. As I turned the page I realized I couldn't remember a word I had read. I had been thinking about Samson Kunene.

I suppose I'd spoken to him only about a dozen times during the last eight years. Sipho had introduced me to him. Sipho is one of the few South Africans I keep in touch with. Like me, he doesn't inhabit the South African exile ghetto; he's married to a Dutch woman and has a young daughter. The last time I'd spoken to Samson was at Sipho's birthday party. He was drunk and pedantic at the time. To humour him I told him I had been born in Thekwini, the Zulu name for Durban. He spent at least half an hour explaining the etymological permutations the word *itheku* (meaning a bay or a harbour) had undergone before it emerged as *ethekwini*. In presenting his case he digressed on Zulu linguistics and folklore. I wasn't sure if he was making it up. He had a round, gentle face and a sparse beard. There wasn't a wrinkle to suggest a life lived or a troubled spirit; just one unexplained scar, no doubt from a knife on a township

Friday night. His hands were delicate and his voice was soft and persuasive. Only his eyes betrayed a restlessness. While he was talking to me they strayed around the room. Apparently he made a scene at the party after I left. Sipho didn't tell me exactly what happened, but I know he avoided Samson after that. Sipho is slow to anger, but when he's angry you'd better take cover. In that regard he's still very much a Zulu.

Whenever someone dies you are reminded of your own mortality. That someone has ceased to exist, the banal realization that it's possible, makes you consider the enormity of the fact that it can, it will happen to you. Samson Kunene didn't exist any longer. How long before his memory would fade away? There is no adequate way of responding to a suicide either. It's an unequivocal challenge. It asks: 'What have you got to live for that's so important?' It's also an accusation; 'we', those who knew him, had failed him. I was having an attack of bad conscience. I had in fact seen him the week before. I was on my way home from work when he came walking towards me along Nes. It's a narrow street and he was staggering from the hoarding on one side to the wall on the other. He was dead drunk and oblivious of everyone in the street. He didn't see me and I didn't go up to him. I remember thinking it would take him more than an hour in his condition to explain the etymological permutations of *itheku* to me. If he tagged on home with me, which was bound to happen if he recognized me, I would have to devote the next day to saving my relationship. Saskia's interest in the anguish of South African exiles has always seemed purely academic and she doesn't respond well to unexpected visitors. In this country hospitality is regulated, measured out carefully by appointments recorded in the diaries of both parties. I believe that doing in Rome as the Romans do is a workable survival policy and have conformed in this and in other forms of social behaviour. When I walked past Samson holding up a wall in Nes I was being practical. As I picked up the phone I knew I was feeling guilty. Sipho was at home babysitting his daughter.

'Yes, I'd like you to come around,' he said.

Sipho and I sat in his living room and stared into our glasses in silence. He had just finished recounting the events of the previous night; Samson lying dead in his bed, his wife in a state of shock, his three-year-old son asleep and unaware that he no longer had a daddy, the police, the ambulance men. He told everything slowly, evenly, with an intonation that suggested mild surprise. I told him about the last time I had seen Samson, about the guilt I felt for passing by on the other side of the street.

'I think you're not the only one,' he said. 'We weren't close, but I knew him. I feel sort of responsible, you know, because I didn't see things were so bad. Not that I could have stopped this, but maybe we could have talked about things. Sometimes things are not as bad as you think they are. I think I let him down. His drinking problem was one of the things that made me stop seeing him. After he buggered up my party he came back the next day to apologize. He sat in that chair and said he was sorry. He just looked at the floor and said he was sorry and kept quiet for a long time. And I was hard, man. I just said, "Yes". I didn't talk to him. Eventually he got up and said he would see me around. And I just said that was okay. And I think this is why I feel guilty. When I think about what happened to him now, I think it was a petty thing. It was so small I could have dealt with it.'

Samson's death had humbled us. It had given him dignity. Samson, whom we had come to regard as a troublesome drunk, had forced us to take him seriously. He'd left us with a question we'd never be able to answer: why did he do it?

'I know his marriage was in trouble,' said Sipho. 'Anita was telling him he must go. She couldn't take the drinking any more. I know she's blaming herself now, but it's not her fault.'

'Why did he drink so much?' I asked.

'I don't know,' said Sipho. 'I know he missed South Africa a lot. I'd been there for a family visit and when I came back he came around and I told him how things are at home. He never missed a detail. He wanted to know everything; how I arrived, what I did, how his family was. He sat there listening to me and nodding. I had brought some magazines and newspapers with me. He said: Well, you know, I'm just going to read these, but I want to take my time. He'd read a bit and then put the newspaper down, like he was saving up some for later. You could see he was really trying to place himself in the stories, rereading them and telling you small details. This is not true, he'd say, because I know that shop was in this street and not in that one. He knew where everything was. It hurt him very much that he could never go back home.'

Could homesickness drive a person to suicide? I found that hard to believe. Everything was hard to believe. I still found it hard to believe that Samson had committed suicide. He didn't seem the type, but obviously my notions of suicidal types had to be revised.

'Why couldn't he go home?' I asked. 'Had he been in the movement?'

'I think he used to be a soldier,' said Sipho, 'but he got out. There had been problems and he was quite cynical. Not about the soldiers, but about the leadership. He never told me why. He used to tell me these things just passing through, you know, not really sitting down. I felt I shouldn't try and dig. I never asked him how did he leave South Africa, but according to the things he told me he must have had a rough life. He's been to quite a lot of countries; Botswana, Zambia, Tanzania, Kenya for some time and I think Ethiopia. He's also lived in East Europe and then he came to Italy for maybe two years, Belgium, Ireland for one year and then he tried to settle down here with the right papers and everything. He spent a long time looking for a country.'

I was asleep before Saskia got back from Breda and I left for the studio before she was up. I remember her getting into bed. Her feet were cold. That night I dreamt I was back in South Africa for the first time in years. (When I first left I used to have nightmares in which I was back there.) I remember a railway station with thousands of people. Then it became a hospital in Soweto. I was with Saskia. We were walking down long, echoing corridors and kept losing and finding each other. I only remembered this dream at lunchtime. The hospital in Soweto obviously meant I was thinking of Samson Kunene. I couldn't get him out of my mind. I kept seeing him lying in one of those fridges, being kept fresh for his funeral. It was affecting my concentration. Trudy asked me what the matter was and I told her. She asked me if I was going to the funeral. I hadn't thought about that. When I did, I decided it was a good idea. Perhaps I was mourning and the only thing to do was to go along with it. The funeral was bound to be the day after next and then everything would be literally dead and buried.

'It's only next week Monday,' said Sipho.

'Why only then,' I asked. 'It must cost a fortune to keep him so long.'

'Samson, he knew lots of people,' said Sipho. 'They must make arrangements to come here from all over; England, Belgium, Sweden and Germany. Also they are hoping someone from the family in South Africa, maybe his brother, can come to the burial.'

'So his parents know?'

'Anita phoned his mother.'

'Does she know how he died?'

'She didn't ask how he had died,' said Sipho. 'She just didn't ask. Anita was crying and the mother started consoling her. Here is this woman who has lost a son she hasn't seen for years and she can't even come to the burial. I know she has a bigger pain and still she was consoling Anita with quotations from the Bible.'

'I still can't really believe it,' I said.

'It's like an unfinished conversation,' said Sipho. 'There are things I would like to say to him now. It's so heavy.'

'I want to come to the funeral.'

'On Thursday evening there's a sort of memorial gathering for the people who've come from other countries. Maybe you can come to that.'

When I hung up I phoned Saskia and told her what had happened. I was surprised, pleasantly surprised, when she said she'd like to go with me to the memorial gathering. She sounded serious and moved and yet she'd only met Samson once. Perhaps it came more easily to her, the appropriate tone and expression, because she was an actress. She was free on Thursday evening.

The memorial gathering was held in a run-down building, which had been appropriated by some refugee group. I think they were South Americans. About fifty people were there and, apart from Samson's wife and someone from the Anti-Apartheid Movement, we were the only whites present. I felt a bit conspicuous and reflected cynically that apartheid perpetuated itself among the exiles by a process of natural selection. Sipho caught my eye and indicated two empty seats near him. I was glad of that. He sort of legitimized my presence. I felt like a white interloper invading their black grief. I felt all that South African shit I'd left behind me. But maybe I was projecting that into the situation. I could hardly expect people to smile at me on an occasion like that.

'Who's that?' I asked, indicating a slight man who looked as though he was about to address us.

'That's Teboho,' said Sipho. 'He is sort of Master of Ceremonies.'

Teboho spoke softly as he welcomed us. He told us that while we were here the Kunene family was gathered in Soweto to remember their son and brother. He said that anyone who wanted to tell us something about Samson Kunene could speak. A speaker took the floor and told us where and how he had met Samson. He told us how Samson had been a brother to him when he first came to Europe. He was followed by a series of speakers.

None of the speakers was nervous. They were not being judged on their performance. They were there to share their sorrow with us and to remember Samson. Songs were sung between the speeches; doleful hymns in Sotho and Zulu. A shudder moved up through my body and I had to close my mouth to stop it escaping. There was something so familiar in the Zulu hymns; something I knew and yet didn't know. I fought back my tears. No one else was crying and I didn't want to draw attention to myself. I glanced at Saskia. She was serious and calm.

A woman was speaking. I heard her saying that Samson was not a traditionalist, but a lover of tradition and culture. She said that he had been brought up in the rural areas and, as a child, had tended his father's cattle. She said he understood and appreciated the rural traditions and culture. She told us how she had gone to his house when his son was born. Her household had been to see his household in the appropriate way. Then 'Nkosi Sikelel' iAfrika' was sung. I hadn't experienced such a sadness since I was a child. It was an empty, almost hopeless feeling. I held the back of the chair in front of me as swell after swell of inarticulate emotion heaved inside me. I wished they would finish singing. I saw Saskia out of the corner of my eye. She knew the tune and was trying to pick up the words as she went along. I saw a few fists clenched in sad and seemingly dutiful defiance.

When it was over Teboho closed the gathering. He said he hoped that by the year 2000 Samson's bones could be taken back to South Africa to be buried near those of his forefathers. He said that was the only way to ensure that the continuity in the line of the Kunenes would not be broken.

'Are you all right, love?' asked Saskia reaching out her hand to touch my face.

'I'm all right,' I said.

'It reminds me of funerals in Brabant. When I was a little girl I went to funerals there with my mother. They were also very emotional.'

We were in a pizzeria. The pizza was heavy, but the chianti was good. At the time I felt Saskia's comparison was misplaced. I know it was unreasonable, but for a moment I felt contempt for her. Had she not understood what was happening that evening?

'What are you thinking?' she asked.

'Nothing,' I said, 'and everything, of course.'

'You're very far away.'

'This whole bloody business has upset me. This evening has made it even worse.'

'I saw you were crying.'

'I wasn't crying. I'm not sentimental. Why should I cry about Samson? I hardly knew him.'

'You were crying for South Africa,' she said.

I let out a short, dismissive laugh. I seldom cry and when I do it's not for abstractions like 'my country'.

'It's nothing to be ashamed of,' she added. 'You should be more honest with your feelings. You're still trying to say goodbye. Perhaps you should go back there and do it properly.'

'If you come with me,' I said. I knew I was on safe ground because a team of wild horses couldn't drag Saskia down to South Africa.

'How could I do that?' she asked. I watched the expression on her face change. It became a sadly caring expression. 'I felt the longing and pain of all those people this evening. If they can't go back to their home, what gives me the right to go there just to satisfy a mild curiosity?'

When she said that, I became strangely proud of her. When I was younger I used to feel proud when I walked down the street holding hands with the prettiest girl in town. Every wolf whistle used to be a feather in my cap. Now I felt proud to walk down the street holding hands with a woman who could outshine the others in moral rectitude.

'You understand that, love?'

'Yes. It looks like you've just taken a decision for me.'

'As usual,' said Saskia. She smiled.

The days leading up to the funeral marked an unaccountable improvement in my sex life. Perhaps the word 'improvement' gives the impression that it was bad before, but it wasn't. What I mean is that Saskia was all over me. It may have been the mood I was in. I was depressed, I suppose, and a bit withdrawn. I've given up trying to understand what provokes an erotic response in women. It's probably more morbid than they'd ever admit. I'd wake up in the middle of the night and realize that she was making love to me. (Something I was well advised not to try on her.) It takes the merest suggestion of pelvic pressure to flatter the male ego and I have learnt to make hay while the sun shines. But Saskia's lovemaking felt curiously calculated, more compliant than passionate. I felt very close to her, but I was aware of her drawing me towards her. During our lovemaking she wanted me to repeat that I loved her, that I loved her, that I loved her.

Then on Sunday evening she announced that she couldn't go to the funeral. She had to meet a director in the American Hotel on Monday afternoon. He had offered her a part in an Ibsen play and she wanted him to explain his production concept to her. We'd always said that work came first.

As I came out of the studio and started walking towards the taxi rank all the sirens and hooters in the city set up a baleful wail. They are tested at midday on the first Monday of every month. I've lived here for eight years and I still don't know what I'm supposed to do if they go off at any other time. If it meant that Russian missiles were on their way, I remember thinking, I was probably doing the right thing then: going to a cemetery. That was the first time I'd laughed in a few days.

The taxi dropped me outside Sipho's flat. He'd said I could drive along with him. I went into a nearby florist and bought the most expensive bunch of flowers I could find. As I paid the shop assistant I imagined Samson looking down from the spirit world and saying: 'Are you trying to buy me off?' The shop assistant pushed a little white card across the counter towards me. I took out my Mont Blanc and wrote: Hamba kahle, Samson Kunene. I was surprised at what I had written and suddenly felt self-consciously emotional. I left the florist as fast as I could and rang Sipho's bell. I must have looked like the rejected lover in a romantic comedy standing on the pavement with that ostentatious bunch of flowers.

'Are you going to take a last look?' I asked as we got out of the car at the funeral parlour.

'No,' said Sipho. 'I don't think I can face it again.'

We crowded into a small room and waited with the coffin. We stood in a silence that was broken by an occasional shuffle or sob. People averted their eyes, not wanting to be drawn into greeting each other. Due to an error in stage management there was a fifteen-minute delay. Teboho asked if we would like to sing softly. The hymns started again and this time the women cried quietly. I placed my flowers on the coffin and looked at Samson. Behind the pane of glass he looked alive, asleep. I was trying to project a thought to him. I don't remember what it was. Perhaps it was just: we know each other.

More people were waiting when we arrived at the cemetery. The service was simple and almost amateurish. Some of Samson's favourite music was piped in from an off-stage taperecorder; Paul Robeson, Dollar Brand, Little Lemmy playing a kwela on two penny-whistles. When I heard the penny-whistles, I began to cry.

We followed the coffin to the grave. It was a cold April day and the weather changed from sun to rain to wet snow. An old man was led forward by Teboho to speak to us. He had travelled from America to attend the funeral.

'Samson's family,' he said, 'is holding a service in Soweto at this selfsame moment. His brother collected the money for a ticket, but he was not able to get a passport in time. The government said it would take three weeks.' I knew that if I'd been lying in that coffin my parents would have been there. They would have been given passports in a day, in an hour. This spite, this perversity filled me with anger and shame.

'I have known Samson since he was a small boy,' said the old man. 'I have come here for the family. In August I will be going home to South Africa. I will go to the Kunene family and I will tell them what I have seen. I can say that everything happened properly and that their son and brother was not buried like a refugee.'

Teboho stepped into the middle of a wide circle around

the grave and started singing 'Nkosi Sikelel' iAfrika', but his voice broke and he fell to his knees with his hands covering his face. Two people helped Teboho to his feet and a woman's voice picked up the anthem, held it high above us like a standard. While the professionals in tails and top hats lowered the coffin into the grave, the April wind scattered the phrases: Lord Bless Africa / Let its Horn of Hope be Raised / Come Spirit / Come Spirit. We all picked up a handful of earth and dropped it on to the coffin. Teboho regained his composure and announced that he would perform the washing of hands.

'African custom says we must do this at the house of the widow,' he said, 'but because we are in exile we have put a fire-bucket and a towel outside the place where we are invited to drink coffee.'

'Maybe I'll believe he's dead now,' said Sipho.

'Do you think they'll take his bones back before the year 2000?'

'I don't know. Did you feel the earth, how cold it was? When I felt it in my hand I just thought I wouldn't like to be buried here.'

'Neither would I,' I said.

A woman of my mother's age came over to Sipho bearing a cup of coffee in front of her. Sipho introduced her to me as Mrs Dlamini. 'He was born in Durban,' Sipho added.

'You come from Thekwini!' Mrs Dlamini exclaimed and she smiled at me. I nodded and smiled at her. Then I remarked that it was a sad day for all of us.

'But Samson Kunene's spirit is with us,' said Mrs Dlamini. 'And his death has united us. Look at all the people who came. You see, he is the one who has brought us together. Through Samson I have also met you.'

Jellymouse

AGNES SAM

I was attempting to hold my own as a single mother, alienated from extended family and friends, while safeguarding the imaginative world my children were living in.

The moment each son approached seven, I watched him hover between a fragile space of living toys and the place where shattered glass was forbidden and impossible to reshape. I wanted to delay each child's progress into the real world for as long as possible, only to discover I was unready for it myself.

It was Lusani's turn to hover at this point — Sinowa was eight, Wande ten — when we moved to a new house. The location contained a mix of colonial and English people, and we were South African. Yet the struggles to reach this point gave me a glorious sense of renewal. We would celebrate.

They spent their days running wild, discovering things, tumbling into the house, talking excitedly, squabbling to be the one to tell me. Football field. Swings. Slide. Rusty roundabout. Icecream man in a van, not on a tricycle. A mad dog jumping at them. Hens in a hen house. Bushes that sting. They located school, chippie, fishing spot, country lanes leading to tadpoles, birds' nests and a tree that made a wonderful den, in the days I took to unpack, leaving the front door wide open just in case the local gang proved hostile.

At night we slept on the floor, together, huddled under one quilt, talking about how Father Christmas would know where we had moved to; what he does if there's no chimney. When the wind blew the windows flew open, and I had to be the one to go bravely to shut them.

And then we were all jolted into the real world by an early morning visit from our landlord. He was not checking to see how we were settling in. He said several used cans of paint and old settees had been dumped in a public area nearby. Someone he could not name reported I dumped the items there.

I was staving off the pressure on my eldest son to assume the role of man of the house. It meant keeping certain things from him, not taking him into my confidence, and yet not sending him away just then, as it would heighten his awareness that we were being harassed. With the children looking on I joked with the landlord, 'We could do with a couple of settees. You can see we've none. Won't you give me a hand?'

He went away leaving us quiet and subdued for the first time since our arrival. The carefree spirit they brought with them to this place was as if slapped away. It seemed a good time for that celebration.

But Wande demanded evidence of what we had to celebrate.

'We're celebrating something you can't see!' I said.

'Is that why the windows are too high?' he asked. 'What don't you want us to see?'

'You must imagine the view.'

'I want a house with cupboards. And an attic.'

'We'll buy cupboards. Stop grumbling. Who's the party for?'

But all our birthdays were past — I'm Gemini, Wande is Leo, Sinowa is Cancer, Lusani is Aquarius — so we agreed to celebrate Lusani's pretend birthday. They were the invited guests. No presents were expected. It would be a good party — provided Lusani remembered not to expect any presents. Hovering on the brink, he might believe it was really his birthday.

They had to be chased out to play — already they were finding excuses to stay home to protect me — while I prepared for the party and waited for the gas man. With a nice sticky mix of margarine and flour on my hands — the mixer was at the bottom of a crate — the sugar could not be found.

I rushed to the supermarket in our twelve-year-old car.

Halfway down the road the sounds of odd banging moved along with my progression. I wound down the window, saw a group of people laughing, looking as if they had been waiting for me to drive my car, and got out. There was a thick chain tied around the axle. It had a notice board at one end. One of the laughing men actually came to unwind the chain.

I was hostile and bristling, by the time I entered the supermarket. Here, there was not a single foreign face — at the checkouts, or doing any shopping. And the staff immediately took turns following me around the store. I smiled first in my bright, hail-fellow-well-met, I-haven't-nicked-a-farthing-in-my-life way. It failed. It must have been obvious to other shoppers I was being followed, if I could detect it. A uniformed security guard brushed close by me several times. If I turned, a woman would rush away from somewhere close behind me. I found the sugar, went to the checkout and three members of staff converged around me. I was unsure what to do in such a situation.

The chain damaged the exhaust. The silencer was now ineffective. The gas man had been and left in the short spell that I was out. I was faced with the prospect of paying for a second call out.

With the cake in the oven, I ran to the telephone booth to phone round for a plumber to plumb in the washing machine.

'You want sixty-five pounds to plumb a washing machine? It cost me fifty! And if it goes next to the kitchen sink? Will it be cheaper? But you said it's the pipes that cost! I can't pay someone sixty-five pounds to work for one hour! What do I need to do it myself? You will say that. It's doing you out of condom money! And the same to you, mate!'

But the plumber's merchant was helpful. He advised me about stand-pipes and waste-traps. I ran home to take some measurements.

The landlord's visit, by now forgotten, heralded the beginning of an onslaught. While I was measuring under the sink, a woman wearing a golliwog badge walked up to the front door demanding her child's baby walker. She was mildly abusive when I said my children could walk. Then a woman called to complain that her children's crayons and powder paints cost a lot of money. Did I think she was buying them for my kid to use? Another called to say the bucket on her son's go-kart was cracked. Wande was too big for the kart. He should not have got in it in the first place. He must have damaged it. I must repair it. Windscreen wipers and car aerials were damaged in the night — my sons must be the culprits. The communal keys were missing. I was keeping them for some criminal motive. The washing machines had been broken into. When I went to use the washing machine someone slipped coins into the machines on my behalf. A freezer had been cleared by thieves — we must have had a feast.

The humorous way I talked to the landlord that morning gradually gave way to fury when anyone approached the front door. All day I vacillated between keeping these incidents to myself, and warning the boys not to play with certain children.

When they returned home we locked the door. The marble cake was baked, cooling on the rack. A pizza was in the oven. And a black cherry jelly in the fridge. They did a 'Bisto kids' scene, inhaling the aromas. The marble cake always has a secret running through the centre: coconut stirred about with yoghurt, chocolate flake, even peanut butter and jam. I was not telling what the secret was that day.

They set the table, rushing from dining room to kitchen for cutlery, plates, real glasses; deciding who will sit where, who will have the largest of the unmatched glasses, who will pour the drinks, who will be served first; while I waited to hear the shattered glass, trying not to think about the past, or the next day, or what appeared to be a crass neighbourhood.

Wande was nominated to be in charge of the ceremony — marching to the table with the marble cake. He hung about, feeling dubious about this honour, suspecting the sponge was too heavy for me to carry.

The pizza was ready, waiting for a lump of parmesan to be grated over it. In the process of taking it to the dining room we heard Wande, about to pick up the marble cake, let out a sound like a wailing siren. 'Mu-um!'

Expecting to see him disappearing down the sink hole, we charged into the kitchen only to find him standing there staring at the marble cake, with a fresh long, deep furrow down the centre — as if a mole had been burrowing underground. A thief had been here.

Each of us looked accusingly from one face to the next. At that moment even I was a suspect. Then my glance fell on Lusani, with real tears in his eyes, his mouth full of something, and cake crumbs around his lips, turned to stone. The others too seemed to be under some spell of enchantment. No one moved or spoke. As long as they remained silent, Lusani could not swallow what was in his mouth. If he was expected to speak, it would be a dead giveaway.

The tension proved too much for him. Without any prompting, struggling to speak with his mouth full, he said, 'Not me.'

His denial was not strong, but there was a distinct sense he was disappointed that all suspecting eyes were focused on him. I awarded him ten out of ten for effrontery, struggling to handle this in a way that was not unfair to Wande who was learning about owning up if he did something wrong, and yet not propel Lusani into feelings of guilt.

Turning to question Sinowa, I asked, 'Where were you when I was bringing the pizza to the table?'

Wande made little attempt to hide his incredulity. He grabbed my arm, shaking me vigorously, 'Mum, look at Lusani!' I pretended he was a gnat and took a swipe at him.

The pressure eased off Lusani. He swallowed what he had in his mouth while Wande looked dismayed, not believing I missed seeing the evidence around Lusani's mouth.

'Do you think Sinowa is innocent, Wande?' I asked.

'If you question him, there must be more to this than

meets the eye,' Wande said, and turning to Lusani asked, 'Why does she suspect Sinowa? Is he your accomplice?'

But Lusani, like a professional, had declared his innocence and refused to say any more. He simply shook his head very, very slowly.

'What about you, Wande? You found the cake. How do we know you're not the culprit?'

Wande, priding himself on being an ace detective, had solved all the codes in the *Super Sleuth's Handbook*, but reckoned he could not fathom how I was doing my sleuthing.

'Why aren't you questioning Lusani?'

We sat down at the table. It was hardly like a celebration to us. We sang 'Happy Birthday' in very subdued voices. 'Hip, hip, hooray!' sounded tearful. Then everyone was quiet. I calmly served the pizza. They prefer curry and rice, every one of them, but I would lose my skill in making bread and pastry without practice. So they had to eat foreign food once a week and at celebrations.

Perhaps because I did not interrogate Lusani, he felt he stood accused. Whatever the reason, he repeated, without prompting, 'It wasn't me.'

None of us paid any attention to this remark. 'How's the pizza?' I asked.

'It wasn't me,' Lusani said, sounding a little cross. 'I didn't do it.' And gradually he became more and more cross and sulky. It seemed the more he denied it, the more he came to believe he was innocent.

As the meal progressed the animosity that Lusani felt at being silently accused began to envelop Sinowa. Even I could not understand how this happened.

'This food tastes horrible! Awful! I wish I didn't have to eat it!' Sinowa said.

Every word Sinowa said, Lusani repeated. 'Yes. It's horrible food! Must we eat it?'

They pushed their food about on the plate, but I noticed they continued eating. Sinowa was more cross with me for suspecting Lusani, even though I had not questioned Lusani at all.

'What about when we serve the cake and jelly?' Wande asked, very pleased at the possibility this presented for him.

'Yes, won't you be having cake and jelly?' I asked, but my voice sounded too sweet.

They knew I was up to something. The prospect of forfeiting cake and jelly had not occurred to them. They began giggling. The mood at the table lightened. The result was that Sinowa took on Lusani's defence. He turned in a kindly, caring way to Lusani and asked, 'Did you do it, Lusani?'

Slowly, with great deliberation, as if emphasizing the certainty of his innocence, Lusani moved his head from side to side. This testimony was all Sinowa needed to be convinced Lusani was innocent. They repeated this question and answer routine, each time Sinowa referring to Lusani directly, 'Did you do it?' and receiving a firm, wide-eyed, 'No!' Sinowa then affirmed his kid brother's truthfulness. 'You see? He's telling the truth.'

The two of them stayed loyal to each other, performing this question and answer tactic until the pizza plate was scraped clean, with Wande sensing that there was something between them but unable to fathom what it was. They cleared the table while I sat quietly pondering some very deep thoughts.

Then I served the marble cake, with them eyeing the chocolate and nuts dripping from the centre. All three accepted their portions with a mumbled 'Thank you' and quickly gobbled it up. Silently they held out their plates and accepted a second helping while I went to the fridge to bring the black cherry jelly myself, since the mould was cold and slippery. A few seconds later I placed the jelly calmly on the table and they stared astonished at a hollow the size of a dessertspoon marring the smooth, wobbly surface.

They were shocked. I, believing in ghosts, fairies and doppelgangers, sat there placid and calm, like a fat frog waiting to be turned into a prince.

Wande chose this moment to tell me, 'Mum, someone hit Lusani today.'

'Who?' I asked, assuming it was a child's fight.

'A woman.'

'What d'you mean a woman? What woman?'

'I don't know her.'

'A woman hit Lusani and you didn't come home and tell me? Wande! What were you doing? Where were you?'

'We were playing Tig.'

'Then? What happened?'

'She just came to us and slapped Lusani.'

'Why Lusani? Why not you?'

'I don't know.'

'And she picked you up and shook you, hey Lusani?' Sinowa said to Lusani.

They stared dismally at the jelly with its marred surface, while I planned another move. Before we moved here, I made excuses for them, whether they were colonial or English. They were not to blame. They were conditioned by stereotypes. Dishonest Arab. Dirty Indian. Loose women. Sly. Cunning. Shady deals. Illegal anything. I made excuses for them. What chance did we have to trust? Leave it to the young generation. They will not have our hangups. It will be easier for them. Wait for this generation to die out. But that day something happened. I gave up on them. Perhaps I hoped — a black South African family would never be treated like this anywhere else in England. It said something for England. From that day I refused to behave as if South Africa had never happened. For that was where they were at. Colonials and English expected me to transplant from South Africa and to meet them as if the burden of reconciliation was not on them.

Wishing fervently to diminish the effect of a strange adult beating a child, I wanted equally to be violent against this woman, against these people who would discredit us, against those who harassed us from day to day. On the outside I spoke about non-violence to the children. About Gandhi coming to help us in South Africa. About my grandfather fearing I would never be given a passport because he had been imprisoned with Gandhi in Bloemfontein.

They drew me back to their world. Sinowa, believing he had trapped the culprit, asked, 'Did you do this, Mum?'

Wande, trying to establish a motive, asked, 'Why did you do this, Mum? Are you trying to get revenge? Or are you trying to confuse the guilty person?'

'If Mum nibbled the jelly, she must have nibbled the marble cake,' Sinowa explained in an aside to Lusani.

The new development seemed like a perfect job for Wande's detective handbook. He slipped from the chair and dashed into his bedroom. I waited until he returned. The incident with the woman had taken second place. Still I felt I must teach them, when they are older, never to tolerate an attack on their person.

While Wande sat flipping through his book, I said with a very straight face, 'There must be a mouse in the fridge.'

At this stage even Wande with all his experience of solving crimes was thrown off the track. The fridge is a piece of junk we picked up for a fiver. In winter it froze over like a freezer. Could a mouse possibly be living somewhere at the back? It feels very hot when they retrieve their marbles. Wande scrutinized my face to see if he could detect a hint of a smile, or guilt, perhaps. But my face was inscrutable.

I continued, 'And the mouse must've nibbled the cake. Sorry, Lusani. You were innocent all the time.'

We sat staring at the jelly. 'This looks like the work of some very professional criminal, to me,' Wande said.

Instead of serving the jelly I began speculating aloud. 'What will we do, because mice carry germs and things? We'll all be sick because the cake is eaten.'

They looked from one to the other, each of them trying to take in the situation. 'What a good thing we haven't eaten the jelly!' I said.

Wande realized I was waiting for someone to own up. But neither Lusani nor Sinowa responded. I went a step further. 'I wonder what poison we can use to kill the mouse?'

Lusani's eyes opened wider.

Wande began playing my game. 'Remember Rahat said some poison makes the mouse want to eat more and more and more.'

'That's very cruel for the mouse.'

Then Sinowa asked, 'Yes, but what about getting ill from the cake?'

'Doesn't the smallest get ill first? Do you feel ill, Sinowa? Or you, Lusani?' I asked.

'Not yet,' they both chimed in together.

'I think the best thing to do is first throw the jelly away before someone forgets and eats it,' I said.

Sinowa and Lusani looked very disappointed with this suggestion. But still neither of them owned up. So I picked up the jelly and moved determinedly to the kitchen. Just as I was about to step through the door Lusani said, very formally, 'Excuse me! Are you telling the truth about the mouse?'

He was still hovering on the brink. What could I do but bring the jelly back to the table and hug him. He did not understand what he had said to bring about this response from me.

But Wande did. 'I don't understand how you solved this case, Mum. Have you been secretly reading my detective handbook?' he asked.

I put out a note in the milk bottle with my first order, locked the door and drew the curtains to shut out the neighbours, hoping that tomorrow the milkman would be whistling and the postman would wish me 'good morning'.

Carlotta's Vinyl Skin

SHEILA ROBERTS

My friend David, a successful lawyer who helped me with my immigration papers for the United States, is unhappy in a niggled, half-tortured sort of way because of the unimpressive salary I earn as an English professor. Once a month regularly he'll phone to beg me to write a lurid romantic novel that might get on the bestseller list and be made into a movie, thus enabling me to buy the house and car he thinks I owe it to myself to own. I have told him over and over again that I cannot write such a novel — I would become immobilized with ennui and self-disgust at my very typewriter. I would waste my time trying, and simply be inserting my hands and head into a stock-like writer's block.

'Sheila, can't you just prostitute yourself for *once*?' he pleads. 'Just once. Then you can keep writing in comfort at least the egghead stuff no one wants to read.'

Sometimes a little inner voice joins its harangue with his. If I have endurance and energy (which perhaps I don't have and am therefore lacking the essentials of a full human being) I could indeed write a money-bringing novel, the voice insists. Think up a simple plot and set it in a foreign country during a time of turmoil. Be prepared to write six hundred pages. Create a beautiful heroine who falls in love with a rebel / renegade / revolutionary / freedom fighter / innocent fugitive from justice / political activist / disinherited son later to be re-inherited / wildcat unionist. Or simply a handsome Dracula-like fellow, eyes heavy-lidded with the boredom of being soul-possessed. Or she could be in search of a lost father. Contrive to have the lovers separated and then bring them together in a grand finale. They are both, or all three (depending on the audience targeted), hot-blooded. Here's your chance, Sheila, to portray the sex act from the woman's point of view. You could do a service to womankind while making money.

Weaving, weaving, I stick a sheet of paper in the typewriter. A foreign country? The only foreign country I know well, whose landscape forms part of my mental baggage and dream-life, is South Africa. My setting will have to be South Africa — it's foreign enough for most Americans (they think Johannesburg and Cairo are just down the freeway from each other) and it's their money I'm after. I couldn't presume to write about America in any case: I know too little about the causes of American turmoil and I'm confused between the names of battle-sites and the titles of songs. But I've no doubt I could recreate in words the look of the Cape coast, the Karoo, the Bushveld, the Highveld, the Natal highlands and the Drakensberge. In fact, if I invented a country, calling it something like Sylvanvakia, or Prinsenmania, or Eendt-sur-Mer, I would only end up describing either the Cape coast, the Karoo, the Bushveld, the Highveld, the Natal highlands or the Drakensberge. Geography is destiny.

Turmoil? If I want this book to sell, I have to keep all racial conflict or discrimination out of it, except perhaps to provide a kindly black sidekick for the hero or have a bit of jungle-enshrouded sex to the beat of tomtoms — but that could come into the subplot. So I could go along with the myth of the 'white man's' war and set my story in South Africa on the eve of Anglo-Boer hostilities. My heroine will be a peaches-and-cream English girl who comes out with her wealthy father to visit the mines and falls in love with . . . an Afrikaner? Ag, no. A descendant of the 1820 Settlers? Bor-ing. A nice English-speaking boy with an open mind? How about that?

I visualize delicate Victorian blouses, thick blonde hair done up in a chignon, large hats, many petticoats, large lacy bloomers, soft white hands, immense blue eyes, a vulnerable but brave mouth. Oh no, I am regurgitating memories of Bo Derek starring in *Tarzan the Ape Man*. Why does schlock always stick? I must start afresh. The image of my best-looking writing student comes to mind. She has slightly curly untidy brown hair, a thin face and slanting cat-like eyes. She usually wears long peasant skirts over Himalayan hiking-boots, or calf-length tights in paisley, Hot Pink or Neon Blue and soft suede boots with a foldover at the ankle, such as medieval pages must have worn, three earrings in one ear and none in the other, oversized T-shirts or fitted fifties blouses. I try dressing her in a Victorian outfit. She looks okay except her shoulders are too broad and she stands rather sardonically and firmly on the ground surveying the desolation of a burnt-down Free State farm as if it's a film-set. Ellie, get those boots off, and for God's sake, wilt a little!

But what's she doing on a Free State farm? She's English, for goodness sake. I'll send her in a donkey cart with her wealthy but dying father into the interior. They are on their way to Kimberley to buy diamonds. But the father dies on the road and she is left a pile of money. I love bumping off fathers in my stories: like other egghead writers I'm haunted by Oedipus, Clytemnestra, Electra and Goneril.

So there she is alone, on her way to Kimberley. But she can't travel alone: she must have picked up some passengers on the way, all decent citizens. Oh, poor girl . . . Look, I'm sorry, but I have to think about these things: how will she wash properly on the road? Wonderful complexions don't stay that way without proper cleansing. How will she be able to urinate and move her bowels out in the bush with all those skirts on? It's hard enough just wearing jeans, I know. Will she just bundle them up? But won't they still get splashed and stained? How much toilet paper does her party have? Did they have toilet paper in those days? Did they have toothbrushes? When was the first toothbrush marketed, hey you Popular Culturalists? What if she gets her period sitting in the donkey cart? Of *course* she'll get her period, unless she's anorectic. But an anorectic girl won't be able to handle the boisterous sex scenes in the book. And what about mosquitoes? I mean, have you ever spent a night out of doors in the summer without netting and that new improved insecticide you rub on hands, face and feet, or whatever parts of the body are exposed? What about days of perspiration? The food going bad?

Let me tell you, I know from experience that when my skin breaks out, I lose all sense of the romantic occasion. I don't feel like going to bed with some guy whose skin is fine and who'll want to leave the light on while we make love. I don't like making love when I'm sweaty or dirty — okay, okay I'm picky: why don't you shoot me? I don't fancy sweaty or dirty men. Also, I find it excruciating to be 'confined' with a man in bed, or even in a car, when I'm suffering from flatulence. Yes, contrary to masculine belief, women *do* fart. Over the centuries we've worked hard to establish the conviction of our continence. But out in the bush the pretence would have to go. Now I simply cannot muster up enthusiasm for romance-writing as I regard Carlotta, my beautiful heroine, waddling like a duck as she squats, searching for a place to hold steady where the tough grass won't prick her bare bum.

As luck would have it, my student Ellie walks into my office. Today she's sporting an old stained braided coat such as major-domos of hotels used to wear, a limp mini skirt and her Himalayas. I know that she (like many other students in these days of recession) buys her clothes from second-hand stores that sometimes stock astonishing antique garments, things people have stolen out of their grandparents' attics, or defunct theatre companies have hawked. Ellie also has on bottle-green tights and a little head-hugging hat from the twenties.

'Why do you want to write that trash?' she asks me.

'To make money.'

'Then you've got to stop thinking about physical discomfort. It's gross! Your heroine has to have skin made of vinyl. Her teeth are white stainless steel and her polyfibrous hair doesn't grow damp and scraggly, and her crystal eyes have three or four necessary expressions, depending on the light, for your purposes, Prof: joy, indignation, love and sorrow. She doesn't have periods, or perspiration, or pee, or poo!'

'I can't write about a vinyl *dummy*,' I say, my own eyes flashing with indignation.

'What's the least you can write about?'

'Well, to begin with, I need to see flesh and blood people in my mind's eye, a woman like you, for instance. Say, what does your boyfriend do?' Deep down in me a little hope is born that she will say he is completing training as an officer in the Air Force Academy. A shadowy Richard Gere starts forming. But would such a gorgeous thing want to date Ellie the Punk in her tights and boots?

'My boyfriend has a degree in Agriculture, but because of the recession he can't find a job in his field, no pun, so he's working as a male nurse at Hannah Hospital. Oh boy, you wouldn't believe the kinds of things he's learnt to do! Give people enemas, stick catheters into them, give them shots in the bee-hind and hold pans for them when they throw up. But it's done him good, especially seeing old people sick and naked and having to wash the shit off them and all that. He's much more sympathetic towards people these days than he used to be. He never criticizes women for their bodies the way most guys do and he doesn't joke about women's weak points.'

'What does he look like?' I ask a bit disconsolately, pulling the paper out of the machine: this may not be the stuff of High Romance.

'He's no Mister Universe. He's okay. He's going to have to go on a bit of a diet because of the tummy he's getting. Twenty-five's too young to get a tummy. Not that I mind, it's just the health of it. He's got a sweet face, but his skin is very pale. He can't suntan at all: he just goes red, mostly his nose. And he was never good at sports at school because of his flat feet. Would you listen to this! No one realized that he was flat-footed until he was about fourteen. He got out of the swimming pool at school and by chance the coach noticed his wet footprint. As flat as a fish.'

'What'll he do? Keep looking for a job in his "field" or settle for nursing?'

'Naa . . . he's decided to go on to postgrad work next year. He may as well. He's saved enough to put himself through, and he still wants to get into some branch of agricultural science, at the higher level though.'

'And you?'

'I'll keep on with my studio art and my writing. Though I wouldn't mind farming. I've always wanted to farm. That's why Percy and I get on so well.' She settles herself on the corner of my desk, running one hand over a pile of books. I see that each fingernail is painted a different colour. She looks at me confidentially. 'You know, Percy my boyfriend had a terrible time as a kid. His parents used to dominate him completely. Even when he was in high school, his mom'd clean his room and go through all his things. He had no privacy whatsoever. She'd even examine the underclothes he'd throw in the wash. And the one time he came home a little shikkered, both his parents created such a scene, even though he was already twenty-one, that now he's paranoid, he simply can't, he *can't* drink. Now his dad offers him beers and beers and beers, but he won't accept them. I've had a lot of trouble getting him to loosen up with me, you know. Do you know that he stayed a virgin until he was twenty-four?'

'Ellie, you don't have to tell me all this.'

'I know you'll keep it to yourself.'

'Of course . . .' I hope my smile looks sincere.

'I had to teach him a lot,' she says coolly, getting off the desk and clumping to the door, her boots heavy against the department's old floorboards. 'I hope you can write your Romance and make some big bucks,' she adds, but without much interest. She wiggles her painted nails at me and leaves. I put the paper back into the typewriter.

My story begins to take form. Percy, my male protagonist (I dare not call him a hero, which is not to say he isn't heroic), will be a civilian helper in a military hospital at Bloemfontein where more British soldiers are dying of diarrhoea than are being killed by the Boers. But I won't go into crapulous details that will nauseate the reader. I might draw a Daumieresque picture of grey skeletal bodies with sombre young faces in overcrowded wards. Percy is a short shy pink-faced fellow with endearing flat feet and a deep desire to be a farmer. He has never known a woman (in the Biblical sense) until he meets Petronella Gous, a farm girl who has had to take on many of the heavy chores at Bloustroom because the men are away fighting in the Transvaal. Times being hard, she has to wear army boots and she hitches up her skirts for ease of movement by means of an old cartridge belt. She ties her hair up in ponytails with string, which causes her cotton sunbonnet to sit oddly on her head. The neighbours think she is eccentric, if not mad (The Mad Woman of Africa — cliché alert!), and no young man comes riding up to Bloustroom to court her when the farmer-fighters are on leave. She is lonely until the day she meets Percy. They happen to stand next to each other at a fence in Bloemfontein, watching some British officers try to play polo on the wrong sort of turf on tired bony horses. Percy is so delighted when she speaks to him that he doesn't notice anything out of the ordinary with Petronella. He too is lonely. His widowed mother, who wielded inflexible control over his life (but what can a forceful woman do when her only son is shy and indecisive?), has herself passed on to the Fathers as a result of a stray shell crashing through Percy's bedroom just as she was about to rifle through the secret things her son stored in a shoebox on top of the wardrobe. Am I killing mothers off too now?

Petronella has great trouble with stomach wind, mostly because of the high-fibre diet forced on all the population, but Percy is unaware of her sneaky farts — because of his job, his hair and clothes are infused with excremental and medicinal smells. One afternoon in her barn she shows him how to make love (this will be my main sexual scene, putting male readers straight about female arousal once and for all), whereafter he becomes insatiably attracted to her. He nearly gets shot by the British at one point because they suspect he is consorting with the enemy, but Petronella can't be the enemy because, as I said, none of the Boers ever come near her. But Percy goes to jail (*sad* scene), and the British decide to burn down Petronella's farm (*tragic* scene: Petronella's unusual silhouette seen against the brilliant oranges and blues of the fire). After the war Percy marries her and takes up farming with her — her father and brothers having died in prison camps set up by the Brits in

the West Indies for Boer prisoners. Yes, kill off all secondary characters, it makes completing the novel that much
easier!

My telephone rings. 'Sheila, honey . . .' (it's David my
lawyer friend), 'I've just been reading in the *Detroit Free
Press* about a housewife in Troy, Michigan, I mean *Troy*,
Michigan! And she's making plenty of money writing these
novels to a formula. Apparently her publisher provides her
with an outline which she merely fleshes out. Now you
could do that. All you'd have to do is some research into the
history and the look of places like say, Belize or San Luis
Potos or Ancient Aleppo and . . .'

The strong picture I have of Petronella and Percy clearing
away the debris of the ransacked farmhouse begins to
dissipate, and I have to fight not to let travel-brochure
pictures hypnotize me. I shake my mind clear and then
behind my two protagonists I see a third figure. It's
beautiful Carlotta, her blonde hair wisping the sides of her
lovely vinyl skin, her lacy petticoats caught up against the
breeze in one small hand, her lips pursed redly in anticipation. She waves. At a handsome horseman on a white
horse? No, at me! I am surprised. Suddenly I see what she
wants. She wants me to bring her to life; rescue her from
that vinyl skin; allow her to experience hot tearful afternoons of toothache, days when she can't get a comb
through her sweating hair, the bloated feeling of bad food
moving through her intestines, messy periods at the wrong
time, just when she wanted to wear a white gown to the
officers' dinner; and she wants me to give her the good
sense to guide her lover's hand and penis so that they move
in ways she wants, instead of having to submit to one of
those writhing grunting quick harsh sex acts always inflicted
on Romantic heroines. I hesitate. I do want to bring her
alive even if she's not a South African. Mmm . . . Carlotta
could be Percy's second cousin from overseas. He intro-
duces her to Captain Coninghame, the Chief Surgeon and
she, in turn, uses part of her fortune to rebuild Petronella's
farm.

'Look, David, I don't think I want some publisher's

133

outline. I can think up my own outline,' I say.

'God, don't tell me I've persuaded you to do it?'

'I have been thinking about . . . a project . . .'

'I mean, if someone in Troy, Michigan, can do it, so can you.'

'Ja, ja, I'm giving it serious thought,' I say, beckoning to Carlotta to come closer.

Sappeur Fijn and the Cow

JAMES WHYLE

Lying on army beds in an army tent in the showgrounds in Bloemfontein they hear a cow: Mmmoooooo. And fall from their beds — laughing.

'Nooit, he didn't. He didn't.'

'He did. He did, ek sê. He did it.'

'Fuuuuuuuuck, he must have stood on a bucket.'

They roll on the floor laughing.

Sappeur Fijn is short and stocky with sly slant eyes and a sailor's swagger. Sappeur Fijn likes to leave the big generator loose in the back of the Bedford. When you brake hard at a robot the generator rumbles forwards under the force of its inertia and the inertia of the taxpayers who paid for it, and commits suicide against the cab. When we unpack for the shows, Sappeur Fijn throws things as far and hard as possible off the back of the Bedfords in the hope they'll break and Minori will have to say: 'Ag nee, fokkit man, Fijn. Wattie fok doen jy?'

Sappeur Fijn gets letters which he claims are from a girl and smirks and sniggers over them before fucking the tangled gritty pile of pipes which leans up against the water purification system. In so far as I fear Sappeur Fijn, I believe I should bend over whenever I see him in a baboon's gesture of sexual submission. Sappeur Fijn is of the Engineers, the Genieskool of the Suid-Afrikaanse Weermag. Sappeur Fijn is a soldier who works day and night to protect South Africans from the dark ruthless AK-47 bearing monsters who are fighting heart and soul to become South Africans like Sappeur Fijn. At the Bloemfontein showgrounds Sappeur Fijn greases his hair back and drinks and drinks and offers girls icecream in a shmarmy deviant unsettling manner which makes the girls suspicious and scared so that they giggle and refuse the icecreams. Then Sappeur Fijn disappears.

The lieutenant is tall and ginger and worried with a ginger moustache and gold-rimmed spectacles. It worries the lieutenant deeply when Pike and Donaldson give black power salutes to black people on the streets as they drive past on the Bedford. The lieutenant is tremendously fit and worried and proud of his two pips which are a direct commission from the State President who had to resign because he lied to the taxpayers who had to pay for the lieutenant's training. The lieutenant once smoked a joint at a party at the university where he became an architect and enjoys talking to Pike and Donaldson who are engineers with strange ideas and no rank and worry the lieutenant when they say they would shoot better if they painted the State President's face over the faces of the dark cut-out monsters they use as targets on the shooting range. The lieutenant is worried because the corporal drank a third of a gallon bottle of Tassenberg which Pike and Donaldson say they found in the toilet and took the Section into town in a Bedford and drove the whole merry gathering over a Porsche and damaged the Bedford's bumper. The lieutenant is worried and ginger and scared about what the major will say when he arrives to inspect the uitstalling and finds that the Bedford is damaged and that the lieutenant has lost Sappeur Fijn. The lieutenant wants to phone his mother, but he doesn't. He goes round to the MPs.

'Môre Sersant,' says the lieutenant.

'Het jy iets van Sappeur Fijn gehoor?'

'O,' says the MP Sergeant. 'Daai ou wat die koei genaai het.'

It's already six years ago that these things happened. In those days they weren't sending soldiers into the townships. In those days the border was pretty much on the border of the country. Now the border goes all over the place. Sometimes straight through the middle of families which is, I suppose, what civil war is all about. Sappeur Fijn was charged and found innocent in a civilian court. I don't know what the charge was. I saw him in camp afterwards and he told me that his defence went like this: 'I was too drunk to get it up, so I couldn't have fucked the cow.'

I heard later that he killed himself in a motor accident in Welkom.

I don't know what happened to the lieutenant, but the cow gave birth to a roaring monster, half man, half beast, which shrieks and jabbers over my shoulder when I watch the news on TV.

Cloete's Revenge

DAMON GALGUT

We didn't dislike him. (There is that about men to be admired: we can be vile, mean, unconscionably cruel, but if circumstances demand it we can get on with each other.) He was a spotty, red-headed boy with warts on his shoulders and a skew, discoloured front tooth. His name was Daniels, and he came from Paarl.

There were twelve of us in that tent and we'd been there two months. After basic training, as in armies world-wide, we had been posted out to bases and installations all over the country, becoming the temporary inhabitants of sentry boxes and guard huts, barracks and messes. Two years, we were told, is a short time to serve your country; but it is long enough to be moved to a lot of places while you wait. (It is also long enough to die in, but that is another matter.) I had been moved to three different camps before this one: Phalaborwa in the Eastern Transvaal, Bethlehem in the Free State, Upington in the Cape.

It was at the end of my first year that I was posted once more: northward this time, to the border. *The Border*, of course, was that of South West Africa; famous once as the site of real war, it had been superseded by the myriad other borders drawn now inside the country. (I speak, naturally, of the townships, but that too is another matter.) People still died there, but their deaths were remote.

We lived in a smallish camp, far from the larger bases that dotted the bush. We slept in tents and shat in holes. There was something primitive about our existence here, as though we had moved closer to nature. Even our clothes — the standard browns — were camouflaged. We were temporary beings in an enduring landscape. In a very strange sense, so far from civilized life, our plight was metaphysical: I became aware of distance and of time. I knew the reason for my — and all of us — being here: war, death and pain. We had purpose after all.

Daniels slept two beds down from me. He'd been sent up from a camp near Bloemfontein; his posting, he told me once, was a punishment for some imagined offence. He was a silent presence in the tent: modest, mild. The only activity that set him apart from the others was an obsession with chess, which he seemed to play against himself, pointlessly, on a faded board.

I went over to him. 'Would you like to play me?'

He looked up, startled. 'Do you . . .?'

'Yes,' I said. 'A bit. My brother's quite good.'

He set up the board. I lost.

We played, after that, quite often. He was a better player than I, and mostly he beat me. I'm not a good loser by nature, but I didn't mind this: the game was the point. We were bored there, in our kingdom of veld. There was nothing to relieve the tedium, the implacable ennui of being alive. We stood guard from time to time. We walked patrol. But, for the rest, we were soldiers off duty and we spent our time as soldiers do: getting drunk, telling jokes.

I had other things to occupy me. My aspirations were poetic. I wanted to write verse. Every night, braving the scorn of my illiterate compatriots (some of them well-nigh speechless in their bid to escape language), I hammered out rhymes in a wire-backed notebook that I kept for the purpose in my locker. They were not good poems and I knew this in my heart; I was, in those days, not lonely enough.

Daniels and I were companions. I use the word advisedly: there was no friendship on the border, and we didn't share secrets. (I have even forgotten his first name, if ever I knew it.) But we accompanied each other on the numerous little missions that go into maintaining a life in the bush: washing clothes, standing guard. Once he showed me a photo of his lover, a tall, thin girl with braces. She was at high school still.

We did not dislike him. There were odder people in the tent than he, but even towards them we displayed no animosity. Normal laws did not apply in the bush: we had, all of us, been sent up here for varying periods of penance and we had no choice but to endure each other. There was no love, but there was tolerance.

So it was that all of us were witness to a most unlikely battle. When I first arrived at the camp, our tent was under the control of a fat but gutless man by the name of Retief. Corporal Retief was due to finish his four-year (Permanent Force) contract in a month; he had no interest in discipline, and he viewed the world through tiny eyes dimmed with benevolence. We stood no inspections. At night, gently drunk, Corporal Retief would lurch into the tent. Balancing himself on uneasy legs, he would lower his distended bulk on to a nearby bed and regale us with tales from his past. Most dull they were too; but they reminded us of a world beyond this one, where people wore civilian clothes and did not carry guns. Under his aimless authority our morale rose high. Dust collected in our lockers. We slept in our beds and made them up, in the mornings, as carelessly as we would at home.

We could not imagine that he would leave. But he did: on a certain day, bearing cases of whisky bestowed on him in parting, Corporal Retief departed the camp in a lumbering Dakota as heavy and shapeless as himself. And in his stead, the very next night, Corporal Cloete arrived.

Let me describe this man. He was small of build, thin, with a luminous scar on his cheek. His eyes were too close together, set deep in his skull. Ginger hair receded from his forehead. His teeth were many and large and perfect, showing, when he smiled, as a bright gash in his face. And his hands — for some reason his most memorable feature — were delicate and small, like the hands of a pianist.

But he played no music. He had been on the border for several years past and in that time had collected into his soul a portion of the dark bush that would never entirely leave him. You could see it in his face. Those close, unblinking eyes gazed out with a single stare, like that of a cyclops.

He despised us, I think. Not because we belonged to him,

but because we were alive. From the time that he arrived, our tent was a different place. Every morning, at five a.m., we stood inspection. He would appear, promptly on time, as scrubbed and spruce as a man who'd been awake for hours. With an intense, demonic energy he would pass through our ranks, scrutinizing every surface for the smallest wisp of dust. Our rifles, newly-cleaned, would lie dismantled on our beds. Though our boots were clean, our shirts starched, he would contrive to find, in some cranny beyond the reach of our fingers, a trace of dirt that was our downfall. Then his clear, high voice would sing: 'PT!' — and all of us were fumbling, in the half-dark, to change into shorts and vests. Under the rising sun we would assemble, glowering in anticipation of what was to come. For two uninterrupted hours we were at his command: running round tents, rolling across the earth, doing push-ups. He stood by, devoid of emotion, watching our little strivings like a god. Eventually, bruised and cut, swimming with sweat, we were permitted to return to our tent.

He knew Daniels from before. On that first night — the night he arrived — he came walking down the central aisle of the tent, between the beds where we stood at rigid attention, and came to a stop in front of Daniels. There was a silence before he laughed, very softly, to himself. 'You,' he said. 'You.'

'Yes, Corporal.'

'Wat maak jy hier?'

'I was posted here, Corporal.'

'Ah,' said Cloete. 'Aha.' And he walked towards me, sucking his beautiful teeth.

After he'd left, vanishing into the night like a wraith, we crowded round Daniels. 'Where do you know him from? What's he like?'

But Daniels wouldn't answer. He only said, 'He also lives in Paarl,' and turned away to his chessboard, a solitary player tonight.

Soon after that, as we stood guard together at the gate of the camp, Daniels kicked at a stone in the road and said, 'I want to ask you something.'

'Mm?'

'Do you believe in revenge?'

'What do you mean,' I said, 'by *believe*?'

'Do you think there's something . . . holy about it?'

'No,' I said. 'No.'

I didn't know what he meant. The moon that night (our shift was late) was full; it shone above us, cold and clear and white. All around us was the bush: unsleeping, black, the whispering skin of a continent.

Cloete hated Daniels. The hatred he had for the rest of us was general: the collective animosity he dispensed to the human race as a kind of benediction. But he hated Daniels with a very particular, highly inspired hate. 'Daniels is slacking, boys,' he would shout at PT. 'Another ten push-ups for all of you!'

Or: 'Daniels isn't drilling properly, manne. You can all take a run round the camp!'

He never spoke directly to Daniels. The punishments he inflicted on him were reflected on all of us. When he referred to him, he did so in the third person, as though he wasn't present. Thus: 'Daniels hasn't prepared for inspection!'

Or: 'Daniels hasn't shaved properly! Ten star-jumps for every bristle I can find on his chin!'

And in time we all came to look on Daniels as the cause of our misfortune. In the tent at night, when Cloete had retired to his room, we would remonstrate with him: 'Daniels, come on . . . Pull your weight, man . . . Don't get us in shit, Daniels . . .' Even I, his chess companion, had my say.

'You've got to try harder,' I told him.

He stared bitterly at me. 'I try,' he said.

'I *know*, but you've got to try more. Look,' I said, weakening, 'we all know it's not you. He's got it in for you, we can see that. But you've got to do better than us so he can't catch you out.'

'He's going to get me,' Daniels said. 'He's going to get me good.'

Daniels had harmed him in the past. This was clear to all

of us. Some awful deed had taken place for which Corporal Cloete was exacting revenge. I tried to imagine what this deed might be: Daniels had crippled his brother. Daniels had stolen his car. Whenever these things crossed my mind, however, I would look across the tent at Daniels — sitting on his bed, alone in thought — and know that they couldn't be true.

Imagine, then, my surprise when I discovered that the cause of this relentless retribution was the thin and blood-less girl in the photograph he'd shown me.

'It's Ilana,' he confessed one night as we walked back together from the bar. 'She's the problem.' Three years before Daniels had stolen Ilana from the clutches of Corporal Cloete — who was then not a corporal, but a boy down the street, the same age as Daniels. Stefan — for Cloete had a first name, I learned — had never forgotten.

It was bizarre: twelve of us, stuck out here in the wilderness, suffering endless persecution for the sake of this high school girl we'd never met.

'And I don't even love her,' moaned Daniels.

We walked on together through the dark.

Then came the patrol.

We had walked patrol before then; it was, of course, the reason for our presence in the camp. Laden with rucksack, radio, sleeping-bag and rifle, we would set out in small groups to prowl the veld. Walking silently, in a long sideways file, we tramped for miles through the dry waist-high grass. At night we slept in a circle, the corporal in the centre. These were longish missions — a week, sometimes — and we would always return to camp exhausted, battered, hollow with fear. Even the benign leadership of Corporal Retief could not lighten our load: if we encountered *them* as we walked on patrol, it was kill or be killed. Suddenly the enemy was a presence with a face, with a uniform like ours. Indeed, I had seen the face of this enemy several times: every now and then a group out on patrol would return, shepherding prisoners ahead of them with their rifles. These — the prisoners — were young black men, sweating as we did in the raw glare of sun. Their hands held high, their faces blank, they were taken to the cell at the heart of the camp; there, behind cold iron walls, they were interrogated one by one. Cries could be heard from that cell, echoing dimly through steel. It was not a good place.

Sometimes these men were brought in as corpses. Helicopters, rushing over the trees like birds, flew in and out with their gruesome cargo. I had seen these too: shattered bodies, stiff in death, unloaded like pigs from the side of the chopper. Consigned to black bags, they too were ferried away, but to where I never found out.

I had never had a contact on patrol. I dreaded this: the nameless exchange of shots in the dark. I was a poet, but I wanted nothing to do with death.

Cloete's first patrol. 'Six of you,' he said, grimacing with mirth, 'are coming with me.'

Two days later we climbed aboard a chopper and were flown north-west, across the border into alien land. Daniels, of course, was with us; he sat beside me on the flight, his knee against mine. I believe he was trembling.

'Is jy bang, Daniels?' Cloete called. 'Are you scared?'

'No, Corporal,' Daniels muttered. We flew on.

We were dropped twenty kilometres into Angola, in an area that had been full of sporadic fighting the past week. As the helicopter flew off, trailing its sound behind it, the wide world opened about us, buzzing with insects and heat. I lay where I had hidden after dropping in the grass, one cheek pressed against an ant-hill. *Please*, I thought. *Don't let me die*.

'All right, boytjies,' Cloete said. 'Let's move.'

In a line, on booted feet, we tiptoed like dancers through the veld.

Three days later, a few hours before we were due to return: I raised my eyes to the horizon and saw above it a rising trail of smoke, like the fumes from a witches' coven. Then the radio hissed. An enemy encampment, surprised by our planes; it had happened barely ten minutes before. We were heading south, towards home and safety; this was not supposed to happen now.

It was just after dawn; the air was cool. The moon was up, a thumbprint on the sky. Our rifles held across our chest, we ran from bush to bush, bent double, carrying on our backs the invisible weight of death. Daniels was beside me.

Like our nightly bivouac, theirs was circular: in this formation, as if at the height of some obscure ritual, they'd died. It was not, as I've said, my first sight of corpses. But it was my first encounter with death so recently bestowed; the earth still smoked. They lay between trees, gnarled and seemingly hard, like coal discharged from the ground. One man (over whom I almost tripped) was still in his sleeping-bag, curled up like a foetus in eternal repose. There was a charred stench in the air.

'One alive here, Corporal!' Daniels's voice was trembling on the air.

'Don't let him move!'

As I too, approaching another of these bodies, saw life: a black hand scuttling like a crab across the stones. 'You!' I screamed, swinging my rifle up: we stared at each other down the shaft of steel.

He was blasted, hurt; his lower body red. His round eyes, somehow, were yellow, like yolks in his head. 'Another here,' I called.

'Don't let him move!'

I stood, statuesque, in the hardening light, holding my rifle in my hands. The man below me was as still; lying propped on one arm, as if disturbed in bed, he watched my face with those amazing yellow eyes.

Behind my back, the scuffling ceased. They had scoured the area and found nobody near. Already poems were rising in me, winding what I'd witnessed into a mesh of words. Cloete crossed to me. He knelt beside me, peering into the black man's face. He looked lower, prodding at his leg. The eyes before me closed briefly, like a light snapping off. Cloete rose. He took his pistol from his holster. He flicked the catch. He shot the man in the centre of the forehead.

(Always I will see this: the body falling back, brains bright as coral.)

I stood mesmerized, my useless rifle pointing, keeping watch over something senselessly departed, gone. The noise of the shot could not penetrate my skull.

'He was too badly wounded,' Cloete said.

He crossed to the other prisoner, lying, like mine, at Daniels's feet. Here too he knelt; performed his perfunctory examination. He stood again. The pistol was still in his hand; he pointed it. A pause. He lowered it once more.

'Daniels,' he said. 'Shoot him.'

'No,' Daniels said.

Cloete was turning away already, feigning indifference. He stopped in mid-stride, his back to Daniels.

'Shoot him,' he said.

'Please, Corporal . . .'

'I'm giving you an order.'

They faced each other now. We stood about them in a circle, silently, watching them.

'Shoot him,' said Cloete again steadily.

Daniels pressed his rifle to the forehead of the man. He shot. A bird rose in terror from a tree nearby, whirring into the sky.

We left them there as we had found them and jogged away through the bush. *It doesn't matter*, I told myself; *nothing matters at all*. Our lives are gestures inscribed upon the void. Like flares fired up into the night, our arc burns brightly for a while, fades quickly, and goes out.

Revenge is a transaction: Cloete was finished with Daniels. After the incident on that first patrol (about which we never spoke), the persecution was over. We continued to stand inspection; we continued to suffer the punishment of PT; but these were never again inflicted in the name of Daniels. Corporal Cloete's enmity remained unchanged, but it had become impersonal: a prejudice directed at us all.

We walked patrol often after that, of course. I saw the

action I had dreaded, and even wounded a man. But on these occasions we took our prisoners alive, and bumped them ahead of us into camp on the ends of our rifles.

I never played chess with Daniels again. We barely spoke, in fact, after that; but I woke once in the night and heard him crying. Time, the priest, absolves us all: the year went past like a season and we found ourselves dispersed once more, southward, become civilians overnight. I met Daniels a year or two after, in the bar of a small Transvaal town where he was a shop assistant and I had stopped overnight on my travels. He had been married, he told me, and divorced. 'To Ilana?' I asked.

'Who?' He blinked. 'Oh, her. No. No. To somebody else.'

We had a drink together; talked about our time up north. I had written many poems meanwhile, some of them published in literary magazines in Joburg. One of these — my first 'successful' poem — was about Daniels and that first patrol with Cloete. On impulse, feeling generous with booze, I scribbled it on the back of a serviette and passed it to him. He read it, frowning, then passed it back to me. 'No', he kept saying. 'It wasn't like that.' I was drunk and irritable, and we parted on bad terms. As I recall it, he vanished down the road in the rain, while I lurched behind, telling him that poetry was beyond him. But I suspected, even then, he was right: it hadn't happened the way I'd written it, and there were things in life beyond the reach of words.

The Barracks are Crying

MATTHEW KROUSE

Parade

When you consider the hundreds of boys who sit, ignorantly, in the barracks crying for their girlfriends, then you will realize the great resource of loneliness that reproduces itself and stalks about here, untamed.

Just before lights out I like to look down the rows of eyes, each pair looking back at me crying for a friend. And I go home with them one by one, I go to their mothers and I say:

'Little Peter has a problem, ma'am, he gets so hard there behind the fence and he keeps coming to me kindly begging me to rescue him from all that cock hanging off all that rank. It's not enough that he has to bow before it, ma'am, it's not enough that he has to suck it. It's not even enough that he has to stick it into his pelvis until his intestines devour that power-hungry come.

'It's more than enough that he has to wake up every hopeless morning with an ache in his heart before he goes out killing those kaffirs, ma'am.'

One of the first things we had to do when we got there was have our dicks inspected. You had to lie on that green bed with your legs spread wide open and someone else with some kind of medical qualification bent over you and certified that the flesh was in a proud and healthy order for the fight. We queued for days, five thousand white boys still in civilian clothing. Days of being processed, dressed for battle, hair cut, all those things that happen in those wild war movies you see. But this wasn't a wild war movie, no, this was war, the true story of how the rank took enough care to post a bunch of fairies to some goddamned border town where we could manufacture our dreams without infecting the proud villains of the fighting force.

We (the new conscripts, fresh, our mothers milk still tasting in our mouths) were standing around all innocent-like, just hanging around waiting to sign the next form. It was day five or six of Basic Training, probably mid-morning, after tea served from mammoth silver urns in the mess, when bells started ringing. There were sirens screaming through the air. Corporals were running everywhere and news travelled fast that the Commanding Officer was coming. So they lined us up in rows on a vast parade ground. All five thousand of us. It was like Belsen, or Auschwitz. Every boy in a brown shapeless overall, carrying a tin plate, standing shivering in the grey winter air. Every boy peering inconspicuously from side to side with rolling eyes, trying not to move the head.

People fainted everywhere, and boys were being yelled at while they cowered over each other, patting the dead face of one who had reached his limit. Already there was some kind of identification between certain blokes who liked the look of each other. It could have been one of those shabby bars downtown where men stare endlessly in fascination at other men, only it wasn't. Rather, it was a dusty playground of horror, perhaps half a kilometre square, teeming with white skin that was goosepimpled and afraid. Arms hung at the sides like empty jackets. And in the freezing cold the hairs on one's legs stood on end, chafing against the rough shapeless overalls that were no different in line to Belsen's pyjamas.

The parade had begun. Suddenly a jeep was seen approaching on the horizon of the road that ran past the ground. When it got to the dusty square of earth at the flagpoles it stopped. A pink, tall, bald man dressed in camouflage jumped awkwardly out of the jeep, escorted by a preacher, a Brigadier and various other ranks. He approached a microphone at the sides of which stood about five adoring corporals, quite informally. They were the superstars. We out there knew nothing, we had never heard the words 'Commanding Officer' in our lives before. Anyway, the speech he delivered was like babyshit. Everyone owed their presence on earth to God. God made South Africa, and God made mommy and daddy. God had also made the South African Defence Force that would let the Jews be Jews, would let Christians be Christians. Everyone could go to whichever church they wanted to.

I watched the backs of the boys' heads, lame and disbelieving. In a way I was exhilarated, I suppose. I wasn't ready for the truth. And it was about to bare its ugly teeth.

Whenever I tell this story I get pissed off. Today as I write it, now six years later, I'm still furious. As far as war crimes go, ours was the crime of ignorance. We knew nothing, besides the fact that we were who we were, our elders were neurotic and paranoid, they had the power and the glory, and we had to sniff their ridiculous holes. The thing is, I want you to get the full picture, I want to leave nothing out, but it's really difficult. It's almost impossible to tell you how those barracks really looked because they looked like nothing, just rows and rows of square blocks in the middle of nowhere. Just pieces of earth, shower blocks, messes, sports fields, rifle ranges, garages of khaki vehicles, thousands of lines of males in unison, running, singing, marching, undoing equipment and reassembling it. Being howled at, assaulting each other, pissing on command, shitting on command, being shown an endless array of trashy American war films to encourage aggression. Hell on earth!

The Commanding Officer stood at the helm of his parade ground with stiff shoulders and an arched back. He went on for about an hour of mirthless wank. And then he promptly turned his back and drove off with his entourage. We were still out there, sizing each other up. People confronting people, with nothing to go by except height, stance and the look of the face when it comes under such bitter pressure.

We suddenly found ourselves left at the mercy of the

Corporals and Captains. We stood in the blistering heat, our crotches and armpits sweating. Someone urinated down his leg. The word spread. Nobody knew the boy's name, of course, but a wave of speculation was whispered from person to person that the pisser was young, really young. I imagined a thirteen-year-old, don't know why. Once the word had got out that the thirteen-year-old had pissed down his leg, everyone was doing it. I tried but I couldn't. So I held it in. I think it helped me stand straight. I shook a little.

A white-haired rotund Captain stood before us. 'There's a problem in this camp, and I'm going to sort it out,' he said. 'Every one of you here has a problem, and I'm going to sort it out right here and now!' he said. 'I'm going to sort out every single problem right now, and then there'll be no more problems!' he said. And then he began to walk towards the five thousand men, two corporals hugging his sides.

From a tremendous distance I saw him out of the corner of my eye. He seemed to be spending a lot of time with each boy, hovering on every word the boy said, it was a little interrogation. Speculation between the boys was growing. 'They're sending people to the border!'

'They're sending people to the Parabats!'

'They're sending people home!'

None of this was true. They weren't sending people to the border, or to the Parabats, or home. They were, in all earnestness, sniffing out queers. It was queer-sniffing going on. It was weird. 'Obviously this camp has this particular problem,' I thought to myself.

I waited my turn, feeling fatalistic, thinking that after all this was a spectacle of incredible theatre. And it was just that. Queer boys started to drop like flies. Truths just came out for the Captain. He heard it all. Hundreds of youths seemed to confess to luscious desires. Some wept, some fainted, many were confronted beyond speech.

To some of the more ignorant boys from the country the Captain became part father, executioner and priest.

The queers were being singled out, as I've said. Each queer being escorted by two Corporals to a newly formed squad that was in two long rows at the back of the field. It was then that I began to feel a sense of envy, and through that sense I grew to understand that many of those there must have been feeling the same as I felt. Feeling that one wanted to be with the queers, on the periphery, on the outside of the madness looking at the madness within. Of course, rare people volunteered themselves out of a sense of solidarity, and out of what they already began to perceive as a lack of responsibility. Young men are like that. They will opt out if things get too tough.

The Captain waded down the rows, coming closer and closer to me. I had recognized three boys I knew from television and theatre. Actors. Boys I had seen on stage and in the local magazines. All three of them were breeding the hunky look, pretty-boy hunky-types. I really was curious to see what the Captain would make of these actors. He approached the first, an Afrikaner named Marais. Marais confessed that he was an actor. The Captain asked if he had been on television. He quoted a drama. The Captain hadn't seen it. He asked Marais if he was queer. Heroic Marais! Hail Marais! He told the Captain that it was none of his business!

It was a dire confrontation. Why Marais didn't just say no, I'll never know. He was strong and sturdy. He could have been anyone, but he just wouldn't budge. It was a moment of puerile dogshit. The poor old Captain sucked and sucked. 'You look like a little girl!' he screamed at Marais. 'You call yourself an actor! You stand like a kaffir girl who hasn't had breakfast!'

Marais got sent to join the queers at the back. The other two actors got sent there too. 'Actors are queers!' screamed the Captain.

I thought, 'Ah, from now on one need not say "I'm queer"; one need only say "I'm an actor".' I decoded it quickly, and decided to do exactly that. But then I decided not to. Why? Because as the Captain neared me I heard him say quite softly to one of the Corporals at his side, 'All of the queers are going to be sent to become riflemen. They're going to Potchefstroom.' And I knew that Potchefstroom was a mean, cold place, and it was one hell of a winter.

And now the Captain drew nearer. Next would be my turn.

I told the Captain my name in a deadpan voice that sounded to me like the flat tone of a stroke victim. The Captain asked me where I was from. Ventersdorp. It was a lie. I had moved out of Ventersdorp and had been living with some bloke in Hillbrow for some time. (A year later the army sent me back to Ventersdorp; but that's another story.) Living in Hillbrow, in the middle of the city, was trashy. I had no money and slept on the floor. I was poor, young and bewildered, and most of all, bored. That is why I obeyed the law and went in the first place. I regretted it now.

The Captain didn't believe that I was from Ventersdorp. He didn't believe a word I said. Noticing the fact that I appeared older than average, he asked me my profession. I lied again, telling him I was a teacher. Then he asked me where I taught. I went cold and just couldn't lie a moment longer. I looked into his eyes and thought, 'What kind of a man is this? Is this man a slut? Doesn't he just want to fuck every boy on the field. He's trying to fuck me right now!'

And then I turned around slowly and took a long sober look at the queer platoon. And in so doing I betrayed myself. I told him where my heart was. Not between his legs, no. My heart was standing in rows, singled out and terrified, at the back of the field. I said to the Captain, 'Sir, I'm an actor.' And without waiting for my sentence I began to walk towards the queers.

'*Where do you think you're going?*' he wailed. I stopped and walked back to him. The Corporals hurried over to my sides. The war was on. I was thrown to the ground and made to do the proverbial press-ups, and let me tell you, I didn't get far. But they pushed and poked and I did more and more. Eventually, when I got to the queer platoon I was limp, asthmatic and blue. The other queers looked at me as if I was Nelson Mandela. For those fifty press-ups, I made fifty new friends.

Once all of the soldiers had been sifted and processed in this manner, the people presumed to be heterosexual were dismissed by the Captain. They wiped their sweaty brows, most of them appearing to feel proud that they had passed the first test of manhood, manifested in the Captain's keen sense of who was what. The queer platoon was left behind, and it waited for about an hour while the Captain went with the real soldiers to eat his lunch.

In other words, that day the queers missed lunch. I don't think anyone really cared. But while the others ate their lunch, a loud young Corporal was posted on the queer front to see that nobody spoke. The Corporal spoke. He told us over and over, in a broken farm Afrikaans, that we were going to Potchefstroom, a tough camp, to be broken, to be built. He told us that he had nothing against us, being what we were. But it would be for our own good. The army would do what it had to, and in the end we would be grateful to The Force. In the end, It alone would be responsible for the fact that we would graduate, from this war, with wives and children.

When the Captain returned from lunch he proceeded to march the queers around the parade ground. Up and down we went. We walked ten paces north, then ten paces south. He tried to catch us out by slurring his commands, words we didn't understand. We went hither and thither. All of us ran and fell for our mistakes. Knees were bruised and bleeding. The palms of the hands bled. The Captain fucked us up completely. And then he posted us to some goddamned border town.

Sad was the night as we lay in our dormitory, waiting for the sun to rise when we would fly off to queer hell.

Posted to some goddamned border town. A miserable little crew of veteran homos out to fight their first war. We were taken from our mother city and placed on the edge of a field in ten rows of tents in a fenced enclosure with one filthy toilet block, within sight of Headquarters. In mid-winter. I said *mid*-winter, in ten rows of tents with one toilet block behind a barbed-wire fence in a platoon of rabbits too fluffy to be serious about this thing called Civil War. Oh the mud was thick that lay at our feet in the rain. We were issued with a metal cup and another plate and some socks and an overall, and we were lectured and inspected and made to clean the crapper six times a day.

We were made to pray for our sins of loving and had to say the lines over and over to protect us from the darkness in ourselves. We were paraded as the Captain's little success story, and we just ambled along with his sordid plan based on the lie that improper conduct can be reformed by squeezing it out of its casing using first degree paranoia and force.

On my third week of basic training I was woken at about three in the morning by some Corporal who stole into my tent brandishing a rifle complete with bayonet, and with his face hidden beneath a woollen balaclava. 'Come we go and make a blowjobbie behind the wall,' he whispered. 'Boy, I'm warning you that you'll lose your arse if you don't come to where I'm standing guard.'

He prodded me with his rifle and I jolted up in bed, my shaven scalp freezing and prickly. He prodded me with his bloody bayonet and I obediently went. I went stealthily to the looming wall, sheltering the barbed wire of a barricade. The back entrance to the camp, where the guard changed. He ushered me into the bushes behind the makeshift guardhouse where I waited for the watch to leave. I could've run or even screamed, but I didn't. I presume I was too scared of the Corporal, armed and frustrated, watching me from the corner of his eye.

When the guard had changed, and he was left alone, he took me to the coalshed, stuck out in the far corner of the camp, from which the geysers were heated. And yes, I had to suck him. It was an experience of intense blindness. There was no light. My overall (quickly slipped over my pyjamas) got covered in soot, my face became smeared with black. And there I sucked him for sure. It was a long, deep and painful suck. It was the suck we all know, that is, the particular suck you feel when you're sucking heavily on authority. When you require some kindness in return. No kindness ever came from this experience. No kindness.

I won't dwell on the months that passed. Six months of fever, exercise, bantering and labouring in the queer platoon that wiped everyone's arses, in the barracks where we were manufactured into a force fit for death. But we decorated our freezing tents with winter flowers and we hung little curtains from the gauze windows in gingham of blue and red. And then every night after physical training we would shower in a huddle of soft unwilling flesh, preening ourselves while moaning about social injustice, our right to be equal. Yes, it was our right. But in earnest, nobody in the queer platoon that year wanted equality, not if it meant that you couldn't go straight from the showers to that pretty khaki tent to put on your make-up and your nice pink frock before humming a sad tune to sleep.

And our singing wafted slightly above the dormitories and kitchens and guard houses. We queens sang sad nostalgic tunes while a lad called Jenny played a melancholic guitar. And then the song we sang went high. It went with a message of reassurance to those virile quarters where the real soldiers slept before their real war, where they rose willingly and crept to our tents for strength and stories and song.

The boys used to come to us; in their sleep they used to tap on the tent-flap and they used to beg us for a little comfort and warmth saying that, yes, you girls of the queer platoon sure know how to invent a genius in your song and your dance, you know how to make a guy feel that home is just a walk away. Always a word and some fine good cheer. Always a story, a true and sad story to ease those welted shoulders, to make them shrug and relax. A story to remind those that might have forgotten that we were perpetrating an essentially rotten and misguided, lonely war.

Funeral

We buried Jacob because he was dead. I know because I touched him. I touched him because I washed him. I was the only soldier there, and I saw about a hundred bullet holes, little flaccid red slits in his skin. It was the first time I had been to the cemetery at night and it was so lonely.

After supper Rabbi Mindel fetched me from the mess and we drove to the cemetery in the rain as he moaned about the limpet mine and the AK-47. The small party of men who washed Jacob's corpse was silent and afraid. All of them wore old creased silver suits, skullcaps and glasses; and they were all short, wrinkled, grave-looking men. They were finally seeing the war in earnest. A son had died, a son of the community — and with a short hose they sprayed and wiped at Jacob's bullet holes.

As I said, it was really the first time that I was made to do this sort of thing, you know, like cleaning a corpse. I was the only Jewboy in the barracks since poor Jacob had been popped off by the enemy. Poor Jacob who in death was to be washed. I think that I began to look very pale, and so the righteous elders of Ventersdorp let me play a kind of secondary, honorary role in the ritual, for after merely touching the corpse I went and stood in the shadows in the corner of the morgue for about fifteen solemn minutes. Eventually I went outside into the fresh air of the cemetery for an emergency smoke.

When Jacob had been dressed and packed in his coffin I was driven back to the barracks outside town by the Rabbi who moaned again about the Intifada and the African National Congress until, at the Camp's white brick guard house, we came face to face with a blond guard who stamped my pass with a growl.

I tiptoed to my bunk, past the sleeping soldiers. And I think I tried to cry, but I couldn't because I was really too tired and pissed off at the army, and at Jacob, and at the withered community crumbling at its loss.

The next day I had to march in Jacob's burial parade. It was at the local cemetery, a small stone-paved myriad of Hebrew script on black stones. Jacob was, after all, my age

— nineteen. We had grown up together and now it was his military funeral. People crowded the grounds. The collision of worlds was a shock to everyone. Afrikaans women in military uniforms stared blankly at elderly Jewish men. The brown pomp of the soldiers and officers was garish. It looked like someone had shitted on the grey geometry, and on the precious stones beneath which lay the beloved dead, a graveyard of predominantly Eastern European Jews.

I thought, 'How strange, an entire community of Russians and Poles who knew one another intimately, lying side by side, even in death, so far away from Poland, yet still together. A community imported from a place far away.'

The irony overwhelmed me. There, in their rows in the ground, lay the dead. And here on earth stood the military funeral, also in rows. Rows stared at rows.

Oh the revelation, it jolted me! The dead are buried in communities, in a symbolic configuration representative of the roles they played on earth. The rich, influential people get big stones. Righteous elders lie beneath significant pagodas. Poor, forgotten people get numbered inside a rusty star. Children lie between parents. Marriages crumble in the soil. Stones of love stare at one another, and we stare back with love, at them, for centuries.

I realized that in death we like to lie beside the ones we loved, who loved us. So that we may decay together. This is the way we have wanted it. To be together, to reach the other side, and to greet one another. I thought of Jacob arriving in heaven and seeing all of the people that he was buried alongside, greeting him, saying, 'Welcome Jacob, Jacob, our son, whose child are you?'

'I'm the Metzinger boy,' he would reply. 'I'm the hero slain in battle, killed by Cubans beneath a dam wall. My father is Metzinger, Metzinger the builder.'

'Ah you are Jacob the Metzinger boy!'

'Oh how terrible for the Metzinger family!'

'I knew your grandmother!' an ancient Russian fossil would croak.

And then, from the depths of heaven, Jacob's grandparents would hobble forward, and they would go on their knees before Jacob, Jacob their darling. And they would hug him and kiss him, they would love this thing that they had known as a son. Jacob, the new hero, fallen in battle, literally shot to pieces by fuck knows who while guarding the border some weeks before.

Jacob's funeral was a serious, orthodox occasion. We conscripts staged a crummy little parade, slouching and coughing through the whole affair.

I was stationed so close to the Colonel and the Rabbi that I just craned my neck a little bit as they shook hands and I heard Colonel 'Shooter' Malan saying to the Rabbi: 'Give me a ring in the next week and we can finalize the payment for the funeral, Rabbi.' And then when they shook hands, they shook and shook.

Oh, and then it was sad and pathetic seeing the mother and the father, the aunts, Jacob's maid (the elderly woman who had spent nineteen years cooking and cleaning so that Jacob could be strong, keen and fine), Jacob's cousins, his brother, Jacob's girlfriend, his best friend, all sheltering themselves behind total fear as various pallbearers wheeled old Jacob down the cemetery aisle amidst davening and salutes, an Afrikaans rendering of the National Anthem and Kaddish, the mourners' prayer. I spent much of the funeral standing to attention in the blistering heat, staring blankly across the graveside drama at my friend Simon who was in the military band, standing hugging his tuba. (It was awful for the band, for when they arrived at the funeral the Rabbi promptly gave the bandleader the bad news that music was forbidden on the cemetery grounds. The band members nevertheless stood throughout the ordeal at attention, instruments poised, but they never played.)

Standing there, like that, amidst all the components that made up my life, I could think only of Jacob. I saw the dark curly hair and the intense eyes. I couldn't help seeing him naked, in the showers at school, at holiday camps, here in the army. I focused my attention on his genitals. I couldn't help myself. I thought of them in decay. How would they look after five days in the soil, after five weeks, five years? For me, I was getting to the essence of life. It was the purest vision of two round testicles, Jacob's testicles, lying side by side in the abundant earth. Like stones that could be picked up, weapons that could break windows. What I'm really talking about are the dreams, I suppose, the capacity for the genitals to remember, long after the mind has forgotten.

I felt a wild upliftment as the sand fell on to the coffin. Thud! Thud! Thud! Jacob's mother and aunt buckling under the hopelessness of this war. The men, attempting to be strong, their pale lips trembling as they said 'Amen' to every call.

Suddenly, in my mind, I was on a beach. There were people basking in the sun, laughing, playing with bats and balls. Little toddlers were swept over by waves sometimes three times their size. I was there, somewhere, on holiday. The war was just a foggy memory of queer oppression, deprivation, of being someone else's enemy. I was on the beach. I was the baby. The waves were crashing about my head. My bonnet was lying in the sand. My father was photographing me. I was cold. I began to cry. The maid cuddled me, took me to the picnic under the umbrella. I, the child, was no one then. I had no existence apart from the love and desire fed to me.

And what if some stranger had then walked up to my parents and said: 'This little boy of yours will one day grow up to be a shameful sinner, he will be banished in war, banished to a queer platoon.'

And what if I was Jacob, and that same stranger had walked up to my parents and said: 'This little boy will one day grow up to be a soldier, and before the war is over, he will be dead!' What then?

Would it have changed the course of this war?

Ngwana wa Azania

MOTHOBI MUTLOATSE

This film has to be shot on location as much as possible, and the musical score shall be regarded as an integral rather than minor part of this Herculean task portraying the lot, or is it heap, of the Black child Azania on celluloid. It will be neither an intellectual nor a fancy exercise: in fact, some or most of the participants will have to volunteer to go through hell first before agreeing to make their contribution, because basically, making a film documentary even on a small aspect of the black man, is sheer agony. One cannot feign pain, it has to be felt again, to put that stamp of authenticity on any documentary, seeing we have no archive to refer to. Again, much of the documentary's success will depend on the imagination, improvisation and dedicated artistry of all those involved in this project.

The director — at least the bum who decides to take up this seemingly impractical proposition — will have to be a strong, patient, open-minded, non-commercial, un-technical artist. He will be expected to do casting himself, from the cameraman up to the last extra. He will have to read the synopsis, which in many ways is also the shooting script, to everybody at a discussion meeting where naturally he will have to be grilled by everybody. Suggestions, deletions, additions or even alterations to the synopsis will have to be made. Concerning the musical score, all the musicians will be required to give their own interpretations of how they view the project, and thereafter agree on the score.

The future of the black child, the recalcitrant Azanian child in South Africa, is as bright as night and this child, for ever uprooted, shall grow into a big sitting duck for the uniformed gunslinger.

From ages two to four he shall ponder over whiteness and

its intrigue. From ages five to eight he shall prise open his jacket-like ears and eyes to the stark realization of his proud skin of ebony. From ages nine to fifteen he shall harden into an aggressive victim of brainbashing and yet prevail. From ages sixteen to twenty-one he shall eventually graduate from a wavering township candle into a flickering life-prisoner of hate and revenge and hate in endless fury. This motherchild shall be crippled mentally and physically for experimental purposes by concerned quack statesmen parading as philanthropists.

This motherchild shall be protected and educated free of state subsidy in an enterprising private business asylum by Mr Nobody. This motherchild shall mother the fatherless thousands and father boldly the motherless millions of pariahs. This nkgonochild shall recall seasons of greed and injustice to her war-triumphant and liberated Azachild. This mkhuluchild shall pipesmoke in the peace and tranquillity of liberation, and this landschild of the earth shall never be carved up ravenously again and the free and the wild and the proud shall but live together in their original own unrestricted domain without fear of one another, and this waterchild shall gaily bear its load without a fuss like any other happy mother after many suns and moons of fruitlessness in diabolical inhumanity.

This gamble-child of zwêpe shall spin coins with his own delicate life to win the spoils of struggle that is life itself. This child of despair shall shit in the kitchen; shit in the lounge; shit in the bedroom-cum-kitchen; he shall shit himself dead and shall shit everybody as well in solidarity and in his old age shall dump his shit legacy for the benefit of his granny children. This very ngwana of redemptive suffering, this umntwana shall but revel in revealing offbeat, creative, original graffiti sugar-coated with sweet nothings like:

re tlaa ba etsa power / release Mandela / azikhwelwa at all costs / we shall not kneel down to white power / release Sisulu / jo ma se moer / black power will be back tonight / release or charge all detainees / msunuwakho / down with booze / Mashinini is going to be back with a bang / to bloody hell with bantu education / don't shoot — we are not fighting / Azania eyethu / masende akho / majority is coming soon / freedom does not walk it sprints / inkululeko ngoku! / The animals are angry.

This child born in a never-ending war situation shall play marbles seasonally with TNTs and knife nearly everyone in sight in the neighbourhood for touch and feel with reality, this child of an insane and degenerate society shall know love of hatred and the eager teeth of specially trained biting dogs and he will speak animatedly of love and rage under the influence of glue and resistance.

This marathon child shall trudge barefooted, thousands of kilometres through icy and windy and stormy and rainy days and nights to and from rickety churches-cum-stables-cum-classrooms with a bloated tummy to strengthen him for urban work and toil in the gold mines, the diamond mines, the coal mines, the platinum mines, the uranium mines so that he should survive countless weekly rockfalls, pipe bursts and traditional faction fights over a meal of maiza that has been recommended for family planning.

This child of raw indecision and experimentation shall sell newspapers from street corners and between fast moving cars for a dear living breadwinning instead of learning about life in free and compulsory school, and shall provide the capitalistic country with the cheapest form of slavery the labourglobe has ever known and the governor of the reserve bank shall reward him with a thanks-for-nothing-thanks-for-enriching-the-rich kick in the arse for having flattened inflation single-handed hands-down.

This child of the tunnels shall occasionally sleep malunde for an on-the-spot research into the effects of legalized separation of families and he shall find his migrant long-lost father during a knife-duel in a men's hostel and his domestic mother shall he ultimately embrace passionately in a cul de sac dikitshining in a gang-bang.

This child of concrete shall record and computerize how the boss shouts and swears publicly at his heroically shy father-boy and how the madam arrogantly sends his mother-girl from pillar to bust. He shall photograph how the superior doctor addresses his unkempt mother in untailored talk as if mother stupid had conceived a baboon-child.

This observant child shall taste its first balanced meal in an i.c.u., and in the very intensive care unit shall he be revived to further life and misery and malnutrition in this immensely wealthy land to loosen up the bones down to their perforated marrow.

This child of the donga shall watch in jubilation and ecstasy and ire as its godforsaken, god-given home called squatter camp is razed through its permission down to the ground by demolishing bulldozers lately referred to as front-enders.

This child of nowhere shall of his own free will join the bandwagon and ravaza its own Botshabelo to lighten the merciless soil conservationists' burden for a place in the sun of uncertainty, he shall show absolute respect for his elders with a hard kierie blow across the grey head and shall be unanimously nominated for the Nobel Peace Prize for his untold, numerous contributions to the human sciences at a local mortuary.

This child born into a callous and individualistically selfish society shall be considered sane until further notice by psychopaths masquerading as men of law. He shall be an unmatched hero with an undecided following, having paralysed parents and preachers alike with his frankness and willingness not only to whisper or speak about wanting to be free but to bloody well move mountains to be free!

This child of evictions shall sleep in the toilets while his offsprings cross the borders for possible m.t.

This child of rags to rags and more rags to riches school uniform tatters shall quench his thirst with dishwater in the suburbs and with methylated spirits in the dead-end street camps to communicate with the gods.

This child shall breastfeed her first baby before her seventeenth birthday and be highly pleased with motherhood lacking essential fatherhood. This child of uneasiness shall trust nobody, believe in no one, not even himself, except perhaps when he's sober. This ghettochild shall excel in the pipi-olympics with gold and bronze medals in raping grannies with every wayward erection and eviction from home resulting from ntate's chronic unemployment and inability to pay the hovel rent.

This growing child of the kindergarten shall psychologically avoid a school uniform admired telegraphically by uniformed gunfighters of maintenance of chaos and supremacy. He shall smother moderation goodbye and throttle reason in one hell of a fell swoop, and the whole scheming world shall cheer him up to the winning post with its courage in the mud and its heart in pink arse. This child of dissipation shall loiter in the shebeen in earnest search for its parents and shall be battered and abused to hell and gone by its roving parents when reunited in frustration in an alleyway.

This child of bastardized society and bastard people-in-high-office and colour obsession and paranoid of communism and humanism, shall break through and snap the chain of repression with its bare hands, and this child, with its rotten background and slightly bleak future shall however liberate this nuclear crazy world with uMveliqangi's greatest gift to man: ubuntu.

This lambschild shall remind the nation of the oft-remembered but never used isintu:

Mangwana o tshwara thipa ka fa bogaleng.
[Tswana: Mother holds the knife by the blade, is the strong one.]

Labour Pains

NOMAVENDA MATHIANE

I got into the taxi and sat next to a pregnant woman, a picture of health. She sat there demurely displaying her happy and healthy state of well-being. For a moment I envied her contented appearance and wished her well.

The taxi went on collecting people. Soon it was full and on its way to town. I had forgotten about my neighbour when she nudged me and whispered, 'I am not feeling too well.' She moved slightly forward and balanced her hand on her hip. I closed the magazine I had been reading and looked into her face. I don't know what I was looking for, but I didn't find it. I looked at my watch, the way midwives do. It was just after 7.30 a.m. I leaned towards her and asked her when she was due. She mumbled, 'Next month.' I asked her if it was her first baby she was carrying. She told me it was the second. We went on chatting about pregnancies and children and related matters.

Ten minutes later she grimaced and held on to her knee. I feared the worst was about to happen. I held her hand and told her not to worry, we would soon be in town and I would ask the driver to take her to the hospital. I also said she need not worry much, as it might be a false alarm. I felt good. I had used midwives' jargon. Clever.

Another pain struck. She held tightly on to my hand. I looked around and counted the women in the taxi — three. The rest were men, eight including the driver. She put her handbag on the floor and moved forward as if to give herself more room to breathe. Fanning herself with one hand and holding on to her knee with the other, she seemed to be in immense pain. I beckoned to one of the women and told her the problem. The man seated in front of me understood what was going on from our looks and exchanged seats with the woman whose help I was enlisting.

No questions were asked as we sat watching the woman writhe in pain. Beads of sweat were running down her face. She no longer seemed to be conscious of her surroundings. The man next to us moved to give his seat to the other woman. The four of us sat there agonizing. Someone told the driver what was happening and he reduced speed. All was quiet in the minibus. We were in the middle of nowhere.

Helplessly we watched cars drive past and wondered what we were going to do about the woman giving birth. We were now on the highway to town when the driver suddenly moved to the extreme left lane, crossed the yellow line and parked his vehicle. We transferred the woman to the back seat. One of the women started stroking the woman's belly while someone suggested we stop one of the passing cars and ask them to call for an ambulance. The driver got out to seek help.

Although the men would not look at what was going on in the back seat, anguish was written all over their faces. 'How far is she?' their faces seemed to ask, or 'Can't you make it easy for her?' We stood there knowing the effort was between her and the baby, and yet we were part of it. One of the women peeked between the woman's legs and said, 'She will be getting the baby in seconds now.' The woman was wailing silently and praying loud. Our nerves were about to snap. The woman kept rubbing her belly while some of us prayed.

Then she screamed. One of the older women took a peek and said, 'Come on now, my child, this is it — push.' The woman held on to our arms and started pushing. We were oblivious to the heavy traffic outside as we joined hands, minds and souls. I felt sweat come down my forehead and spine. I held tight to her hand as she clung to mine. She was sweating, grimacing and pushing with all her might when slowly the baby started appearing. It was like watching a movie, while at the same time being part of it, as the head gently broke out, made a turn and one by one the shoulders and wham! the legs were out. One of the women caught it, turned it upside down and gave it a slap. The little thing released such a scream. We all started. And it was over.

I've thought of that morning, those many years ago, when the lives of so many strangers came to a standstill. I have thought of how the pain of birth, initially confined to the woman, had gradually engulfed the rest of us. I still carry the mental pictures of how we wrung our hands in desperate helplessness as she writhed in agony. We prayed with her and we suffered the pain with her.

Isn't it strange that none of us, as we got into the taxi preoccupied with the thought of our various destinations, had an inkling of what would befall us? How were we to know we would be part of a happening of such importance? Isn't it true that if we had been asked as we boarded the taxi if we wanted to share in such an experience we would have refused? But we did share in it. We were destined to experience the birth in that fashion and at that particular time.

Childbirth is unique with every woman. And every child has a route and manner different from other children. They may be born of the same woman but their circumstances are not the same. Some take days while others take minutes. Who dictates? It is a struggle and nobody can decide or dictate the form, shape or duration.

I have lived with the 'struggle' all my life — long before I could understand its meaning. I heard the struggle being pronounced by men at work. I have heard women mention the struggle as they carried on with their chores at home. To me, the struggle became synonymous with liberation. 'When the struggle is over . . .' I heard as a young girl when Jomo Kenyatta was fighting the British in Kenya. I heard it when Kwame Nkrumah led his people to independence in Ghana and I also heard it when he went into exile and there was talk of the country 'going to the dogs'. I was to hear it again at the Rivonia trial followed by the exodus of people leaving the country.

I have heard it many more times as I have grown older. At first it was not any of my business as one by one people in the struggle were detained or died. One mourned those one knew and hoped the whole nasty business could be sorted out. Gradually, like a net, people got dragged in. It was no longer Mandela or Sobukwe on Robben Island. 1976 came and went. Maybe it was the first pains. Perhaps the false alarm. The midwives looked at their watches, peeped and went back to the waiting rooms, continued knitting and reported the patient's progress simply as 'one finger dilated'.

They went on with their business: crocheting and knitting and talking about their families or discussing patients. Who cares? 'That woman in bed 5 is going to be here for days,' they said. But the woman in bed 5 was not just lying there and enjoying the comfort of the hospital bed. The moment for her to stop everything and begin the long process of delivery had come. It was just a matter of minutes before the nurses, the doctors, as well as people at home would join her in the marvellous and painful task of bringing a life into the world. A matter of time.

During the Carter administration a number of black congressmen visited South Africa. At an informal dinner held in their honour by one of the activists here talk veered, of course, to South Africa's independence. Questions were thrown about and answered. Then one of the Americans, Congressman William Gray asked, 'But are you blacks ready for it?' The question bordered on arrogance. Typical of all self-styled facilitators, he had given the situation a cursory peep and concluded the patient was far from delivery. But a Soweto leader, Mr Mosala, in his gentle and wise manner of talking, saved the night. 'Does an expectant woman make an appointment with the baby to be born?' asked the man. While the woman may have a say in so far as conceiving, she has absolutely no say on how and when the child is to be born. How does one, therefore, say to people, 'Now get ready, a new society is about to be born?'

A new society is not born by magic. It moves at its own pace. It determines the pace. It takes shape according to the specifics of its needs. For some countries the period was much shorter. Ours seems to take an eternity. Could it be the real pains or just a false alarm that we see the South African society disintegrate, and we watch our children become aliens to us, our culture and tradition? Whether it be false or real, the fact is that something to do with the new order is happening. A new society is being born and we are all sweating, writhing and pushing.

It begins humbly with individuals. Those who conceive of the idea, develop it. They get detained, skip the country, while the rest of mankind refuses even to talk about it. The architects continue while some fall by the wayside. And yet the seed already in the womb continues to grow. The individual tosses with the uncomfortable feeling of carrying. The rest of the people watch with apparent disinterest as the society changes. And soon, one by one, they begin to hold hands.

Metamorphosis

MIRIAM TLALI

The narrow streets tapered even more towards the west where the sunken sun had left a beautiful golden glow barely visible in the grey smog. Velani noticed the crimson ardour only because he — out of impulse — had decided to remain seated in his Volkswagen Golf. One never really noticed the setting sun's beauty in Soweto. He shut his eyes and tried to listen to the music from the car radio.

He was waiting. He looked around. His car was parked near the gate of house No. 2249. In this township of Mapetla there were no numbers on the doors. They had been erased with white paint. The houses were faceless, mute matchboxes, Velani thought, smiling. The comrades had done a perfect job of it. It was amazing how these youths thought of everything to befuddle the system. If he had been a stranger and did not know his uncle's house, he would have been completely at a loss as to which one of the rows of similar matchboxes on either side of the dusty road it was. His wife, Mavis, a district nurse, had often spoken of developments in and around the townships but he had never really taken everything seriously. All she said had been just a lot of woman-talk. Even at the spot which he frequented, the Suzzie's Haunt, people had alluded casually to 'incidents' but he always thought there were more serious matters a man could think of. He recalled that Mavis had once said that it was important for the struggle that we be one thing, no one should be labelled 'good' or 'bad' by the authorities, that injury to the one must be injury to the next. 'After all,' they say, 'we are all black; we all belong to the soil. Besides, we are all oppressed. An attack on the one must be an attack on all.'

Velani tried to listen to the music but the kids in the street were excited. They were frolicking around, jumping and chasing one another. He looked through the window and clicked his tongue loudly. He shut the window and closed his eyes. It was becoming dark and he was sitting there waiting for his mother — affectionately known as Aunt Tillie (for Matilda) — and his sister Tembi. He spoke to himself: 'Waiting . . . Ngisalindile namanje, I'm still waiting even now. You always have to wait for abantu bes'fazane, womenfolk. They never seem to get over what they are doing. It doesn't matter whether it's talking, washing their faces, exchanging greetings, even praying . . . I bet they're on their knees right now, praying "Nkulunkul' olungile-e-e-eyo . . . Nkulunkul' olungile-e-eyo!" (merciful God . . . merciful God!).' He shook his head vigorously. And this was Friday mind you, he thought regretfully; Friday, the day on which he and the 'MaGents' would normally be 'in conference', enjoying good music, chatting the night away over a c-o-o-l beer.

It was his own fault, Velani thought regretfully. What on earth had made him go via his mother's house anyway? Somehow his dear mother never seemed to hesitate to send him off on one errand or another. On this day, he had tried to dissuade her. He had emphasized, 'You know, Ma, that I never refuse to drive you to U-Malume (Uncle's place). But *today* . . . it's not safe to drive to Deep Soweto, surely you *know* that Ma. Moreover, travelling there with two abantu bes'fazane . . . If you were *men*, yes: but abantu bes'fazane . . .' He shook his head . . . 'Hayi, hayi, hayi.'

To which his mother replied, 'But Velie, you rarely ever come except in the late hours. In fact, this time you're early. And you *know* that unless you drive me to U-Malume's place I can never hope to see him. Besides, I don't think I can have a good night's sleep when a message came this morning that your Uncle Bafana is very ill indeed. Who knows what can happen? Even *he* would rush here if he received news that I was on the brink of . . .' She dared not mention 'Death', no: not her beloved brother Bafana. She had pleaded, 'Please my son, drive me there. Your sister Tembi can help me walk.'

Velani tried to drive his point home. He added, smiling, 'But you three are the ones . . . Your daughter-in-law Mavis, your daughter Tembi and *you*, Ma . . . You three are the ones always speaking about ama-necklace, a-Makabasa, ama-Comrades yonke lento and now . . .'

His mother interjected, waving apologetically, 'Velie, Bafana is my own brother, my mother's and my father's only other living child. His end is near; I can feel it. You don't seem to realize that it's only the two of us left now. When he goes, I'll be left alone.'

Tembi, who had been busy in the bedroom, was now standing at the entrance to the dining room, listening and smiling. She anticipated what Velani was going to say and the two were amused. He said, 'Why Ma always says "only the two of us are left" I don't know. Doesn't Ma also have another brother in Eldorado Park? What about *him*? Just the other day I passed at the coloured township with a friend of mine who wanted to have his car panelbeaten by Uncle Boetie — Uncle Mbuti to be correct. Isn't he also your very own mother's and father's son? Why do you always exclude him as if he doesn't exist?'

Aunt Tillie's two children were relieved that in spite of their mother's sadness, there was a smile on her face as she replied, 'You two know the answer to that one. I have told you on many occasions that it is because we all have to remember always to refer to him as Uncle Boetie McCabel and not Mbuti Mkhabela. He does not want to be exposed and known as unyana ka Mkhabela (son of Mkhabela). That, as you very well know, would take the bread out of his mouth. In this country, it is only the fairer ones who eat, don't you know?'

The three were now ready to go, Tembi following her brother on whose arm their mother was leaning. As she clung to the strong biceps of her son, Aunt Tillie felt safe and she moved slowly and confidently over the uneven bricks of the pathway leading to the Volksie. When she was seated comfortably on the back seat, Velani took the travelling rug Tembi was holding and tucked it gently around his mother's knees. He smiled into his mother's face. It was a strong, stoic and steadfast face which, to both her children, never seemed to yield to the vicissitudes of life and the inevitable hazards of ageing.

The radio blared away and Velani listened and watched as the red arm on the car-watch ticked the seconds on and on. His boot tapped almost unconsciously to the rhythm of the song and he kept his eyes closed. When the music stopped, he opened his eyes and looked through the windscreen into the thick grey smog which competed with the dotted heaps of garbage, ash and rubbish of every description. The unsightly mounds formed a screen on the narrow end of the road where a short while ago he had watched the rosy hue of the setting sun. Velani clicked his tongue again and kept his eyes focused on the faintly illuminated dashboard. The record had stopped. Velani wished that the rather too enthusiastic announcer would stop his remarks and let the bands play on without stopping. He stretched his arm, clicking his tongue once more. He reached for the dial-knob and moved the needle from so-called Radio Zulu to so-called Radio Bophuthatswana. He scoffed loudly, 'These howlers should be fired!'

On Radio Bop a drumming thumping hit was playing and Velani smiled as he twisted his torso, rolling his eyes dreamily in sheer ecstasy. The boredom he had experienced a while ago seemed to wear away.

When Velani opened his eyes again, the sun had gone completely, leaving the sky dull and murky, with the thick smog hanging as if suspended in mid-air from some invisible frame. He knew that no breeze would clear the dense menace.

It was quite dark outside in the street now, and the people kept passing. Their footsteps were more brisk. Velani could only just make out from their obscure silhouettes that they were men, women and children. He remembered that it was Friday, and on Friday night people hurry home to the safety of their matchboxes. Only the brave and daring ones remain. The footsteps were awkward and now and again Velani could hear a woman's voice groan, 'Ichuu-u!' as she stumbled, apparently knocking her toes against a stone. The rocky roads had been eroded by the rains into uneven footpaths and the jutting rocks were everywhere, merging with the wire fences on what should have been pavements but were now sloping irregular banks.

There was a loud thud on the window and Velani started. The knock was so close that it felt like it was from inside his own head. The dark figures on both sides of the car were peering eagerly. A quick glance around made Velani realize at once that the car was in fact completely surrounded by a number of youths. Most of them were wearing balaclavas with brims lowered over their eyebrows. Velani was shaken, but something within him told him that there was no need to fear, that he was not going to be intimidated because he was not born yesterday. He switched off the radio and asked furiously, 'What's the matter?'

There were several hard taps on all four side windows, and impatient shouts of, 'Vula, bula, bula!'

'What is it?' Velani asked.

'Vula, vula! Open the window or we break all of them!'

The youths meant business but Velani was no Mafikizolo. He would not give in to their demands. He looked around and asked, 'Why?'

Some of them replied, 'We would like to borrow your car. We have to attend a vigil of one of our boys who was shot dead by the police in Emdeni. Are you going to give us the car or not? Just open and let us in. You can drive us there if you want. Open!'

'No; I won't!' Velani shouted back, determined to hold his ground.

The car rocked uncomfortably on to one side and he felt his stomach fold into a knot. His heart beat faster and the sweat ran down his temples and forehead. There was an even louder chorus from outside: 'Open!'

This was real trouble. Had his ancestors turned their backs on *him*, Velani, who was never a coward? But even if he tried to fight the mob he would never overpower them. They were too many. They were wielding knives, sharp instruments and iron bars. He just could not understand it. The stark shocking reality of what he had up to then only imagined was happening to *him*; he, Velani, a 'clever' of Soweto . . . No, it can't. Not to *him*. He shouted stubbornly, 'I won't open!'

Again the car rocked uneasily as if it were resting on foam; and his entrails felt like they were suspended in a jelly-like fluid. He felt sick. What was he to do? According to what he knew, from what he heard from his wife, his mother and his sister, in fact all those who made it their business to attend the people's meetings, no right-thinking comrades would do that, not to *him*. Wasn't he a well-known clever with all the power of a real man? He *had* to be a man. He challenged them, 'Do what you like; I won't open!'

Crash! came the violent sound. Velani looked back and saw that the rear window was now a mosaic of broken glass. In the centre was a gaping hole as big as the fist of a full-grown man where a heavy steel bar had landed. The bloodshot vicious eyeballs of one of the assailants peered at him through the window next to him. He pointed a clenched menacing fist at Velani, threatening, 'Sizak'nyova thi-ina, grootman uyezwa? Uyacu-u-uga ne?'

A whistle . . . a whistle . . . If only he could sound a loud SOS. Call someone, everybody, anybody to come to his assistance. Had his mother, his sister, his wife, all those who attended the people's meetings not warned him to carry a whistle wherever he went? And *that* he thought was only woman-talk . . . sheer cowardice. But now he had to act. His life, his beloved Volksie . . . All these thoughts raced through his mind in a flash. He *had* to do something. In that state of uncertainty and fear, his manly thumb groped for the hooter and pressed it down . . . hard. The car came down with a clamorous bang, and only then did he realize that the youths were going to turn it over.

His call had aroused people inside nearby houses. Doors and windows were flung open. Tembi was the first one to emerge, from his uncle's home nearby. Her shrill voice pierced through the dark night, making an urgent appeal

for help. Whistle sounds from windows all around perme-
ated through the thick smog, sending alarm signals in all
directions.

Velani knew that it was the women — mothers, sisters,
wives — who were blowing the whistles. At that moment he
seemed to hear the voice of his wife sound the resolve of the
people in distress: 'The system does not care. All they want
is to exploit us. They will never go out of their way to
protect us. Stand together and fight as one. They are
guarding the borders and hunting for so-called terrorists
like you look for a needle in a haystack. Blackman, you're
on your own. Only *you* can root out the evil in your midst
and its hired lackeys who are only there to confuse the
people; to distract them from the real enemy . . .'

It was bad for the marauding youths. Velani watched
them still in a state of complete paralysis and shock. They
sauntered away in all directions, some dropping their
weapons as they scaled over the dilapidated fences into the
adjoining streets and vanished.

'Cowards!' Velani cursed, spitting through the window
which he had now opened to assure the converging people
that *he*, Velani, was safe and sound.

'Soweto is a jungle. I don't know what you want there. You
should come to Eldorado Park. We coloureds here are
safe!'

Velani remembered the words of hope his uncle had
often whispered to him when he paid him a business call.
None of Boetie McCabel's neighbours and friends had ever
suspected that he was in fact an African who, according to
the South African divide-and-rule laws, should have been in
Soweto. Who could have known that he was Mbuti Mkhabela? On his not-so-frequent visits to his uncle in Eldorado
Park, Velani had been like all McCabel's African customers
from Soweto. From a struggling start, Uncle Boetie's
panelbeaters had flourished over the twenty-five years in
that township. Only his fair-skinned wife had known the
secret and she had vowed to keep it from anyone's 'prying'
ears.

Very often now, while he lay in bed thinking, Velani became increasingly uneasy. All right, he had fitted on a new rear window to his Volksie . . . But what of the future? He was a traveller and often he did not sleep at home. The fences surrounding his house were not so good either. It would cost a fortune to erect good ones. The people were not paying rent. To do that would be to risk getting a necklace. The signs were all over . . . 'YOU PAY, WE BURN'. Who would risk that? Perhaps it was a good thing to leave Soweto and go to Eldorado Park after all.

Once while he lay awake in bed with his mind besieged by these thoughts, he patted his wife Mavis's shoulder gently to make a suggestion to her. She had just fallen asleep lightly. She grunted, 'Hm?' Her eyelids already heavy, she asked, 'What's the matter?'

At least Mavis was willing to listen, Velani thought, his mind already excited by what he had to tell her. He asked, 'What if we pack up everything and go to Eldorado, May?'

Mavis was now fully awake. She replied, 'Velie, are you dreaming? Eldorado is somewhere in North America. Where have you ever heard of someone leaving Soweto to go and live so far away . . . even if one were crazy enough to think he or she could afford the plane ticket, let alone get a passport from the Boers?'

Velani answered anxiously, 'No. I mean the Eldorado next to us; next to Soweto, on the other side of Kliptown, May, please. Things are so difficult for us here now. Look, the car, the house, everything.'

'Heyi wena, are you crazy, what's wrong with you anyway? Why do you think you can run away from the struggle?'

Mavis shook her head in disbelief. Somehow she felt grateful. 'At least he is worried,' she said to herself. That silly suggestion he had made meant that he was restless. How long had she wished that Velani would stop floating around in a cloud of self-deception and concern himself with what was happening? He would never even listen to what she had to say whenever she came from the people's meetings. She sighed, 'The struggle is everywhere, Velie.'

'But the people in Eldorado lead normal lives. They pay rent, electricity bills and water. Their houses still have the numbers. Everything is going on smoothly.'

'So you think if you do that — run away to Eldorado — you'll be safe? Okay, you want a house with a number so that the police, the army, the council messengers can spot you easily. You want to eat, sleep and drink in their safe hands . . . What about those who cannot run away? Do you think you can build an island of comfort and safety around you when everyone else is oppressed? Not even the Boers still think they can.'

But Velani's coloured uncle's voice haunted him, and the harder he tried to forget it now of late, the more it goaded him: 'Leave that Soweto and come to Eldorado. The Immigration Control Laws, the 101 (a)s, (b)s, (c)s are all suspended.[1] They are scrapped for good. You can live anywhere you like now. Save your neck and your property. Come to our coloured township. Come to Eldorado.'

Velani could not remember when he finally fell asleep.

Whether Velani's ancestors had turned their backs towards him, he did not know. It had happened again. His beloved Volksie had gone — grabbed from him at gunpoint. This time he decided that he would take his uncle's advice.

It had been seven months since he had last spoken to his Eldorado uncle. The fact that Uncle Boetie had not even bothered to attend the funeral of his own brother Bafana in Mapetla, Soweto, had made him bitter towards him. If Eldorado made him insensitive towards his own people then it was not worth living there. Perhaps Mavis was right after all. That was before the whole 'ibadi' (bad luck) happened again.

But now it had happened. His nice little Volksie had gone, taken from him by an unscrupulous mob of youngsters in broad daylight. Where did they get the guns from

1 These are the different clauses which stipulate the legal required conditions under which a black person (African) may or may not qualify to stay or remain or work in the urban or so-called 'white' areas.

anyway? He had been chatting away at Suzzie's Haunt and some time late in the afternoon, he decided to go to S'godiphola. In the bare veld overlooking the township he saw the youths who came into the road blocking him from passing. Something within him told him to run straight into them, but his dazed mind would not think straight. He slowed down when something inside him snapped with anger. He thought that if they attacked him outside, then he had a good chance of confusing them. It was only after he had slowed down that he realized they were armed.

It was the next day. Velani could think clearly. He asked Mavis to go to work and leave him to his thoughts. If he were left alone, he would be able to figure out just how it happened.

He sat alone, his mind putting the pieces together.

After the no-good hoodlums had knocked him unconscious, they sped off in his Volksie leaving him lying there. Some good Samaritan — also a regular customer at Suzzie's Haunt — recognized him and picked him up. With some of their friends, they decided to take Velani first to the police station to report the loss of his car. When he, Velani, had regained consciousness, he pleaded with his friends that he would rather go and report the matter to the police than go home 'on foot' to face his wife Mavis. They immediately rushed him to the nearby Moroka Police Station.

Never in his life had Velani seen so many people lined up in a small room waiting to be served. All of them had lost their cars. They all had sad stories to tell. Even sobbing women were there. Some of them had also been raped. It is only when you have your personal share of pain that you know what it is like to be pierced. Velani listened. His sense of loss had made him sober. He wondered how it was still possible for some of these people to speak about the pain at all, with their hearts still bleeding. He listened, absent-minded. The two men next to him, with homemade bandages tied around injured limbs, one an elbow and another his shin, rattled on in whispers, 'A friend of mine had his car interfered with and pushed away right out of his yard, mind you; and he could do nothing! They were armed, so what could he do?'

The other confirmed, nodding all the time, 'I *know*. Others are hijacked at intersections. And when you come to report here they tell you that there are no policemen to come to your aid, that they are short of them. I'm not surprised. How can they be everywhere? Zambia, Malawi, Zimbabwe, Botswana, the Bantustans, Swaziland, Lesotho, the border — all over . . . What are they — an octopus?'

'It is dangerous these days to stop at a robot. Even when it is red, just dash on!'

Some sat looking hopefully at the official on the other side of the desk. The bespectacled policeman looked up at the rows of anxious, exhausted faces while he kept reaching for dockets. He seemed polite and Velani wondered what had happened . . . He was thinking . . . A so-called 'kaffer-konstabel' polite? Never . . . or was it in keeping with the so-called reform process? . . . So this was what they meant by 'reform', eh? It was a rather annoying revelation; especially because he kept on reiterating to one complainant after another, 'We can only try to do our best, but we cannot make promises that you'll get your cars. Soweto is bad. Most of you I know have no insurance cover. Too many cars are stolen. The thieves work fast. They use false number plates and they spray the cars almost immediately. It is difficult to spot any stolen car from the descriptions you give . . . We are your friends. We are here to protect your property and your lives.'

The whole rhetoric sounded meaningless and hollow. The sad people's eyes and ears were open, but they remained stern and unimpressed. Velani knew that he would never see his car again. It was gone for good. He could feel it in his blood.

Velani knew what he would do. He would ring his Eldorado uncle and ask for advice. Perhaps he was right after all. What was the use of staying in Soweto? Who cares what happens to people in Soweto anyway? Certainly not the police or the so-called councillors or the lawmakers in Pretoria.

As he sat alone, thinking, he became more and more certain that Boetie McCabel was in fact his best adviser. He only had had the common sense to look into the problem facing the blacks — especially the Africans — and arriving at the best solution to it. Escape . . . escape from the jungle and draw closer to the well-provided-for world, the privileged one.

He reached for the telephone receiver and dialled the number impatiently, his brow sweating with excitement. It was the voice of a woman — possibly Mrs McCabel — which answered, 'Hello, kan ek u help?'

Velani replied, 'It's Mkhabela here, Ma'am. Can I speak to Mr McCabel please?'

'Just hold on please, I'll call him . . . Boetie!' she yelled, placing the receiver on the table. McCabel rushed from the kitchen into the lounge.

Velie recognized his uncle's voice immediately. He whispered into the receiver, 'Hello, it's Velie, Uncle Boetie. I want to come to Eldorado. I have decided to take your advice.'

'Why now?'

'My Volksie is gone. They took it. Nothing is safe here. I want to come and live in Eldorado if . . .'

Before Velie could continue, McCabel interrupted, 'It's no use, Velie. The disease has spread all over. We also have comrades here. They want solidarity with the people of Soweto. They say they are returning to their roots. They have wiped off the numbers from the houses. They say unless we are one the struggle against the settlers is for ever lost.

'Stay where you are. Injury to one oppressed is injury to all, they say. We all have to change. Just like the police say, they cannot keep up with all the cases. Gangs of hooligans, encouraged and armed by the police themselves, are on the rampage and nobody really cares. All the police and army are really concerned about is tracking down the so-called terrorists. It comes from the police themselves. They say they are tired, overworked. People are no longer joining the police force. The few who are still there also want to go on strike. They want to run away and they don't know how to do it . . . Are you still there Velie?'

Without another word, Velie dropped the receiver and sank on to the sofa next to him. He sighed and whispered to himself, 'It's no use. Real protection will come from the people themselves. From now on, I'm with the people.'

Death of a Son

NJABULO S. NDEBELE

At last we got the body. Wednesday. Just enough time for a Saturday funeral. We were exhausted. Empty. The funeral still ahead of us. We had to find the strength to grieve. There had been no time for grief, really. Only much bewilderment and confusion. Now grief. For isn't grief the awareness of loss?

That is why when we finally got the body, Buntu said: 'Do you realize our son is dead?' I realized. Our awareness of the death of our first and only child had been displaced completely by the effort to get his body. Even the horrible events that caused the death: we did not think of them, as such. Instead, the numbing drift of things took over our minds: the pleas, letters to be written, telephone calls to be made, telegrams to be dispatched, lawyers to consult, 'influential' people to 'get in touch with', undertakers to be contacted, so much walking and driving. That is what suddenly mattered: the irksome details that blur the goal (no matter how terrible it is), each detail becoming a door which, once unlocked, revealed yet another door. Without being aware of it, we were distracted by the smell of the skunk and not by what the skunk had done.

We realized something too, Buntu and I, that during the two-week effort to get our son's body, we had drifted apart. For the first time in our marriage our presence to each other had become a matter of habit. He was there. He'll be there. And I'll be there. But when Buntu said: 'Do you realize our son is dead?' he uttered a thought that suddenly brought us together again. It was as if the return of the body of our son was also our coming together. For it was only at that moment that we really began to grieve; as if our lungs had suddenly begun to take in air when just before, we were beginning to suffocate. Something with meaning began to emerge.

We realized. We realized that something else had been happening to us, adding to the terrible events. Yes, we had drifted apart. Yet our estrangement, just at that moment when we should have been together, seemed disturbingly comforting to me. I was comforted in a manner I did not quite understand.

The problem was that I had known all along that we would have to buy the body anyway. I had known all along. Things would end that way. And when things turned out that way, Buntu could not look me in the eye. For he had said: 'Over my dead body! Over my dead body!' as soon as we knew we would be required to pay the police or the government for the release of the body of our child.

'Over my dead body! Over my dead body!' Buntu kept on saying.

Finally, we bought the body. We have the receipt. The police insisted we take it. That way, they would be 'protected'. It's the law, they said.

I suppose we could have got the body earlier. At first I was confused, for one is supposed to take comfort in the heroism of one's man. Yet, inwardly, I could draw no comfort from his outburst. It seemed hasty. What sense was there to it when all I wanted was the body of my child? What would happen if, as events unfolded, it became clear that Buntu would not give up his life? What would happen? What would happen to him? To me?

For the greater part of two weeks all of Buntu's efforts, together with those of friends, relatives, lawyers and the newspapers, were to secure the release of the child's body without the humiliation of having to pay for it. A 'fundamental principle'.

Why was it difficult for me to see the wisdom of the principle? The worst thing, I suppose, was worrying about what the police may have been doing to the body of my child. How they may have been busy prying it open 'to determine the cause of death'?

Would I want to look at the body when we finally got it?

To see further mutilations in addition to the 'cause of death'? What kind of mother would not want to look at the body of her child? people will ask. Some will say: 'It's grief.' She is too grief-stricken.

'But still . . .' they will say. And the elderly among them may say: 'Young people are strange.'

But how can they know? It was not that I would not want to see the body of my child, but that I was too afraid to confront the horrors of my own imagination. I was haunted by the thought of how useless it had been to have created something. What had been the point of it all? This body filling up with a child. The child steadily growing into something that could be seen and felt. Moving, as it always did, at that time of day when I was all alone at home waiting for it. What had been the point of it all?

How can they know that the mutilation to determine 'the cause of death' ripped my own body? Can they think of a womb feeling hunted? Disgorged?

And the milk that I still carried. What about it? What had been the point of it all?

Even Buntu did not seem to sense that that principle, the 'fundamental principle', was something too intangible for me at that moment, something that I desperately wanted should assume the form of my child's body. He still seemed far from ever knowing.

I remember one Saturday morning early in our courtship, as Buntu and I walked hand-in-hand through town, window-shopping. We cannot even be said to have been window-shopping, for we were aware of very little that was not ourselves. Everything in those windows was merely an excuse for words to pass between us.

We came across three girls sitting on the pavement, sharing a packet of fish and chips after they had just bought it from a nearby Portuguese café. Buntu said: 'I want fish and chips too.' I said: 'So seeing is desire.' I said: 'My man is greedy!' We laughed. I still remember how he tightened his grip on my hand. The strength of it!

Just then, two white boys coming in the opposite direction suddenly rushed at the girls and, without warning, one of them kicked the packet of fish and chips out of the hands of the girl who was holding it. The second boy kicked away the rest of what remained in the packet. The girl stood up, shaking her hand as if to throw off the pain in it. Then she pressed it under her armpit as if to squeeze the pain out of it. Meanwhile the two boys went on their way laughing. The fish and chips lay scattered on the pavement and on the street like stranded boats on a river that had gone dry.

'Just let them do that to you!' said Buntu, tightening once more his grip on my hand as we passed on like sheep that had seen many of their own in the flock picked out for slaughter. We would note the event and wait for our turn. I remember I looked at Buntu, and saw his face was somewhat glum. There seemed no connection between that face and the words of reassurance just uttered. For a while, we went on quietly. It was then that I noticed his grip had grown somewhat limp. Somewhat reluctant. Having lost its self-assurance, it seemed to have been holding on because it had to, not because of a confident sense of possession.

It was not to be long before his words were tested. How could fate work this way, giving to words meanings and intentions they did not carry when they were uttered? I saw that day how the language of love could so easily be trampled underfoot, or scattered like fish and chips on the pavement, and left stranded and abandoned like boats in a river that suddenly went dry. Never again was love to be confirmed with words. The world around us was too hostile for vows of love. At any moment the vows could be subjected to the stress of proof. And love died. For words of love need not be tested.

On that day, Buntu and I began our silence. We talked and laughed, of course, but we stopped short of words that would demand proof of action. Buntu knew. He knew the vulnerability of words. And so he sought to obliterate words with acts that seemed to promise redemption.

On that day, as we continued with our walk in town, that Saturday morning, coming up towards us from the opposite direction was a burly Boer walking with his wife and two children. They approached Buntu and me with an ominously determined advance. Buntu attempted to pull me out of the way, but I never had a chance. The Boer shoved me out of the way, as if clearing a path for his family. I remember, I almost crashed into a nearby fashion display window. I remember, I glanced at the family walking away, the mother and the father each dragging a child. It was for one of those children that I had been cleared away. I remember, also, that as my tears came out, blurring the Boer family and everything else, I saw and felt deeply what was inside of me: a desire to be avenged.

But nothing happened. All I heard was Buntu say: 'The dog!' At that very moment I felt my own hurt vanish like a wisp of smoke. And as my hurt vanished, it was replaced, instead, by a tormenting desire to sacrifice myself for Buntu. Was it something about the powerlessness of the curse and the desperation with which it had been made? The filling of stunned silence with an utterance? Surely it ate into him, revealing how incapable he was of meeting the call of his words.

And so it was that that afternoon, back in the township, left to ourselves at Buntu's home, I gave in to him for the first time. Or should I say I offered myself to him? Perhaps from some vague sense of wanting to heal something in him? Anyway, we were never to talk about that event. Never. We buried it alive deep inside of me that afternoon. Would it ever be exhumed? All I vaguely felt and knew was that I had the keys to the vault. That was three years ago, a year before we married.

The cause of death? One evening I returned home from work, particularly tired after I had been covering more shootings by the police in the East Rand. Then I had hurried back to the office in Johannesburg to piece together on my typewriter the violent scenes of the day, and then to file my report to meet the deadline. It was late when I returned home, and when I got there, I found a crowd of people in the yard. They were those who could not get inside. I panicked. What had happened? I did not ask those who were outside, being desperate to get into the house. They gave way easily when they recognized me.

188

Then I heard my mother's voice. Her cry rose well above the noise. It turned into a scream when she saw me. 'What is it, mother?' I asked, embracing her out of a vaguely despairing sense of terror. But she pushed me away with an hysterical violence that astounded me.

'What misery have I brought you, my child?' she cried. At that point, many women in the room began to cry too. Soon, there was much wailing in the room, and then all over the house. The sound of it! The anguish! Understanding, yet eager for knowledge, I became desperate. I had to hold on to something. The desire to embrace my mother no longer had anything to do with comforting her, for whatever she had done, whatever its magnitude, had become inconsequential. I needed to embrace her for all the anguish that tied everyone in the house into a knot. I wanted to be part of that knot, yet I wanted to know what had brought it about.

Eventually we found each other, my mother and I, and clasped each other tightly. When I finally released her, I looked around at the neighbours and suddenly had a vision of how that anguish had to be turned into a simmering kind of indignation. The kind of indignation that had to be kept at bay only because there was a higher purpose at that moment: the sharing of concern.

Slowly and with a calmness that surprised me, I began to gather the details of what had happened. Instinctively I seemed to have been gathering notes for a news report.

It happened during the day, when the soldiers and the police that had been patrolling the township in their Casspirs began to shoot in the streets at random. Need I describe what I did not see? How did the child come to die just at that moment when the police and the soldiers began to shoot at random, at any house, at any moving thing? That was how one of our windows was shattered by a bullet. And that was when my mother, who looked after her grandchild when we were away at work, panicked. She picked up the child and ran to the neighbours. It was only when she entered the neighbour's house that she noticed the wetness of the blanket that covered the child she held to her chest as she ran for the sanctuary of neighbours. She had looked at her unaccountably bloody hand, then she noted the still bundle in her arms, and began at that moment to blame herself for the death of her grandchild . . .

Later, the police, on yet another round of shooting, found people gathered at our house. They stormed in, saw what had happened. At first they dragged my mother out, threatening to take her away unless she agreed not to say what had happened. But then they returned and, instead, took the body of the child away. By what freak of logic did they hope that by this act their carnage would never be discovered?

That evening, I looked at Buntu closely. He appeared suddenly to have grown older. We stood alone in an embrace in our bedroom. I noticed, when I kissed his face, how his once lean face had grown suddenly puffy.

At that moment I felt the familiar impulse come upon me once more, the impulse I always felt when I sensed that Buntu was in some kind of danger, the impulse to yield something of myself to him. He wore the look of someone struggling to gain control of something. Yet, it was clear he was far from controlling anything. I knew that look. Had seen it many times. It came at those times when I sensed that he faced a wave that was infinitely stronger than he, that it would certainly sweep him away, but that he had to seem to be struggling. I pressed myself tightly to him as if to vanish into him; as if only the two of us could stand up to the wave.

'Don't worry,' he said. 'Don't worry. I'll do everything in my power to right this wrong. Everything. Even if it means suing the police!' We went silent.

I knew that silence. But I knew something else at that moment: that I had to find a way of disengaging myself from the embrace.

Suing the police? I listened to Buntu outlining his plans. 'Legal counsel. That's what we need,' he said. 'I know some people in Pretoria,' he said. As he spoke, I felt the warmth of intimacy between us cooling. When he finished, it was cold. I disengaged from his embrace slowly, yet purpose-fully. Why had Buntu spoken?

Later, he was to speak again, when all his plans had failed to work: 'Over my dead body! Over my dead body!'

He sealed my lips. I would wait for him to feel and yield one day to all the realities of misfortune.

Ours was a home, it could be said. It seemed a perfect life for a young couple: I, a reporter; Buntu, a personnel officer at an American factory manufacturing farming implements. He had travelled to the United States and returned with a mind fired with dreams. We dreamed together. Much time we spent, Buntu and I, trying to make a perfect home. The occasions are numerous on which we paged through *Femina*, *Fair Lady*, *Cosmopolitan*, *Home and Garden*, *Car*, as if somehow we were going to surround our lives with the glossiness in the magazines. Indeed, much of our time was spent window-shopping through the magazines. This time, it was different from the window-shopping we did that Saturday when we courted. This time our minds were consumed by the things we saw and dreamed of owning: the furniture, the fridge, TV, videocassette recorders, washing machines, even a vacuum cleaner and every other imaginable thing that would ensure a comfortable modern life.

Especially when I was pregnant. What is it that Buntu did not buy, then? And when the boy was born, Buntu changed the car. A family, he would say, must travel comfortably.

The boy became the centre of Buntu's life. Even before he was born, Buntu had already started making enquiries at white private schools. That was where he would send his son, the bearer of his name.

Dreams! It is amazing how the horrible findings of my newspaper reports often vanished before the glossy magazines of our dreams, how I easily forgot that the glossy images were concocted out of the keys of typewriters, made by writers whose business was to sell dreams at the very moment that death pervaded the land. So powerful are words and pictures that even their makers often believe in them.

Buntu's ordeal was long. So it seemed. He would get up early every morning to follow up the previous day's leads regarding the body of our son. I wanted to go with him, but each time I prepared to go he would shake his head.

'It's my task,' he would say. But every evening he returned, empty-handed, while with each day that passed and we did not know where the body of my child was, I grew restive and hostile in a manner that gave me much pain. Yet Buntu always felt compelled to give a report on each day's events. I never asked for it. I suppose it was his way of dealing with my silence.

One day he would say: 'The lawyers have issued a court order that the body be produced. The writ of habeas corpus.'

On another day he would say: 'We have petitioned the Minister of Justice.'

On yet another he would say: 'I was supposed to meet the Chief Security Officer. Waited the whole day. At the end of the day they said I would see him tomorrow if he was not going to be too busy. They are stalling.'

Then he would say: 'The newspapers, especially yours, are raising the hue and cry. The government is bound to be embarrassed. It's a matter of time.'

And so it went on. Every morning he got up and left. Sometimes alone, sometimes with friends. He always left to bear the failure alone.

How much did I care about lawyers, petitions and Chief Security Officers? A lot. The problem was that whenever Buntu spoke about his efforts, I heard only his words. I felt in him the disguised hesitancy of someone who wanted reassurance without asking for it. I saw someone who got up every morning and left not to look for results, but to search for something he could only have found with me.

And each time he returned, I gave my speech to my eyes. And he answered without my having parted my lips. As a result I sensed, for the first time in my life, a terrible power in me that could make him do anything. And he would never ever be able to deal with that power as long as he did not silence my eyes and call for my voice.

And so, he had to prove himself. And while he left each morning, I learned to be brutally silent. Could he prove himself without me? Could he? Then I got to know, those days, what I'd always wanted from him. I got to know why I have always drawn him into me whenever I sensed his vulnerability.

I wanted him to be free to fear. Wasn't there greater strength that way? Had he ever lived with his own feelings? And the stress of life in this land: didn't it call out for men to be heroes? And should they live up to it even though the details of the war to be fought may often be blurred? They should.

Yet it is precisely for that reason that I often found Buntu's thoughts lacking in strength. They lacked the experience of strife that could only come from a humbling acceptance of fear and then, only then, the need to fight it.

Me? In a way, I have always been free to fear. The prerogative of being a girl. It was always expected of me to scream when a spider crawled across the ceiling. It was known I would jump on to a chair whenever a mouse blundered into the room.

Then, once more, the Casspirs came. A few days before we got the body back I was at home with my mother when we heard the great roar of truck engines. There was much running and shouting in the streets. I saw them, as I've always seen them on my assignments: the Casspirs. On five occasions they ran down our street at great speed, hurling teargas canisters at random. On the fourth occasion, they got our house. The canister shattered another window and filled the house with the terrible pungent choking smoke that I had got to know so well. We ran out of the house gasping for fresh air.

So, this was how my child was killed? Could they have been the same soldiers? Now hardened to their tasks? Or were they new ones being hardened to their tasks? Did they drive away laughing? Clearing paths for their families? What paths?

And was this our home? It couldn't be. It had to be a little bird's nest waiting to be plundered by a predator bird. There seemed no sense to the wedding pictures on the walls, the graduation pictures, birthday pictures, pictures of relatives and paintings of lush landscapes. There seemed no sense any more to what seemed recognizably human in our house. It took only a random swoop to obliterate personal worth, to blot out any value there may have been to the past. In desperation, we began to live only for the moment. I do feel hunted.

It was on the night of the teargas that Buntu came home, saw what had happened, and broke down in tears. They had long been in the coming . . .

My own tears welled out too. How much did we have to cry to refloat stranded boats? I was sure they would float again.

A few nights later, on the night of the funeral, exhausted, I lay on my bed, listening to the last of the mourners leaving. Slowly, I became conscious of returning to the world. Something came back after it seemed not to have been there for ages. It came as a surprise, as a reminder that we will always live around what will happen. The sun will rise and set, and the ants will do their endless work, until one day the clouds turn grey and rain falls, and even in the township, the ants will fly out into the sky. Come what may.

My moon came, in a heavy surge of blood. And, after such a long time, I remembered the thing Buntu and I had buried in me. I felt it as if it had just entered. I felt it again as it floated away on the surge. I would be ready for another month. Ready as always, each and every month, for new beginnings.

And Buntu? I'll be with him, now. Always. Without our knowing, all the trying events had prepared for us new beginnings. Shall we not prevail?

Ike and Phindi

SIPHO SEPAMLA

When Ike married Phindi Wattville people said it was 'the wedding of the year'. That was ten years ago. People talk of the event now and again. They cannot forget how the bride landed at the Wattville soccer field in a helicopter just for the image of things. They speak as if they hear the drone of the machine, they wave hands to illustrate the dust clouds that swept over the convoy of cars carrying Ike and others waiting on the tarred street a few metres away from the field. 'Mercy! Mercy!' they cry, 'Ike was the bride on that day!' They think of how he took orders from Phindi's family. He married for love; he married Nyawuza's money because Nyawuza is one of those sinfully rich blacks. The most mischievous never stopped to say how Ike was as thin as the 'I' in his name but had hurled himself on a buxom lady ready to overwhelm him with naughtiness. Ah, location gossip!

Phindi stood over the coal stove pondering. It was a Friday evening. Alone in the house at that time she felt lonely, a failure. She retreated on to one of the kitchen chairs and sighed. She had come home from Troy Manufacturers at 4.30 p.m. hoping to kill the hour separating her from Ike's arrival by tidying up and preparing the evening meal. Ike was punctual. If he came late it was for some extraordinary reason. She never liked what he termed 'extraordinary' and if she tried to probe he became belligerent. Or he would clam his mouth tight.

Phindi tossed an eye around the kitchen. Doing so always pained her. The kitchen was small. And that reminded her of what she had first revealed as a secret to her workmates that they were about to build a dream house on a plot near Magalegase School. When she first mentioned this at work the delay was caused by the Administration Board. Then came the excuse of her father's shop in Maseko Street damaged by fire. Finally Mr Lewis was said to be holding back some of Ike's wages. So years rolled on without the house coming up.

Mr Lewis, the one of Madison Avenue Furnishers, with a balding head and a quick step, paid Ike a fair wage by general standards. And Ike tried hard to maintain his wife at a reasonable level. He was able to carry home every Saturday midday a parcel — it could be meat, groceries or brand-new ashtrays, all bought back door. For a while, these acts of a good, caring husband seemed always to please Phindi. Trouble with her was that she wanted everything she had known in a twelve-roomed house to be in a four-room. She complained of slow progress despite the bedroom suite and sewing machine given her by her parents.

Ike never replied to her. At least not in a way that would offend her. He just sneered and went on to count in his heart his bachelorhood acquisitions: the Ellis de Luxe stove in the kitchen (it was smokeless, wasn't it?), the old wardrobe in the spare room, knives, forks and spoons. Ag, women!

There was no mistaking the dark mood of Phindi on such evenings. She would remain sulky till bedtime. Ike tended to be silent for a long while. He had begun drinking 'the waters of immortality'.

On this Friday it was apparent that the gods had deserted Phindi. She remained alone in the house until she became uneasy about the non-appearance of her husband. Her heart gave a thud when she realized it was late and she had not fixed anything for him. It was late even to send for a piece of fish from the shops down the street. 'I am tired,' that's how she saw it all in her mind.

Ike came home humming. It was one of those nonsense tunes which refuse to develop beyond a certain inspired start. Anyway Ike repeated and repeated the tune until energy seemed to desert him.

He sat at the kitchen table and looked up at Phindi. She was staring down at him as if intending to say something. She couldn't place a finger on her fears but certainly there was something strange about Ike. Her first reaction to his humming would have been to scream at him to shut up but she didn't. Then there was the unusual look in his eye.

'I don't know what to give you for food,' she said tentatively. She was standing near the cupboard at this stage.

'Fish!' said Ike with an impatient edge to his voice.

'God knows there's no fish in this house.'

'Meat!'

'Meat? But it is only Friday today. You bring meat on Saturdays.'

Bang went a fist on the table as Ike yelled, 'I am hungry, woman!'

Phindi was shocked and she held one hand firmly on the cupboard. She yelled back, 'I can't turn myself into fish or meat. You should have come early!'

All the same she bent forward and brought out a porcelain plate, put it on the table near Ike. He was all the time looking menacingly at her.

There was one thought which gave Phindi comfort, making her feel fairly safe in the house despite the heavy atmosphere. Ike had never threatened her physically. She brought out a tin of baked beans. She was going back to the cupboard when a sudden loud noise shook her. Ike was on his feet, the porcelain plate crushed on the floor.

'Am I a cock or a hen?' he yelled, advancing on her. 'You are spiteful, woman!' he said, lashing at her with his right fist. The blow grazed Phindi on the side of her head but she screamed as if she had just set eyes on the devil himself. Ike tried to hold her with one hand but she wriggled free of him and stood near the kitchen out-door, arms clasped on her breast. Shock more than pain blunted her mind because she stood there petrified, seemingly unable to think further.

Ike took another step towards her but she was able to dart outside the house.

'Go away, man,' said Ike, 'you think I care!'

She fled to her home.

Nyawuza opened his arms to his daughter. 'That thing is useless,' was his comprehensive comment.

197

Weeks went by without a new development between the young couple. Ike continued to serve Mr Lewis faithfully while Phindi remained punctual at Troy Manufacturers.

One evening Ike found the house too large and empty. He felt his enforced celibacy was just too much. But first he had to find a way to convince Phindi of his turning over a new leaf. He was aware deep down somewhere in her heart she loved him and no one could take his place.

He moved from room to room to find something to put in which would smite her immediately.

'Damn it!' he said aloud, 'a TV set of course.'

In two weeks' time the house had acquired a brand-new TV. And for two weeks thereafter he made sure that the world was aware of his having given up the bottle. Neighbours conveyed the change in him to Phindi.

The stage was now set for Ike to make the next move. On a Saturday afternoon he went straight to Nyawuza's place after work. Every part of his body revealed that here was a changed man. He was solemn. He was humble. Even as Nyawuza gave him a tongue lashing, Ike sat there seemingly very repentant. What he did was to clear his throat now and then like one about to say something. But Ike said not a word. Instead, when his father-in-law had finished speaking, he produced a small parcel which he placed before Nyawuza's eye and waited patiently for it to be torn open. It revealed a brand-new pipe. For Ma-Nyawuza Ike had brought a pair of coloured sheets.

Phindi spent the first evening back in her house cleaning. Ike was glued to the TV set. An undefined peace prevailed for the nights and days that followed. The parcels on Saturday became part of the events of the day. Phindi was kept guessing about what was contained, never doubting there would be one. Ike was totally exemplary.

Neighbours picked up another point for gossip as if they condemned Ike for being level-headed: they said he was afraid Nyawuza would break up the marriage with Phindi if he dared go astray again. All that talk make Ike miserable.

But he stopped short of complaining or discussing this with his wife.

Overtime at Troy Manufacturers was not common. What with the economic recession management played it safe. No one wanted to stockpile goods. Yet out of the blue Phindi and her colleagues were asked to work overtime. That day Ike was home before his wife. And wanting to kill time with friends, he set off telling himself he wouldn't be away too long.

Phindi had taken advantage of a loving and repentant husband to visit her parents. 'He's so sweet,' she actually remarked to Ma-Nyawuza as they parted company in the street. There had been no particular reason to drop by her parents' place — just a longing to see them.

He wasn't home as she arrived. That didn't bother her. The moral boost from her mother and his recent gentleman's behaviour combined to lull her suspicions. Besides, the meat parcel was in the fridge, so there was no reason to be upset, just this once.

Ike came back home many hours later than he had hoped. Some teasing by buddies made him prove a point or two. He drank beer and stayed long with old friends to show that there was no external force in control. One buddy said something like there was no overtime at Troy's, Ike was being fooled. That statement fuelled the fire burning in him as a result of the many things friends had said on this brief encounter.

Phindi was surprised by the question, 'Where have you been?' asked by Ike. It was strange because she should have asked it.

'What's this rubbish of saying hello to your parents on your way from work?' he wanted to know.

'Awi, Ike,' she pleaded, sensing war, 'I'm telling you the truth.'

'Truth, rubbish!' he snarled. 'You are a liar, bitch!'

'That's an insult, Ike,' she cried, her hands going up to shield her head. It was the cue Ike had been waiting for. He began to pummel her like a punchbag, working on her body. But then there was just this one blow, a stray one. It landed on the left eye. That made her scream madly. Ike withdrew as if contented, as if his manhood had been restored at that moment.

Phindi stormed out of the house.

Nyawuza was dumbfounded. His wife said her child must never go back to that hooligan again. Nyawuza spoke rather vaguely as if not addressing himself to his daughter when he asked if Phindi had taken in her mother's words. He went on: 'I wonder why the law is hesitant to lock up such things.'

Phindi's blue eye cost Troy Manufacturers a couple of days' lost time.

Ike cried inwardly every day. He couldn't understand what went wrong that he actually took to drinking that one day — friends? Yes and no. How did it all start? He shut his mind to that one. He couldn't believe that he was so simple-minded not to have distinguished truth from lies on that day. As if to punish himself he kept away from friends and shebeens. For weeks following he behaved correctly.

Neighbours expressed the change in him with compassion to Phindi. But she said she was not interested in her husband any more. Yes, she was through with Ike.

It was like thunder and lightning when Ike heard of Phindi's resolve. Impossible, he said. Yet he knew in his heart it could happen. In that same heart he experienced a twitch of fear. The house became large and empty. The TV set was a nightmare. All acts on it were child-like, senseless and uninspiring. It remained switched off.

He went to bed early but took long to sleep. The house held a fear for him though he couldn't pinpoint where it lay or in what form it was. It was fear he lived with. Dreams were contorted into nightmares. He began to wonder if he was still sane. What accentuated his concern over his dreams was what he had heard said as he grew up, which is what every location child knows, that one should never ignore dreams. There's a meaning behind all dreams.

Ike became a worried man. And it was through the maze of worry that he resolved to bring Phindi back into the house. A tall order!

Every time he looked at the question how, he came up

with the same answer. Phindi was of an insatiable nature. She liked the world and its material things. He merely had to find one item for the house which would satisfy her. And then buy it by hook or crook. The list was long. That made things slightly easy for him.

He settled on a washing machine. At Nyawuza's place there was one which was housed in the garage. He cracked his brains to find a place for it in their house, the kitchen was small; it would be silly to put in it the dining room. The spare room — sometimes referred to as the visitor's room — luckily no child had been born to their marriage yet. Visitors would understand its presence in the room.

Ike's spirits took a dive when he faced the issue of purchase. He owed Mr Lewis for the TV set. Asking for the machine would make Mr Lewis remind him of economic realities, as he put it to his staff every time they borrowed money from the shop. And once Mr Lewis spoke of that, no one could make him budge from his resolve not to part with a cent. No, Mr Lewis was out.

Ike decided the machine could be bought by a relative on his behalf. He raised a loan from the same generous relative.

For days the washing machine remained in the kitchen on display. He spoke freely about its advantages especially since he and Phindi were working people.

The news of its purchase was bandied about in the neighbourhood. Wattville is a small location, it was therefore unavoidable that Phindi or Ma-Nyawuza would hear of this addition to Ike's place.

Ike's new worry was how to enter Nyawuza's house without deflecting missiles in the process. Love doesn't die, he believed. For this reason he was content that Phindi would listen to his pleas. But there was no guarantee on how the Nyawuzas would react to the sight of him. I want my wife, became a chant of resolve. Armed with it he thought he could face Nyawuza. When he remembered that Nyawuza relied heavily on lawyers, Ike gave the matter a second thought.

It wasn't easy for him to settle on the services of the same relative who had helped him buy the washing machine. But he laid it on thick for the relative: he fetched his family history from the Eastern Cape; settled the family in Doorn-fontein and Vrededorp; told how his parents died and the hardships attendant on him as a result; how his marriage was dogged by misfortunes because his relatives were not strong enough to demand from Nyawuza that certain rituals be conducted. Phindi's behaviour was traceable to the neglect of his family, but he was grateful to this relative for his assistance every time he called on him.

The relative was smitten with a sense of guilt. He volunteered to accompany Ike to Nyawuza's place in order to resolve their marriage problems once and for all.

It wasn't easy for Ike to enter Nyawuza's big house. Walking through the kitchen to the sitting room was like groping through a dark tunnel. Fear accompanied every step he took forward. Even the smile he tried to wear just fizzled out so that in the end he wore a very blank expression. The two parties sat at two ends of the room. Preliminaries were uttered by Ike's relative whose humble-ness and solemn behaviour would have impressed all the gods of Africa. For some reason Nyawuza was without words for a while. In that silence Ike ambled across the room to hand his wife a small parcel. To enhance its value he smiled at her. She remained glum but undid the wrap-ping. Phindi couldn't contain her joy. Oh, she cried, jumped up and went to her mum to show her the present: it was a gold-plated ornament in the shape of a butterfly. A brooch of green and white and brown wings. Gots! it was very pretty.

Phindi crossed over to her husband and planted a kiss on his cheek. That resolved their differences. Nyawuza sounded hollow with his 'Keep away from the bottle, mkwenyana!'

'I'm seeing A. A. on Monday,' replied Ike as he and his wife and the relative trooped out of the house.

The washing machine can be heard moaning in the spare room now and then. As for Ike, he has become a TV fanatic.

After six months of peace in the house it is no wonder. He does not seem worried by neighbours. He says if they are worried by the peace between him and his wife, there's no way in which he could be bothered. He has the accounts of the house to look after and that's enough to keep him busy. Why, at times he feels like screaming just to ease the frustrations of paying such heavy accounts. But he's big enough to know that the accounts will not disappear as a result.

One evening Phindi joined her husband to watch TV. It surprised Ike because it was not *Dallas* night. To his relief she did not do one of those naughty things one reads of in fiction, like sidling up to one's man coquettishly. She sat away from him but assumed a mischievous smile. When she spoke there was a slight trace of a face wrinkled by joy.

'Tell me dear, what used to happen to you whenever you boxed the daylights out of me?'

'Ah Phindi, please,' he pleaded, 'why be so hard? Let's forget those things.'

'I'm not fighting. I'm not angry. Every time I recall how the TV set was bought those things crowd my mind.'

'All right, all right,' sighed Ike resignedly, 'I'll say something. I hope it will be the truth. I have myself thought about these things. How, for instance, I am able to go back to work every morning. Haven't you bumped into someone and said you're sorry, but the other person says not a word of apology? I don't claim to be good or saintly but I feel rotten inside if I don't say I'm sorry to the next person. Maybe I come from a nowhere background, you know, no money, no food, nothing like luxuries. And you — the world's being at your command.'

'My father is a strict man,' chipped in Phindi.

'Strict? That's nothing. He gave you peace of mind — a meal, pocket money, stuff like that. You didn't have to hustle in life. You bought over the counter. I — bought back door. Sometimes I never paid.'

'You are bitter.'

'Bitter? No, not bitter. I just failed to adjust to normal life. It was difficult for me.'

'And you beat me up to teach me a lesson of life to level us, in other words?'

Ike tried to face up to his wife. In a way she's a tough girl, he thought. He stole a look at her and felt embarrassed by what she was able to face without a blush. He closed his eyes, clammed his lips. That was a cue for her to retire.

This little encounter was like a cleansing hand. Phindi had not sought victory over her man. There could have been none under the circumstances. She had gained a glimpse into his make-up and for her that was all she wanted.

Ike and Phindi live fairly happily together. They are still in Wattville. They fight sometimes but mostly they are happy to be together after all the tribulations of married life.

Flat

CHRIS VAN WYK

I was standing on the first storey of the block of flats listening to the women cackle and skinder between the lines of washing down below. Mrs Adams, a double row of clothes-pegs stuck to her huge damp chest, heaved, hands on hips beneath dripping shirts. 'Instead of getting off his black bum and going to look for work, he spends that fifty cents every day on . . .'

'That cheap wine.' Mrs Peacock spat into the dust to endorse disapproval.

'Maar my Here!' a grey head uttered scornfully behind a white sheet.

'I just knew it,' Mrs Adams waved a sanctimonious finger at a damp trousers. 'I knew he was sommer a gemors.'

'Ag, yous know, I feel so sorry for Lydia,' muttered the head behind the sheets.

A brief silence followed. I took a swig of beer.

Then Mrs Peacock wanted to know: 'What's 7½%?'

There followed a mental splashing and rinsing.

'Seven and a half cents,' answered Mrs Adams.

'So little!' Mrs Peacock gasped.

'Oh yes,' Mrs Adams assured her.

'Why do you want to know that?' the grey head was curious.

'Ag, Joseph got a increase of 7½%.'

'Good for you, old girl.' Mrs Adams hung up a boy's shirt.

'Ja.' Mrs Peacock heaved disappointment. Then she lifted an empty blue dish against her hip and strode out of the mud and wet clothes towards the steps.

Mrs Adams allowed a few impatient seconds to pass before she warned: 'If my husband comes home with seven and a half cents, klap ek hom nie een hou mis nie.'

I turned and went into my flat. Gail was standing at the sink, cleaning rice in a colander.

'You had enough of that skindering?' she asked.

'Ja.' I fetched a beer from the fridge in the corner. 'Pass me a glass, please.'

Gail slid a glass across the table to where I was sitting on the one stool we had left.

'How many are there left?' she asked, not looking up.

'There's only this one. The other two broke last month when we moved . . .'

'I'm talking about the beer. How many've you got left?'

'Oh, probably three or four.' I leaned back and opened the fridge. Three cold necks of beer stuck out from a broken pack.

'And it's only Saturday.'

'Ag, don't worry. There's always the shebeens.'

She gave me a sharp look. 'Six-packs used to last you all weekend.'

'Oe, die wind!' we heard one woman shriek from downstairs. 'Die stof!'

'It's the stof, Gail,' I clutched my throat in mock agony.

Gail glanced up from a pot she was stirring and chuckled. 'An answer on the line.'

'Clever.' I took a gulp of beer. 'Now tell me, what's 7½%?'

'Of what?'

'Doesn't matter,' I said, relieved. 'Mrs Adams says it's seven and a half cents.'

She giggled. 'How did this explanation come about?'

'They were talking about an increase that Mr Peacock got. She asked them how much 7½% was.'

'And Mrs Adams told her?'

'Ja, clever Mrs Adams.'

'Well, Mrs Peacock's in for a pleasant surprise.'

'Ja,' I nodded. 'Unless of course Mr Peacock earns R1,00. But with a wife as gullible as that woman, he might just take out his increase and leave 7½ cents in his pay packet.'

'Sis, Raymond,' Gail berated me. 'Only you'd think of

something like that. D'you like some tea?'

'No thank you I'll . . .'

'Have another beer?'

'Jesus! How'd you guess?'

'You realize how much you've been drinking since we moved in here?' she asked, hands on hips.

'Ag, not so much. It's summer, man. It's hot.'

She glared at me for a few seconds, sighed heavily and poured boiling water over a teabag in a cup.

'I'm going to see if there's any letters,' I rose and pushed the stool under the table. 'Postman must've come. I don't trust those laaities, specially that Early Boy Adams. Must be the naughtiest bastard in the world. I wish his mother would send him to a reformatory . . . or to the gallows.'

'Hah!' Gail gasped. 'Don't say such things about a child.'

'He must've committed a crime bad enough to warrant that surely.'

And for the umpteenth time the cistern in the Adams's flat flushed. I could hear the peristaltic action loud at work as water pushed the wastes of somebody's bowels through the long thick porcelain throat that passed through our kitchen.

'Okay,' I retracted. Maybe he should just get lifelong constipation.

'Don't forget your shit passes through Mrs Johnson's kitchen. Yours and Early Boy's.'

'But I don't shit as often,' I reminded her. 'That bastard's stomach is as loose as a whore.'

'Your language!' she shook her head disdainfully. 'Here,' she handed me a dish of potato peels, 'you might as well throw this away for me.'

I walked along the balcony which was polished in red here, black there, as the women fancied, or not at all before some doors. The dustbins were downstairs near the washing lines, the letterboxes near the stairs. The sun shone determinedly down on the stoep, melting some freshly smeared polish. I felt wheezy in its heat, my legs wobbled. I had drunk a lot of beer since this morning.

Down below children squealed and cursed, disappearing

and reappearing between the hundreds of blocks of flats that stood all around in desolate grey parallels. A drunk staggered in the maze of damp washing, cursing incoherently. A group of youths looked up at him from a circle of dice to laugh and lampoon.

Somewhere children began to chant, 'Daar's 'n man by die busstop, hy hou my sister se boude dop!' Why they were singing this I could not begin to understand, but as soon as they grew tired of that they would sing another one much more scurrilous from their vast repertoire of ribald rubbish.

Mrs Peacock's door was open. A radio blared cheekily. The adjoining flat was Miss Philips's. The woman whom Early Boy's stomach was as loose as.

The smell of hops drifted out from her open door, and wanton laughter. In my curiosity to see whom she was entertaining, I stumbled over some brat's tricycle. Two peels flew out of the dish I was carrying. I was about to pick them up when I remembered that Early Boy might slip and do himself an injury, a small one on his spine. I left them sprawled on the balcony.

And as I turned the corner there he was in the company of all his cronies. Early Boy Adams and his friends on the landing, squeezed between the railings, their penises exposed in a stiff peeing competition.

I remained hidden awhile to watch. Early Boy and a scrawny sandy-haired kid called Charles pinched their foreskins for effect. A dark-skinned Muslim boy, Rashaad, did not have a foreskin but would not be outdone.

Early Boy's sidekick, a vile-tongued five-year-old in a dirty frock who could not participate in the game for obvious reasons, stood aside clapping and rooting for her man.

'Hey!' I shouted, trying to frighten them.

Two of the competitors withdrew immediately.

'Earl Adams!' I tried to put some menace into my voice. But the arc only spurted higher.

'Aw,' he sneered through pouted lips, 'I'm only pissing.'

'I can see that, but don't you have a lavatory at home?'

He nodded.

'So why don't you use the toilet?'

'My mother was shitting.'

I winced. His mother hadn't even equipped him with the genteel vocabulary of the toilet.

Surlily he put away his prize-winning penis, still sneering at me.

I shook my head and walked down the steps. I held my breath for the stench at one of the overfilled dustbins, disturbing a buzzing circle of green flies as I toppled the peels on to the heap of rubbish.

I checked the letterbox for letters. There were two; one was addressed to me. I recognized it to be a bill for a furniture account with which I had fallen into arrears. The other one was for Mr September, the previous tenant of my flat. It was a bulky, white official looking envelope. Money?

I went back upstairs. On the landing Early Boy and his friends were huddled in a serious meeting. He was grimly addressing them.

Soon after I had passed them I slipped on forgotten potato peels, hurting my shinbone and sending an enamel dish careering across the long stoep. Jeering laughter followed.

I limped the rest of the way home.

'You're drunk!' Gail declared reproachfully.

'I'm not,' I dabbed my shin.

'Why did you slip then?'

'I dunno, anybody can slip, there was something in the way there.'

'Something like potato peels?'

'Ja, maybe.'

'Well, if you dropped potato peels then you are drunk.'

'Ja, maybe I am drunk.' Then with a daring lurch I took another dumpy from the fridge. 'But I'll have this to make sure.'

Gail folded her arms and laughed wryly.

I felt foolish now. I wasn't sure how to react.

'Where's that letter of September's?' I said, for want of something less embarrassing.

She pointed with her eyes to the fridge.

I placed it on the table before me and lit a cigarette.

Gail spread a tablecloth across half the table and began to dish up.

'Maybe it's money,' I speculated, holding it against the light.

No response.

'A cheque,' I decided. 'Must be a cheque.'

She fetched tomato sauce and chutney.

'Wonder how long he lived here.'

'Come and eat.'

'Maybe since the flats were built.' She began to eat.

'Wonder where he lives now.'

'Oh,' she said finally. 'Why don't you go and find him!'

'I will, I will!' I cried with mock impatience. 'Just give me a chance to eat please, woman!'

She glared at me from across the table.

'I'm sorry,' I smiled, holding her wrist penitently. 'You take your tablets today?'

She nodded.

'When you going to the clinic again?'

'Thursday.'

We ate in silence. Afterwards Gail offered me some tea. I refused it. I still had some beer left.

Suddenly the silence was broken by the shrill familiar sound of the cistern overhead and the slurping down the long pipe in the corner of our kitchen as the sewerage system swallowed and digested one more time.

Gail glanced up at me expectantly. But this time I made no comment. Maybe I had been too irascible lately, too touchy.

I often heard old folks say how husbands experienced the symptoms of pregnancy whenever their wives were pregnant. Gail mentioned the other day that I was proving this to be true. 'Rubbish,' I had told her. All the more reason why I decided now to be more patient in future, with Gail, the neighbours, Early Boy.

I thanked Gail for the lunch. 'Can I clean up for you?'

'It's okay, thanks.'

I lit a cigarette and went to sit in the lounge. I was about to settle into a comfortable position when I heard terrible swearing come from outside. Early Boy and Co. were at it again. I struggled out of the settee and closed the window. The swearing sounded far away now.

I settled down once more and began to flip through the latest issue of *Living and Loving*. It contained advice on baby and child care and had pictures of women in various stages of pregnancy; foetuses curled up contentedly in bright pink placentas.

Soon it was three o'clock and time for the sports programme on television. I switched on the box, lit another cigarette and lay back. Two bulky wrestlers were pummelling each other before an enthusiastic crowd. The bald head seemed to have an edge over the blond one. I pretended that I was the bald one and Early the other one.

It was very pleasant until Early Boy stamped on my stomach and tried to wrench a limb from my body.

Before we learnt the outcome of that bout we were shown some show-jumping. This bored me so that I drifted to sleep.

I had a dream. A faceless Mr September was promoting this wrestling match. He was offering a big envelope full of money as a prize. Early Boy and I had agreed to do battle for this generous purse.

I was in the ring, loosening my limbs, getting ready to beat the living daylights out of Adams when he snatched the envelope and ran away. Suddenly one thousand police appeared and together we gave chase. Early ran lithely up and down the staircase, jumped through windows, slid down pipes, all the while cursing us in the foulest language imaginable.

The police drew their whistles to summon help, but when they blew, instead of whistles I heard a thousand cisterns.

I woke up cursing. Gail was singing a hymn at the kitchen sink. It was 5.00 p.m. Time for *The Star*. I put on a windbreaker because I felt cold.

'Going to buy the paper, hey,' I told Gail. 'Want anything from the shop?'

'Yes, please. Some Coke. And a chocolate: Mint Crisp.'

'Give me some more money then. I've only got . . .'

'There's some money in my purse, in the white bag.'

I knew she'd say that. I took more than enough.

'Lock the door, hey!' I called as I walked out. 'And don't open for anyone.'

The sun had begun to set. Its last rays painted the high flat walls a drab yellow. People slouched against the darkness. I trod carefully down the stairs. I saw a man slip here once, in his own vomit. He looked ugly as he lay there, blood oozing from somewhere underneath him. He groaned through his stupor for help. And just as I had plucked up enough courage to help him, his friends came to his rescue. I was relieved.

That was last Saturday. And the stains of it had been douched from the cracked cement on a rainy night. Now it had been replaced by the rough maps between the rails. And the stench of a pissing contest.

I stopped by my car, a reliable blue Volksie. I checked the doors and kicked a tyre. I decided to wash it tomorrow.

Two lovers passed me. They had been arguing but now paused. But before they were out of earshot the man insulted her. She said he must be referring to his mother and sisters, whereupon he slapped her twice about the face.

After I had done my shopping I took a detour. I had only a few days earlier discovered the inevitable watering place.

I knocked. The door opened and I glinted in a rectangle of dull yellow light.

'Ja?' said the shebeen queen, blowing smoke into my eyes.

'Half a jack brandy, please.'

She snatched the money from my hands.

'Er, can you make it two nips, please?'

She gazed at me quizzically, nodded and disappeared. Clever tannie, I mumbled; two nips are easier to hide.

She shuffled back to the stoep and shoved two small

bottles into my hand. The rectangle of yellow shut into rude darkness.

'It's me, Gail, open up.'

She opened. 'Where were you so long, then?' she was annoyed.

'Shop was full,' I said, as I used to say to my mother.

'Can I help you with something?' I had to do penance for pilfering.

'Like what?'

'Anything you like.'

'No, there's nothing.'

I poured Coke into a glass and went to the lounge where I topped the glass with brandy.

We sat watching television for a while.

Then later, as on most other Saturday nights, it began. Loud banging at the door.

'Who's it?'

'Myrtle!'

'Who's it?'

'Ek soek vir Myrtle!'

'Myrtle doesn't live here!'

'Ag tog Myrtle.' Beseeching.

'No Myrtle here!'

'Ag Myrtle, don't be funny!' Annoyed.

'Myrtle bly nie hier nie!'

'Jy bly hierso!' Insistent.

'Ek bly nie hier nie . . . ek bedoel ek bly hier, nie Myrtle nie!'

'Ag my Myrtletjie,' Slurring, maudlin.

'Fuck off, get away.' Angry.

'You fuck off.' Indignant.

I decided to remain silent. He curses me and Myrtle and somebody called Danny's mother. Eventually he slouches back into the night of uneasy distant sounds. I stand still to make certain, my mind wanders to rent, groceries, a new-born baby, layettes.

And suddenly an overhead cistern strikes me out of my reverie. 'Bastard!' I shout beyond the ceiling.

I crawled into bed long after Gail, drunk.

The next morning it woke me. After three weeks of living in this flat, one thing I could say for the Adamses: they are more punctual than a farmer when it comes to putting nature to work.

I lay in bed, smoking.

Knock knock knock.

I hopped out of bed. I knew who this was.

'Koeksisters, uncle?' he said as chirpy as last Sunday.

'No.'

'Thank you, uncle,' he said, as if I had bought a dozen.

'Pleasure.' I shut the door.

I went back to the bedroom and got dressed. I could hear his knocking grow fainter and fainter.

Over coffee Gail and I decided to visit her parents in Riverlea.

'I'll sommer go and wash the car now. But first I want to buy the papers.'

Outside Eldorado Park was at it again; drunks, gambling, arguing and Mrs Peacock adding colour to it in a garish nightie and pink slippers, each topped by a fluffy purple cat or lion.

'Good morning,' I greeted.

'Good morning,' she yawned and her jaws creaked open like an ungreased door.

Downstairs a shock awaited me. All four tyres of my car were flat.

Early Boy. It must be! A dirty matchstick in each valve said so.

I ran back up the stairs. I was livid, ready to commit murder. This was my big chance to bludgeon him to death. No! Wait! A better plan.

I ran up to the third storey and there they were, the entire team with Early in the centre seriously addressing them.

They looked up when they heard my step. Some made to run. I quickly replaced my malevolent expression with a subdued, avuncular one.

'Hello, outjies,' I greeted, smiling.

Early Boy frowned suspiciously.

'I've been looking for you children. Guess what I got at home?'

Nobody guessed.

'Sixteen packets of sweets, twenty chocolates — big ones — and sixteen packets of biscuits and other nice stuff.'

They stared at me in awe.

'S'true, I'm not lying,' I crossed my fingers against my lips. 'And all those who want to come can come.' I grinned and turned to go.

It worked. They got up and began to trail behind me, at first in an unsure patter of feet, then bursting into unrestrained excitement.

'Have Uncle got those chocolates with the cream in, Uncle?' enquired one.

'Of course!'

'Are we all gonna have a full glass of colddrink?'

'Yes.'

I ushered them into my flat, giving Early Boy a special grin as he shuffled in behind the dirtier ones.

Gail gaped in bewilderment. I gestured to her to wait and see, beckoning her into the lounge.

They sat along the settee, their feet dangling above the floor.

Gail watched from the doorway, bemused, her hands on her distended tummy.

'Right,' I started, trying hard to sustain my grin. 'Who flattened my tyres?'

An uneasy silence.

I produced sweets, a big bar of chocolate and some cooldrink.

'If you don't tell me, nobody gets . . .'

Eventually saliva exposed the culprit.

'Him!' they pointed at Early.

'Early?' I asked in mock surprise.

Nobody dared say it again.

Early sneered insolently.

I handed sweets and cooldrink around to all except Early. One four-year-old was so grateful that he swore witness to the crime.

'He do it wid der matches, Uncle,' he sniffed up mucus.

I handed out more sweets. And Early's sneer turned to sullenness.

'More chocolates?'

Woe.

'And Coke?'

Disgusted, Gail went to the kitchen.

'Out now, all of you, the party's over.'

They trooped out. I began to clear up the mess. I felt wretched.

'Sis, you're cruel!' Gail reproached me.

'To hell with cruel!' I shouted.

'You could've given him a sweet.'

'That bastard, that brat!'

'What does he know, he's only a child.'

A diffident knock at the door punctuated the argument. 'Come in!' Gail called.

A small man stood hunched in the doorway self-deprecatingly. In his hands he gripped a shapeless hat so that veins showed on the back of his hands. He was grey at the temples. Heavy bags hung from underneath his eyes. Flecks of alcohol had burnt their way through his gullet, and lay branded on his neck in cauterized patches of pink and purple. He opened his mouth to speak and a gust of stale wind emanated from his dry mouth. 'I, er, I come here for a letter.'

I took the envelope from the fridge.

'September, er Abie Ronald September. I think that's my disability money . . .'

I was uncertain but handed him the envelope and the other mail addressed to September.

Just as he feverishly began to open the white official envelope there was a loud crash of glass down below. A car! My Volkswagen! Oh God!

Mr September buried his emaciated face in his hands and gasped hoarsely: 'Early Boy!'

A Passion for Wealth

KAIZER NYATSUMBA

'I am going to write a play!' Victor Moeketsi exclaimed.

He had never tried his hand at playwriting before. Nor had he ever scribbled on a blank page a few disjointed lines which could be called poetry. Not only did he not write any fiction either, but he also read no fiction at all. He simply had no time for such elitist and, let's face it, pretentious diversions. Like now, he spent his free time boozing with his friends.

'Gents, I am going to write a play,' Victor said again when neither of his friends said anything. He emptied his glass of beer in one gulp, placed the glass on the coffee-table in front of him and looked at Jack and Peter. The men looked at each other and smiled.

'Listen gents, I'm serious. I am serious. I am going to write a play which will be a phenomenal box-office success both here and abroad, and shame Mbongeni Ngema's *Sarafina*,' Victor said with a serious face.

'Kyk nou, bra Vic, you must be joking, man. You know that man is a playwright par excellence, and no one in this country can write as well as he does, let alone do better than him,' said Jack.

'I'm gonna be rich, Jack. Stinking rich,' Victor said, standing up. He stood in the middle of the modest lounge, put his hands in his pockets and walked towards the big window. Once there, he opened the window wider and peeped through it. There, on Pretoria Street, were people moving up and down. They were in a hurry as usual. Others, however, sauntered up and down the street hand in hand with those they loved. Cars hooted and sped up the street. There was nothing unusual about it. It was all typical of a normal Saturday in Hillbrow.

As Victor looked down from the fifteenth floor of

Highpoint, the tallest block of flats in Hillbrow, he thought of how the play he wanted to write would be published and later adapted for a movie. It would rake in a lot of money, no doubt, and he could even end up becoming a millionaire. It would be a hit in every country which would see it. Maybe he would even get so rich that he would resign from his job as a showbiz reporter on *The Star*, the Johannesburg daily newspaper. Maybe he could even get married then.

For Victor flat number one-five-seven-zero Highpoint was home. It had been home for the previous eighteen months since he had left home in Soweto to get a place of his own. As he told his colleagues at work, and his friends, he wanted 'to own' so that he could have the privacy he wanted. And so here he was today entertaining two of his closest friends, Jack Lusiba, a lawyer, and Peter Mpachoe, a school-teacher. They were listening to pleasant music and drinking beers as they chatted about all sorts of things.

The idea had occurred to him quite unexpectedly, and he was fascinated by it. It crystallized further as he stood at the window, inhaling fresh air and looking at the street. The title was quite clear in his mind.

'You know what I am going to call it?' he asked as he turned away from the window and walked back to the sofa where he had been seated before. '*Twenty-Seven Lonely Years*. How do you like that?'

'Stop pulling our legs now, bra Vic. What play are you talking about? You know as well as we do that you have never written a play in your life. Whence gettest thou this inspiration?' Peter spoke for the first time, and he and Jack smiled. Victor, however, did not smile.

'I may not have written a play in my life, but I *am* a journalist. I have seen and reviewed more plays than I care to remember, and so I know what makes a good play,' he said. Then he added, 'And don't use that stupid form of English when you talk to me. I know you teach Shakespeare's plays.'

They all laughed.

'But seriously now, bra Vic. Why the sudden desire to dabble in the Thespian art? You know as well as we do that you are no Ibsen or Shakespeare or . . .'

218

'Athol Fugard or Mbongeni Ngema? Is that what you wanted to say, Mr English-master? Well, I can write as well as any one of those guys. Just wait until I put pen to paper!'

'Kyk nou hier, bra Vic,' said Jack after clearing his throat, 'writing a play is different from writing for a newspaper. For instance, while the language of journalism is passive and simple . . .'

'Passive and simple? Who told you that, bra Jack? You make it sound as if being a journalist is the easiest thing in the world, you know!'

'Kyk nou hier, my bra, what I wanted to say is that writing a play, as far as I know, is very demanding. The language used by your characters has to be powerful if it is to elicit any response from the audience. Your . . .'

'Bra Jack, please,' Peter chipped in. 'Please don't scare Victor away from playwriting before we have even heard his novel idea. Don't confuse him with characters and characterization. Let's find out first if he knows what dialogue is?'

'Listen to him, listen to him. "Let's find out first if he knows what dialogue is," he says. What arrogance on the part of the teacher! One doesn't have to teach Shakespeare to matric pupils to know what dialogue is, you know. A good dialogue is one of the things I look for when I review plays.'

'How you never forget the fact that you are a theatre critic. One would be forgiven for thinking that it was a great achievement. Let me remind you of what that great and extremely talented eighteenth-century writer, Alexander Pope, once said about critics . . .'

'Please spare us the . . .'

'He said:

Some ne'er advance a judgement of their own,
But catch the spreading notion of the town;
They reason and conclude by precedent,
And own stale nonsense which they ne'er invent.
Some judge of authors' names, not works, and then
Nor praise nor blame the writings, but the men . . .'

Jack, who had been listening attentively all along, cleared his throat to talk. 'Kyk nou hier, gents,' he said, 'let's move on with the discussion, shall we? Let us not indulge in academic ostentation.'

Before Victor could say something, Peter was speaking again. He was now pacing up and down the lounge as he spoke.

'Alexander Pope was himself a critic. If you still want to know what he said about his fellow critics then, for your own good, listen:

Some praise at morning what they blame at night,
But always think the last opinion right.
A muse by these is like a mistress us'd,
This hour she's idolized, the next abus'd.'

'Okay, bra Peter,' Victor said as soon as he got a chance. 'I will take your reservation about critics. But you will have noticed that in the two passages you have recited like an excited pupil, Pope talks about "some" critics, and not all of them. I am not one of those he wrote so disparagingly about.'

The three friends laughed. Victor was cornered. They were good friends — had always been good friends from the time they were classmates at high school at Pace College in Jabulani, Soweto. Like all boys their age they were naughty, but they were also the best students at the school. They always aimed for, and attained, the top three positions at the school.

When they matriculated they went their different ways. Victor studied journalism at Rhodes University, Peter flew to Cape Town to read for a degree in teaching at the University of Cape Town, and Jack remained in Johannesburg and read for a law degree at the University of the Witwatersrand.

The three men always had a chance to see each other when they were on vacation. After finishing their studies they all worked in and around Johannesburg, thus getting a chance once again to cement their friendship. Whenever they were together they liked to poke fun at each other.

'Kyk nou hier, gents . . .'

'You and that cliché of yours, bra Jack. Can't you say anything without first prefacing it with that boring kyk nou hier of yours. Do you also say that in court?' Peter asked, laughing. Jack had always used the phrase for as long as they knew him. Peter was just trying to tease him now.

'There the teach goes again,' said Victor.

'I have no time to waste answering your question, bra Peter. Nou bra Vic, kyk nou hier, what is this play about? This play that you so desperately want to write!'

'Oh. It is about Nelson Mandela. His experiences in prison.'

'What?' Jack and Peter said simultaneously.

'About Mandela.'

'You can't be serious.'

'Why not, Jack? Of course I am dead serious.'

'But . . . that's a violation of something sacred. You know Mandela is a sacrosanct figure in our struggle . . .'

'Use your fucking lawyer's mind to think, Jack, will you? Use your mind, man. And if you want anyone to preach to, then I suggest you talk to all the bubblegum musicians, the poetasters and the second-rate writers who use Mr Mandela's name for no other motive than profit.'

'Surely you don't want to stoop to that level yourself, or do you now, Victor?' Peter asked.

'You guys amaze me,' Victor said. 'You really do. Since when are you such high priests of morality? Look, the man walked out of Victor Verster Prison a free man in the glare of the international media last Sunday, and today — a mere six days later — one is hassled at every corner of the city by people trying to sell one a poster of the ANC leader, and ANC flags, and a whole lot of other Mandela memorabilia. It's all business, man.'

'Ja, but . . .'

'Ja but what, Peter? What? If I don't act now very soon local and international musicians will be flooding the market with Mandela songs, books will be written and movies will be made on him. It's a question of timing.'

My God, he is serious, Peter thought. The man is serious. For a moment quiet descended on the lounge of the High-point flat like death striking when it is least expected. A tense atmosphere pervaded the lounge, and each man shifted uncomfortably in his chair. Smiling, Jack was the first to speak.

'Kyk nou hier, so go for it, bra Vic. I see your point now. There is a lot of money to be made here.'

'I knew you would come around.'

'You know me. I know a good thing when I see, or hear of one.'

'That's my man.'

Peter was unimpressed. 'Do you hear yourself, bra Jack?' he asked. 'Are you actually encouraging Victor to go ahead and use Mandela's name for money?'

'Kyk nou hier, bra Peter. I don't see anything wrong with that. Everybody is doing it.'

'To hell with those guys, man,' Jack said. 'You don't care about those clowns, bra Vic, do you?'

'Me? I couldn't be bothered at all by hypocrites. God knows those guys have used and continue to use Mandela's name in all their public utterances to get where they are now. They have written line after line on Mandela, apartheid and what-not and called it poetry, and it has sold simply because Mandela's name was in it and it was therefore seen to be anti-apartheid poetry. And now they have the brutish audacity to issue injunctions calling on people not to use Mandela's name for money. How typical of them!'

'How typical indeed,' Jack said. 'They want to have a monopoly over the struggle, a monopoly over the use of words such as "progressive" or "democratic", and now they want an exclusive monopoly over the use of Mr Mandela's name. Fuck them, man.'

Again quiet, like dusk, descended on the lounge. Music kept pouring out softly, quietly and pleasantly from the stereo, and one bottle of beer after another was emptied and put aside. During the gripping discussion, the men each took a turn in changing the LPs on the record-player. As they thought over the issue at hand now their attention was on the music. They allowed themselves to be carried away to unknown lands by the sweet and seductive voice of Ruby Turner as she wailed out: 'I'd rather be blind than to see you walk away from me.'

'Are you still with me, gentlemen?' Jack asked when he saw his two companions looking absentminded.

'Yes I am, bra Jack,' Victor responded immediately.

'Me too,' Peter nodded nonchalantly.

'Okay. Now, Victor, please tell us more about this get-rich-quick dream of yours.'

'It's not a dream, bra Jack. It's as real as the coffee-table here in front of us. Not abstract, but concrete, man.'

'Tell us about it, then.'

'I will do so in a minute. But it looks to me bra Peter does not want to hear my great literary plans.'

'No, I'm listening, gents. I'm listening.'

'Good. Now this is my plan, and you are the first privileged two to hear about it. It is . . .'

'Privileged, did you say?'

'Yes, privileged, Peter. Now please don't disturb me until I have finished.' They all laughed.

'All right, go on Victor,' said Peter.

'Good. The idea is simple, really. It is going to be a play on Mr Nelson Mandela. Of course you already know that. Now, a lot has been said about Mr Mandela before he was sentenced to life imprisonment, and a lot will be said about him in the period after his release. And so I want to focus on the period in between. I want to focus on the twenty-seven years he spent in prison.'

'But what are you going to write about, Victor? Those are the man's lost years, buddy. How do you hope to positively reconstruct them?'

'That's the point, bra Jack. That's the whole point. Here I can write absolutely anything about the man without any fear of being accused of falsifying facts or history. That's the best thing about it. I will have complete licence, you see.'

'Ja, but what are you going to write about? You still haven't answered bra Jack's question.'

'Easy, Peter; easy man. To start with, I intend calling it *Twenty-Seven Lonely Years*, a play exploring African National Congress leader Mr Nelson Mandela's life in prison, written by *The Star* journalist Victor Moeketsi, which will open at The Market Theatre in Johannesburg next Tuesday. Just imagine it, man. People will certainly flock to the theatre to see it.'

'Again I must ask, Victor, what is it going to be about? What new insights into Mandela's life are you going to give?'

'Insight? Who said my play was going to give anybody any insight? Plays do not have to do that, you know. I must ask you again to hold your horses, Peter. Let me tell the story at my own pace.'

Victor kept quiet and thought for a while.

'Now you know what its title is going to be, *Twenty-Seven Lonely Years*,' he continued. 'I don't quite know yet how I am going to develop it, but I do have an idea. I think I may have Mr Mandela reflecting on a number of things — his youth, his family, his political ideals, his future, etc. It will all fall into shape once I start writing.'

'Good idea, bra Vic,' Jack said. 'Good idea. The whole thing sounds very interesting. I like men who make use of a golden opportunity when they see one.'

'Yes. That's me. I have seen a wonderful chance to be rich and famous, and I am grabbing it with both hands.'

'Can I be your legal and financial adviser, bra Vic? You will certainly need one since the world of showbiz and entertainment is full of sharks and massive exploitation of artists, as you probably know. You will need a good lawyer, my friend.'

'Welcome aboard, bra Jack. Consider yourself a financial and legal adviser to the author of the potentially phenomenally successful, record-breaking and, let's be bold enough to say it, the prospective multi-award winning *Twenty-Seven Lonely Years*. Let's drink to our coming success, my friend Jack.'

The two men were frighteningly serious and seemed certain of their project's success. Failure was neither in their vocabulary nor was it in their minds. As they proposed a toast to their dreamt-of success, Peter looked on incredulously.

He was shaken. His friends had total faith in the play which was still to be written. What if it failed? Or, were they on their way to wealth and fame, and was he deliberately disqualifying himself from benefiting together with them, he wondered. He should act while he still had the time.

With an unsure, quivering voice, and hesitantly, he spoke.

'Bra Vic, if you need a director for your play, I am available. Speech and Drama is one of the courses I took in my first year at university!'

In Court

ROSE MOSS

They began as adversaries.

Karl Meyer liked tennis — the dedicated field of action marked with clear white lines that defined where to stand, where to serve, to answer, to run, in a world made human and sane by rules; the dedicated clothes, white, formal and fit for action; the dedicated language, slightly arcane, historic, precise and shared in the comradeship of the courts.

On a Saturday afternoon, when the sun shone crisp on the cleared space of hours, he walked toward the pavilion where friends waited. Birds with melodious notes sang in the trees, bright flowers edged his path. The racket he held at the leather shaft and delicate neck felt poised with promise. 'Hello, Karl.' Jamie, Willem and Herman waved greetings. They offered a few sentences, like wine poured to the ground, and then they were on the court, bouncing, running in the dense dance of air and light, movement and control.

Scraps of conversation survived the trance of concentration, the sky, the net, the lilt of serve, bounce, run, rally. Movement with grace, effort with joy. 'They're destroying the country.' It was always surprising to Karl that Jamie, built so burly and tall, spoke in a thin treble. 'There'll be nothing left here but a ruin,' and Karl knew what he meant. He had driven past burned out oil tanks. The news had too many scenes of rubble, soldiers and the higgledy-piggledy of shoes and shopping bags and hands.

Karl disdained politics as a game not worth its prizes. Too many politicians swelled as their names appeared in head-lines. Time on TV pumped them smooth like brown paper bags schoolboys puff and explode. Bang. The class laughs and the teacher swells with anger.

But the conversation in the tennis pavilion wasn't politics, it was patriotism. Soldiers sent from borders with other countries to borders within the country. Battlefields all over the land. Law and order lost. In milk and wool country, in wine and orchard country, in factory and mine country. Students. Unions. Church groups. Unruly and incessant. Coordinated. Cumulative. The peaceful country of his childhood was now at war on every hand and in every field of action. 'Total onslaught,' Willem said. Willem liked to use phrases readymade by the press and politicians. Karl watched the spotted guineafowl he had brought from his farm pecking on the lawn between beds of yellow, orange and red cannas. The sky, a deep blue Karl had never seen anywhere else in the world, held its peace. Doves were talking to each other in a dialogue one did not have to understand, like the Saturday afternoon talk of servants in the backyard. Karl wanted to be done with war, and talk of war.

Sarah set the tea tray on a bamboo table and departed, the bow of the white doek at the nape of her neck a small bird in flight.

'They're talking about big trials,' Jamie looked meaningful.

'You think that'll do it? I don't.' Herman crumpled his embroidered linen napkin and dropped it in the centre of his plate. 'They spin out these trials for years. As far as I'm concerned, it's just expense and waste.' Herman always liked the role of critic and sceptic. Nothing ventured, nothing lost.

Karl wanted to disagree with the narrow greyness of his safe position. He wanted to say something in sympathy with the passionate cannas and the elegant spotted fowl wandering so calmly among them. 'We've had incompetents handling them. People who don't know how to keep order in court. The case dismissed last week — it was a travesty. People don't see what the country's facing, don't understand what's going on.'

'You think a good judge could keep a political trial short?' Herman scoffed, recognizing Karl's subterranean challenge.

'Why not? If I had one of these cases, I'd have it wrapped up in two months.'

'You would?' He couldn't tell whether Jamie was impressed or jeering with Herman.

'Why not?'

'We all know these lawyers are clever, and paid by foreign money. The international anti-apartheid set.' Jamie's younger brother, a reporter on *Nuus*, had recently joined that set and the chorus of carping that wore out the nation's pride as its critics travelled abroad and made safe names for themselves as foes of apartheid. 'It's the fashionable thing to give money, and from the lawyers' point of view, why not? The longer the trials last the better. Maybe you don't know their tricks, Karl. You've never touched a political case. They know how to make delays last years.'

Karl was almost speechless at this patronizing lesson. 'They wouldn't trick me.'

'Come on, Karl! You don't know anything about politics! The last time you attended a political meeting, you were a student.'

'That was enough.'

A lilt of township jazz wafted from the servants' quarters next door. Saturday afternoon. A time for relaxation and licence.

They were on the courts again before Sarah returned to take the smeared and crummy plates, the bowl where orbs and scabs formed when a careless guest took sugar with a dripping spoon, the delicate stained cups.

On Saturday afternoons, Themba prepared for funerals. He was often asked to talk to the mourners at the house of the bereaved and in the ceremony by the grave. Sometimes it was a long drive to the township. Dusty roads, hovels made of mud and plastic and sheets of naked iron. He honed his spirit to give heart. Let the mourners leave with songs in their mouths, confident in their strength. Victory was certain. Their cause was just. When he spoke and the elders nodded assent, he felt as though his father had just smiled at a good report from school.

His three companions were enjoying the idleness of passengers, joking with each other and talking about who would make what power play at the next regional meeting. Themba listened. He foresaw a harsher future than they. It could only be a few days now before the police came to the office. Or soldiers. Or worse. He listened with professional attention to the youths' speculations. When he spoke for these young men and to them, they would raise their voices to cheer: Viva! Amandla!, resolved to fight until the struggle was won. He must know how to sustain courage in their hearts.

Themba swerved. A mother had pushed her child forward to cross the road. He honked and shouted at her. How dare she set the child in danger before herself! His heart raced as the mother restrained the shoulder of the girl with a pink bow proud in her hair.

Themba's own Magdalena was nine days old today. This morning when he dandled her, her chubby feet, still creased and soft, had danced on his hand like rain. Her toes had not touched the earth yet. When he put his finger in her hand, her fingers furled around his index with a soft bird grasp he would never escape. He looked at Lily with proud despair that they were both caught, servants of love. Lily did not meet his eyes.

She was hiding something from him.

He was feeling unbearably thirsty, tormented by the blue smears of mirage dancing on the road ahead. False promises.

At last week's funeral, police in yellow vans parked under bluegum trees watched the proceedings. Some walked about, talking to each other on walkie-talkies, thinly disguising a disrespect for the dead and the mourners Themba found brutish.

The mourners barely had time to scatter earth on the coffin when the police warning came. Before older people had time to get away, choking smoke. Some of the youths covered their faces with wet rags. They had prepared, sure the police would shoot teargas. They were growing more canny about violence, less careful to avoid it. Experience. Common sense. And forewarned provocateurs? It was getting more difficult to know who was what. He must talk with Kunene about provocateurs pulling mass action toward riot. It had never been easy to inspire hope without turning people's confidence into impatient rage. After last week's funeral, there were two more dead. And after this week's?

He focused on the emotion he wanted to create, concentrating and planning as he had learned in childhood. Teaching gardening, the teacher said, first, you prepare the soil. When the soil is good, everything grows well. When the soil is poor, everything grows sick. What was the right soil here?

The youths in the car must also learn to listen — to old people who remembered the past and had learned wisdom. And to adversaries, to hear how they would act. They must hear people's fears and calm them, hear hopes and bring people together. Their listening and self-command would prise open the jaws of the state and release those mangled by its teeth. Meanwhile, the government was still taking hundreds into detention, and threatening more political trials.

They would take him. The questions were, when? charged or simply detained? If charged, with what? If detained, how long? Some of these political trials took years, and the leadership on the ground was dangerously thin.

He turned off the main road on to a side road. Golden dust followed them like a dwarf pillar of smoke. It would not do to think too long. He saw no way to evade the police with dignity. At first, he and Kunene had avoided the authorities. Dressed like servants and delivery men, they seemed invisible. Rallies and meetings continued. After some, people turned from outrage to stoning and burning. The President accused the organization of treason and blamed it for terrorism. With Kunene, Themba prepared a press release. It warned that the police and army were tormenting people beyond endurance. The government's unjust policies and officials were responsible for the country's violence. Their own organization was non-violent. They did not criticize supporters who became provoked, or turn a back on those in exile and prison who had lost hope in non-violence and chosen armed struggle.

Yesterday, he had gone to the office and worked through a pile of correspondence. They had to show that their organization acted within the law and in good faith. The authorities knew where to find him and Kunene. They would come.

But, holding Magdalena to her own body, Lily would not look at him.

He was thirsty. The road turned toward a low bridge over a muddy stream. Rolls of glistening barbed wire blocked the bridge. A handful of soldiers patrolled with guns tucked between chest and arm. Dry eucalyptus leaves whispered and their shadows skittered along the road. On both sides of the bridge, army vehicles flanked the road. Young men sitting in trucks, under arches of khaki canvas, looked out with bored faces. They would rather be playing soccer or joking with girls. At their age, Themba had spent Saturday afternoons rehearsing with the choir. 'Jesu, joy of man's desiring.' The older choirboys snickered about other joys of man's desiring. Across the muddy stream, behind the glittering wire, a metal sign, Coca-Cola, rusted from the corners where it had been bolted to the wall of a country store.

A small winter wind shuffled through dry grass, husks of a summer past.

At the arraignment four months later, Karl did not notice Themba. His eye was more caught by the publicity director, Kunene, showing off for the gallery. Kunene did not plead a simple not guilty, like the others. He took the occasion to make a little speech on the justice of their cause. That kind of thing would have to be stopped. Also the Anglican priest who insisted on blessing all present before the proceedings could begin. He would not allow them to turn the court into any more of a circus, with policemen at every door, the dock, the bar, the stand and the gallery. The opposition press were relishing the pictures they were getting, subversive suggestions that the unarmed prisoners held the state in terror, while the government, armed but ineffectual, could not withstand the righteous virtue of their cause.

To these reporters, Karl knew, he was the guilty one. He would show them. He would not let this trial run for years, a punishment before sentencing. He would not allow bias on either side. He had gone out of his way to be fair, and they would have to admit it.

Jamie could not understand why he insisted on inviting Nico Veenendal, a known liberal, to assist in judging the facts of the case. Sure there was Ben Marais, a reliable country magistrate, on the other side. Why complicate things? But Karl believed in fairness. Fairness visible to all was the only way in this case.

Nico would bring to the case wisdom, the prestige of his career and the strength of a God-fearing life. Nico was an old friend. He had been Karl's professor in law school. Principles he had instilled still guided Karl in thorny cases. Nico and he respected each other. When Sipho Ncube could not find anyone willing to rent him office space, Karl insisted on fairness — if a qualified lawyer, even a black, wanted to practise in the city he must have chambers like anyone else. Nico was almost the only other lawyer who agreed. They both convinced the municipal authorities to make space available.

Things were better since those days. People were heeding the advice Nico had been giving for years. There was even a new constitution. But now Nico had moved out on a limb again, asking for more. For all. Too fast. Neither blacks nor whites were ready yet.

But Karl had found it good to invite Nico to dinner. After the food and wine, in the mellow time after the meal when Nico accepted a small cognac and swirled the golden liquid with appreciation, contemplating the beauty of the Cape wine country, and of its oaks imparting character to this magnificent brandy, after a silent toast, Karl said quietly, 'Well, Nico, could I invite you to sit with me in the Matthews case?' He saw surprise and pleasure in Nico's eyes and found it good to be reciprocating Nico's invitation, years before, to join the faculty of the law school.

Robed for the arraignment, with pudgy Ben Marais on his left, Karl felt Nico's presence on his right hand like a guarantee of probity, a gold standard. It would be a good trial. The lawyers for the defence were the best in the country. They too were champions who had dedicated their lives to the law. Karl was eager to watch how they handled the rules and the play of wit and stamina that would shape history in this dedicated field. He waited for the ceremonies of opening with bridal nerves. Let the real trial begin.

He did not notice Themba among the twelve defendants in the oak dock.

Themba observed Karl. Seated in the centre of the bench, robed in red as though he dressed every day in fresh blood. The lawyers manoeuvred. The court recessed and met again. Days passed. Weeks passed. In late spring, when jacarandas were blooming outside the prison, Lily brought Lena to court in her carrycot. During the break Themba saw her still sleeping with clenched baby fists, a born revolutionary.

Soon, fallen jacaranda blossoms browned the streets. Summer heat glared from building to building. Themba enrolled at UNISA, but found it difficult to concentrate on economics and sociology. He thought about the case. He thought about Lily. She did not come to court like the other wives and rarely came to prison. A few newspapers noted the first anniversary of their imprisonment. One afternoon Kunene's wife broke off speaking in a low voice when she saw Themba. He thought she looked at him with pity and curiosity.

At Lily's next visit, she would not meet his eyes. He asked gently, 'Are you lonely?'

She bent her head and turned it askance.

'Why don't you look at me, Lily?'

She looked at the hands she held in her lap like an empty boat.

'Where's Lena?'

'Your aunt's looking after her today.'

'Why don't you ever come to court?'

'I can't bear to see you in their power like this.' Her mouth twisted like a child's about to cry.

'Don't come then, Lily darling. Don't come to court. But come here to see me. And let me see Lena. This trial could take years more. I won't know her when I come out.'

The defence lawyers were angry. The judge was denying every petition. He's trying to be fair, Themba thought, appointing Nico Veenendal. He saw that the judge feared the lawyers would outwit him. They knew him as an addict of fine music and fine wine, of books and paintings and Persian carpets, a connoisseur who travelled to Europe every year, a proud man impatient of weakness, a self-made man who believed that every man could make himself. A man comfortable with the way things were, and ready to dismiss critics as ill-informed or ill-willed. He believed they would try to trick him. He would not let himself be tricked.

Themba wanted him to see something else: their cause was just. They would not challenge the law's legitimacy. They would not appeal to a higher law. They would not defy. They would argue, as they had always done, that their organization was lawful and they had always obeyed the law. Let the judge see that they respected the law although they opposed specific laws. The new society they worked for would need the law's protection. Let him see that they were not terrorists, careless of the future. Let him understand that they respected his office and his choice of life. Let him not fear. Even when their cause was won, the new society would need fair judges.

The new society would be Lena's. 'He's got a daughter, hasn't he?' Themba asked.

'She doesn't live at home. She preferred boarding school to living in the same house. Even his wife can't stand to live with him. She spends most of the year in Europe.'

234

In the panelled chamber where they took tea, Nico listened to Karl talking with Ben Marais about the news of the day — more violence, boycotts, strikes, multiple dangers to the state posed by a total onslaught. Ben expressed opinions with rustic certainty, and in a moment alone with Karl, Nico said, 'I'm troubled by that kind of political talk. It might prejudice the case.' Karl flushed deep red until his face seemed as bloody as his robe. When he regained his voice, he said, 'Thank you, Nico. I know how to run a fair trial in my own court.'

Nico dropped the matter until Karl seemed more calm.

A stubble of frost grew daily on winter's jaw. The prosecution presented its witnesses. Themba observed the judge's impatience, straightening his papers with meticulous long fingers, leaning forward to ask the clerk for a reference or exhibit, leaning back to listen. He aimed at a judiciously inscrutable face, but his attention quickened when senior defence counsel spoke. Although they addressed him as M'Lord, it was he who respected them. They disliked him. Every few weeks he brought cake for the defendants. 'Stale leftovers,' the lawyers scoffed. 'The slave-owner wants to feel good,' Kunene said.

Themba also suspected the appearance of generosity, but there was more to the judge than their sceptical disdain admitted. When one of the younger defendants asked permission to train for and run in a marathon, he granted permission with admiration for the young man's spirit. When it came to the law, he thought, this man would be scrupulous and judge by principle. He began to feel some hope. They had always acted within the law.

In the cage of a police van hurtling them towards prison, Kunene said, 'I am not going to say anything to discourage you. You are a man of discernment.' Themba felt trapped as if inside a bullet targeted to kill.

The prosecution finished its parade of witnesses in time for a summer break. The defence asked for a recess. In the panelled room, afternoon sunlight was sloping on to the table of heavy oak where Ben pushed aside the dirty teacups. 'It's a strong case. More than a hundred witnesses.' Ben had been more of a support than Karl had expected, but as he set his briefcase on the table to pack his papers Karl noticed his new double chin and popping buttons. Too many good lunches and teas. Ben should play more tennis. Or something.

'I don't think they'll call the defendants to the stand,' he said. 'A scruffy lot.'

'Oh, I don't know,' Nico said. 'Some make a good impression.'

'You think so?' Karl sounded more amazed than angry.

'I do.' Calm and firm. 'I think they've got a story to tell, and will use the court to tell it.'

Karl remembered Kunene's impudence at the arraignment. Well, he'd shown he wouldn't put up with nonsense in his courtroom. Nico was wrong. 'I bet you a bottle of whisky they won't take the stand.'

That shut Nico up. He looked upset, and left the room.

During the summer recess the pains around Themba's heart increased. They took him to the prison hospital. They prescribed rest. Themba slept during the day and dreamed of times on the run when he drove all night and slept in strangers' houses by day, and of a childhood time of illness when he had slept in the room assigned to his aunt, a servant in a white suburb. The dogs had learned not to bark at him. His aunt interrupted his naps with cups of steaming tea and soup. The mornings were strangely silent, except for the sounds of birds and occasional footsteps and conversations in the concrete courtyard behind the house. It felt like a time of unaccustomed solitude, ease and care. At night, when she slept head to toe on the same bed, he felt her body offering comfort through its simple being and warmth. He dreamed of her now, and took the interruptions of nurses and orderlies with a patience they did not expect from men unless they were very ill, least of all from men reputed to be fiery leaders with dangerous views. When friends brought Lena to visit him, he chuckled at her inquisitive prowling about the ward.

'Like father, like child,' a friend said. 'She wants to know everything that's going on.'

But Themba's appetite for knowledge had dimmed. When the visitors left, he just wanted to sleep in the clean bed of the prison hospital, opening his eyes from time to time to see that the sunlight had moved across the room.

When Jamie asked how the case was going, he did not rub in its length, nearly two years now. Karl was doing a good job. Other high profile cases had either collapsed or were also proceeding slowly. The gang of defence lawyers who took on these cases had mastered the law's delay.

Among the white lines of the courts' defined rectangles, they ran and hit and leaped in harmless play.

Sessions resumed when the late summer fruit was coming in — Hanepoot grapes, Kakamas peaches, grannysmith apples. The defence laid out its argument. The prisoners would take the stand in their own defence.

'I hope you bought that bottle of whisky a while back,' Nico could not resist. 'The price has been going up.' Karl despised him for the weakness of the jab. Next morning he had his clerk take the fifth to Nico. He saw no point in talking.

The case ground on. Themba took the stand and, led by his lawyer, presented his childhood poverty and the indignities inflicted by police, extreme and, he claimed, shared with many; he spoke of listening to his people's pain and of his work to give them political voice, of his faith in eventual victory and negotiation. He spoke modestly and, Karl thought, truthfully. At times, he almost acknowledged that violence might not be avoidable, but denied that his organization was responsible. He looked beyond, to reconciliation in a unified country.

Karl noticed Themba's quiet acknowledging glance when a dignitary entered the courtroom during his testimony, his fingers setting papers straight when the lawyers handed him papers and other exhibits, his meticulous grey suits. The man bore himself calmly, like a leader who knows that others wait for his words. They did. When he spoke, the crowded courtroom fell still. During intermissions, Karl knew, dignitaries crowded round Themba and Kunene as though they were already leaders of the country, their ambitions fulfilled. During sessions, Karl listened and took notes. Occasionally he interrupted, disgusted that the careless prosecution did not understand Themba. They were not dealing with an unprincipled demagogue like Kunene, a communist revolutionary or one who claimed a right to pick and choose which laws to follow, which to break. No. This was a man who respected the law as a safeguard of decent society, concerned for the future. A man they should have on their side.

He dreamed he was playing tennis in the courtroom. Themba was his opponent. Or, sometimes, his partner in games against Jamie and Ben. The walls of the court gave way to walls of forest, like the thick green valleys near the coast where indigenous hardwood hung with vines gave shelter to white rhinoceros, and birds of purple plumage and brilliant song.

He woke, rose and went to the bathroom, but the harsh light hurt his eyes. He drank water from the tap and felt relief. He slept again and dreamed. The dry court was vast as a desert cracked with drought. They played from a tense distance hardly bridged by the ball spinning at their blows. Lizards slipped into the cracks between them. Grass thrust up and spread with spider arms in all directions. The country cracked into rubble, the concrete split like a broken fruit and thick blood poured slowly from its skin.

Themba sometimes thought he would faint on the stand, but he summoned his strength and stood with a straight back like a free man. This was what he had lived for — the right to declare himself and speak for all who spoke through him. They had given him courage and purpose. They had entrusted him with hope, to speak for their old age, their children. He spoke, and saw his words move the prisoners with him, supporters who filled the gallery, the press, diplomats come to represent their countries' concern, church officials come to show God was listening, celebrities drawn into the trial's wake. Even the lawyers. Even the judge.

From time to time the judge lost patience with the prosecution. Couldn't they do a better job? He asked questions, followed up on cross-examination. Sometimes it seemed he wanted to convict. Sometimes it seemed he wanted to protect.

The lawyers noted his interventions. If he found against them, they would appeal, saying he had intervened not like a judge but like a prosecutor.

They kept Themba on the stand for three weeks. Karl developed a slight tick of the cheek under his right eye. His doctor suggested sleeping pills, but Karl refused. He promised to exercise more and sleep more. In his dreams now, women cried out in terror and triumph, guns clapped open the sky, smoke obscured the lines, and the ball became a rock thrown into store windows and schools. Themba, inside, ran like a shadow from classroom to classroom, hunted. It was Karl who was hunting him. He tried to wake but sleep held him. He had to play another interminable set.

Kunene observed his perturbation with a sardonic eye. 'You're giving him nightmares,' he told Themba.

When they turned to Kunene, Themba sat with relief on the foam pad friends had brought for the men consigned to the dock's hard oak. He saw that the judge looked worn. His clerk was doing crossword puzzles at a desk set so far under the bench Karl could not see what he was up to.

Jacarandas were blooming again as the defence summed up. Karl interrupted senior counsel, 'But why didn't they protest the violence? Why? I am really troubled by this question. How do you answer? Wasn't it their responsibility?' It did not occur to him to look at Themba or Kunene in the dock.

Themba's lawyer bowed slightly, as if in courtesy. He had no intention of exposing his clients through unwariness.

The question, he said with deference, raised new issues not proposed in the indictment. He asked M'Lord for time. The law's delay. The trial was now in its third year. Karl was sick of it. He wanted it to end. He wanted to go to Europe, to a concert, to read a book. The country's turmoil had grown ever worse during the years that kept him prisoned on the bench. Although he had stopped reading newspapers — the trial consumed all his time — headlines and brief talk with old friends were enough to show him the trial had accomplished nothing to bring order.

In the panelled room, behind closed doors, Nico said, 'They can't be held accountable for the violence others committed while they were in prison.'

'You've always shown you're on their side,' his irritation erupted.

'Karl, for goodness sake, what are you thinking?'

'I haven't been able to rely on you for anything. You've been partisan from the first. They just can't do wrong in your eyes.'

'You're insulting me, Karl, and I demand an apology.'

'An apology! Are you crazy? I had no idea I was asking for unrepentant prejudice when I invited you to serve as adviser.'

'I demand an apology, Karl.'

'Excuse me!' Karl picked up his briefcase, walked past Nico to the door and closed it firmly. Nico looked at Ben, who avoided his eye.

'What do you have to say about that?'

Portly Ben replied, 'I wouldn't take it too seriously. Karl's tired. We all are.'

'Do you think I've shown prejudice?'

'I'm not going to get into it, Nico.'

'I'm not going to let him get away with it.' Let Ben tell Karl.

It took Karl nearly two months to write the verdict. He worked on the farm. After a rapid walk through the fields each morning, he settled down to writing and did not stop until the late evening radio programmes turned to Schubert and Mozart. From time to time he looked out at the golden sweep of grassland, the peach orchard and the guineafowl pecking in the grass under the trees and felt his love for the country swelling like a wound. He turned his back and returned to the desk and the soft scratching of his pen on paper.

On the day he read the verdict, a man two blocks from the court aimed his gun at blacks in the street, shooting to kill them one by one. A hawker wrestled him to the ground. Although police clustered thick around the court, it took a while to reach the scene. Some recognized the gunman, a past member of the force. When the clerk said, twelve dead, eighteen wounded, Karl covered his eyes with his hands. An involuntary gesture.

Security in the court, tighter than at the arraignment, presented him with a small audience of luminaries. He explained the issues. He cited precedents. He described the historical context. He analysed the evidence and the arguments. He could not read his whole decision in one day. On the third day, after all his explanation and care, the verdict was met with a gasp. What had they expected?

In the panelled room where he did not look at Nico, he did not speak to Ben. He was spent.

He wanted nothing but sleep, blessed extinction, but the telephone rang incessantly. He was astonished. When Jamie called and commented in his treble voice, Karl said, 'I don't understand your reaction.'

'I don't understand you, Karl. Don't you know what's been going on in the country? Don't you read the newspapers or watch the news!'

'You're not asking me to interpret the law to conform with politics are you?'

'Karl, you're a baby.'

If only he could sleep like a baby.

'What's this I hear about Nico bringing a suit against you?'

'Nico's crazy.'

'You've done yourself a lot of harm, Karl.'

He poured himself a whisky and remembered that Themba's younger brother had just died. Cirrhosis. For a moment he looked into a lifetime of pain and numbing drink. He closed his mind's eye. But not before remembering that damned wager with Nico. Whose dark life had he looked into? He drank the whisky like medicine, not caring for the taste.

The President did not call him, but what was it, if not a signal, when he pardoned ten other political prisoners? Karl wondered whether to defy him, and invited Jamie to dinner.

Afterwards, they drank, and talked about the world situation, and the situation of the country.

'You've been too busy with this case to appreciate what's been happening,' Jamie said. He swirled the brandy in his snifter and held it up to the light. 'Best in the world, I'd say.'

Sarah entered quietly, took drained coffee cups from their end tables, asked, 'Anything else, master?' and left them alone in the large house.

'It's the end of an era,' Jamie mused. 'We're in the last years of our history, you know.'

'That's absurd.'

'No man, Karl. From now on, this country's history will be written by those men you had in the dock. Didn't you see it? Didn't you see who the press came to cover? Who the diplomats talked to?'

Karl felt as if his skin had been torn off.

'Bear it in mind, Karl, when you sentence them.'

The President pardoned more political prisoners. Everyone said what Jamie said.

The case went to appeal, and the lawyers brought up his whisky wager with Nico to show that Karl had been prejudiced against the defendants. They brought up his criticism of Nico. The press was publishing stories about hit squads led by police he had trusted and cited in the verdict. By the time the appellate court heard the case, Karl knew how the verdict would go. Colleagues passed him in the corridors and did not stop to talk. Even Jamie could not join him for tennis this year. He was not surprised when the prisoners were released.

He went on with his work — a labour case, a land case, things as they had been before. But now he was alone as he had not been since the bitter days of childhood when other boys scoffed, he kept his nose stuck in books and no girls.

The prisoners moved into the centre of public life again, their pictures under newspaper headlines, their opinions in interviews on the television still controlled by the state they had defied.

Karl planted oak trees on his farm. Let them know, after a hundred years, that he had done something right. Then he saw a programme that decried planting imported trees instead of fine indigenous varieties. Sometimes Karl considered work in Europe or the States, but these were just dreams. His tic grew more constant. His doctor told him to drink less and to rest, but work was still a comfort, so he ignored the doctor. Violence throughout the country multiplied, and now it seemed no one could control it, not even those who had invited it. Karl planned a rose garden to replace the tennis court.

Themba wondered how the man who had condemned him saw things now. At odd moments in the car, in the bathroom, he found himself thinking about Karl. He wanted to speak with him. The wish grew. He did not want to answer questions about why he wanted to see Karl. They would not bump into each other in the ordinary course of things. Where then? The wish slipped into darkness, like the wish to spend more time playing with Lena.

Karl threw the invitation into the wire wastebasket under his desk. A poplar's uneasy leaves by the streambed caught his eye — silver coins slipping through merchant hands. All judges in the area must have received the invitation. An opportunity to hear leaders newly returned from exile or released from prison, on the judiciary of the future. He had heard enough and feared the worst. Kangaroo courts, show trials, venial and political judges, officials running petty tyrannies, indulging personal tastes, sometimes perverted . . . The rule of law would follow the sad script of the rule of power. A few lawyers of the recent generation who had protected defendants with the rule of law might stave off darkness for a year or two, but even they would find that politicians they had protected, once in office, understood opportunism, not principle.

Silver leaves shuffled through gambler fingers quicker than the eye. The poplar seemed still untouched by drought. Doves called from branches that showed no sign yet of the drought branding the continent from north to south. A little wind rose a few feet, twisted dust round itself like a dog making its bed, and lay down. The doves had nothing to say. A dry time. A dying time. If he went . . . He did not need to court the simulated sightlessness of colleagues who would not care to be seen talking to him. He turned to other letters in the meagre post.

Falling into a nap after dinner, he swung his racket to meet the ball's parabola. In a quiet court white rules held them until the lines inverted like photographic negatives turning opaque transparent, light dark, dark light. In a pliant, electric game he served, and ran, and rallied in a space wider than the sky, waiting for the deep hit of ball on string, still, hold, swing, hit, his opposite dancing to the same beat, run, leap, swing, hit, deuce, love, love, deuce, deuce, game.

He woke to the discomfort of his body slumped in its chair, his neck cricked and a moist stain on the cushion. His teacup was gone. Sarah had taken it while he was collapsing on himself with open mouth a-dribble like an old man. He walked quickly to the bathroom by his study, washed sleep out of his face and found work on the labour case he must decide by the end of the month.

About to set the cap back on his pen before a nightcap of brandy, he pulled the wire basket from under his desk, found the invitation, accepted, tore a stamp from its sheet, pulled it over the damp sponge and fixed it in its corner. He screwed the pen closed, no word in his mind. He could have been asleep, walking.

He bore the evening's slights with numb obedience, colleagues who did not greet him, a past clerk who waved from a distance and took no nearer step, a moment when both the barrister on his right and the magistrate on his left were turned to other conversations, and he saw himself talked about at the other end of the table — a glance in his direction before a bite of fish confirmed something, a nod and answering grin, another bite and chew. He felt immune, a patient under local anaesthetic who sees the surgeon expose and cut his intimate thigh without hurt, only nonchalant curiosity.

After the icecream and speeches, the guests moved to the hotel lounge for coffee and brandy. Small groups settled in armchairs. A few lingered near the cups and urn of coffee.

He saw Themba in the flux of people. He had put on weight. As Themba turned from the table, a steaming cup in his right hand, Karl caught the moment. 'How are you?'

Themba stopped and looked at Karl. 'No, things are good. I'm very busy.' He moved another step away from the table.

'You're active again, I see. I expected it. You'll be playing a big role in the country's future.'

'Yes. You said so in the verdict.' Neither moved now. 'I appreciated that.'

'You understand, I had to sentence you. I did think you broke the law.'

'No, man. I thought you were struggling.'

'I was.'

They fell silent as though they had lifted a heavy beam together and now stopped to rest. In the uneven knit of conversations and ting of teaspoons on saucers, a quiet ring around them felt like the moment Karl had seen himself discussed. He looked at a silver bowl on the table piled high with decorative fruits and realized he was waiting for Themba to take the lead.

Someone brushed by them. Themba said, 'Your timing was unlucky.'

'It wasn't really my timing.' He was thinking of the lawyers, and the headlong rush of events he had not seen, catching him blind.

Themba heard unaccustomed helplessness, bitterness. A course of self-destruction. 'No. History was moving its own way.'

Seeing something, Karl recognized, beyond the range of his own eyes. 'I heard you were ill again in prison. Are you better now?'

'No, all that's over. I'm fine.'

Karl could not stop. 'They say conditions on the Island have improved a lot.'

Themba, also aware of people watching, heard Karl's pleading undertone and laughed sadly. 'Who says so? You should go yourself and see. Spend a night in a cell. Eat cold mieliemeal and samp on a tin plate. Live without rights, for a day. Even one. A judge should know these things.'

Karl did not see how to continue.

Themba did not want to end with rebuke. 'This time, yes, the authorities were trying to treat us right. I mean, the leaders, not ordinary prisoners. They're still in misery. But we had newspapers. TV. Books. Sports.' He smiled, knowing his man. 'Kunene taught me to play tennis in prison.' He laughed.

'I play tennis,' Karl heard his own confessing, astonished.

'I know.' Their eyes met. 'My wife left me, you know. She couldn't take the fear, the long time alone.'

'I heard.' He raised his eyes to Themba's. 'You've got a daughter. Did she go with her mother?'

'No, I've got custody, but Lena's still learning who I am.'

Karl nodded, grave. 'She lives with you?'

'I'm too busy. Too much travelling. She's with Kunene's children.'

Karl did not want to talk about Kunene. Voices from other conversations flew against the net of attention between the two of them, and Themba's stance showed Karl what he had not seen in court — careful listening, the

246

wellspring of his activism. As though Themba could answer and speak for him too, he bared his fears. 'What do you see happening in the country? There's all this violence. Do you think . . . How do you think it'll come out?'

Themba did not answer. Wary of his recent adversary? Then, 'I don't know. The younger people don't always listen to older leaders now. Our organizations were almost destroyed while we were in prison. We lost leadership on the ground, where it matters.'

A plum in the silver bowl, Karl saw, had ruptured and was oozing, broken by its own ripeness. He straightened his shoulders. 'Will you be able to bring order into the situation?'

Again Themba paused.

'Well, your silence answers me.'

Taking a step away from the table to show he was ready to end their exchange, Karl gestured towards the fruit and a platter of cake.

'No, thank you.' As friendly as though the half-hidden exchanges of sympathy and accusation had never happened, Themba continued, 'My doctor says this must go.' He pointed to his shirt stretched tight, like Ben's. 'More exercise, he says.'

The roomful of talk fell away from Karl. 'Would you . . . I, er . . . We could . . . Well, why don't you come over . . . We could play a game of tennis.'

'Thank you, but, you know, my schedule's really heavy.'

Burning Dog

PETER WILHELM

Where the land fell away in smooth green folds from the house to the river, Derek enclosed the horses. They ran free in a green triangle: the black horse, the dappled horse, and the chestnut horse. Jill loved to wander down to the wire fence and feed them, plucking up tufts of grass and holding out the sweet ends for their loud chewing mouths. When it was misty their big shapes clattered towards her alarmingly and she feared being bitten, they were so greedy.

The enclosure was successful. There were no stables but it was not difficult to carry saddles and such from the house, so they could offer riding for the guests. Jill believed in offering a wealth of choice for guests; she did not accept Derek's simpler hope that they would all make their way into the great dark cavern that was the pub and drink away their expensive hours listening to his tales. She reckoned it was not always misty, it did not always rain, the snow had its own attractions.

But Derek was right: few guests rode and she would always find a small crowd in the pub after Derek unlocked the door at eleven each morning.

She wondered if the horses were lonely. Sometimes she took them apples and they were enormously pleased.

She had little time to consider her own loneliness. Each event and circumstance which led to their possession of the farm was logical, but it was the logic of dream: their eight-year marriage had begun with the hope of such an outcome, built on the powerful base of his prowess. 'I can't play cricket for ever,' he had said. 'One day we'll go to the countryside and run a hotel.'

Now that they had the farm, on the expanses of which his dream had unfolded, she knew she had ceased wanting it.

She had ceased wanting Derek. His sly infidelities and drinking had seen to that. On the day he had come to her, tremulous, and told her the outcome of his discussions with the bank, she had been planning to leave him. As he spoke, her desire to leave fell into that blank well of inanition he discerned and valued in her: the character she had presented to him when she was twenty-four and he thirty-two. His amiable, leathery face was insouciant then and now; he had a cloudy eminence that dazed her.

Returning from the paddock she skirted the oblong pond he had constructed and stocked with trout. This was a failure; the lie of the land was wrong and subterranean seepage from the concrete washroom brought a rainbow shimmer to the water's surface and poisoned the fish with warmth and detergent. They lay belly-up in the shallows, slimy and swollen, snared in the black rot of twigs. The pond had the look of death. Jill's retriever Callie, coppery and fierce, protective of children, shook her fine head in disgust and loped away through the waving lace of a weeping willow tree.

Derek had such power when he took the bat, he shivered with it. His lithe form in white fulfilled the image of captaincy and he played boldly in the sun. When he was forced into error he raised his glove and struck his forehead and the crowd would breathe laughter. How could you help but love him?

Jill lay in bed reading, or attempting to read, troubled by the laughter and roaring from the pub. Each day exhausted her: her duties were so far-ranging and repetitive, so much a pushing against the intractable facts of the hotel and Derek alike, both unwilling or unlikely to be tamed, regressing to older patterns. There was a horrible tale of the previous owner — that debt and isolation had driven him mad and he had set fire to the main house, incinerating his family, and fled to the river's edge where the police had found him crawling in mud and taken him away. No one would speak of this history; the charred walls were silent. For years the place had remained desolate until Derek had heard of it and secured it.

The enforced intimacy of the first year — the year of rebuilding and planning, working in a shell — had been dreadful but exhilarating. She would never believe Derek's terms of endearment again, too much damage had been done; but she had seen him happy at times and believed this might restore the marriage. She was one to find fault with herself for the estrangement that had corroded their life. Now she could hold him tightly against the night.

But since the guests had begun to come — mainly parties of German or Swiss tourists, coarse, basic people — the management of the farm fell into distinct domains, his and hers: hers to tend the kitchen and the servants, the logistics of cleaning rooms and changing linen; his the flow of drink and sociability, telling all the old stories and jokes, florid and pointing at the triumphs commemorated in newspaper cuttings behind glass of which he was the absolute focus. When she went into the pub she caught sidelong glances and felt herself infringing on his mastery: the laughter grew a little less until she left.

He would not discuss finance. That, too, was her domain, the ledgers and headaches, fending off the bank. And his follies were so expensive: the ruined fish pond, the extravagant food he ordered by telephone when he was in the mood, the free rounds in the pub. She saw the cash drain away; the iridescent surface of the dead pool had the precise corrupt and dazing effect of their bank balance. When she raised the issue he flared and frightened her. It was like the time she had heard him on the phone arranging an afternoon liaison with some woman and, seeing Jill listening, let something savage show through his charming eyes.

Now he drank so late with strangers that when he crawled into bed with her, all slippery and stinking of whisky, she lay rigid with her back to him.

'As long as everything's all right in bed, it'll work out!' her mother had advised at the time of their troubles; but now she saw this as a stupid and modish thing to say, something taken from the glitzy magazines her mother had forced upon her in adolescence instead of the truth. She thought of sex as something very difficult to do even with someone you loved, and frightening when Derek was consumed by rage, drink, self-pity and remorse.

And he smoked all the time: endless cigarettes like fuses in his soft mouth.

That was why when the rushing, guttural clatter of the pub diminished around midnight, and she knew Derek would soon mount the stairs and weave towards her side, she carefully marked her place in the book, laid it beside the bed and switched out the light. She lay unmoving as if deeply asleep.

Of course they were not alone. Even in the dreariest months someone who had heard of the hotel would make his way by car through the steep white oceanless cliffsides and green feathery fields of this remote area. Finding them. Perhaps he was a solitary traveller wanting a bed for the night and Derek would be restless, sipping whisky, yearning for company. More often there were people he could entertain, people who had heard of him.

Above all, there were the servants. They came with the land, had always been here in their decisive, eerie way. There were perhaps a dozen of them under the dominance of a patriarch: and each had devolved upon him or her a precise area of labour, field or house, washroom or flower bed. At the end of each week Jill paid an agreed sum to the patriarch which he would dispense in turn to the extended family in proportion to their value in his private calculations. She always felt breathless at the operation, handing over the cash, seeing him count the notes. She felt she was being judged and wanted to please him. They had always been here, it seemed.

Yet the sounds of Saturday night laughter and music from the cluster of huts where the servants lived estranged her even further than the boozy riot of the pub. She and Derek held only the authority the unknown servants gave; and the authority might in an unknown circumstance be taken away.

In the games room she showed a solitary child how to trace the patterns of a magnetic field. Over a plain white piece of paper she sprinkled iron filings and then held the magnet beneath the paper; and the filings rearranged themselves, following the invisible lines of force. But the child grew bored and there was nothing to explain. There was a lack of children here.

She took apples to the horses. It was July, the day cold and threaded with grey murk. There was no way of telling whether the greater sky had taken on that pearly, leaden colour which meant it would snow. Callie was with her, her fur silvery with wetness. Jill stood at the fence and looked for the black horse, the dappled horse, and the chestnut horse. Huddled in wool with awkward hair, she called out to them, making hollow sounds with her tongue, wishing to furnish comfort.

Callie began to whine. It was a strange, scraping sound she gave out, almost a high mutter. 'Sshh! Callie!' said Jill, but the dog crawled between her feet and would not be still. Jill looked about: the mist was close now, denser than before, and she could not see the horses. Listening, she heard the blood in her head and far, stony sounds.

The sounds were those of some heavy, hard stuff like nail or hide being moved uneasily over rock: a shifting, pausing, laborious pattern. And the sounds were distant, perhaps down at the river at which the field ended, a marshy place where the grass grew high and black-shaded on its inner blades. The grass cut flesh readily.

Jill believed she could hear the trickling of water over stone, but concentrating on this sound made the other sounds dissipate; and she could not be certain she had heard anything.

She called out to the horses by name. A terrible sense of isolation seized her, something like the anxiety of waiting for Derek to mount the stairs but sharper, far less easily understood. The misty swirls around her drew off meaning like air: air taken from her lungs: a violent appropriation. Within the sphere of her vision objects sprang into unique prominence, stones and twigs and stumps of grass, the fallen apples she had brought. She crouched to cradle the whimpering dog and smelt burnt fur. Callie's fur flared, its coppery colours bent in wrong ways and under it the flesh twisting in agony; she howled high and pitiably with straining eyes.

The dog was on fire.

Jill breathed in blue flames and in a spate of horror hurled the writhing animal away from her; broken, it fell back and where it lay shuddering seemed to make the grass hiss and steam.

The palms of her hands were burnt; the front of her white sweater was barred with soot in the shape of what she had held. What was left of Callie rose up on twisted legs and over all the beast's body a rippling, crushing sequence of waves moved back and forth; and the legs gave way and she fell again, head shaken violently from one side to another. The sound she made was not in nature.

Jill's mouth filled with a hideous taste and she screamed. Where was help? She broke away from the scene and ran to the house, grass stalks slapping her body. Hysteria was swollen in her, she could scarcely see.

'Derek! Derek! Help!'

He was stoking the fire in the pub, bent over in livid light, a dark formless mass: the sound of steel on red pulsing coal like the sound in the mist. But his face lurched at her with concern and his arms enfolded her. He somehow lit a cigarette on his way to her, match flaring. Where did he hold it when he held her?

She had an impression of huge, pink Germanic faces aghast in rows: the drinkers of the cold afternoon taking her in with discord.

'It's Callie, something horrible's happened to her!'

'Wait, sit down, have a drink, take it easy.'

'Callie,' she insisted, 'you must look, please look.'

He murmured to the group and they seemed to look

away. She had a glass of brandy in her hand; drank it. Inappropriately, she thought: *He's embarrassed. He's trying to keep the business running.* Callie had loved children; but there were no children here now.

Later, in the room, in bed, she was stared at in a distancing way. He was not in bed: he was on his feet, swaying, exuding a kind of insistent male rationality. He had searched, found some marks, nothing more. Callie, he said, must have gone after a rat or a snake. Try as she might, she could not describe what she had seen, not quite tell the truth, *Callie was on fire.* Something horrible had happened to the dog; she had to repeat that, chattering and stained with feverish unreality. And the horses — had he seen the horses?

'Christ, Jill, it was dark out there! I couldn't see more than a few yards. But even if something attacked Callie, the horses are so much bigger, they can take care of themselves. Are you sure you didn't see anything else? Another dog, maybe?'

'No, no, we've been over that.'

Solicitous, but a little cold, deflected from duty, he came to see her from time to time, bringing more brandy. From somewhere he had grasped the idea that brandy was medicinal but she accepted the glasses he gave her because she was numb and drunk, wavering in and out of sleep, and brandy helped her to stay there.

Awakening abruptly in the dead of night to utter clarity of mind and unspeakable thirst, she had vividly in mind a tumult of sexual behaviour from which she flinched: but it was a memory of her and Derek earlier, at the end of the night when he came up the stairs and she was not asleep. The memory was clear and shocking, a rare, uninvited paroxysm of acts and penetrations. Now she felt on fire, but it was shame and in the bathroom when she examined her nakedness in the mirror she could no longer be sure it had happened: and if not, why the pain and wretchedness, the intimacy of violation?

Her hands would heal slowly.

They entered the time of the emigrating birds: across the stone-like, impassively bleak sky — a coarse, blue fabric — silent formations appeared, moved and disappeared, not so much sliding down to the horizon as they followed the curvature of the earth, as maintaining their elevation. When Jill stared after them, her eyes betrayed her and she was unable to reckon them as either immeasurably high and distant or as tiny eddies or echoes, motes in her eye.

She went into the pub, early one morning, in search of a pen, and found Derek already there with a guest. The air was dense with cigarette smoke, but the men were not drinking though they were amiably close, Derek's face white in the gloom, smiling, attentive. The other man was big, looming in black leather that folded the light away.

Jill greeted them and searched a drawer, took a pen. The visitor's voice was deep and pebbly. He said: 'So you have good business here, ja?' and Derek agreed, and the man, an Austrian, or perhaps a Swede, went on: 'And maybe soon a new government?'

'Maybe.'

'That is good, too. I mean for business. Don't you agree?'

Derek watched Jill; his tongue flicked out, back. 'What do you mean, exactly?'

'Well, you see, in my country, in Europe, some say that your changes, your reforms, will make more conflict. But my opinion is that in Africa nothing ever changes, only the public relations.'

The men laughed. Their cigarettes steamed. Jill was out of the room.

She discovered that Derek had become a compulsive gambler. Once or twice a month he would be away on 'business': it was as vague yet precise as that. Certainly, there were reasons for him to be away. There was an aged mother he had put away in a retirement village on the coast and she would phone them in desperation, forever losing things, losing her memories and her mind. Derek needed to see her. And he needed to go to the big towns to buy hardware or replacements for the many things that failed in the hotel; and to speak to bankers and such.

She suspected him of infidelity. But when he returned she could tell at once it wasn't so: he was clean in that department. Something shaded his accounts of his travels, but she assumed, with a certain logic, that it was just the forgetfulness of drunkenness.

He must have been diverting his own credit card accounts from the mass of bills with which Jill dealt. For when she found that she had opened one, happily ripping it into view with a fingernail, the warnings of overshot limits and legal threats were recorded for months past. She had never seen anything like this before, this history, and she had seen and scrutinized his hotel bills, reading those simple statements for evidence of another woman and not, of course, finding it. But now she found that there were days when he had been far away, in a neighbouring state, and had repeatedly drawn cash from a casino cashier.

The sums were staggering.

They had no money whatsoever left. The credit card account was a black hole into which everything would eventually fall: the farm, their possessions, their life. This, then, was his secret.

It was perhaps ten in the morning when she found this out. Derek was still upstairs; the servants had seen to breakfast; and it was not yet time for the pub to be opened and the beer to flow. She put the evidence down and went outdoors, finding the wind bitter. Streaks of dirty snow lay in the lee of trees. But it was clear, the sun starry and consuming in the lower third of a sky the exact colour of Derek's eyes when he looked at her in lamplight: a fragile, smoky blue tinged with red. The three horses were on the far side of the field, the river side.

Around the corner of the hotel three Germans paraded: heavy father, heavy mother, a little boy with mad eyes who looked like Hitler. They greeted her and she waved, hobbling down an incline to a small forest, junk pine, seeking secrecy. Behind a tree she leaned back and found herself drenched with fear and sweat; a deep grief assailed

her, for Callie, for herself. She was near the place where —
memory was evasive — the dog had seemed to burn. Now
she clutched her stomach with revulsion and was sick, her
mouth full of strands of coffee and half-turned cereal.

'You fucking fool! How could you do it?' Her chest was
so sore and she was so miserable she could hardly speak.
What was she to do?

The wind rose up and pushed strands of mist into the forest:
each sound, each falling branch and scuttle of a small
animal was hollow. Big birds with dramatic feathery crests
clambered through leaves and rapped the bark for insects.
Tap, tap: anybody home? The beaks were like steel on stone.

Frosty flecks swarmed in the air, not rain, not snow,
something between the two. Jill sat on a mat of pine needles
with her back against a tree as the day became dark and
yellowish, sunlight touching tips of leaves and the edges of
spiderwebs slung like parachutes into the breeze to trap
drifting flies, making them intense and silvery. Everything
that was green became a darker, avocado colour, brown
stems and bark pale against it.

She must have drowsed, for abruptly she was aware of
the declension of light, the advent of that mid-afternoon
waning of the force of heat which was the time to stack logs
on the fire and stoke it in a shower of exploding sparks;
time for the guests to sleep off the long effects of after-lunch
drinks, port and ale drunk with Derek whose red eyes
would now be sunk in exhaustion. At this hour the hotel
would always be still, each cabin closed off against the
swirling mist.

Jill had difficulty rising. Her hands were painful, fingers
stiff but curved in where she had been burnt, as if the
burning had been a lifelong wound, as she had feared in the
days of healing. Then as now she fought a stifling frustration — a profound inarticulateness — because no one
would listen to her, or did not wish to hear what she had to
say. She had seen the big Aryan heads of guests sway in
commiseration with Derek when she tried to describe what
she had seen; so now she merely smiled and shrugged when

they asked about the blistering. She was the mad wife of the owner.

'I'm a mess!' she thought, aware of the piquant, silly-girlish tone, as of some schoolgirl who had inadvertently lost her virginity and, what is more, was late getting home. She must have penetrated deeper into the woods than she remembered for she found herself in an open mossy depression ringed by tall gently swaying trees, and could not remember ever having been here before. A small burr of voices came to her, and sounds of (it must be) washing; evidently she was near the washroom. The ground she stood on was marshy and where water oozed into view it had a corrupted chemical sheen like that of the dead pool.

She followed the lure of voices and stood in shadow looking at the square concrete washroom, like a big grey stone with holes in it, windows like eyes. With the dark upright doorway the windows formed a face. There were two or three people inside, invisible servants. Jill caught the rustle of movement. Where the land was open, each stone, root and stalk was luminous, stained with unusual light.

She was about to step forward into the clear space of grass and low bushes that lay between her and the wash-room when she saw that not only did the washroom resemble a face, it was a face and from its mouth emerged a long, fibrillating tongue, low down and lank across the earth, and this brought such an onrush of fear that her head pulsed and she fell back into shadow as if struck by an immense hand.

The hotel was hushed, utterly. She stood in the entryway and looked at the tidy but somehow brown and old rooms that led off from here: the dining room and lounge with its padded green chairs; a games room that was seldom used, magazines and jigsaw puzzles stacked on rickety tables for the vanished children; the well-lit little room with a bay window that she used to do accounts and where this morning she had opened Derek's credit card account. All this was new, newly-built or restored, but it struck her as being disgusting: an attempt at disguise. There was a more ancient presence here.

In the bedroom she found Derek asleep on his back. She might have found him pitiable — his face bloated with unconscious terror and hidden things — but the last leavings of her love stirred her to rage instead.

She drew up a chair and sat looking down at him, the leathery, wrinkled look of him as he entered middle age with the gallantry of failure deferred or bought off with a thousand tales or misalliances of which she would never know; the veins in his neck and big hands pulsing too rapidly, floridly; and his flesh actually dragged off him by gravity so that his face, big and grey, was shapeless and had no resemblance to the tall, shining eminence he had presented to her heart so long ago. The corruption of intent remained: that to which she had given herself.

Beside the bed, the overflowing ashtray and the drained whisky glass with a dead fly in it. She had a vision of them, years hence, perhaps in some filthy coastal room in a dying town where he taught schoolboys how to play cricket.

She had believed in the possibility of change, its reality. But she remembered the iron filings scattered over a sheet of paper and the magnet held beneath it so that the flecks of iron formed into the shape of the lines of invisible force and were held in that pattern for ever unless the magnet was removed and they became random and scattered again; until, putting back the magnet, the lines of force would appear again, the old pattern unchanged. In nature itself.

There was something in each one's soul that would for ever shape identity with its lines of force, dark and compelling, for ever and ever. Here lay Derek, so shaped, reverting to intrinsic decay; and beyond him the whole lie of the land, unalterable, not theirs.

One by one, she began to light the matches.

A Place of Killing

ANDRIES WALTER OLIPHANT

Come, then, my men,
To pluck wild garlic,
To pluck wild garlic,
And on our road,
The fragrant-scented
Orange tree in flower,
Its topmost twigs
Withered by perching birds,
Its lowest branches
Snapped and killed by men.
Emperor Ōjin, AD 710-94

I raise my head apprehensively. The cloudless sky is bright indigo. A fierce but invisible sun spreads its light over the edges of the staggeringly high outer wall, infusing the area with an intense luminosity. Behind me the lower inner wall rises. The sky slants downwards as it passes over me and is blocked out by the buildings rising behind the inner wall where I am kept.

My arms dangle at my sides. My feet huddle together in the soft grass. The slip in which my body is wrapped hangs motionless from my shoulders. Out here between the high walls it is windless. From this courtyard I watch the square chunk of tilted sky. I wait for a bird or cloud to traverse it or ruffle it but nothing happens. Eventually my neck tires. I have to drop my head and cast my eyes downward.

The kikuyu spreading out around me absorbs the light, tinting my shadow and the lower part of my body in deep saturated green. My bare feet are happy in the soft grass. The edge of the garden is lined with shrubs, pampas grass and flowers. A botanical scent fills the air.

I stand at the centre of this walled-in space with its hypnotic tranquillity. I listen intently, like one expecting to hear the earth's cranking as it revolves around its axle. Faintly, from afar, or from the earth's depths, a sound rises. It evokes the squeaks of a wheel faltering as it turns around a rusted shaft.

Then I see them. A flock of guineafowl as they emerge cautiously from the shrubs and flowers. They come out into the sun, moving slowly, their dropped hindquarters swinging rhythmically as they call to and fro, assembling in groups all around me. Some peck the grass for seeds and insects. Others ruffle and stroke their feathers with their yellow culmens. Here and there some bask in the warmth of the sun. Light plays over the white and pale blue spots in their dark plumage.

I listen to their atonal calls. I am pleased by the fact that they are not afraid of me. Their indifference affords me a closeness which enables me to listen carefully to their muted calls. I study and absorb it until the sound echoes through my body. I listen beyond the surface effect of melancholia which they evoke in me, suspecting a deeper but as yet elusive and indeterminate message in the rasping consonants. I am alert to tragic possibilities in the calls of these terrestrial birds. I try to isolate each sound before linking it to the pattern of their calls. Its meaning, which escapes me, I sense lies just below my full awareness. This quest for meaning drives me in hours of wakefulness and sleep.

I am about to kneel in the grass, to listen more intently, when a door, squeaking on its hinges, opens and shuts. Startled, I sit up. The coarse fabric of the blankets and the hard surface of the bed remind me where I am.

I am temporarily blinded by the glare of the unshaded bulb suspended from the low ceiling. Day and night it remains on, obliterating my sense of time. Since my transfer to the 'pot', as this place in the final stage of my journey is known, I am not permitted to leave its confines. Neither for exercise nor for fresh air. I am kept indoors, shut away from the world. I know that a final visit has been scheduled but I do not know when it is due to take place nor do I know whom I will be seeing.

I get meals three times a day. I shape my tenuous sense of time around these. But monotony of bad food and my sudden loss of appetite have shattered even this rudimentary frame of reference. Time lies in ruins in the depths of my flickering consciousness. Afloat in this tiny space, I brace myself against the demands of a sudden and unexpected intrusion.

I rub my eyes and stare in the direction of the door. The hazy outlines of a figure loom in front of me. As I leave the bed the figure speaks.

'Sorry to wake you. But it's long after breakfast. I didn't expect to find you in bed.' It is a woman's voice. I squint involuntarily as my eyes struggle to adjust to the glare. An ageing woman in a uniform stands at the door with a friendly and benevolent expression on her face. The smile tucked into the corners of her mouth enhances the expression of kindness written over her face. When she speaks again this impression is confirmed by the relaxed and jocular tone she strikes.

'Well, that's one of the privileges of being in the pot. You can sleep for as long as you like, you can make as much noise as you wish, in a word, you can do just as you please.' I am drawn by the playfulness in her voice. Then she bends and places a flat, slab-like object on the floor and unfurls a tape measure.

'The only requirement is that you cooperate with us over these last few days. We need your weight and your measurements.' She articulates this with such emphasis that it belies the friendly smile, now clearly rippling her ageing face.

I am struck by her use of the collective pronoun and the emphasis placed on it. Did 'us' refer to herself and me? Or did it include the corporate identity of the institution? I am not sure, but when she speaks again her tone is considerably colder.

'Will you please undress and get on to the scale.' She points to the flat object on the floor. I look at her and hesitate. Suddenly her attitude becomes rigid and commanding. 'Come on. Don't just stand there. We don't have all day. This, after all, is not a social visit. I am not the chaplain. If you need one, put in a request. Undress!'

The harshness in her voice matches the surroundings. I look hard into her face. Her smile has become a grimace.

I remove my slip while she paces the confined space, humming a familiar tune to the beat of her heels. When I approach the scale in the loose-fitting, bulky bloomers issued to me, she intervenes.

'No, off with it!' She points at the bloomers. I oblige without any sense of outrage or humiliation. Over time I have become accustomed to this. I do not feel stripped of my dignity when I am instructed to bare myself to my captors. At first anger and agony overcame me. My hands always moved to cover my sex. However, once I had overcome my shame, on which their instruction to strip is premised, I discovered the power of accepting my body.

I remove my bloomers and step on to the scale. I look down over my chest. I see the swellings of my breasts. The dark, pointed nipples are so close to my face, if I wanted to I could put a hand under one breast, lower my head, and raise it to my mouth. Through the gap between my breasts I see my flat belly and the tuft of hair where my thighs separate. My feet, far below, are placed squarely on both sides of the aperture where figures spin past a needle and come to settle on the number thirty-five.

'You are rather thin, considering your race.' She mutters this as if to herself and jots down my weight on a form clipped to a board. 'Good, now let us see how tall or rather, how short you are.' She holds out the tape measure.

I step off the scale and stand erect. She bends down behind me and inserts the end of the tape under my right heel before raising the rest of it to the crown of my head. I feel the tape touching my buttocks and the back of my shoulders.

'That will be all for today,' she says and jerks the tape from under my foot, jots a figure on to the form before rolling up the tape. 'We'll be back same time tomorrow,' she says with the old friendly smile back on her face. She picks up the scale and is about to leave.

'Why did you measure me?' I ask, in a strange-sounding voice.

She looks at me thoughtfully before replying: 'To ensure an effective drop.' She leaves and locks the door.

I dress and am alone again. I think about her parting words, wondering why she took my weight without any clothes on. One must surely be clad for the occasion? Or do they hang one naked? I have heard stories so grisly that I do not wish to recount. But I can't recall whether the victims were dressed or not. I have no fear, but a feeling of immense loneliness overcomes me. I move to a corner with my back against the wall and slide on to my haunches. I stare into the empty space in front of me.

I am out in the inner court. The guineafowl are waiting for me. I look up into the heavens. The sky is spotlessly blue. The grass under my feet is soft. I walk among the birds, my slip billowing with the movement of my legs. When I reach a group of fowl sitting close to each other in the sun, I kneel and observe them from close by. They sit quietly and undisturbed as if they do not see me. Am I invisible?

I see the red flesh moulded over their crowns and the ochre-coloured casque rising from it. The blue rubber-like flesh loosely draped around their napes, cheeks, necks and throats. I look into the eyes of an old hen basking in the sun. I see the sensitive and wrinkled skin of her eyelid, the light-brown eyeball motionless in its socket, the dark iris shining in the sun. Right at the centre of the eye the microscopic aperture of the pupil enlarges under my gaze. I am transfixed.

The river with its wide banks, sunk deep into the earth, is almost dry. The stream running over the smooth stones is barely audible where we walk hand in hand through the rooigras under bare trees. We hardly speak.

The dry grass bristles in our wake. Then something snaps underfoot. We stop and look, discovering that he has stepped on the dry bones of a bird. He kneels, picks it up and carefully tries to reconstruct the broken skeleton.

I watch him. His lanky frame is bent into a triangle where

he sits. The light falling through the branches plays over his dark face which is held still as he concentrates. I see the fire in his light-brown eyes. I reach out and stroke his head, his neck, his face. He smiles as his breathing becomes audible. He laughs, puts the skeleton aside and embraces me.

I recline in the crisp grass, cradling him in my arms and with my body. His lips are soft. The moisture from his mouth mingles with the thick, lustful juice welling from the walls of my mouth, covering my tongue. When he enters me gently I see the sky: an unmade bed strewn with crumpled sheets. I groan and sink my finger into his smooth buttocks. He sighs. The sheets float through the slate-blue heavens.

We stir again when the grass rustles. There is a commotion in the underbrush. We sit up, startled. A dog barks close by and suddenly around us we hear shrill calls and wings flapping as crested guineafowl fly up to the overhanging branches.

'Pheasants?' he slurs, close to my drowsy head.

'No, they are guineafowl,' I reply.

'Oh, yes. Impangele,' he says as he rises unsteadily, pulling up his pants and looking up into the trees. 'The white spots over their bodies make them appear as if they have been struck by tiny hailstones.'

We look at the birds in the swaying branches. It is quiet, the dog we heard has gone away. He looks at me. We smile.

We get up and wander through the dry veld towards the edge of the township which is shrouded in the late afternoon smoke rising from a multitude of chimneys. It will soon darken. We step up our pace.

A sharp ache shoots up my spine. I must have dozed off squatting in the corner after she left. I am sitting on the floor. My arms are resting on my thighs. When I try to move my knee joints hurt. There is a wet spot on my slip. I realize that I've been drooling. I rise slowly and wipe the spittle from the left corner of my mouth and chin with my sleeve. I am cold and stiff.

The air is filled with the smell of food. On the floor close to the door there is a tin plate of food. I move towards it and see that it contains some samp and a dark gravy. My back hurts as I bend to inspect it more closely. Ants are crawling all over the samp, some are thrashing in the gravy, a few have drowned. I can't remember when last I had something to eat. My stomach feels empty but I do not have any appetite.

I stick a finger into the gravy. I bring it to my nose before tasting it. It has a pungent smell and a vile meaty taste. I retch. My empty bowels hurt at the sudden contraction.

I pick ants from the samp and the gravy and clutch them in my left hand. When I rise my head spins. I panic and move to the bed where I lie on my back, staring at the naked bulb until my eyes become moist and hurt, compelling me to shut them. The bed rocks. The pampas grass ululates.

The pampas grass and the shrubs rock gently in the breeze tugging at my slip. The scent of the forget-me-nots drifts through the air. I walk along the borders of the flowerbeds. The colours are dazzling. The pastel blue of kingfishers, the bright yellow of everlasting, the white and red of bidens and in a small rock garden the love-lies-bleeding are a blaze of colour. I wonder who tends this garden? I look around but there is no one in sight. Obscure hymns rise from the grass.

With my one fist closed tightly I peek between the shrubs and the pampas grass, but there is no sign of the fowl. I listen for their call; but for the singing leaves, there is not a sound alluding to their whereabouts. Have they fled from the garden? Have they abandoned me?

I part the branches of shrubs, look into the dense underbrush and see a hollow in the ground cradling small oval objects. Ah, a nest with eggs, I think. On closer inspection I am disappointed. What at first sight I took to be a nest is a heap of coiled dead growth and dry bulbs.

I leave the borders and walk to the centre of the garden where I sit on the lawn with my legs crossed. My slip, stretched between my knees, forms a basin in which I place the ants. They form a little heap of mangled bodies. Except for one stirring at the centre of the heap, they are all dead.

I listen for the call of the guineafowl but the air is still and

I am alone under the tilted sky between the rising walls. To the far end of the high outer wall, half concealed behind the pampas grass, I detect a huge black sheet of metal. I get up, hold the front of my dress in such a way that I can carry the ants like so many tiny bodies in a makeshift stretcher, and approach the sheet in the wall.

When I get closer I see that it is a huge metal door big enough for a truck to pass through. Massive steel hinges attach it to the wall. Three big brass locks secure it at the top, middle and bottom. There are tyre marks in the dark soil under the gate. I have been out here several times but have never seen or heard any vehicle come or go.

Almost involuntarily I inspect the tracks and notice that they run along a sand road behind the shrubs and pampas grass. I follow it all along the outside wall and realize that it cannot be seen from the lawns on the other side of the garden. The humus of rotting leaves is suffocating. It is as if I am walking along a path deep in a jungle. I warn myself against the danger of self-deception by looking at the heap of ants which I cradle in my dress.

We enter the township walking hand in hand. The late afternoon air smells of anthracite and burning wood. The sky is crested with vermilion. We hear singing and see a crowd in the distance toyi-toyiing down the street towards us. We are holding hands, listening to the singing grow louder as it approaches us. The chant and martial dance is familiar. I've sung it many times. I've moved in the folds of the dance on numerous occasions. I hum the tune. My hips and feet start moving. I free my hands from his grip and join the crowd. The sky is red and filled with the sheets of smoke.

Then suddenly it seems as if the crowd turns on itself. There is a collision of bodies as the chant becomes screams as stones rain into the heart of the crowd. I stumble over a body as I struggle to free myself from the thrashing multitudes. Then the smoke which fills the sky springs from the earth itself. I choke, fall to the ground, bruising my knees. Something strikes the back of my head. Night falls.

I awake to the sight of the concrete ceiling. I avert my eyes from the glaring light by staring at its edges. How many times have I stared at that rough surface before drifting to sleep or after waking? Recently I have taken to sleeping on my back. Now, staring at the ceiling, I cannot help but feel that I am lying in a massive stone coffin.

'You have a visitor.' It is the voice of the one who has been weighing and measuring me recently. I assume she has arrived for another session and rise to undress. I didn't hear her at the door. She must have entered while I was asleep. Has she been watching me? Do I speak in my sleep?

When I grab hold of my slip with the intention of pulling it over my head, she speaks again. 'No, we've been through that today, don't you remember?' She clicks her tongue and shakes her head like one who takes pity on a wretched fellow being. 'You have a visitor. Come.'

I follow her. We walk through several doors along a passage until we arrive in the visiting room where he is waiting.

I sit down next to him. The warder withdraws to a corner where she watches us. He touches me. I look hard into his face. His eyes avoid me.

'How wonderful to be able to touch you,' he says. 'How strange for them to allow it. In a way I can understand it. It's a kind of concession. Something they feel obliged to concede. I mean, that's not what I want to speak about. I mean to say, I am here for your sake. To tell you that I love you, that this is a mistake. I mean, I am here to help you not to lose hope. It's difficult, I know, even if I know.'

He strokes my arms, caresses my face, his hands feel cold and lifeless. When he speaks again, his voice sounds far off and incoherent. 'Do you remember the afternoon at the river, when we woke to the commotion of the impangele in the grass, fleeing from the barking dog?'

I look into his eyes. Under the vowels and consonants woven into the stream of his speech I hear other sounds. I hear the call of guineafowl and see a flock emerging from the shrubs and the pampas grass, their dark bodies marked by the white and pale blue spots as if struck by hail.

They converge on me where I stand in the middle of the garden. They raise their heads slightly as they call. At first

I think they are warning me. I look up into the sky and see a strange circular cloud shaped like a noose drifting in the slanted heavens. Then I hear a mocking tone in the voices of the earthbound birds around me, like the chanting of a crowd.

'*Andikhathali, andikhathali,*' I hear them say as panic seizes me. I look up into the sky which is closing in on me. I want to respond. I want to scream 'No!' but my lips repeat their chant.

'I do not care,' I say after them. Suddenly, it's quiet.

Ginger

ELLEKE BOEHMER

They were all at the airport to welcome her. They were the friends who had stayed. They still lived in their old haunts, brick buildings in green streets where night-long parties were once held. At some stage years ago, they'd thought about leaving, about Perth, Brisbane, Auckland, but something had held them, inertia maybe. They stayed on.

She spied Liz first, Liz craning her body over the chrome barrier, the big nest of her hair. And there was Ingrid, waving, and behind Ingrid the dark purple patch of Clare. Alison pushed her luggage trolley more slowly, lifting the handlebar slightly so that the brake was half on. She didn't want to burst in on them. They all needed a bit of time.

But now Ingrid was coming round the barrier, her arms open. Her scarlet shirt was voluminous. The trolley veered off to one side.

'Welcome to the sun, Ali.'

'Man, do you need it.'

'An English woman, that's what you look like.'

Those were Clare and Liz's voices beyond Ingrid's soft shoulder. The men stood further off, Jannie of course in a leather jacket, Chris looking more like a GP than ever. Chris had brought his Indian wife. He introduced her as Susie, which didn't sound like her real name. She was thinner even than Clare. She looked shy, he looked proud, proud maybe of his advanced brand of marriage.

'We're into this new nation thing, Ali,' said Ingrid. 'It's like it's the fashion. I have white friends looking for houses in Coloured neighbourhoods. A girl at work, a white girl, has called her baby Sizwe. We're trying loving and living together these days. In spite of the politicians. It's great.'

Ingrid was talking fast, especially at the traffic lights. She was driving. She cursed the slowness of the lights, calling them robots. Alison had forgotten they were called robots. She had forgotten other things too. Like the smell of bare skin her friends had, also the intense sweetness the women carried on them, the smell of a spray-on deodorant. It was taking time to come back to her, the bright light, the bright tar, her friends' sunglasses, greasy frames.

Liz looked for new things to point out, new developments, improvements. There was the extension to the mall, a new flower and crafts market, those townhouse clusters, and white men in their usual short haircuts strolling and shopping with black girlfriends. Further away on the horizon, Alison saw, the big Anglo-American buildings in the middle of town still shone blindingly, like a supernova, like glory.

Jannie was leaning his head against the window as though sleepy. His hair left a fuzzy sweat patch on the glass. After a while Liz gave up talking. Maybe they didn't have much to say to each other, Alison thought, they were pulled back together only by this visit. She looked round to where Chris and the woman he called Susie were following them in a shiny white Honda.

'They're doing okay, those two,' Liz said.

Lunch was at Jannie's house because he was the one who had the space. Look at the tiled patio and walk-through fitted kitchen, Ingrid said, pointing with a raised arm. Jannie's band, still called the Namib Diviners, were doing well. She guided Alison to a frail-looking plastic chair beside the laden table.

The food was mainly mayonnaise salads in Tupperware tureens, side-dishes for a braai. Clare was spooning cream on to a large pink and white fruit pudding in a pottery bowl. Alison recognized the bowl from the time, nearly seven years ago now, when they shared a house.

'That must be Palmerosa pudding,' Liz said. 'I read about it in an American cookbook the other day.'

'Once I thought I would bath my baby in that bowl,' said Clare, pouring herself white wine from a box.

Liz raised her eyebrows at Alison.

In their final year at university Clare tried to have a

child. She told everyone she wanted to be a single mother. Every four months or so, regular as a menstrual cycle, she informed them she'd miscarried again. Sometimes she shouted the news from the toilet. Then she spent days locked in her bedroom. Ingrid would leave cups of black tea mixed with Johnny Walker outside her door.

'I wanted us to have the party round the pool,' Liz said. 'But James didn't go golfing today. So he would've been in the way. And the kids too. We wanted to have you to ourselves, Ali.'

'All's not well with the marriage,' whispered Ingrid, giving Alison white wine in a beer glass. She was reciting from one of her most recent letters.

'It must be so strange for you not to have family in this country any more,' Liz was saying. 'Your dad's still in Canada?'

'Yes,' said Alison. Her father was married to a hand and foot model in Toronto. He lectured at the university there about soil erosion. He still used the slides he'd taken years ago in the Transkei. Pictures of red dongas.

'Not so strange as for us to have friends in just about every Western capital of the world,' said Jannie.

The remark was abrupt, it sounded out of place. Liz brought Alison more wine in a plastic party cup decorated with yellow and sky-blue squares. She sat on the carpet beside her chair. She was pretending it was comfortable to sit cross-legged in high sandals.

'I usually don't smoke,' said Liz, waving her cigarette in the air. 'Only on special occasions.'

'We still smoke far too much in this country,' said Clare. 'It's killing the nation.'

She spoke from the kitchen door. Behind her the chicken pieces and chops were blackening on the oven grill. Jannie had forgotten to buy charcoal for the braai.

Chris came in carrying bottles of wine, Susie behind him, also carrying bottles.

'We took a detour to the off-licence,' said Chris.

'They don't drink box stuff,' said Clare.

'We're allowed to smoke and drink without guilt,' said

Jannie. 'We're a Third World country after all.'

Liz poked his calf with her sandal heel.

'What is it you do in London, Alison?' said Susie.

She handed Alison a glass of wine, a proper glass this time. Alison now had three helpings of wine on the table beside her, two portions of box wine and the glass.

'Believe it or not, I still do temping,' she said. 'I've been doing it nearly four years.'

'But you earn well on it, Ali,' said Liz, as if she wanted the reassurance.

'This place must look a bit different after all these years,' Chris said.

He didn't look straight at Alison even though he faced her. Chris, Susie, Liz, Clare at the kitchen door were silent now, glasses' rims at lips, lips pressed flat and pink against the glass, looking at her. It was time to declare herself, she saw, tell a story, reward them for the occasion.

Chris arranged mouthfuls of different kinds of salad on a plate. He passed the plate to Susie.

Alison wanted to say, it's not that different, none of you are very different. She wanted to lighten the situation. It was an ordinary thing this coming back, just for a holiday, to see friends. I haven't changed, she could say. When you temp, you don't change, there's no time.

But because she paused Chris must have thought she needed to be filled in. He spoke from where he stood at the table, he had helped himself to three pieces of meat. There was a time when they used to tease him about being serious. Now they listened, no one teased.

'Things are definitely on the mend,' Chris said. 'We can shake the mothball dust off our old green-back passports. Even India will let us in.'

Alison wondered if he said that for Susie's benefit. His eyes were fixed on his plate.

Liz peeled a drumstick like a banana and held it so that the loose bits of skin flopped over her fingers. She tugged them off with her teeth one by one.

'If we try we could all be one happy family,' she said.

'The country needs psychoanalysis,' said Clare.

Clare was on her second bowl of Palmerosa dessert. She had eaten none of the main course. Alison remembered Clare's food fads at university. One week she was a fruitarian, the next week she lived on powdered protein drinks. The protein powder smelt of lavender and soap.

'We desperately need the confidence of the international community,' said Chris slowly, as though making a delicate point. 'We need cash, aid. We don't want to become another poverty-stricken African nation.'

'I don't see the problem,' said Jannie. 'We are an African nation. Let's have black-outs every night. I mean, what will we lose? What has all that wealth done for America?'

'We all need psychoanalysis,' said Clare.

'Anyway, Alison, what do you think?' asked Susie. 'From your outside perspective?'

Alison didn't know what to think. She smiled, she glanced around. Everyone was looking at her again. Plates were empty. They wanted to be put in the picture. There was her life in London, in the ground floor flat off the Holloway Road.

'I've saved a pile of *Weekly Mail*s, Alison,' said Chris. 'The most interesting ones from the past few years. If you like you can catch up on our news.'

'I've been following the news,' said Alison.

'But there's nothing like the *Mail* for hands-on opinion,' said Chris. 'I mean, to know about South Africa you really have to be here, you have to see it from inside.'

Clare winked at Liz to fill her glass. She didn't want to interrupt Chris by speaking.

'Anyway, you're looking okay even though you haven't seen much sun,' Ingrid said suddenly.

'I like your top,' said Susie.

She bent over her tightly-folded arms as though over a ledge to look more closely at the appliqué design on Alison's white sweatshirt. The picture was an African mask done in bronze and silver sequins. She had bought the sweatshirt on holiday in Greece.

Everyone bent forward to look at the mask.

'Yes, even I think it's okay,' said Clare. 'And my taste is usually horrible.'

'We have things like that here too,' said Liz. 'Remember the malls? I can take you along whenever you want. I know some of the stores where Winnie Mandela used to buy clothes for her overseas trips. Where Joan Collins shopped when she was here.'

'Thanks,' said Alison.

Jannie's eyes were closed. Clare took the cigarette that was burning between his fingers and stubbed it out in her dessert bowl.

'Your pudding was lovely, Clare,' said Ingrid.

'Yes, you must give me the recipe,' said Liz. 'I want to discover more about foreign cuisine.'

'What shall we do now?' said Chris. 'Remember what we planned? Shall we take Alison on a tour?' His chops were chewed down to the raw bits congealed in the crevasses of bone. 'She can see how town has changed,' he added, responding to the silence.

They had spent time planning this reunion, Alison saw. They didn't want to run the risk of getting bored during the first meeting. Clare now said let's see Soweto, Liz said the Zoo.

'Personally, I'd like to see round Jannie's house,' Ingrid said crisply. 'The times I was here before, I've only been shown the front rooms.'

Jannie stirred at the mention of his name. 'The rooms are really untidy,' he murmured. 'They haven't been done in days.'

'Maybe Alison just wants to come to my house to unpack and settle in,' said Liz.

She was trying to speak cosily but her heart wasn't in it. She sprayed more box wine into her glass.

'Liz said you had some nice garden paving round the back, Jannie,' Ingrid said. 'I'd like to see that.'

Alison decided to help with the planning. 'I'm happy just to sit around,' she said. 'We've hardly even seen each other.'

'That's right,' said Jannie.

Ingrid pulled him out of his chair.

'At least show us your yard,' she said.

They crowded at the kitchen door. To see, Alison had to look to the side of Clare's head. The paving in the yard outside was of silky dark slate. Along the house wall were flowering azaleas in wooden vats. Under Alison's nose was Clare's shirt label. It was sticking out. It said, Cool Wash, Remove Promptly, Made in USA.

'Yes, attractively arranged,' said someone, words from a magazine. Jannie said it must be a professional job. He bought the house this way, with everything that was in it, the furniture, azaleas, the lot.

'Even the dog house came with it,' he said. 'Any of you can take that thing if you want. I don't like dogs.'

To the left of the kitchen steps stood the blue dog house. It had Swiss chalet-style windows painted on either side. The painted curtains were red and white polka-dot. Over the entrance was written, Dom se plek. A heavy chain trailed out of it, as if looking for an anchor.

'The words mean Dom's place,' said Chris.

'Or Dom's spot,' said Liz.

'I'm sure Alison remembers how to translate,' said Clare.

'But if she didn't, she might feel left out if we didn't say,' said Liz.

'No, I remember,' said Alison.

She looked around the yard for something else to say. There were the vats, a hosepipe, a white fence that looked as if made of polystyrene slabs, the outhouse to the garage, painted blue. On the top step of the door to the outhouse a woman was sitting, her legs were stretched out. She wore high gold sandals, stilettos, and an American baseball cap the wrong way round. She was drinking out of a paper cup patterned with yellow and sky-blue squares. On the step beside her was a half-loaf of bread. Chris looked at Alison watching her. He turned away from the door.

'You haven't introduced us to your maid, Jannie,' he said.

'That's Ginger,' said Jannie. 'She's not my maid. She works at a place down the road, a dentist's or something.

276

She must be an assistant. She sleeps here. It's better for her than going all the way home to Soweto.'

'That could be a good idea,' said Chris, 'to turn maids' kayas into boarding rooms.'

He stepped back into the kitchen, bumping against Alison. He was somehow uncomfortable, not as confident as when eating. He began to glance over in Susie's direction. She was leaning against the doorframe, her back to him.

Alison wanted to move. Chris had forced her up against the side of the rubbish bucket. A smell rose up out of the bucket of half-digested food, Palmerosa and vinegar, a smell of young babies.

The other women were still collected in the doorway, talking. Something out in the yard continued to attract their interest. It seemed to be the curtain of plastic-coloured strips that hung in the doorframes of Ginger's room. Individual strips blew out, dirty pink and dirty yellow, occasionally flicking Ginger's shoulders. Ingrid remembered they had curtains like that in the sixties in places like butchers and hairdressers. Susie said they had one hanging up in her old home, at the entrance of her parents' bedroom. When she said this Chris breathed loudly.

There was also Ginger's little starched half-moon apron. Ingrid pointed to it. I wonder why the dentist makes her wear that, said Clare. Ginger was using the apron to collect the soft pieces of bread she was plucking from the inside of her loaf. She was eating out of her apron. She was not looking at them. Then the person furthest out, it was Liz, mentioned the garden hose coiled among the azaleas. Everyone liked it, it was transparent, very slender, it looked state-of-the-art. Like transparent straws, said someone. Transparent Coke cans next, said someone else.

Chris nudged Susie by prodding the arm leaning up against the doorframe. He startled her. Her eyes looked back large and confused. Alison dropped her gaze, pretending not to have seen.

Then everyone began to stroll back in the direction of the living room, gathering pieces of food as they went, nibbling.

Alison was the last to move. They all filed past her. The rubbish bin edge was wet against her knee. She picked a lettuce leaf off a place and it doused her hand in dressing. She saw that the woman out in the yard, Ginger, had gone in too. She left her paper cup on the top step.

Liz and Jannie were in conversation at the entrance to the living room. The conversation looked private, Liz's voice was low. 'It's the kids. I could do with a nanny a few days a week. She looks very clean and neat,' Alison heard Liz say as she walked by.

'I've told you what her work is,' said Jannie. Then he dropped his voice.

Ingrid handed Alison another glass. It was box wine again.

'Even Ginger was drinking this stuff,' said Ingrid.

'What I want to know is where she got a name like Ginger,' said Clare. 'What do you think, Alison? Ginger? It's not right somehow. The name's from American movies. It's not African. It doesn't really belong in South Africa.'

Tender Sentiments

RIAN MALAN

Maybe it was the hot weather, maybe it was festive spirit, maybe it was just irrational, but there was a time there in early January when I thought everything was going to come right. The feeling lasted a few days, and I remember the exact moment it ended — ten o'clock one Saturday morning, when I turned on Radio 702 and the bad news came down like hammerblows: thirty-nine dead in Sebokeng, arsonists on the rampage in Khayelitsha, sectarian battles in Komga and Oliver Tambo bewailing an appalling atrocity in a place called Umgababa.

The Umgababa event was the last straw, because I couldn't find out what had actually happened there. There were two newspapers on my kitchen table, but neither of them mentioned the place. There was simply too much violence; at least fifteen people had been killed in Umgababa, and their corpses had just fallen through the cracks. I thought, nooit, this is too much, this is overwhelming, and fell once again to pondering Bernoldus Niemand and the immortal question he raised: 'How do I live in this strange place?'

How indeed? I know mild suburbanites who have joined vigilante movements, agnostics who now go to church and pray. I know blacks who've signed up for township defence committees in search of salvation, and blacks who've ducked to the white suburbs because they're terrified of the SDUs. And then I know an ou who's trying to do it his own way.

His name is Ernest Oelofse, and I met him years ago in the corridors of Joburg's magistrate's court, back when we were both cub reporters.

He was wearing leathers and carrying a motorcycle helmet, so I knew right away he was a man after my own heart. We sneaked straight into a toilet and smoked a poison, an insanely dangerous thing to do, considering the swarms of boere around, but what the hell, we were young and foolish. After that, we were like brothers for a while.

Oelofse was wild. He was a breker from the West Rand, the son of a goldminer and had been a miner himself for a while. He knew his way around motorbikes, drag racing and bars of the sort where lightbulbs were naked and dart games ended in brawls. His brain was a confusion of macho images, the cowboy superimposed on the biker superimposed on the Trekboer. He smoked Luckies, drank tequila and told stories like Oom Schalk Lourens on acid. Most of them were tall, of course.

We once fell in love with French sisters, he with the younger and I the elder. One blazing summer day we all dropped acid on a mountaintop in the Stormberg. We took our clothes off and sat on a huge rock in the sun for hours, like lizards; immobile. Then Oelofse put on his boots and his hat and took off on a death-defying run across the krantzes, leaping from boulder to boulder, penis slapping his thighs, a kaalgat breker in a floppy farmer's hat with leopard-skin band, silhouetted against the hot blue sky. He was windmilling his arms and playing air guitar — going 'Kerang, ketchang,' you know, and sing-shouting ecstatic nonsense: 'Boogie met die wind o ja innie Moordenaars Karoo baby.' That is how I remembered him. I remembered him well.

He phoned me once in the States, but after that I lost touch with him, and when I got home eight years later he seemed to have vanished. Whenever I asked after him, noses wrinkled in disgust. There were rumours of unsound method, as Marlow said of Kurtz; of dope-running, guns, gambling and violence; of stints in jail, and most chilling of all, a pack of killer dogs that had torn a black woman apart.

He had been a good china of mine, though, so I kept at it, and in the end I tracked him down. He was living in a redoubt that lay beyond fear and guilt, in a landscape of rolling hills and thorn trees north of the city. The house had a nice Third World feel to it, all rundown and dilapidated and surrounded by chicken hoks. The lawn had long since reverted to veld. Chickens scratched in the abandoned flowerbeds. There was a squatter camp at the bottom of the garden.

As I cut the engine, my ears were assaulted by a great barking of dogs and clanking of chains. There were four tall thorn trees outside the house, each with a heavy iron chain dangling from its boughs, and at the end of each chain, a pit bull. As I stepped out of the car, the dogs charged, moving with such velocity that when the chains snapped tight the dogs were yanked into the air and went sailing across the garden like acrobats on a flying trapeze.

And then Ernest appeared, and these slavering, howling beasts rolled over to have their tummies tickled. He was still lean and mean, with eyes cold and blue. In his thirties the hairline was receding, but he'd grown a beard to compensate. Otherwise, nothing had really changed. He was still buckling his swash, still riding high and walking tall, a Boer Marlboro man in boots and jeans.

We sat down on the stoep, had a dop for old times' sake and did some catching up. Ernest had quit newspapers a year or two earlier to write a novel. The novel was about ten pages long. Meanwhile, he was breeding pit bulls and gambling for a living. He almost brained me for referring to the birds scratching in his garden as 'chickens'. They were a killer strain of fighting cock, hatched from eggs illegally smuggled from Puerto Rico. Ernest liked illegality. His idea of a good time was a game of high-stakes backgammon in one of Hillbrow's gambling dens, his idea of a good woman was one who didn't throw up at a cockfight.

After a while, he disappeared into the house and came back with his newest toy — a Kit Carson throwing knife, ideal for cloak-and-dagger jobs. He also had a Czechoslovakian shotgun, a nine mil Star, and a high-tech steel catapult with a mealie-bag full of ball-bearings, for use when the ammo ran out. I observed that he seemed to be arming himself for an apocalypse, but Ernest didn't want to talk about that. He wanted to talk about his dogs and birds, and about courage — about the way a fighting cock staggered to its feet and fought on, even though it was dying, kicked full of holes by its opponent's steel spurs.

'That's courage,' Ernest said. 'I'm into courage. Courage for courage's sake. Courage because I'm a man.'

Ja-nee, Oelofse was fuller of bluster than ever. Talk of chickens led to talk of dogs, so I asked about those beasts chained to the trees. He said he'd bought his first pit bull in the Seventies, back when he was still a liberal living in the suburbs and working on *The Rand Daily Mail*. One afternoon, hitching home from work, he was picked up by a crew of reporters from *Beeld*. They were on their way to check out a police report about a fatal dog attack. The nearer they drew to their destination, the lower Ernest's heart sank. In the end, they pulled up right outside his doorstep. It was his dogs that had done the killing, and the victim was his servant, Elinda Ndyabazi, aged twenty-one. The dogs had somehow broken loose from their chains and torn her apart.

As he told this story, Ernest's eyes veered away from mine. 'It was the worst day of my life,' he said. He was found not guilty of criminal negligence, but he wished he'd been sent to jail. Rather that, he said, than have to face the dead girl's father.

'What could I say?' he said. 'I told him I was sorry. I gave him all the money I had. What else could I say? I felt sick.'

Maybe so, but he didn't stop keeping pit bulls. The killer dogs were destroyed by the police, but he still had a bitch, so he took her out to the plots and bred another pack. This was the end, as far as his — our — friends in the suburbs were concerned. If Ernest walked into a party, they walked out the back. He was considered to have become a reactionary, a racist psychopath. On the basis of what I saw on the day of our reunion, the lefties had a point. Still, his attitude made an interesting change from the morbid wringing of hands, so I unrolled my sleeping bag on his living room floor and stuck around for a week or two.

Lying on my back in Ernest's living room, this is what I saw: a stereo, a few sticks of furniture, a wooden box full of LPs, mostly Dylan and the Stones, and walls papered with an intriguing collage of newspaper clippings and political bric-a-brac. There was, for instance, a picture of a dark-skinned starveling, all protruding ribs and huge suffering eyes. 'This is Asif,' read the caption. 'He lives in Bangladesh in total poverty. He gets hardly any food to eat. Tough luck, Asif.'

Right alongside Asif was a UDF poster, and alongside that a design for what looked like a Cosatu-type struggle T-shirt, emblazoned with slogans and a big clenched fist. On closer inspection, however, the fist had a thumb sticking out of it and the union was called FUCUSA — the mass movement of exasperated management. FUCUSA's slogans were, 'Redistribute Guilt!' and 'An Injury to One is No Concern of Mine'. I chuckled whenever I read them.

I also got a chuckle out of the adjoining item, a wry parody of the standard SABC propaganda line, typed on authentic SABC news stationery. The headline read, 'How's This For Objectivity?' and the body copy described an attack on a police station. The 'socialist freedom fighters' responsible were being hunted down by police 'armed with guns of European origin' and travelling in 'capitalist American vehicles'.

This was no doubt the work of Piet, one of the stranger members of Oelofse's strange household. Piet was an Afrikaner who came from a family so poor that they used to park on the hill behind the drive-in and watch the fliek without sound. The state had given him a university education, though, and now he was writing news for the SABC in return — an extremely odd job, I thought, for a razor-sharp theoretical Marxist. But then Piet was a very strange ou. He used to sit around in short pants and a Tukkies rugby jersey, puffing on a skyf and discussing heerskappy van die werkersklas — dictatorship of the proletariat — in Boland Afrikaans. I used to fall around laughing. It killed me to hear Marxist jargon with a brei.

No, it wasn't cruel. Piet had a sense of humour, which is probably why he was forsaking Marx for Malatesta and other apostles of anarchy. He and André, a pale, tormented draft dodger who also lived in the house, were hatching a diabolical anarchist plot. They were going to write a bulletin announcing the assassination of Nelson Mandela and plant it on a live newsreader's desk. The aim was to trigger an uncontrollable explosion of black rage.

Why on earth did I like these ous? They were all half-mad, but that was the point, I suppose. You could experience all the contradictions and weirdness of the country at large without ever leaving their home. All the essential elements were there — a racist psychopath, a Boer Marxist, an apartheid war resister, scores of homeless blacks at the bottom of the garden and sundry drifters passing through. I'd often wake up to discover a strange life-form snoring on the living room sofa. Once it was a dope runner from the Cape Flats with tattooed tears falling from the corner of one eye, marking him as a member of some murderous prison gang. On another occasion it was a toothless biker. Several draft dodgers crashed on the couch on their way to Amsterdam, only to be followed by a soldier named Deon, camouflage uniform, automatic rifle and all.

This oke Deon was a Recce, a member of the toughest, most secret, most deadly unit in the entire SADF. Recces go to places they can't name, where they do things they can't talk about. They go into darkest Africa in sticks of six — two Portuguese, two blacks, two Boers — wearing enemy uniforms and carrying enemy weapons. They blow up railway bridges, sabotage industrial installations, assassinate ANC cadres. Their standing orders are to kill themselves rather than submit to capture, or so Deon claimed, at any rate. I wouldn't know. Deon was totally insane.

The first thing he did, on the morning of his arrival, was jam a toothbrush into a vice on a workbench. 'I'm going to interrogate this toothbrush,' he said. In the next ten minutes he delivered as withering and sidesplitting a parody of Afrikaner militarism as has ever been uttered. Then he started drinking. He was drunk before the dew evaporated from the grass. By midday he was so drunk he fell down and went into a coma. It was midnight before he came out of it.

By then a small party was underway. Oelofse had made a fire on his stoep, and a dozen or so of us were standing around it, drinking beer. On the stroke of midnight Deon came running out of the house in his underpants, brandishing that automatic rifle and screaming, 'Kontak! Kontak!' He opened fire. Tree boughs danced in a hail of bullets. The crowd hit the dirt and clung to it. When we lifted our heads Deon was laughing his head off. It was just a joke, you see. Everyone assumes that Recces are bosbevok, bushmad, so he put on a bit of a show to gratify our expectations. After that, he got drunk again, and passed out on the couch. In the morning he was gone.

In his place came the cockfighters, an entire pack of them, in town for a clandestine cockfighting tournament. Ernest hosted a braai in their honour. A dozen or so white savages with Brylcreemed hair and combs in their socks took up position around the fire, making jokes about blacks as the missing link.

They were farmers or security guards, for the most part; strong men in short pants with borselkop sons in tow. They talked about the state of things, which they felt was bad. Indeed, most of them thought it was time to break out the heavy weapons and have a tweede Bloedrivier. Someone asked my opinion, and I ventured an extremely cautious dissent. In a flash, the cockfighters turned on me.

'Listen to this rabbit!' screamed a fat thug in a safari suit. 'He doesn't do his army, he splits to America, and now he wants to tell us what to do!'

One of his drunken buddies planted himself in front of me, clamped my temples between his vice-like hands and said, 'I'll go you with the head, china!' These okes were serious battlers. They would have stomped me unconscious just for fun. They closed in around me, urging their man into action. 'Go him!' they cried. 'Go him!' I was groping for a carving knife on the table behind my back when Ernest intervened.

'Animals!' he yelled, stepping between the pack and me. He was six-six tall and dangerous when angry, so the pack fell back before his excoriations. 'You're stupid!' he shouted. 'You're worse than blacks! That's why you're scared of them, because you're too dumb to compete!' This was a lethal thing to say to such men, all the more cutting because it was true. The battlers were aghast, but Ernest wasn't done yet.

'They're coming for you!' he continued. 'They'll marry your daughters! Your grandchildren will all be half-breeds!' The cockfighters were so taken aback that they forgot all about me and shook their heads in disbelief. They had assumed Ernest was one of them.

But he was nothing, really. He had simply read the wind and seen a storm coming. It had been bearing down on us for centuries and there was nothing to be done about it, no way to avert it, no point even talking about it. I mean, I knew the man. His whole life had been shadowed by the waiting, and he'd finally grown tired of it. He held no brief for apartheid, but he could no longer stomach the indecisive dithering of suburban white liberalism, so he'd simply declared himself independent and retreated into the countryside. He didn't do camps any more, and declined to obey or even acknowledge most laws. He just drew a line in the red dust of the plots, ranged his dogs and guns behind it and dared strangers to cross at their peril.

And God knows, many must have been tempted, because Ernest was truly an outlaw now. When he was broke he poached guineafowl, and there were rumours of sheep rustling and dope deals. He harboured draft dodgers and squatters. He hosted illegal cockfights. The guns and dogs were intended to discourage prowling lawmen, but if they also scared off chicken thieves, burglars and marauding comrades so much the better. 'Whip them till they piss blood.' That was Ernest's prescription for everyone — ANC, AWB, SAP, PAC, animal rights activists, feminists and Greens.

And he did — did whip them, I mean. There was a cluster of shacks at the bottom of his garden, housing fifty or sixty squatters. Each of them might have earned Ernest a R500 fine if the police had known they were there, in the heart of a 'white' area, but he didn't care. If he wanted squatters in his garden, he would have squatters in his garden. They were a pretty desperate lot, those squatters, all poor and hungry and steeped in fatalism. They brewed skokiaan and spent their weekends reeling around in a collective stupor.

One Friday night, a nosebleeding woman came pounding on the kitchen door, wailing, 'Baas, baas, die manne slat my' — boss, boss, the men are hitting me. Cocking an ear out the door, we heard more thuds, clangs and screams of calamity coming from the squatter camp. A full-scale mêlée seemed to have broken out down there. The Marxists and I tuttutted, frowned concernedly and considered calling the police. Ernest vetoed that suggestion. If the police came, he stood to be fined, and the squatters taken away. The screaming continued, though, and it seemed impossible to just sit there.

The writer V. S. Naipaul once found himself in a similar predicament, in some lawless corner of the world. 'Either you go among them with a bullwhip,' he said, 'or you do nothing at all. To do anything in between is ridiculous.' I had no stomach for violence, so I was invariably ridiculous. Ernest, on the other hand, was a breker. He tucked the shotgun in the crook of his arm and set off for the squatter camp. The gun went off, silence fell, and Ernest came back with bleeding knuckles.

There was an awkward silence around the table. On one hand, we were appalled by this display of baasskap and kragdadigheid. On the other, we weren't entirely sure that this was the right place, the right time or the right country for tender sentiments. There was a sneaking suspicion that we'd just been shown up as cowards.

And I suppose we had. Around noon the next day, a hungover skollie with a split lip came knocking on the back door, bearing a quart of beer and a zol as a peace offering. He and Ernest shook hands and split the beer, laughing and drinking from the bottle. More black men drifted up from the camp, and the living room filled up. Soon there was a party going, the regular Saturday afternoon dice party. The previous night's unpleasantness wasn't even mentioned.

Ernest would gamble on anything, with anyone. He was one of the few whites who knew the variant of craps that black men are always playing on pavements. He hunkered down with his guests, spat on the stones, chanted rhymes for luck and hurled the dice down on the slasto with an ear-splitting cry of Tsa! He was considered to have great luck, was Ernest. The black men often duplicated his bets, because they tended to lose if they bet against him. A tattered sheet of paper stuck to the refrigerator kept tally of what they owed him. It was a small fortune, but Ernest let it ride. I suppose there was a vestige of liberalism left in him, after all.

So the dice tumbled, bottles passed and I sat there thinking about this renegade and his enemies in the white suburbs, some of whom remained friends of mine. They were good people, with hearts in the right places, striving to be good New South Africans. They always invited a few English-speaking Africans to their dinner parties, and tried hard to make them feel welcome, to be sensitive and sympathetic towards their socio-political concerns. Maybe they tried too hard. Maybe that's why it was so often forced and false.

And then I looked at Oelofse, kneeling in a circle of noisy, reeking peasants, and I thought, no, those lefties have got it wrong. Those agonizing 'non-racial' seances around their swimming pools aren't authentic South African gatherings — *this* is. This is how most of us are — crude, uncouth, sometimes violent and preferably drunk. This is how it will be in the end, when we finally come together.

In his macho moods Oelofse used to complain about being born a century too late, but I sometimes wonder if he wasn't born too soon. There is too much killing in this country, too much crime, too many volatile forces at work and too little hope of taming them. The smell of anarchy is in the air. I don't know for sure, and I pray I'm wrong, but I think Oelofse may have reached a place where the rest of us are still going.

Holding Back Midnight

MAUREEN ISAACSON

The night is shooting past. It is bright jet and hot. The air is as smooth as the whisky we sip on the veranda of the old hotel that has become my parents' home. We are safe from the faded neon and slow-moving traffic lights outside. The bubbles of fifty chilled bottles of champagne are waiting to spill as we touch down on the new century. In our own way, we each believe that from that moment on nothing will ever be the same.

Anything could happen at midnight. President Manzwe has said that he has a surprise for us. What can it be?

'Cheers!' shouts my mother. Old opals shine dully against her sagging lobes, her webbed neck. She is flushed, like a dead person who has been painted to receive her final respects.

'Cheers!' echoes her friend Ethel.

Smoke and disillusion have ravaged their voices. Their tongues are too slack to roll an olive pip. They walk slowly among the guests, in silver dresses that were fashionable once. They teeter on sling-back stilettos. They offer salmon and bits of fish afloat on shells of lettuce leaves.

Don't the people at this party ever think about AIDS? Out there in the real world, they give you cling paper gloves in restaurants lest you should bleed from an unnoticed cut. Waiters wear them. Doctors. Environmentalists, like my husband Leon and me. The lack of sterility makes me queasy tonight.

'What is the time, Dad?' I ask.

'Be patient,' he says.

Hopefully the moment we are waiting for will release him from the grip of history. History is ever-present in my father, like the patterns that shimmer from the chandeliers over the cracked walls. It is trapped in the broken paving outside this hotel where angels of delight once fluttered eyelashes as if they were wings at white men. History hovers, with the ghosts of the illicit couplings that once heated the hotel's shadowy rooms. It is funnelled through my memory.

Here comes my Uncle Otto, ex-Minister of Home Affairs, glass in hand. Looking at his ginger moustache, I am seven years old again. I am sitting on his lap at the bar. Don't tell your mother, he is saying. His hand is on my knee. I feel the closeness of flesh. Angels are rubbing themselves against the men. Men against angels.

'Why angels?' I want to know.

'Because they take the white men to heaven,' says Uncle Otto.

Like the street names that have been removed for their Eurocentricity, my parents and their friends are displaced. They do not understand the new signs. Their silhouettes glide across the garden, outlining their nostalgia. Through the shrill chirp of the crickets, I catch the desolation in the voices. The talk of lifts that no longer work, of the rubbish that piles up. There goes our old dentist Louis Dutoit and his wife Joyce, speaking of 'Old Johannesburg'. For all the world we are still there. Except for Leon and me, of course. We could not have married in the old days, him being Coloured and all. Doctor Dutoit would not even have filled Leon's teeth.

How graciously they tolerate us now. We have breezed in from our communal plot in the outer limits of the megacity these people are too afraid to visit.

'Not without an AK-4777 rifle,' my father has said.

Instead they ruminate in this, the last of the shrunken ghettos that began to decline when cheap labour went out. Not for them the spread of shebeens and malls that splash jazz from what used to be poverty-stricken township to the City Hall. The place we now call Soweto City. Connected by skyway and flyway, over and underground, as steady as the steel and the foreign funding on which it runs. Talk about one door closing. The Old Order was not yet cold in its grave and the place was gyrating, like a woman in love.

290

And the people out there? There are millions of us — living the good life advertised by laser-honed graphics that dazzle the streets. We are fast-living. Street-wise. Natural. We till the land. Our food is organic. See this party dress? It's made of paper. Tomorrow I'll shred it. Recycle later.

I thank heavens for Leon. I envy him his equilibrium. Forgive and forget. That's what he said before we came here tonight. His kind of thinking has helped me cope with the effect my parents have on me.

'Thank the Lord Leon's surname is also Laubscher. Some people will never know,' is all they said when I told them about our marriage.

Dad is the perfect host. But earlier this evening his sentimentality got the better of him when Uncle Otto reminded him of the New Year's Eve parties, five times the size of this one, held at our old house. Foreign diplomats, caviar, black truffles in Italian rice. Now he embraces Ethel. One-two. One-two. He dances a little jig with her on the veranda, cooled by the breeze that fans the palm tree. I squirm, reminded of the way he used to cavort when the hotel was in its prime.

'I'm a miner at heart,' he used to say, insisting that the place was a private sideline of no consequence.

Was anyone fooled into believing it was anything but a thriving business? We had more maids than rooms that needed polishing in our double-storey house. My parents had owned three game farms and four cars. A relic of the Old Regime, my father will never forgive the New Order for destroying his lifestyle. I am sure that in his dreams he still sells the kisses of angels to those who would cross the forbidden colour line by night, endorse it by day.

'Would you like to dance?' asks Paul Schoeman, once the Minister of Law and Order. 'Mona Lisa . . .' sings Nat King Cole. I shuffle. Our feet collide. He holds me close, looks into my eyes and says, 'How can you live in the native township?'

I am unable to persuade old Schoeman that the change has brought with it a downswing in crime. I say all the things my father will not hear. But like Dad he does not grasp a word about redistribution. About progress. How can they when they insist without blinking that English and Afrikaans are still the official languages?

'You talk too much,' he says and pulls me towards him, gripping me so tightly that my left nipple sets off his security panic button, the kind my parents pay a fortune to wear round their necks. A siren wails. Up here on the veranda men remove the fleshy fingers they have been rolling over their wives' naked, sagging backs. The whites of the wives' eyes show. Paul Schoeman grabs my breast. I scream. I put my hands to my ears. I want to block out the wailing. The barking of the Rottweilers. The jibbering of the guests. Four armed response security guards appear. Their sobriety creates a striking contrast.

They are not amused when my father says, 'False alarm. Who let the dogs out?' Leon is nowhere to be seen.

'Have a snack,' mother offers. It is anchovy tart and salty.

'Is it nearly time for champagne?' I want to know.

'It won't be long now,' says Dad, as if he were meting out a punishment.

'What is the time?' shouts someone. One minute to midnight says my watch. My father pours me another whisky.

'Be patient,' he commands.

Any minute now, I tell myself.

'To the year two thousand!' I shout. 'To the future!'

'There is nothing to look forward to.' Dad's voice is weighed down. Now two of him are saying, 'This is the future.' The thick curl of his cigar smoke throws me back into a time when I believed that he had power over the planets. Now I am starting to believe that my father is actually capable of holding back midnight. I want to call the security guards with their military boots and pistols to return.

'Do you want to see the real danger we face here tonight?' I will ask. Then I will see what they can do about the fear that washes this party like a backward-moving current.

I am standing alone when it happens. The blackness of the sky is split as fire crackers explode brightly into two million broken stars. An ethereal chorus resounds above the voice of Nat King Cole, above the marabi jazz that plays on Station Nnwe in the background. As the heavens shift, time dissolves and my rapture rises.

Down below the profusion of papyrus plants, the bed of lobelia, chrysanthemum and wild hydrangea, the lawn that is overrun with weeds are illuminated by an unearthly light.

'Happy New Year!' Leon embraces me from behind. 'Did you hear what Manzwe said?' he asks.

From a great distance I hear my father saying that there is still one minute to go.

Glossary

bioscope cinema
bladdy, blerrie bloody
breker tough-guy
ubuntu humanness, humanism
china friend
dagga marijuana
deurmekaar confused
doek, doekie headscarf
donga ditch
dronklap drunkard
ek sê I say
hamba kahle go well
isintu African culture
kaalgat bare-arsed
laaities children, boys
larney posh, classy
maiza maize beer
malunde homeless
mkhulu grandfather
uMvelinqangi the Creator
ngwana child
nkgono grandmother
nooit never
ntate father
ou, oke fellow, bloke
robot traffic light
samp mealiemeal
shebeen drinking den
skinder gossip
skoffel to hoe
skolly, skollie delinquent
stoep veranda
stof dust
tannie auntie
toyi-toyi processional dance

uitstalling exhibition
umntwana child
vula open
zol handmade cigarette

Notes on Contributors

ANTHONY AKERMAN, born in Durban in 1949, read English and Drama at Rhodes University, Grahamstown. Trained as a director at the Bristol Old Vic Theatre School. Settled in Amsterdam in 1975 and worked in Dutch theatre, directing many South African plays in translation. His own plays include *Somewhere on the Border* (1983), included in the anthology, *South Africa Plays*. 'The Exile' first appeared in *Contrast* in Cape Town in December, 1987. Returned to South Africa in 1992 and lives in Johannesburg.

DAVID BASCKIN, born in Johannesburg in 1944. Studied in Natal and Bristol. Has worked as a copywriter and since 1976 has lectured in psychology at the University of Natal, Durban, where he researches animal behaviour. He is also a columnist for *The Sunday Tribune*. He is married with two children. One of his short stories was first published in the anthology, *Firetalk*, in 1990. Other work has appeared in *Upstream* and *Staffrider*. 'The Wreck of the Santa Maria' was first published in *New Contrast* in September, 1991.

ELLEKE BOEHMER, born in Durban in 1961 of Dutch parentage and studied at Rhodes University; on a Rhodes scholarship in 1985 she went to Britain, where she is now resident in Oxford and teaches in Post-Colonial Studies at the University of Leeds. Her first novel, *Screens against the Sky*, was published in 1990 and her second, *An Immaculate Figure*, appeared in 1993. An early story of hers about childhood in South Africa, 'Kaya', was launched in *Kunapipi* in 1989. 'Ginger' appears here for the first time.

AHMED ESSOP, born in 1931 in Dabhel, India. After taking a B.A. he taught at private schools in Fordsburg, Johannesburg, and later until 1974 at government schools in Lenasia, where he now lives. His first book, *The Hajji and Other Stories*, appeared in 1978, followed by two novels. His collection, *Noorjehan and Other Stories* of 1990, brought together works regularly published in journals like *Staffrider, Contrast* and *The English Academy Review*, in the first number of which 'Shakespeare's Image' first appeared (in 1983). He is one of the few writers in this anthology also to have appeared in *The Penguin Book of Southern African Stories*. He is now a full-time writer.

DAMON GALGUT, born in 1963 in Pretoria and educated there. On completion of his national service he was appointed the first resident playwright of the Performing Arts Council of the Transvaal (PACT). He has since taken a performance diploma in Speech and Drama at the University of Cape Town, where he teaches part-time. His first collection of five long stories, *A Small Circle of Beings*, was published in 1988. The story included here, 'Cloete's Revenge', was first published in *Upstream* in Spring, 1989.

MAUREEN ISAACSON, born in Johannesburg in 1955. After graduating from the University of the Witwatersrand, was a copywriter for advertising agencies and researched for Bailey's African Photo Archives. For the last five years has been a full-time journalist on *The Star* in Johannesburg. Her first collection of a dozen stories, *Holding Back Midnight*, was published by the Congress of South African Writers (COSAW) in 1992. The title story, 'Holding Back Midnight', first appeared in *Leonardo*, a publication for the Seville Expo 92. Other works of hers are included in *Raising the Blinds* and *The Vita Anthology of New South African Short Fiction*.

FARIDA KARODIA was born in 1942 and raised in Aliwal North in the Eastern Cape which was to provide the setting for her first novel, *Daughters of the Twilight* (1986). After teaching in Johannesburg and in Zambia, she emigrated to Canada in 1969, where she lives as a freelance writer. Her collection of nine stories, *Coming Home*, was published in the Heinemann African Writers Series in 1988; 'Cardboard Mansions' is taken from there.

MATTHEW KROUSE, born in Germiston on the East Rand in 1961, studied theatre at the School of Dramatic Art,

University of the Witwatersrand, and has worked on the fringe as a writer and performer. Until recently employed by the publishing house of the Congress of South African Writers in Johannesburg, for which he has been the chief editor of *The Invisible Ghetto: Lesbian and Gay Writing from South Africa* (1993). A selection of his poetry has appeared in their *Essential Things* (1992). Some of his works for theatre and film have been banned.

RIAN MALAN, born in Vereeniging on the Rand in 1954. Worked on *The Star* in Johannesburg until in 1977 he left his homeland to live in the United States as a freelance journalist. Eight years later he returned from exile to face his origins and heritage, as recorded in his bestselling autobiographical work of reportage, *My Traitor's Heart* (1990). He has published similar work in *Esquire* and *Granta*. 'Tender Sentiments' first appeared in *Frontline* in February, 1991, in a slightly cut version. He has settled in Cape Town.

NOMAVENDA MATHIANE, born in 1944. Based in Chiawelo, Soweto, with her children, she has been a journalist on *The World*, *The Voice*, *Frontline* and *The Star* in Johannesburg in turn; her collection, *Beyond the Headlines*, brings together some of her major recent reporting. Currently she works for the Institute of Multiparty Democracy in Durban. As a creative writer she made her debut in *Hippogriff New Writing, 1990*, in which 'Labour Pains' and other pieces were included.

ROSE MOSS, born in Johannesburg in 1937. Taught at the University of Natal and at the University of South Africa in Pretoria, and emigrated to the United States in 1964. There she has taught creative writing at Wellesley in Massachusetts and at other colleges, and currently at Harvard. Her long story, 'Exile', is included in *The Penguin Book of Southern African Stories*. Her non-fiction compilation, *Shouting at the Crocodile: Popo Molefe, Patrick Lekota and the Freeing of South Africa*, appeared from Beacon Press in 1990 — this presents testimony and other aspects of the notorious 'Delmas Treason Trial' of the late 1980s and has a bearing on 'In Court', the story here. This was first published in *Agni* in Boston in 1991, and subsequently was nominated for a Pushcart Prize.

MOTHOBI MUTLOATSE, born in Western Township, Johannesburg, in 1950. He has edited several influential anthologies of the black heritage and of contemporary works. Currently he is head of Skotaville Publishers in Johannesburg. His first collection of a dozen short stories, *Mama Ndiyalila: Stories* was published by Ravan in the *Staffrider* series in 1982; 'Ngwana wa Azania', which first appeared in *Staffrider* as a film concept in 1980, was the concluding piece there and was illustrated with photographs by Mxolisi Moyo and others.

NJABULO S. NDEBELE, born in 1948 and grew up in Western Township, Johannesburg, and later in Nigel. He took his B.A. at Roma in the University of Botswana, Lesotho and Swaziland as it then was, and went to Cambridge and Denver for further studies. He has lectured at Roma and at the University of the Witwatersrand, was recently Vice-rector of the University of the Western Cape and now is Vice-chancellor of the University of the North. His first collection, *Fools and Other Stories*, appeared in 1983. His *Rediscovery of the Ordinary: Essays on South African Literature and Culture* was published in 1991 by the Congress of South African Writers, of which he is president. He has also written a work for children, *Bonolo and the Peach Tree* (1992). 'Death of a Son' first appeared in *TriQuarterly* in 1987. He is married with three children.

KAIZER NYATSUMBA, born at White River in the Eastern Transvaal in 1963, educated at the University of Zululand and Georgetown University in Washington, D.C. Lives in Johannesburg where he is a political correspondent on *The Star*. His collection of poetry, *When Darkness Falls*, appeared in 1990. His first collection of ten short stories, *A Vision of Paradise*, was published by COSAW in 1991; 'A Passion for Wealth' is taken from there. His work has also appeared in *Staffrider, Classic* and *The Vita Anthology of New South African Short Fiction*.

ANDRIES WALTER OLIPHANT, born in 1955 at Heidelberg in the Transvaal. Educated at the Universities of the Western Cape and of Oregon, where he was a Fulbright scholar in Comparative Literature. He has been resident playwright in the Space Theatre, lectured at the University of the Transkei, and in 1988 published a collection of poems, *At the End of the Day*. He is currently editor of *Staffrider Magazine* and general editor of COSAW publishing in Johannesburg. 'A Place of Killing' first appeared in *Tribute* and in *New Contrast* in Spring, 1990.

DEENA PADAYACHEE, born in Durban in 1953. Graduated from the University of Natal as a medical doctor in 1991, and is in private practice in Phoenix, near Durban. 'What's Love Got to Do with It?' is the title story of his first collection of ten, *What's Love Got to Do with It? and Other Stories*, published by COSAW in 1992. Another of his stories, 'The Finishing Touch', has given its title to the anthology of the 1991 Nadine Gordimer Short Story Awards, also published by COSAW. His work has also appeared in *Kunapipi, New Contrast* and *Staffrider*. He is married with two children.

TONY PEAKE, born in Johannesburg in 1951. Took his honours degree at Rhodes University in Grahamstown in 1973, and moved to London where after various occupations since 1984 he has lived as a literary agent. He has regularly contributed to Constable's *Winter's Tales* annuals of short stories; 'Necessary Appendages' first appeared there, in the new series No. 7, in 1991.

SHEILA ROBERTS, born in Johannesburg in 1937, but was brought up in Potchefstroom, educated at the Universities of South Africa and Pretoria. In 1977 she emigrated to the United States, where, currently, she teaches creative writing at the University of Wisconsin at Milwaukee. Her first collection of stories, *Outside Life's Feast*, appeared in 1975, followed by *This Time of Year* in 1983 and *Coming In and*

Other Stories in 1993, 'Carlotta's Vinyl Skin' being included in the last. It first appeared in *Kunapipi* in 1985.

AGNES SAM, born in an Indian Catholic family in North End, Port Elizabeth. From school she went to study in Lesotho and Zimbabwe, then worked as a teacher and freelance writer in Zambia, before going to study in York, where she currently lives with her children. Stories of hers first appeared in *Kunapipi* in 1985. Her first published volume of fifteen short stories, from which 'Jellymouse' is taken, *Jesus is Indian and Other South African Stories* (The Women's Press, 1989), is due as a paperback in the Heinemann African Writers Series. She has had radio plays broadcast by the BBC. Her first return visit to South Africa in twenty years occurred in 1992.

SIPHO SEPAMLA, born in 1932 near Krugersdorp and has lived since the 1950s in Wattville, near Benoni, on the East Rand with his wife and family. Although substantially published as a poet and novelist, his short stories have not been collected. An early one appeared in *On the Edge of the World* (1974, revised as *Modern South African Stories*) and another in *Forced Landing* (1980). 'Ike and Phindi' was first in the revived *The Classic* in 1984. Since 1980 he has been the director of the Federated Union of Black Arts (FUBA) near the Market precinct in Johannesburg.

MIRIAM TLALI was born in 1933 in Doornfontein, Johannesburg, and grew up near Sophiatown. In 1975 she published *Muriel at Metropolitan*, a semi-autobiographical account of her life as a clerk in the city — the first novel by a black South African woman. Once *Staffrider* was established in 1978, she became for a while a key contributor of new journalism and interviews; the collection *Mihloti* (1984) brings some of these pieces together. In 1989 Pandora in the UK published her *Soweto Stories*, which in the South African edition from David Philip is known as *Footprints in the Quag: Stories and Dialogues from Soweto*; 'Metamorphosis' first appeared there. She lives with her husband and family in Soweto, and often in Lesotho.

CHRIS VAN WYK, born in 1957 in Soweto; lives in Riverlea, Johannesburg. Married with children. Writer of educational material, co-founder of the short-lived *Wietie* and for several years editor of *Staffrider* when it was still attached to Ravan Press. An early story of his appeared in the anthology, *Modern South African Stories* (1980). 'Flat' appeared in *The Bloody Horse* in March-April. 1981.

IVAN VLADISLAVIĆ, born in Pretoria in 1957. Graduated from the University of the Witwatersrand in 1979 with an honours degree. Has worked at Ravan Press, where he is a member of the editorial board, and is a freelance editor living in Johannesburg. 'The Prime Minister is Dead' was first published in *TriQuarterly* in 1987 and in *The English Academy Review* in 1988, then became the opening story of his first collection, *Missing Persons*, in 1989. He has since published new stories in *Staffrider* and *Soho Square V*, and his novel, *The Folly*, is due from David Philip in Cape Town and from Serif in London.

JAMES WHYLE, born in 1955 in the foothills of the Amatola mountains, Eastern Cape. Pursued his education at Rhodes University in Grahamstown, and has since his national service lived in Johannesburg with his wife and children as an actor and dramatist (*National Madness, Hellhound*). 'Sappeur Fijn and the Cow' first appeared in the collection of anti-military satires, *Forces' Favourites*, in 1987.

ZOË WICOMB was born in the Cape in 1948. She completed an arts degree at what was then the University College for Cape Coloureds and went to Reading University in Britain in 1970. She has taught in Nottingham and Glasgow, and recently returned to teach English at what is now the University of the Western Cape in Cape Town. Her first book, a collection of connected stories under the title *You Can't Get Lost in Cape Town*, was published in 1987. Her later story, 'In the Botanic Gardens', appeared in *Icarus* in 1991. 'Another Story' first appeared in the anthology, *Colours of a New Day: Writing for South Africa*, in 1990.

302

PETER WILHELM, born in 1943 in Cape Town. Has lived most of his life in Johannesburg, training as a teacher but practising journalism, chiefly on *The Financial Mail*. To date he has published three collections of short stories, *LM and Other Stories* (1975), *At the End of a War* (1981) and *Some Place in Africa* (1987). 'Burning Dog' first appeared in *New Contrast* in June, 1992. At present he is executive editor of *Leadership* magazine, based in Cape Town.

Acknowledgements

For permission to include the items in this anthology, acknowledgement is made to the following copyright holders:

to David Basckin for his 'The Wreck of the Santa Maria'; to David Philip Publishers (Pty) Ltd for 'The Prime Minister is Dead' from *Missing Persons* by Ivan Vladislavić and the author himself; to Shelley Power Literary Agency Ltd for Stephen Gray's 'Letters to Pratt'; to Deena Padayachee for his 'What's Love Got to Do with It?' from *What's Love Got to Do with It?*, published by COSAW, Johannesburg; to Heinemann Educational Publishers (Oxford) Ltd for Farida Karodia's 'Cardboard Mansions' from *Coming Home and Other Stories*; to Shelley Power Literary Agency Ltd and Zoë Wicomb for her 'Another Story'; to Ahmed Essop for his 'Shakespeare's Image' from *Noorjehan and Other Stories*, published by Ravan Press, Johannesburg; to Jennifer Kavanagh for Tony Peake's 'Necessary Appendages' and the author himself; to Anthony Akerman for his 'The Exile'; to The Women's Press Ltd, 34 Great Sutton Street, London EC1V 0DX, for 'Jellymouse' from *Jesus is Indian* by Agnes Sam (1989), used by permission of The Women's Press Ltd; to Sheila Roberts for her 'Carlotta's Vinyl Skin'; to James Whyle for his 'Sappeur Fijn and the Cow'; to Peake Associates, London, for Damon Galgut's 'Cloete's Revenge'; to Matthew Krouse for his 'The Barracks are Crying'; to Mothobi Mutloatse for his 'Ngwana wa Azania' from *Mama Ndiyalila*, published by Ravan Press; to Nomavenda Mathiane for her 'Labour Pains'; to Peake Associates, London, for Miriam Tlali's 'Metamorphosis'; to Shelley Power Literary Agency Ltd for Njabulo S. Ndebele's 'Death of a Son' and the author himself; to Sipho Sepamla for his 'Ike and Phindi'; to Chris van Wyk for his 'Flat'; to Kaizer Nyatsumba for his 'A Passion for Wealth' from *A Vision of Paradise*, published by COSAW; to Rose

Moss for her 'In Court'; to Peter Wilhelm for his 'Burning Dog'; to Andries Walter Oliphant for his 'A Place of Killing'; to Elleke Boehmer for her 'Ginger'; to Rian Malan for his 'Tender Sentiments'; and to Maureen Isaacson for her 'Holding Back Midnight' from *Holding Back Midnight*, published by COSAW.